HINT OF COPPER

HINT OF COPPER

STEVEN R. BURT

Ridge View Partners

Amazon paperback edition / November 2021
Ridge View paperback edition / March 2022
ISBN: 9780578369419

Cover photo used by permission,
Utah State Historical Society

Cover design by Bre Hunt

Dedication

For Mom and Dad,
who taught me the value of reading

I

Wilson Hotel, Salt Lake City, Utah
4:10 p.m., Sunday, July 18, 1948

I told her I'd be there by four, but vapor lock killed my car at the stop sign. As the afternoon sun pushed the mercury over the century mark, the gas in my fuel line bubbled into a scalding mist, unable to reach the carburetor. I rolled the dead Ford to the roadside and hurried down an empty sidewalk on foot.

Just past the Trailways station, I cut under a hotel portico and pushed through a set of double glass doors. The woman waited near a cold lobby fireplace, sitting with her knees together and clutching a cloth handbag. When she spotted me, she smoothed out wrinkles in her puckered, off-white dress and stood up. Her right eye sported a shiner, blue gray but fading, and she turned sideways, hiding it from me.

I looked her straight in the good eye and said, "Your last name wouldn't be Ecker?"

"You have my camera?"

"Right here," I said, slipping the leather case from my shoulder. I held it out where she could get a better view.

"Where did you find it?"

"Your ad in the *Telegram* said $25 reward, no questions asked."

Color flushed in her cheeks, and she looked down. "But you're sure it's mine?"

"Well, if *you're* not sure—"

"Look," said the woman, twisting the bag in her hands, "I don't know quite how to put this, but how do I know you're not just some guy who stole it from me? You know, so you can sell it back?"

"Lady, I'm a licensed investigator, and there's not a single complaint in my file—"

"You have a license for this kind of work?"

"That's right, and when I find stuff, people pay up."

"May I?" she asked, holding her hand out. I passed her the camera, and she unsnapped the strap, taking it out to examine it.

A bald man sat nearby chewing on a gray cigar and listening in. He stood up and stepped between us, saying, "Look, pal, it's her brother's camera, so how about takin' fifteen? We need to give it back to him, so will you go fifteen?" He blinked and poked the cigar back in his mouth, like an exclamation point.

"Your ad said twenty-five."

He stuck his hands in his pockets and looked up at the lobby wall, searching the mounted deer heads for ideas.

"Will you take a check, then?"

"I'm not your bank."

He yanked the cigar out and scowled at it, like it suddenly tasted foul.

"Fine. Money's in our room, up on four."

But I wasn't gonna make that mistake again.

"You know what?" I said, "I have this absurd fear of heights, so why don't you just bring the money down and me and the lady'll wait over there, in the dining room." I pointed to the Chinese café, through a door on the other side of the narrow lobby.

He looked anxious.

"I'll be fine," she told him, snapping the case closed. She followed me through the doorway, where smells of pan-fried fish, ginger and hot cooking oil filled the room. I took a chair at an empty table, waiving off the waiter.

She sat across from me.

"My name's Jack," I offered, but it didn't make much of an impression. Her blond hair reminded me of thin straw, the kind left behind on the ground when you baled it for winter feed. I noticed her face was sunburned, and her small hands were rough and calloused. She set the camera on the table between us and turned away again, nervously bouncing one crossed leg off the other.

I studied Chinese hieroglyphs on a bottle of soy sauce, waiting her out.

"So, this is your job, then?" she asked finally. "Sifting through Lost and Found notices in the paper, taking bounty off somebody's bad luck?"

"Sometimes," I answered. "But I work nights too." I couldn't tell if she was trying to shame me or storm some sort of moral high ground. When she didn't ask what else I did, I told her anyway.

"I'm the night watchman over at Auerbach's, the department store on Broadway. And I take cases on the side: divorce work, missing persons—that kind of stuff." I handed her my business card and touched my finger to my left eye, hinting.

"I'll keep that in mind, Mister ... 'Hammer,'" she said, reading from the card. She reached in her cloth bag for a cigarette and fumbled with a book of matches, ruining two before catching a light.

The tobacco smoldered in her hand. Its thin gray smoke line swirled toward me.

"You know what?" I said, waving the smoke away with one hand and pulling the camera case toward me with the other. "Why don't you go see what's taking him so long? I'll keep this baby safe right here."

She took her cigarette and most of the smoke with her.

The hovering waiter sensed an opening and thrust a menu at me like a sword strike. "You liking lunch now?"

"Some water, please, with ice."

He bowed and stepped away while I passed a few minutes with the dinner specials: Sea Slugs with Black Mushrooms, Pan Fried Noodles, Chicken Chow Mein ... rice.

This was taking way too long.

The waiter came back with a small glass, no ice.

"Watch my stuff," I told him, pointing to the camera.

I stepped back into the hotel lobby and called to the deskman. "Did you see a blonde gal come in here a minute ago? Or that bald guy I was just talking to?"

He turned.

"Their name's Ecker," I said, "with a room on four."

"They dinnae have a room here, sir," he said, rolling his R's. "Oot the front door they went, in some mighty hurry."

I rushed to the front glass and looked both ways. Heat shimmered off the empty street.

She'd been holding that fabric handbag—

I ran back into the cafe and popped open the camera case. Three five-dollar bills were wrapped around one of the hotel lobby ashtrays, nestled inside the felt liner where the camera should have been.

2

Karrick Building, Salt Lake City
3:30 p.m., Monday, July 19, 1948

Detective help is what I offer, tracking down stray husbands or locating heirs to Grandma's estate—whatever the cops can't touch, or won't, so long as it isn't another lost dog or missing wristwatch. I have plenty of those cases already, filling my slow days by responding to ads in the local Personals column—anything that has the word "reward" in the copy.

It was a bad business plan.

The loss of the camera punched a hole in my ego, but fifteen bucks covered my costs, so by Monday I was ready to climb back in the saddle. I lifted the sash on my office window. The Venetian blinds rattled in the warm breeze. Near the front door, an Indian warrior slumped on his horse, silhouetted in colored print against an orange and yellow sky. The artwork came with the office I rented on the third floor of the Karrick Building, on Main Street. I straightened the frame, pulled two folding chairs to the edge of my desk, and plugged a stainless-steel desk fan into the wall socket.

Then I sat near the open window and ate an egg sandwich, willing the temperature to go down.

Aunt Edna called to say the lunch-hour thunderstorm was going to make her late. She was bringing a friend who needed my help. Edna married my mother's brother, Jim, in '22, when he was a beat cop in Sugar House. After twenty-five years he'd risen to the rank of captain, but the two of them never had kids. Edna said it was because Jim spent so many nights on duty, away from home, but I noticed she never laughed when she told the joke.

I closed my eyes.

Edna knocked twice and opened the hallway door before I could get to it. Short breaths punched out through her nostrils and her navy blue, polka-dot dress showed sweat stains. Her friend followed, a much younger woman with straight brown hair showing a hint of copper. She wore a green dress that matched the green of her eyes. I motioned for them to have a seat and gave them a minute to catch their breath.

The younger woman locked her fingers around the edges of her seat, looking away.

"Jack," Edna said, "you really should have an elevator in the building." She took off her gloves, pulled out a compact mirror and touched her hair.

"I'm getting one," I lied. I filled two paper cups with water and offered them to the ladies. "That was some downpour."

"It was, but we can use the rain."

"And this is—?"

"My friend, Yasa Cvito; that's C-V-I-T-O. We're neighbors, and we shop in the same market, around the corner."

I made a note.

"She needs your help, Jack. I told her about how you were starting up your new detective business, and how good you were at finding things."

Yasa glanced my way but looked down when our eyes met.

"Anyway," Edna continued, "about three months ago she moved into the house two doors down, to be with her uncle, Bosko. He's the one who has all those antenna wires sticking up from his roof ... lived in New York before he showed up here in '43 and told us all he was an inventor. They're both from someplace over in Europe. So, last Sunday she came by our place right after church, says she knows your uncle Jim is a policeman and could he look into something privately. Turned out her own uncle had up and vanished!"

I watched Yasa, who listened carefully.

"What did Jim say?" I prompted.

"'Not a police matter,'" Edna finished. "That was his opinion. He said it's not a crime for a sixty-year-old man to be away from home for a few nights."

Yasa leaned forward, putting her hand on my desk. "Yes, Bosko is my uncle, but now he is missing. When our big war ended, I traveled to this country to look for some family. He is my only one, so now I am coming to Salt Lake City to take care of him. But he is gone away, so I must find him back again. I cannot be here without him."

She looked over at Edna.

"What makes you think he won't come back on his own?" I asked.

"Two nights ago, he filled up some boxes and left from our house. He acted so much secret. I have not seen him since that night. But this is not—how do you say it? Not his way of acting."

"Comes home every night, does he?"

She nodded yes, but said, "Not *every* night."

I made another note. "What about his friends?"

Yasa looked at Edna again.

"Sometime he goes out to see his friend Peter. He tell me, '*Yasa, I am going to Peter's place tonight,*' but I do not know about this Peter."

"Did he always tell you where he was going?"

She seemed puzzled, then shook her head. "He just say, 'See you' and laugh, like he was saying some joke. Then he get into the truck and drive away."

"You said he filled up some boxes?"

"With papers, electrical things ..."

"Speaking of electrical things," Edna piped up, "you should see the workshop set up in his basement. Did I tell you he's an inventor? With all those wires and tubes, it's a wonder he hasn't burned the place down!"

Yasa leaned toward me again. "Yes. To know Bosko, you must look in his workshop, in his cellar."

"W-O-R-K-S-H-O-P." I wrote that down too, then sat back and tapped the eraser on the notepad.

The telephone rang.

Edna glared at me, but it rang again anyway.

I picked up the handset and said hello.

"Jack," said a voice. "It's Woody. Did I wake ya?"

I looked at the ladies and answered carefully, "You think I sleep all day?"

"I don't know, I don't work nights. Listen, I've got a couple of Bee's tickets—"

"I'm with somebody. I'll call you back."

I hung up and put the telephone on the floor, under my desk.

"Sorry about that," I said, looking through my notes.

Yasa dabbed at the corners of her eyes with a handkerchief. Edna put a hand on her arm.

"He'll probably turn up," I said. "Is there some other reason to worry? To think he might be in danger? Maybe a medical problem? Alcohol?"

She stole a sideways look at Edna. "He plays ... pool games, with some little balls and numbers. So maybe is trouble for him."

"She means gambling, Jack."

"I caught that Edna, thanks."

Yasa mentioned he was living on a pension, but she wasn't sure where it came from. "And I have this photo," she said. "I made it. I have this camera for myself. You can see it." It was a grainy snapshot. The old man in the picture appeared to be thirty years older than Yasa. He stood in front of a shabby truck with wooden sideboards.

I turned back to Edna. "You said she wanted Jim to look into it privately?"

"She's alone here, Jack," Edna said, speaking as if Yasa wasn't in the room. "We think—Jim and I think—she might have visa issues. And by the way, she doesn't have much money to pay."

"I have some money," said Yasa, unsnapping a beaded, white coin purse. Her hands shook. The purse contained a couple of silver dollars and a tenner.

"I thought maybe you could just ask around," Edna interrupted, "in your normal daily rounds. See if he's taken up with ... I don't know, a woman, perhaps."

"Is there a woman?"

"Just ask around," Edna said, "while you work on all those other things you do."

I reached past the paper and took the coins.

"Expense money," I explained. "If he shows up on his own in the next day or two, I'll return it, less money for gas."

We chatted for a few moments about Edna's garden and Jim's work schedule—back on days from the sound of it.

Yasa was quiet, except to ask politely if I'd keep my inquiries confidential. If she had other ideas about her uncle's disappearance, she wasn't in the mood to share them. I wondered about the parts of her story I wasn't hearing, and I tried to imagine coming to a foreign country without adequate cash and few friends, then having the one person you came to visit disappear. I made a few last notes and we stood up. I walked them both to the door.

"I'll stop by later on, to check things out," I told Yasa.

"Good idea," said Edna. "Maybe there'll be a clue or something that'll help you figure out where he went."

I smiled and gave her a hug, then shook Yasa's hands, holding them between mine.

"Thank you," she said. "This is so important for me. I will watch for you."

Her eyes glistened. She needed the hanky again.

"And show that photo to some folks around town, to see if anyone's seen him," Edna reminded me.

"Thanks for the tip," I said. I could see why my uncle didn't take up the case.

I closed the door and looked over my notes. "Peter's Place" was local shorthand for Peter Pan Billiards, just up the street. I'd spent time there myself, losing money. I had a strong hunch that Bosko was simply off on a bender. He'd probably wander home on his own before I could even spend the silver.

I leaned back and studied the photo Yasa gave me.

Bosko appeared unremarkable, somewhere around five-and-a-half feet tall, judging by the truck. Balding on top, with a slight build, he wore round eyeglasses with metal rims. It was a description that probably fit ten thousand men around town. With a hat on, double that number.

I called Woody back. "What's up?"

"Free tickets are what's up tonight! Third-base side, in a box."

Woody was a high-school buddy who worked as a sports reporter at the *Tribune*, always coming up with free tickets. I weighed the likelihood of finding Bosko tonight against sitting in a box seat, for free.

"Who're they playin'?"

"Portland."

Maybe he'll be at the ballgame, I reasoned.

I thought about Yasa and the lousy hand life had dealt her. I'd seen plenty like her during the war, trudging along dirt roads, families torn apart. She was one of the lucky ones, here and now, but it seemed like she was holding back, and I needed more time to cogitate on her problems.

"I'm workin' at the store later," I told him, "but I'm good till 9:30 or so."

"Bring a poncho then—it looks like it might rain again."

I hung up, clipped Bosko's picture into my notebook and put it in the desk drawer. Sadie smiled at me from her own picture, propped in a frame on the blotter. I picked it up and ran my thumb along its gold, braided edge.

Horns honked out in the street. I switched off the desk fan, closed the window and slammed the door on my way out. From the hallway I heard the Indian slide to a more comfortable position on the wall.

3

⟨⟩⟨⟩⟨⟩

The Beehive Café
7:10 a.m., Tuesday, July 20, 1948

Stars faded over the Wasatch as I finished my shift at Auerbach's. Mountains east of the city gathered detail, emerging gradually from smoky silhouette shapes set against a lime-white sky. I spent my nights protecting department store dummies. That was my real job, the one that kept me afloat in '48. I clocked out and made my way up the sleepy morning edge of State Street to Sadie's place. Of course, it wasn't really her place, just the place where she worked. But Sadie was my girl, and to me it was her place. To everyone else, it was just the Beehive Café.

Across the street, a Ford and a Buick backed out of parking spots along the sidewalk like black beetles, slow, shiny and round. The Buick coughed up a bluish cloud and died shuddering. Up ahead, the Tuxedo Hotel sheltered its own chop house and barbershop. I stepped around puddles and passed them by.

The Beehive was bright, a contrast to the morning outside. Tobacco smoke swirled around the ceiling, looking for a way out.

Its smell lay sharp over the mix of bacon, toast and coffee. High-backed booths clad in tan leather lined the wall on my left. A ten-stool lunch counter on the right fronted a giant mirror, partially obscured by glassware, taped signs announcing specials, and a brass cash register. Conversations rumbled under the sound of dishes and silverware clanking. I breathed deep, taking in the morning smells of breakfast.

Sadie was wearing a pink apron, white dress, and matching half-cap. A yellow pencil perched behind her right ear. Her dark hair was pulled back in a ponytail. A hint of recognition crossed her face, betraying a dimple.

"Mornin', babe."

"Jack, your eggs'll be up in just a minute. I think there's a couple of open spots down at the end of the counter." She turned to another customer.

The booths were packed with breakfast plates, the counter was nearly full. I climbed onto a padded stool near a door on the back wall that led to someplace called the Twilight Lounge. A crystal ash-tray reminded me of a recent visit to Ely, Nevada, that nearly ended in disaster when I lost all my gas money playing craps. I picked up the morning paper: "Truman Confers with Top Aides Over Berlin Crisis." Somebody else had the sports page. I could hear George, the owner, barking out orders to the cooks in the back. I liked the counter. I could stare into the mirror along the wall and take in the entire café. A couple of new punch boards caught my attention, standing erect by the napkins under the mirror. I stared at the nickel board, a five-cent chance to win a donut or a piece of pie, imagining the feel of the tiny roll of paper pushed out by the key.

Sadie found me again. "Three eggs, over hard and smashed flat, with a side of bacon." She rolled her eyes as she set them down.

"What?" I asked. "You don't like eggs?"

"They're not eggs anymore, Jack. They're like ... coasters or something."

"You know how I like 'em, babe."

We'd been dating since May when I met her on the dance floor at Saltair, an amusement park hovering over the edge of the Great Salt Lake, west of town. When we slow danced, she hung close, smiled impishly and told me how she worked the lunch counter at the Beehive Café. After I left her that night, I penciled a beehive into my notebook. I showed up there for lunch the next day, but she didn't, so I asked around. George told me she worked mornings. "What a coincidence," I said. "I eat breakfast."

A shadow appeared next to me.

"Mind if I sit down, Jack?"

I glanced up from thoughts of Sadie and beehives and eggs to see a tall, thin man in a tan suit take the empty stool on my right. As he leaned on the bar, his jacket fell open. He carried a gun. Although I couldn't see it, I knew he carried a badge too. It was my uncle Jim, captain of police. He set his hat on the counter.

"Mornin', Sadie. Bring me a cup of Postum," he said, "and some cream if you have it."

She cocked her thumb and pointed her finger at him.

He pulled the paper his way and frowned. "How'd our Bees do last night?" he asked.

"Wet field. They didn't play."

He nodded and pushed the paper back. "Well, we can use the rain."

"That's what Edna said. So, is it a coincidence seeing you here, or are you tailin' me?"

"Tail you? Why would I tail you? You're here every morning at 7:10 sharp."

I felt color rising to my face, but Sadie had already turned away.

"Besides," he added, "why shouldn't I stop in here? My office is practically across the street."

"You're here for the free coffee," I countered.

Sadie came back. "One cup of Postum," she said, setting down a cup and a thimble-sized metal pitcher of cream. "On the house, Captain."

He looked up, a self-satisfied smile on his face.

I turned to Sadie. "You're luring him in here with free food?"

"Well, what brings you in, Jack?" she said. "You're here every day."

They exchanged grins. I went back to my eggs as she bussed plates from the counter.

"Listen," Jim said, "Edna wants to know how the Cvito case is going. What have you got so far?"

"Cvito is a *case* now, is it?" I asked.

"Call it what you want," he said. "She said Yasa went straight home after your little visit yesterday and waited on the porch for you until well after dark. She thinks something is really wrong there."

"It hasn't even been one day," I said, feeling a little guilty, "and it rained!"

He held up his cup and stared across it, into the mirror.

"Look, just do me a favor. Stop by, look at Bosko's things, and show a little interest. It might turn out to be nothin', but you did take her money."

"Who's Bosko?" asked Sadie, who'd wandered away and back into the conversation.

"I'll tell ya later," I said, turning to Jim. "Look, tell Edna I'll stop by Bosko's after lunch. I'll have a chat with Yasa and check out his stuff in the basement. By the way, she doesn't have much to say, you know."

"Edna?" he asked.

"Of course, not Edna."

"Just go along with me on this, Jack. Edna's taken a liking to her for some reason, a lost dog kind of thing. Not that I'm sayin' lost dogs are your thing."

"Oooh ... a big case, huh?" Sadie teased. She often joked that I should find a regular day job. "How am I ever gonna explain you to my family?"

"Too late for that," I said.

But humor masked her real feelings. She wasn't sold on my career as a private eye. At first, she thought it was exciting, but my night schedule at Auerbach's made it hard to spend time with her during the week. Saturday nights, Sunday nights and breakfast— some weeks that was all we had. We'd had words about it.

Sometimes.

Often.

She'd come around though, when I got busier and made more money.

I left two bits on the counter and said my goodbyes. Then I walked Jim to his office and headed over to Main for some much-needed shut-eye.

4

꧁꧂

A few hours later I splashed cold water on my face, grabbed my notebook and pulled my '38 Ford out of the alley. Jim and Edna made their home in one of a dozen pre-war, brick bungalows along both sides of 11th East. Bosko and Yasa were two doors south. I pulled up in front of number 864, where the grass needed mowing and the front porch had been overtaken by pyracantha bushes. I left the keys on the dashboard and stepped outside into the heat.

Could eggs really fry on a sidewalk?

A dirt-colored Hudson sat at the other end of the street, windows down. A shadow slumped in the driver's side. The Beeline station on the opposite corner pumped gas quietly. I walked up the front steps and knocked. An empty metal porch chair, the color of clay pots, sat facing the roadway. A tin mailbox, painted black, had an outgoing letter in a blue envelope held tight by a clothespin.

When no one came to the door I knocked again, louder. Same answer.

I stepped down and followed the gravel alley downhill to the back of the house. A wooden garage faced the alley further on, its door closed. Rain-battered laundry hung on a clothesline, slack and unmoving. The remains of a once-great tree stood sun-bleached and naked, bark and branches all removed. Cicadas buzzed under the hot sun.

Higher up, behind a screened window on the sleeping porch, a shape moved. I tried the back door below. It was locked.

"Who you lookin' for, Mister?" came a voice from above.

I squinted up at the window. Sunlight glanced off the two-story, white-washed porch addition.

"Yasa ... Cvito. Is she home?"

The voice's owner moved. Footsteps echoed on the wooden stairway inside, and a shape appeared at the screen door. The shape was a short, heavy man with dark curly hair, late thirties. Sweat stains under both arms ruined his otherwise dapper appearance, but the holstered handgun under his left arm lent a certain confidence.

"What do you like with Yasa? Are you some neighbor?"

"I am," I said. *Like the Good Samaritan.*

"But you drive your car to visit your neighbor?"

"Sometimes."

He stared at me, unsure if I was pulling his leg.

"She is not here now," he said, opening the screen door slightly. He had an accent like Yasa's and pronounced every word carefully. "She took holiday, I think."

"My name's Jack ... Jack Hammer," I offered. "And you are?"

He looked at me, then around and past me, searching for someone else. "I am her brother."

He was dark and soft-spoken like Yasa, but he was a liar.

"But I thought—"

"Please, go away now," he ordered, closing the door behind the screen. *And don't come back* was his clear message.

5

Beeline Gas Station
2:00 p.m., Tuesday, July 20, 1948

I walked back up the alley, crossed the street and dropped a nickel into the pay phone on the far side of the service station. The switchboard put me through to the desk sergeant, who told me he hadn't seen my uncle Jim since earlier that morning.

Something was off.

Yasa said she had no family except Bosko, and I didn't buy the trip scenario one bit. I mulled over my options. Maybe there was more to this Cvito case than I'd first thought. A guy answering the door with a gun flashed trouble, like a neon FREE BEER sign in the ward-house window.

Behind me the bell clanked as a car pulled up to the gas pumps.

I dropped a second nickel in the slot and called another number.

"Hello!"

"Aunt Edna, it's Jack."

"Jack, how are you? Did you get over to see Yasa?"

"I'm trying. Have you seen her today?"

"No, should I have?"

"Edna, listen, I'm at the pay phone just down the street. Is Uncle Jim around?"

"A pay phone?"

"At the Beeline, across the street ... is Jim home?" I pulled out my notebook and pencil to write down the name and address from the blue envelope, before I forgot it. Oxford something. In the city. I paused at the beehive on the first page and drew a heart around Sadie's name.

"No, he's working days now. Why are you calling me from a pay phone?"

A hand settled roughly on my shoulder and turned me around, into the sun. A fist smashed into the left side of my face and another one hit my gut, taking the wind from me. I hunched over and dropped the phone, then went down on the pavement. I couldn't catch a breath. Hands ruffled my pockets. Somewhere far away, Edna was calling my name. Then I rolled over, sucking wind from the hot pavement and took a short nap.

"Mister! Hey, Mister, are you okay?"

The station attendant, a pimply-faced kid in a gray uniform, shook my shoulder and helped me to my feet. I rubbed my jaw and leaned against the station wall, trying to keep upright. I reached down. The .38 was still there, strapped to the inside of my left leg. I spotted my wallet on the ground, its contents scattered along with spare change and the bullets for my gun, but my notepad was nowhere to be seen.

"There were two of them," he said, "funny accents, like in the movies. A big guy and a short guy, in suits. They pulled up and I thought they wanted gas, but they said they needed help starting that car across the street. I took a look and it started fine."

"That's my car," I told him. "Keys still in it?"

"They should be. When I started back this direction they hopped in their own ride and took off, headed west down Ninth South like a house on fire. I thought they hit the cash drawer, so I ran the rest of the way back here and found you."

"You did okay, kid."

I gathered my things from the pavement. "Dammit!"

"They take your cash?" asked the kid.

"No, my license."

"Should I call the cops?"

I nodded. "Send 'em across the street. Tell 'em my name is Hammer and tell 'em not to shoot me."

6

I pulled the Colt from my ankle holster, chambered five .38 caliber rounds and kept it in my hand. The kid said the two guys headed toward town, but that didn't mean the house was empty. I marched back across the street, looking for answers.

Whatever Yasa wouldn't say in front of Edna, I was getting the idea it was more than a worry that her uncle went out for a long weekend of billiards and booze.

The front-porch window opened to the dining room and the kitchen beyond. An oak buffet sat by the wall, its drawers open and cutlery scattered on the floor. The front door was still locked. I banged on it, but nobody cared. The blue envelope was gone.

I moved off the porch, heading downhill around the back of the house where the tree stump stood sentinel and cicadas droned on. When I tried the screen door again, it was unlatched.

I stepped inside, listening. A stairway led down to a make-shift cellar door. The workshop could wait until I'd dealt with her "brother." I crept upstairs to the main floor, half expecting the guy to pop out like a jack-in-the-box, each step bringing me closer to confrontation. A mattress stood tipped against the wall at the top of the stairs, longing for the useless bed frame across the room. From the sleeping porch, the kitchen was visible through a window in an unlocked door.

"Come out, come out," I whispered, stepping inside. "Wherever you are ..."

A tea-kettle-shaped electric clock on the kitchen wall showed a quarter past the hour. Two open bins stood under the countertop, one filled with potatoes, and one half full of flour. White powder was splashed everywhere, like someone had scooped out handfuls and flung them into the air. Potatoes littered the counter, surrounding a single, flour-covered envelope containing a two-inch stack of C-notes. I picked it up and put it back down.

Money like that was trouble.

Blackout shades at the windows were rolled up, and sheer white curtains filtered the afternoon sun. I moved slowly, trying to get a sense of the layout. The dining room and parlor stood between me and the street.

To my left, a line of light showed under a door down the hallway. There were three doors, two dark. My gun went ahead, and I looked in the first. It was a bedroom, wallpapered with a floral print. The mattress was partly off the bed frame, its blankets piled in a heap. The roller blind was down. I switched on a light. A few dresses hung in an otherwise empty closet. Nylon stockings and assorted undergarments filled the partially open top drawer of a chest and spilled out onto the floor.

I stepped back into the hallway. The second door was open, leading to an empty washroom.

I paused in front of the closed, third door, watching the light at the floor. It was steady. Hugging the frame, I pushed back the door and quartered the room with my gun. The black and white tile floor was slick with water from a claw-foot bathtub, full to the top. A woman's leg, shoe still attached, dangled over the porcelain side. It was Yasa, swimming in her green dress. Her unblinking eyes stared up at the ceiling. I put my gun on the floor and reached in, feeling her neck for a pulse that clearly wasn't there. Her face was marked like somebody had beaten the life clean out of her.

A thump sounded behind me and when I turned, the floor tile to my left erupted in pieces. A second bullet from below careened off the bottom of the bathtub. I stumbled, brushing wood and bits of tile away, falling back to the hall as another bullet tore upwards through the wooden floor between my legs. I fumbled again for my own gun and pointed it at the floor, two-handed. I fired three times, downward and blindly.

It took me a moment to realize the last bang from downstairs was the screen door slamming. My ears echoed from the sound of the shots in the small hallway. I dashed back to the sleeping porch just as a car engine roared to life. I watched through the high windows as a plum-colored Chevy coupe crashed through the garage door. It skidded on the gravel, careened down the alleyway and disappeared around the corner.

7

11th E Between 8th S and 9th S
3:00 p.m., Tuesday, July 20, 1948

Cops showed up with lights and sirens.

I sat outside on the curb, in wet pants, while they roped off the porches, front and back. A hawk-faced detective named Nichols went through his list of questions, making notes. He wiped the sweat from his forehead with his rolled-up shirt sleeve and collected my gun, hooking his pencil through the trigger guard.

"You're a private dick?" He looked me over, wagging his head. It was more challenge than question. "Where's your license?"

"I already explained that, when I handed you my gun," I said. "It was stolen. Talk with the kid at the Beeline. I told him to call you guys."

"Are you even old enough to—"

"—to what? Grow a mustache?" Sweat dripped from my own hairline. I rubbed my head. I needed a haircut.

"Watch your mouth," he said. "And the dame inside?"

"She was my client."

"What kind of client?"

I thought for a moment. "Unhappy."

He looked up from his notes.

"Yesterday, she hired me to look for her uncle. The guy went missing last Saturday."

"And you found him?"

"I just came by to ask a few more questions."

A crowd gathered on the grass in front of the house next door. I surveyed the faces, old, young and sunburned. Edna was there, no doubt wondering why I was being questioned. She caught my eye, but I quickly turned the other way. She was going to have to get her explanations from Uncle Jim.

Rainclouds were building again in the south, warning of another thunderstorm.

"You'll have to come down to the station and make a formal statement."

"I know the drill," I said.

When I looked over again, Edna was gone.

8

Karrick Building
8:30 p.m., Tuesday, July 20, 1948

I spent the afternoon in an interrogation room, alternating between short bursts of two cops asking questions and long periods
of nobody but me in the room. My car was stuck in impound until
the crime lab guys finished making sure it wasn't evidence. My gun
would be there even longer—a week, maybe. Having a police captain
for an uncle expedited some things, but others, not so much. At
least he offered to drop me off back at my place.

"Anywhere along here is fine," I said, as we turned onto Main.

The sun set behind rainclouds. Tall buildings made the storm-
darkened street seem darker. Striped canvas awnings gathered to
shop fronts, and neon signs flickered on above the sidewalk. Jim
pulled the car into an open space in front of a jewelry store.

"Thanks," I said, "for getting me out of there so fast."

He switched his windshield wipers on and off again. The mist
came and went. He was quiet.

"You ever think about doing anything else?" he asked. "Maybe go back to college and get a degree in something?"

I waited to see if he was kidding. "What? Like architecture or accounting?"

"Well, maybe something else."

"That door closed years ago," I said, "with the war. Besides, I like what I do."

He sat back in the driver's seat and gripped the wheel with both hands.

"I gotta apologize Jack. I got you into this ... me'n Edna."

"I knew what I was doing."

"Maybe, but you're not Sam Spade—not yet," he winked. "Sure you don't have time for dinner? I know Edna would love to grill you."

He smiled at his little joke.

"I get it," I said, "but no. I have to be to work soon." I opened the door to step out.

"Hold on a second," he said, grabbing my arm. "What about Bosko?"

"Bosko?"

His face darkened, suddenly serious. "Jack, you need to step away from this—that's direct from the chief. Leave it alone."

I made a face like I'd tasted bad medicine.

"What's it to him?" I asked.

"I don't know, but something's up. The FBI moved in, asking questions. They want to tie it up in a package and make it go away without any outside interference from us. They meant you too."

"The FBI?" I said. "What's their angle?"

"Don't know, and frankly it leaves me uneasy. But you need to *stay out*. Those were the FBI's words, not just mine, and if they come around here asking questions, you let me know. You got paid in advance?"

I nodded. "Good night, Captain."

I passed the now-empty display windows of the jewelry store on my way to the stairs in the back of the building. A dentist moved in last month on the second floor: Painless Modern Dentistry. Since I hadn't heard any screams, I guess he lived up to his billing.

I thought about finding Yasa's body floating in the bathtub. Despite the damage to her face, her eyes looked peaceful somehow. But I was sick inside. She'd asked me for help, paid me for it, and now she was gone. I hadn't done much to earn her two bucks except to show up.

Late.

I climbed to the third floor. Light showed in the workshop where Edison Krogue, the half-blind watchmaker, worked odd hours. Besides me and him, the rest of the top floor was for rent.

My office faced the street, at the front of the building. I paused just long enough to pull my pockets inside out. *Keys.* They were still on the chain with my car key, impounded. My extra keys were in the cigar box in my bottom desk drawer.

But it didn't matter.

The door stood open, and my life's stake was piled up out in the hallway. The cigar box sat on top of the water cooler, next to my cot, and the Indian print leaned against the wall.

9

Karrick Building
8:45 p.m., Tuesday, July 20, 1948

My first thought was rent.
Did I get my rent in on time?
My wallet was nearly empty so, yes, and the lease had a thirty-day grace period anyway. My heart thumped in my ears. Inside, I switched on a ceiling lamp. Lacking my meager furnishings to spruce things up, the office seemed bare and lonely. Plaster walls showed their age, with shadows of missing pictures in spots marked by nail holes with chipped paint edges.

A double-hung window faced Main Street. Another window in the back room faced the alley, a view for the sink and the toilet. An iron fire escape snaked down the outside alley wall. The wood floor was scuffed and worn, something I'd never noticed because the rolled-up carpet out in the hallway usually covered most of it. The shaving kit I'd left on the sink in the back room was gone too; everything was in the hallway except my desk, the telephone, and the gold frame lying face down on the desk.

I sat it upright.

A chill ran down my back.

Yasa's picture of Bosko, the one that I'd clipped in my missing notebook, looked back at me from where Sadie had been. But the photo had changed: His eyes had been scratched out with something sharp, like a pin or a knife. And Sadie's photo wasn't just hidden behind Bosko's—it was gone. *Gone!*

"Doing some deep cleaning, are ya?" a voice asked.

I flinched and twisted around.

I hadn't noticed anyone come through the door, but there was Old Man Krogue with his thick, wire-rimmed, walking-around glasses that made his eyes look huge. He pulled an envelope out of his green apron pocket and shoved it at me.

"I think this must be your bill. The cleaning folks said to give this to you when you got back—your key too."

"Cleaning folks?"

He tilted his head and narrowed his eyes.

"Yeah, they showed up in the afternoon, started moving furniture and such. They seemed real thorough-like. I'm surprised they left all this out here, though."

"Thanks, Eddie," I said. I put the key in my pocket.

"You okay, Jack?"

"Sure. Long day. Hey, about these cleaners: What kind of crew did they send over?"

"You know, two guys in white shirts. Foreigners. They said you'd be a while. I didn't have my regular glasses on, but I figured it was all good since they had your key. Do you need a hand gettin' all this back inside?"

"I got it, no problem," I said. "Listen, was one of them a short, thick guy with dark hair, by chance?"

He smiled and said "sure" in a way that made me suspect he hadn't paid any attention.

I collected the Indian print and stepped inside, slipping the frame's wire over the nail by the door. Whoever these guys were, they must've pulled the office key off the chain while I was on the telephone with Edna. *How did I miss that?* I sat down and tore open the blank envelope. My license fell out onto the desk, followed by a single sheet of paper that contained a short, hand-written message:

"BRING ME CVITO DEVICE OR LADY WILL END UP LIKE YASA. SATURDAY. NO POLICEMAN."

There was no signature, no one to contact, and no three days in advance. It was a hell of an engagement letter, and it was Sadie's photo that was gone.

My heart jumped.

I direct-dialed her house but couldn't get through.

I tried the operator. No luck.

Damn party lines.

10

Near Layton Avenue
9:20 p.m., Tuesday, July 20, 1948

I dragged my stuff into a pile in my office and dug out a Walther PPK from the tin trunk where my Army uniforms were hidden away. The smell of mothballs stabbed my sinuses. The PPK boasted an eagle and swastika molded onto the grip. I'd bought it off a drunken soldier I'd arrested in a bar in Belgium, four years earlier. I swapped out the .38 rounds left in my pocket for the 9 mm shorts in the cigar box.

I tried calling Sadie again. *Busy.* I tried getting the operator to break in on the call. She wouldn't.

Sadie lived at home and had two sisters. One was married and one was still in high school. She idolized the older sister and tolerated the younger one. Her father was a bank teller, small and quiet, but he'd been a sergeant in the army during the Great War. When I picked her up one night, he pulled me aside.

"Sadie tells us you're a private investigator."

"I'm trying," I said.

He took off his glasses, stepped close to me, and with a face as serious as a funeral, said, "Keep her out of your business, Jack, and I'll let her keep seeing you."

Then he put his arm up and around my shoulder and squeezed. I got the message.

The family lived a few blocks south of downtown, just past Derks Field. On Sundays they all went to church. I wasn't going to let him down.

I tried calling her a third time. *Busy.*

She was too far away. I couldn't wait for a bus. My best bet was a taxi. I ran downstairs and caught the next one headed her way. The rain let up. I leaned up close to the driver, telling him which lights to run.

Why threaten me? Or Sadie?

I didn't have any idea where Bosko was, or what a "Cvito device" could be.

The driver let me out on the corner, by the market. It was a brick affair with a hip roof and white trim that matched the rest of the street's houses—except for the blue-and-red neon beer signs announcing Lucky Lager had come home. The market was closed. Clouds parted. A full moon had crested the mountains, rising slowly.

The street was quiet except for crickets. Young sycamores lined the sidewalk. Somewhere, a woman laughed. I walked down to Sadie's house with its canopied front porch and the house lights off. Lights winked out in other houses along the street too. It was a working-class neighborhood where people went to bed early, woke up early, and went to work.

I thought about knocking on the door, but stepped into the shadows behind some bushes instead, watching. Nothing moved. Far off a dog barked, then stopped. With a full moon I could barely make out the time on my watch.

I moved to the side of the house, where Sadie's bedroom window was wide open to the humid night. I tapped on the frame and moved back. A wooden stepladder leaned up against the house wall. Underneath it, someone had dropped what looked in the dark like a sweater, maybe Sadie's. I leaned down to pick it up, but it was heavy, and the texture was wrong. My hand was suddenly wet and slippery, prompting me to drop it, fast.

A cat's face stared up from a pile of fur, motionless eyes catching the moonlight. Its belly had been split, neck to tail, spilling entrails onto the grass from the still warm body.

My heart pounded again.

Another message ... or neighborhood dog?

I spun around, searching the shadows.

"Jack!" whispered Sadie, through the bug screen, "what're you doing out there?"

I turned back to the window, thinking fast. "I ... I was just missin' ya," I lied, standing up. It was getting easy.

"You know, I stopped at your office, but some cleaners were there."

My heart jumped again. "You didn't talk to 'em?"

I could hear whispered voices further back in the house.

"I can't talk now, Jack," she said quietly. Her hair was rolled in large curlers. "Don't you work tonight?"

"Later. Listen, Sadie, you should probably close this window. It's supposed to rain again," I lied.

Her life and mine seemed miles apart. That was a good thing. She smiled, then pushed down the sash and vanished.

I waited a few more minutes, standing in the shadows. Nothing moved. I grabbed the cat's body by the tail and flung it into the bushes next door, then wiped my hands on the damp grass. Nothing else seemed out of place. After a while, I made my way back to the market and caught the last bus uptown.

Bring me Cvito Device ... Saturday ...

I tried imagining what a Cvito device could be, but couldn't. And I didn't know where to find it, or who I could bring it to if I did.

Dead cat?

Through the bus window, I could see lights at the ballpark. My mind filled in the blanks, and I thought, just for a moment, I could hear the crowd roar.

11

Auerbach's Department Store
9:55 p.m., Tuesday, July 20, 1948

I stepped off the bus near the Judge Building, on the corner of Main and Broadway, and hurried down shopping row, empty of shoppers this late. I knocked on the door at the employee entrance at Auerbach's.

"Where've you been?"

It was Jonny's standard question, no matter when I showed up for work.

"You lost your key again?" he asked.

"I got a spare somewhere. Why don't you go home and tell your wife she's been missin' ya?"

He was wearing my lucky Bees cap.

"I'm gonna do that, chief. Everything's locked up tight. The maintenance guys were working on the new elevator in the back, but they're done, gone. You should have a quiet night."

Jonny was the regular house detective and worked the afternoon shift. He was a former cop from Ogden who took a bullet in his belly and retired out on disability. He was my boss in every sense, except that he called me "chief." He hired me, I think because I knew his wife in school. He turned back to the desk in our pint-sized security office and picked up an envelope.

"By the way, somebody dropped this off for you. It came down from the mailroom."

We didn't typically get mail, even private letters, delivered to work, so two hand-delivered messages in one day bordered on unbelievable. My name was the only writing on the envelope.

He waited for me to open it.

Instead, I hung my sports jacket on the coat tree and dropped into the other swivel chair at the desk.

"You okay, Jack? You look ... bushed."

"Everything's fine," I lied again.

"Well, you don't look fine to me. I'll get out of here so you can take a walk around, catch a few z's."

What? Sleeping on the job was against all the rules.

"You'll still have to sign in at every station," he said, glancing at his watch.

"Sure. Look, I want to get your take on something ... about Sadie."

He waved me off. "Marry her."

"But—"

"No buts, Jack. If I miss my bus, I'll be stuck here for another hour." He hung my cap on a peg and walked out.

I locked the door behind him and switched on the radio to listen for the news, then picked up the envelope and stared at it.

Who were these guys? Mailmen? I tore it open, and another paper slipped out.

"MEET ME AT TINY'S CHOPHOUSE, ALONE, AT NOON TOMORROW."

I knew the place. It was a whitewashed barbecue joint, shoe-horned between a two-pump Texaco and a grove of elms out on

33rd South. It was near the city edge, where buildings thinned out and farmland thickened.

I pulled out the first letter from my jacket and compared it with the new one. The handwriting didn't match, but what did that prove? There were two guys who jumped me.

I followed Jonny's suggestion and took that walk around midnight. I inspected all the doors and the elevator and signed off at each check station, finally stopping at the women's department on the second floor. It was a funhouse of full-length mirrors, full-length furs, and plush red carpeting. Rich dames loved it. I sat under a crystal chandelier in a red upholstered chair and talked things through with two of my favorite mannequins.

So, ladies, do I turn this thing over to the cops?

They considered it, but the way they stared back reminded me there was that part about "No Policeman."

Then should I take a chance, solve this myself, and hope Sadie and the cops never find out?

One of them had a hand on her chin like she was listening closely, but nothing useful came of it.

They were both blondes.

I fell asleep in the upholstered chair while they thought things over.

12

The Beehive Café
6:55 a.m., Wednesday, July 21, 1948

Next morning, I clocked out early, locked the side door, and ran the entire three blocks up to the Beehive. George was out front helping with the breakfast crowd.

"Where's Sadie?" I asked, out of breath.

Before he could answer, she backed out of the kitchen, arms piled high with plates of pancakes and sausages. I raised my hand in a feeble wave. She smiled, showing her dimple again.

"Spot in the back, Jack," she said. "You're early, aren't you?"

"Maybe a minute or two."

"I have something for you," she said, walking away.

George came over and held the counter with both hands, as though he were steadying it. He leaned over like he was going to tell me a secret or an off-color joke.

"How are you two doing?" he asked with a sly smile. He turned and watched her work.

"You see more of her than I do. What does *she* say?"

"She says you're the most thick-headed shamus she's ever dated."

"I'm the only shamus she's ever dated!"

"You sure about that?" he asked. He rolled a toothpick in his teeth and stood back up straight. "Take care of her, Jack ... you ever considered a nice desk job somewhere?"

"What is that supposed to mean?"

Somebody dropped a plate in the kitchen. It shattered, by the sound of it. He turned and shook his head, then leaned close again.

"Couple of guys were in here this morning makin' her laugh. Young guys, business types. It's probably none of my affair."

"It ain't," I said flatly, guessing at his advice. "Goes with bein' a waitress. You should know that."

He looked down at the counter and pulled out the toothpick.

"Okay, Jack. Sounds like you're on it," he said. He hit the counter softly with his fist, a punctuation mark that said he'd spoken his piece and disappeared into the kitchen.

I searched for a paper to look at until my eggs were done.

Waitresses flirt. I flirt with waitresses. It don't mean nothin'.

I scanned the front page: "Alien Agents Enter U.S. By Hundreds. Truman Sets Draft Registration Date." Nothing about Yasa.

In the mirror, I watched a well-dressed old woman wearing a hat sip orange juice with two hands from a small glass. Across the bar, young single businessmen in white shirts and neckties anchored the stools along the counter, reaching over each other for salt, pepper, and ketchup.

The smell of Folgers drifted past, and I thought of my first visit here, of finding Sadie at lunch and her smile when she realized I'd tracked her down after the night at the dance.

She stayed away until my order was up.

"You ever eat a pancake?" she asked. She'd arranged the eggs and bacon on the plate in a way that made two eyes and a mouth, then rotated it around to look at me. Her own eyes studied my face for something. "Aren't you gonna even smile?"

I smiled, but inside I was uneasy.

"You and I need to talk. You got a second?" I poured ketchup on the eggs and wolfed down some bacon.

"For you," she smiled. "By the way, there were a couple of guys here this morning, early." She walked to the cash register and came back with a tan envelope. "They left this for you."

I thought about asking her if these were the guys George mentioned, but I kept my mouth shut. I undid the string on the envelope and emptied the contents onto the counter. My hands started to shake.

"Who gave you this?"

She moved down the counter filling coffee cups, then came back.

"I don't know. They said they were business associates, that you were doing some job together." The contents of the envelope caught her attention. "Hey, isn't that my photo?"

I slid her picture back in the envelope before she noticed the eyes were scratched out. *Like Bosko.* If I was unsure about the cat, I knew what this was. They were sending me a message. They knew where Sadie worked, and Sadie was safe because they let her stay safe.

"Sadie, I need to know which guys they were."

"How would I know?" she said. "They're your friends."

"They're not. Were they tall? Short? Did they have accents, what, Sadie?"

She backed away.

"Sorry, Jack. I wasn't paying that much attention," she said, thinking. "Maybe not from around here, but I don't remember any accent. They were wearing suits, carrying their hats. And one of them smelled bad, like stale vinegar. I was too busy to chat."

"They didn't make you laugh?"

She gave me a puzzled look.

"Look, if you see 'em again, keep your distance," I said. "They're bad characters ..."

"And you gave them my picture?" Her voice rose and cracked.

"What picture?" It was George, back from the kitchen, sticking his nose into things.

"A photograph of me," she said. "It was Jack's."

"Was?"

"You gave it away!"

"No, I didn't. They broke into my office and took it."

George raised both hands in mock surprise and backed away. I put the envelope on the counter and took Sadie's hands in mine. "Listen, babe, I need to explain about something."

"Involving those two guys?" she asked, biting her lower lip.

Café noises faded away. The world seemed small and cramped, just Sadie and me. After my conversation with the mannequins, I'd decided to tell her everything. But now I had to reconsider. Her picture showing up here changed things. They'd been right *here*. Today. How could the cops protect her? I wasn't even sure I could protect her. This is exactly what her dad warned me against, and if he found out I'd involved her in something ... I might never see her again.

"Jack, say something."

I gave her the outline of finding Yasa, leaving out the gunshots. I told her about my furniture stacked in the hallway but stopped short of mentioning the letter or the dead cat. From there my story walked a crooked line, telling her some of the truth and leaving other parts out. It was a balancing act, somewhere between protecting her and scaring her.

"What is it you're not telling me, Jack?" She pulled her hands from mine.

I managed a smile anyway. "It's just business," I said, trying to be confident. "That's all."

She looked into my eyes, searching.

"Your job scares me," she said.

I already knew that.

13

Public Safety Building
8:11 a.m., Wednesday, July 21, 1948

I left her a nice tip and jaywalked across the busy street to the police station, where two young cops looked me over and headed out a side door.

I stepped to the desk. "I'm looking for Jim ... sorry, Captain Burt," I said. "We were supposed to meet up."

The desk sergeant made a call. "He's over in impound, around the corner and behind the fire station."

"I'll find it."

The impound lot was surrounded on three sides by buildings, including the police building. Jim stood next to my car, examining the driver's side door. The morning sun ignited a brilliant orange hue in the fire station brick behind him.

"Eggs again?"

"You're guessing," I said.

"Hmm ... I got pulled into a briefing this morning about Yasa. I thought I better check on your car."

"So whad'ya know?"

"Coroner took a look at her, and—don't tell anybody I told you this—she'd been beat up. Homicide found a nylon stocking with a potato in it. It makes a nice weapon, non-lethal."

"Jesus," I breathed. "Thanks for that, but I meant whad'ya know about my car?"

"It'll be out after lunch. We lifted some prints off the steering wheel, but that was all," he said.

"Great, and what if I need it before lunch?"

"No can do, Jack."

"How am I supposed to do my job then?"

"I thought I told you to stay out of this," he said. His face went dark.

I wanted to tell him about the letter, explain about Sadie, but the words "No Policeman" stopped me. That, and the fact they'd just been to the Beehive.

"Prints might belong to the station attendant at the Beeline," I said. "Did he give you descriptions of the two guys who jumped me?"

"Yeah, a taller one and a shorter one." He hesitated before telling me more. "Homicide thinks they're all connected somehow: Bosko, Yasa and the guy in the house. Too big a coincidence not to be. The working theory is that somebody was looking for Bosko and found Yasa instead. Gambling debts is what Edna thinks. Maybe Bosko had a premonition and took off."

"Nice uncle," I said.

"We're not all like that."

"Didn't mean you."

He leaned against a shady part of the brick structure with his arms folded and rubbed a circle in the gravel with his Florsheims.

"Hey, when do I get my .38 back?" I asked.

"Not today," he said. "I'll check on it. Stop back after one o'clock and ask Kissell about your car. It should be ready."

"You worried about something?" I asked.

"What do you mean?"

"This Cvito case. One day you want me looking into it, the next day you want me to sit it out."

He shrugged.

"Things change, Jack," he said. "And you never follow my advice, anyway."

14

The Beehive Café
10:35 a.m., Wednesday, July 21, 1948

I needed a shower.

The Deseret Gym was just up the street. I'd washed the cat blood from my hands at Auerbach's, but I'd been wearing the same clothes for almost twenty-four hours. Then I remembered the gun in my waistband.

I crossed back to the Beehive, where a few old-timers still sat at the counter, killing time. One of the back booths was full. I spotted Sadie sitting in a front booth, polishing silverware. Her eyes brightened.

"I thought you'd be back," she said.

"You *did*? Well, I decided to run up to the gym for a shower, before hittin' the hay. But I need a paper sack. A big one."

Her smile changed to confusion. "What for?"

I ran my eyes around the room before I showed her the pistol. She stepped into the kitchen to find something and came out with a shopping bag.

"Put it somewhere safe," I said. "I'll be back for it in about thirty minutes."

"And you'll show me how to shoot it?" she asked.

"Sure, but ... maybe not today."

She pouted, running her fingers over the grip. "This isn't your regular gun, is it?"

"Hey, don't be foolin' around with it," I said, as she took aim across the room. "And don't be flashin' it around where people will see it."

"What if I need to use it?" she asked.

"It's not loaded." I took it back and popped out the clip to show her. "You know I don't like carryin' loaded guns."

"So, this is why you stopped by?"

She squinted her eyes, pinched up her nose, and put it on a shelf under the cash register behind the counter.

"I won't be long, I promise."

I blew her a kiss and hurried out the door.

The gym was public, church-owned, and tucked behind the Hotel Utah. I piled my clothes into a wire basket, and the kid at the counter traded me for a towel and a safety pin with a number. I let the warm water run down my back, dried off, and made it back to the café in two shakes of a lamb's tail. But when I came back, Sadie was gone. So were the rest of the customers.

The café was empty.

Then I smelled gunpowder.

George must've heard the bell. He stepped from the kitchen into the dining room, sleeves rolled up, and wiping his hands on his apron.

"She's not here, Jack. I sent her home." He pulled a rag from his back pocket and started polishing an already clean counter.

"I didn't think things were that slow," I said looking around.

"They weren't. Not until that fool gun of yours went off!"

I started to say I was sorry.

"Sadie showed it to one of the other girls, and they accidentally blasted a hole through the floorboards, behind the counter, right over there," he said. "We were just lucky nobody got killed."

"Geez, I told her it wasn't loaded." I leaned over the counter to look.

George shook his head. He had his own gun in the back and probably carried one under his apron somewhere too.

"I'll take care of it, George," I said, headed out the door to find her. "I mean the damage. It wasn't her fault."

"Don't I know it," he said. "It's yours."

15

Karrick Building
11:43 a.m., Wednesday, July 21, 1948

I knew she'd be there, waiting.

She was sitting in the hallway outside my office, holding her skirt tight around her knees. The pistol was still wrapped in a twisted bag beside her. Sunlight reached in from the back stairway and reflected off the wood floor. She didn't move, even though I knew she could hear my footsteps.

"Sadie?"

She looked up. Tears streaked her cheeks. "You said it wasn't loaded."

I unlocked my office and went to the back room. I wet my handkerchief, then came back out and sat next to her on the floor, brushing the cloth softly against her face.

"Sadie, I am so sorry. I thought I checked. There must have been one left in the chamber."

She stared at her knees.

"But I swear, I didn't know. I would never—"

"You left this," she interrupted.

I felt a jolt, like I'd stuck my fingers into a light socket. In her other hand was the envelope with her picture in it.

I'd left it behind.

She pushed me away and stood up, sliding the picture out. "Tell me what this is all about."

Her hand shook as she held the photograph toward me. The hallway light was dim, but I could still see scratch marks on the photo where her eyes had been.

"It's ... your picture." I fumbled for words as I climbed to my feet, regretting those three almost immediately.

Her mouth closed and I could hear her breathing, heavy and measured. "You know what I mean, Jack. *What did you do to my picture?*" she said in a controlled manner. "And why did those guys have it?"

"I didn't do that—! I told you, they broke into my place, and—"

"And what? Stole my picture so they could toss darts at it? And my eyes ... somebody scratched out my eyes? You saw *that*, and you didn't say anything?"

"I know. I don't understand that."

I wanted to say something now, something comforting, something true and wise, but nothing came to mind. Instead, I stared at my shoes, feeling the blood pound through my veins.

"Jack, it's more than just the fact that you can't be honest with me about things. It's that ... sometimes you make me feel like I'm ... just an afterthought, something left behind, like the picture."

"Well ... I was ... gonna get your photo when I came back for my gun," I said.

Tears glistened in her eyes. "Why can't you just admit it, Jack? You forgot about it. You never even asked ... you just left it on the counter and walked away." She measured her words. "Because you know what I wanted you to say? What I hoped you'd say was that you were gonna get your gun when you came back for *my picture*."

"Sure, babe. That's what I said."

She turned and stared down the hallway, starting to cry again but hiding it.

"That's just it, Jack—that's not what you said, and you don't even get that it's not. Just like when you get locked in on something, a lost watch, a mining claim, a divorce case, and I start to wonder where I fit in, or *if* I fit in. Because all I see right now is how your gun fits in."

She stopped.

I couldn't think of anything to say, so I put my arm around her in the awkward silence.

"You know I like you," she started again.

My heart dropped. "Sadie don't ..."

"But you know it?"

We hugged one of those hugs where each of us looked away, sideways; a hug like one of us was going away somewhere and not coming back.

"Sure," I said. "I know it. And I guess maybe the whole thing with Yasa just shook me up, more than I wanted to admit. And sometimes I don't ... can't tell you things I know, because I do care about you. I just don't want to worry you, and I especially don't want you being pulled into my business. But Sadie, you have to know that you are the one I come back for, always."

She leaned into me again. Her body shivered in staccato bursts as she quietly cried into my shoulder. It passed in a few minutes, and her breathing calmed.

"Jack, what if I'd shot somebody on accident?" she asked.

"But you didn't. Things are gonna be alright."

"Are they?"

Two women came out of the watchmaker's office, glanced down the hallway, and then headed toward the back stair, embarrassed at their intrusion.

"I try, Jack. I really try to believe you. And I can only imagine how finding Yasa like that could shake you up. But lately, I feel like you're holding back on me, and there's a part of you I can't seem to reach."

She was right. I knew it, and she knew it. And if I explained it to her now, that I'd possibly involved her in something dangerous, even accidentally, it could only make things worse between us. It played right into her fears about me and my work. I couldn't see a good way forward except to find this guy Bosko and his device, and end things ... *or lady will end up like Yasa* ... and I didn't even know who she'd be safe from.

"I said, *I'm sorry*, Sadie."

She leaned into my shoulder and cried. "The gunshot scared me," she said, without looking up. "A lot."

Our conversation was interrupted again, this time from the floor below by a cry of pain and then a long, stuttering wail that rose up the back stairway and subsided into distant sobs. She stiffened in my arms. Her eyes grew round, and she stared down the hall. I could feel her heart beating.

"So much for painless dentistry," I said, and we both laughed. The tension broke then, not just of the moment but of the entire morning. She laughed and cried. She told me more about the gunshot and the silence that followed at the Beehive, and we laughed at how George ran out of the kitchen with his shotgun in his hands.

"Jack, I was so embarrassed and so scared at the same time."

"I wish I could've been a fly on the wall."

But the moment couldn't last. I could feel disaster approaching, like a car on a road, in a dream. It was a car you couldn't swerve away from, and somehow you just knew it was all going to end in a terrible wreck.

It happened faster than I expected.

"Take me to lunch, Jack, to Keeley's, and tell me what's bothering you. Tell me about Yasa, and the Beeline, and my picture ... tell me the whole story ... get it all off your chest."

I loved Keeley's, the lunch counter near the Rialto Theater, and next to the hat shop. We went there after the first picture show we saw together when I'd told her I was broke and all she could have was a Coke. I was joking, but she got even: when we ordered dinner, she only had the Coke. The taffy-pulling machine in the window was making something pink, so I bought her taffy on the way out.

It was a great memory, but I was going to spoil it. I didn't want to. I wanted to tell her that I'd always take good care of her. But to do that, the letter said I had to be at Tiny's in twenty-five minutes.

Alone.

I'd run out of lies but couldn't worry her with the truth. Not yet. God only knows what the truth would do to her. To us.

"Listen, about lunch?" I said. "You know I'd love to, but ... it's just that I've gotta ... get the oil changed in the Ford just now."

I should have thought of something better.

She pushed me away without a word, tore her photograph in half, and dropped it there on the floor.

"Sadie, wait!"

But instead, she turned and ran down the back stairway.

I picked up the pieces. Maybe I cried too, inside. I kicked open the office door and slipped the two halves back in the gold frame on my desk. Then I waited a few minutes, followed her down the stairs, and caught a bus headed south.

16

Tiny's Barbecue and Chop House
Noon, Wednesday, July 21, 1948

The destination sign said OUTBOUND-MURRAY. I took a seat on the driver's side, across from the rear exit, and pulled out the note.

"MEET ME AT TINY'S ..."

The gun was in my waistband, pushing hard against my back. When we got close to the crossroad at 33rd I pulled the cord. The bus slowed, and I stepped off onto the gravel shoulder in front of a corner drugstore called Utah, which offered fountain service and Coca-Cola.

Tiny's was across the street, nestled between tall trees and the Texaco. The clapboard café was all signage, not much bigger than the gas station. The windows were open, and the smell of wood-smoked meat drifted toward me. I jaywalked straight to the front entry.

I was late, and the place was lousy with workmen there for lunch. They stood outside in groups, picking their teeth in the shade, hooking their thumbs in denim coveralls. A gravel drive ran back into the trees. Whoever sent the note must already be inside. I hoped they knew me on sight because I wasn't too good at matching handwriting with faces.

I was overdressed, especially for a hot day, but I needed the sports coat as cover for the gun in my waistband. I missed how easily the .38 fit my ankle holster or slipped into my pocket.

A short, steel counter ran across the front of the kitchen. A half-dozen booths crowded the west wall. An opening had been cut between the kitchen and eating areas to pass plates. It was noisy, smelling of ribs and beer.

A little guy with a white paper hat and a mustache found me. He appeared to say something, but I couldn't hear him above the din of the diners.

I cupped my hand to my ear.

"Here for lunch?" he asked, speaking louder.

"I'm supposed to meet a guy."

He nodded. "Pin game's in the back, that way."

He pointed to the back wall. There was a door painted out like the wall, between the two sets of booths. It had a peephole but no knob.

So that was the setup: ribs in the front, gambling in the rear. The rib business seemed prosperous on its own, but a uniformed cop sat near the back in a booth with a blonde. He had a plate of rib bones on the table. When I headed to the door, he stopped paying attention to her, never taking his hand off her knee while he looked me over. He nodded, almost imperceptibly, and turned back to the woman.

The door stayed shut. I knocked, shave-and-a-haircut. It opened. Somebody took my arm and pulled me inside. The light was dim and smoky. When the door closed, the noise of the chophouse vanished.

"First time, bub?" It was a doorman. He stood up and by the

low light of the desk lamp made sure I saw how big he was. Nobody patted me down.

"I'm Tiny," he said. I resisted the impulse to laugh.

"Of course, you are," I said. "I'm Jack, and I'm meeting somebody."

"Of course, you are," he said, mocking me. "Have a look around, pal. The girl in the corner can make change for the pinball." He indicated a row of noisy machines to the right. "And if you cause any trouble ..." His voice trailed off as he touched a baseball bat leaning against his stool.

My eyes adjusted slowly. The darkened room had a high ceiling and a three-blade fan that turned noiselessly on a pulley to clear the smoke. A line of red neon ran high around the walls. Bells sounded, but voices on this side of the door were hushed. Nobody putting down money seemed to care I was there.

I drifted further inside. Two guys worked the handles of a game where a pair of mechanical boxers were slugging it out. A low-hanging light illuminated a long wooden shuffleboard table, keeping players' faces in the dark. As the puck slid, a low groan came from the crowd. I headed over to the pinball machines, all bells and lights.

A hand took my forearm, again. It was connected to a pretty redhead, the gal who made change.

"This way," she said.

She led me to an alcove containing a hidden back door. She opened it, and I was blinded momentarily by the bright sunlight as the door closed behind me.

Black flies buzzed around a long row of dented garbage cans. A gray Chevy coupe with a paint job like worn-out sandpaper sat waiting, windows down, door open, and engine running. The driver leaned over to the passenger window. It was Yasa's "brother."

"Get in, neighbor; I have been waiting in the hot sun."

I hesitated, trying to control my anger and fear.

"Well, why are you waiting for? You have your gun."

He was right. I slid onto the hot bench seat and closed the door.

17

Road Trip
12:35 p.m., Wednesday, July 21, 1948

We headed south, then made a U-turn, towards town. My right hand instinctively braced against the window frame, angling my body to face him.

I eased away from the door and reached back under my jacket. The Walther came out but snagged on a belt loop and clattered to the floor at my feet.

He glanced down. "Maybe you expected ribs for lunch, yes?" he laughed.

"Not my worst moment today."

"I can call you Jack?" he asked while checking his rearview mirror. His voice had the texture of gravel, like he needed to clear his throat.

"Suit yourself. Where are we headed?"

He didn't answer but made a sharp left down an alley between two brick warehouses and pulled over behind a wooden garage. He stopped the car where shade from a row of tall poplars cut the sun's midday shine.

Before the engine was even quiet, he'd pulled his own gun from the holster under his left arm.

"I have no wish to harm you," he said in a matter of fact, almost casual way.

"You mean, not like yesterday?" I had a momentary surge of fear-driven adrenaline but held my hands and my eyes as still as I could.

He looked puzzled.

"When you killed Yasa and shot at me through the floor?" I prompted.

"I would never hurt Yasa."

He pulled the magazine from his gun, popped the bullets out, and cleared the remaining shell from the chamber. He placed the empty mag and the gun, a model I didn't recognize, on the dashboard between us, daring me to pick it up.

I hesitated, then hefted the heavy gun, admiringly.

"FEG 37M, is made in Hungary and can shoot some 9mm," he said.

"That's a rare thing."

"To shoot 9mm?"

"No," I said, "to hold a gun that's been fired at you."

"Was mistake, I think," he said. "I did not know it was you."

I took a couple of 9mm rounds from my own pocket and pushed them into his clip, then slid it into the grip. I twisted on the seat and put the gun back on the dash, a little farther from him. I picked up my own gun now and set it on my lap. He didn't know I kept all my bullets in my pocket.

He pulled the FEG off the dash and we drove off again, for a few minutes in silence.

"I think I like you, Jack Hammer. Call me Marko, if you like," he said.

"Marko?"

His smile showed a gap between his front teeth. He twisted the steering wheel hard to make another quick U-turn.

"We can trust each other, yes?" he asked, glancing left and right. He seemed nonchalant, almost casual about our previous encounter. I was on edge, breathing fast, not knowing where this was heading. He wasn't just thick, he was solid, like a brick. A wrestling match wouldn't end well for me. He smelled of garlic and cigarettes.

He glanced in the wing mirrors again, checking the road behind us.

"All this driving and turning ... you think somebody's followin' you?"

He didn't answer but gave a sly smile my way.

"You think somebody's followin' me?" I guessed.

He chuckled at that.

"I will speak directly, as you Americans like to do. I know that Yasa asked you for help. You and I, we are strangers to one another, but I ask: Do you still look for Bosko? Because in this, our minds are together. You can help me also to find Bosko, and then perhaps together we can find who killed Yasa."

"But you are the one—"

He held up his hand to stop me.

"I said, I would never hurt her. We have shown trust in each other, and now also you know my name. So, let us go someplace where we can talk about our business."

"Business? You mean Sadie?"

His left eye narrowed. "I do not know about this Sadie."

We made several more loops, backtracking our route. He was still checking his rearview mirror for a tail.

18

Napoli Café
1:05 p.m., Wednesday, July 21, 1948

We ended up in a café on the southern end of Main Street, nearly as far south as the ballpark. It was small and quiet, with eight tables and an empty lunch counter. Black-and-white art photos of nude women, backs facing the room, hung in slick ebony frames. A chair rail with a shelf ran along one side of the room. Tiny, hand-painted ceramic birds perched along its edge.

"Now, I hope you do not prefer the counter," he said, gesturing with his hands to the rear of the café. "I so much like this place. Clean cloth on tables, it seems suitable for two men like us to discuss business arrangements."

Business?

We sat down at a four-top, jockeying for who sat with their back to the wall, settling for neither. A little waiter cleared off two place settings and brought out a beer for Marko and a ribbed glass jar filled with hard, thin breadsticks. His ears stuck out. A wall fan installed above the front door blew hot air from outside toward the screened door at the back.

"Where're your friends, Marko?"

"Friends? I have many friends."

"C'mon, your *friends*, the ones who sandbagged me, at the Beeline ... your muscle."

"What is this muscle you speak of?" he asked. He was sweating again. He took a white handkerchief from his pants pocket and wiped his forehead while he smiled. "You would like some beer?"

"I don't drink beer," I answered. "Mormon."

He acted surprised. "I do not know if I can trust some man who drinks no beer."

"Even after our little gun game, back there in the alley?"

"But no beer ...?"

He ordered me a Coke and then lunch for both of us in a language I didn't recognize. We sat for a few minutes, sizing each other up. I could tell he knew the waiter personally, perhaps in the way a good customer comes to know service help.

I pushed a breadstick into a slice of butter.

"What're we doin' here, Marko?" I asked. "Why were you in the house, and how are you connected to Yasa and Bosko?"

"You see, I too am the investigator."

"Come on," I sniffed at that. The little waiter returned, delivered the Coke and a small bowl of olives and cheese, and then scurried back into the cloud of steam coming from the kitchen.

"No, is true. You see, I come from Serbia, the country of Yasa and Bosko, and our most famous citizen, Nikola Tesla. Do you know about this man, Tesla?"

"Let me guess," I answered. "He's a private investigator too?"

"No, of course not! Tesla was genius inventor."

Inventor ...?

"You see, many years ago, Bosko worked in some New York City laboratory with Tesla where he had access to very many of Tesla's ideas, but Tesla died. Your government came and took many of his belongings, and many papers went missing. But Bosko also took some of Tesla's most valuable ideas. Those things rightfully belonged to my client, so now he is most anxious to have them back again."

He signaled the waiter for more beer.

"So, you're saying you have this client who is an heir to Mr. Tesla's estate?"

"Yes, of course! He is the nephew."

"And you're looking for Bosko, because he stole some of Tesla's ideas?"

"And papers, yes. Will you help me?"

"Ha! Why would I work for you?"

"Because I can pay you." He laid a spread of ten-dollar bills on the table. I considered them carefully as he gathered them back into his shirt pocket.

"You already know more about Bosko than I do—"

"Perhaps, but here is a true thing, Jack: I am stranger here. To me, this city is not so familiar. So why not? Is there someone else I should be asking for help?"

A tall waiter carried two hot plates with a towel and set them on the table. One was filled with oblong meatballs and flatbread, the other with small bits of pasta surrounding mashed potatoes.

"You will enjoy," he said as if it was an order. "Ćevapi and pierogis."

"Tell me about Yasa?"

"Yasa ... yes." He stopped and poked at his food. "When Tesla died, Bosko disappeared and left no trail. They were here, in your country. But this was 1943, when the war was still very much in my country, and we had many accounts still to settle."

"German accounts?" I asked.

"And others," he said, leaning forward as though warming to the role of storyteller. "You see, Tesla was true genius. Before war came, he told people about some grand new invention, some amazing application of magnificent electrical power. These people, important people in my country, believed him. He had already invented so many useful things."

"Name one," I said.

He busied himself with ćevapi and bread, held up a hand, took a drink of beer and cleared his throat. "Wireless radio. Tesla developed wireless radio."

"Marconi invented wireless radio," I said. "Everyone knows that."

"You are wrong, Jack, but we must not quarrel over such details. When war ended, my client had become some important person to my country, with so many duties. Yet always he thought about Tesla's ideas, and how they could help our country, and always he remembered Bosko's theft. Our plan was his idea."

"Okay, but I asked about Yasa."

His face brightened.

"Of course! You see, Yasa was our plan! Because Bosko had gone to hiding here, and we could not find him. Instead, we searched for some family at home. We hoped to gain information about where he went. But the war changed many lives and ended so many others. We found only his niece, Yasa."

"And she knew Bosko was here?"

"No," he said, shaking his head, "but she remembered his name. Our hope was that she had friends who could help her search for him in America, to help their family to be together. So, my client gave her money to travel. I followed her here."

"So, when she led you to him, you killed *her* and not *him*?" I couldn't help myself.

He sat quietly for a moment, rubbing two fingers on the table. "Why, Mr. Hammer? We knew that Bosko would never come from his hiding except perhaps for family, and now I have much regret to the fate of Yasa. But she did find him. I ... we helped her to leave

Yugoslavia at so much expense. So, you must believe, I would never hurt Yasa."

"I thought you said Serbia."

He held up both hands, slid back from the table, and walked to the cigarette machine. It was waist-high black porcelain with a chrome insignia on the front and a half-glass top. He leaned over and spent a moment surveying the contents, tapping a finger on the edge. Then he dropped two dimes into the slot and pushed the button for Pall Mall.

"Do you like smoking?" he asked.

"I don't."

"Some of my friends, they say is for good health to smoke."

He sat down again and pulled an ashtray close. He tapped the pack end on the table, pulled out a cigarette, and struck a match. For a moment, we both watched the sulfur burn off.

"They come for Morava cigarettes, from my country, but I so much prefer American cigarettes."

"Yeah, and we were talking about Yasa," I repeated, shaking off his dodge.

The little waiter appeared again and cleared off the table, brushing crumbs into his gathered apron. He spoke with Marko in his guttural language and hurried away. Marko blew smoke over his left shoulder.

He turned the package of cigarettes over and over, eventually tapping out another one.

I took the package from his hand and set it aside. "Okay. If you didn't kill Yasa, who did?"

19

Napoli Café
1:45 p.m., Wednesday, July 21, 1948

If Marko was stage acting, he was talented. His voice quivered as he spoke. "I do not know, but I will find out." He cleared his eyes with his handkerchief. "And I fear Bosko is also in much trouble."

"What kind of trouble?"

"The kind that gets him dead." He paused. "We must find him first."

I stared back into his eyes. They were black, like a painting of dark eyes pasted into his tan face. To find Bosko, I had my own reasons, but Marko? He crushed out one half-smoked cigarette and lit another one.

"Did Yasa know about your plan?"

"Yasa was smart. If we used her, she also used us. We told her that she was receiving help from the government, some special relocation benefit for orphans of war. But she knew something else. When I followed her to New York, in springtime, she disappeared. Only two days ago did I find her here again, in Salt Lake City."

"The same day I met her?"

"Of course! I followed her to Bosko's house. She was afraid when she saw me again, and told me she had found her uncle, but he went away."

"To where?"

"She did not know. She was expecting your visit and said you would help her to find Bosko again."

"What else was she afraid of?" I asked. "It sounds like she knew more than you're telling me."

He paused and thought for a moment. "She feared being here, alone."

"What time was this on Monday?"

"Evening time, while it rained. We sat together under some ... outside roof. We had not spoken together since being together in our old country. I told her I also would like to meet this Bosko. We sat and talked of home. I said goodbye and waited across the street until dark, but you did not come."

"Then she was alive when you left? You swear it?"

"Of course. I returned in morning, and her door was open. I found Yasa as you found her."

He crossed himself with the cigarette, head, down, right to left.

"Why didn't you just call the police?"

"Would they have helped me, or arrested me?"

A gust of hot wind blew through the screened door at the back.

"Was it you who found the money?"

"Of course, but I was not looking for this money."

"And you didn't take any."

"I am not some thief!" he said. "I am searching for Bosko."

"Why didn't you just tell me this, when I came to the back door, instead of that story about being her brother?"

He tapped ashes from the cigarette into the ashtray.

"I knew you only by name, Jack Hammer. You did not know me. If you could be in my place, a stranger from another country, a dead woman in that house, much cash on her cabinet—it looked for me to be guilty, yes?"

His story seemed plausible enough on its face, but then he could have found out my name by beating it out of Yasa.

"Then why did you shoot at me?"

He appealed with his hands, upturned and apart.

"I did not know you had come back. Policemen make their own sounds, so I knew it was not some police. In my idea, footsteps above belonged to someone else, perhaps Yasa's true killer."

"So, you just shot blindly, through the floor?" I asked.

"Perhaps I acted foolishly, but a man who steals valuable things makes many enemies. People get hurt, and Bosko is, how do you say, playing with fires. I do not wish to get burned too. You must understand, other people also would not stop to be killing him, or me, to get what he has stolen. They are bad people."

"Others? What others? Americans? Russians? Who?"

"Not from here, I think." The cigarette machine caught his eye again.

"So, all that crazy driving, on the way here ... that was for these bad people?"

He exhaled heavily and nodded his head.

"And your friend, Bosko ... he knows your face too, doesn't he?"

Marko wagged his finger at me, smiling. "Yes! You Americans are so clever. I met Bosko many years ago. But he would take much care to avoid seeing me again. I still search, but you must be my eyes."

Bird dog ... just like Yasa.

He put out the cigarette and stuck out his beefy right hand. "Shall we do business, Jack? For Yasa?"

A clatter of dropped pots echoed in the kitchen.

"Swear to me you're just recovering stolen property, that you're not gonna hurt Bosko if I find him."

He ran his tongue around his lips, mulling it over, then crossed himself again.

Was that a yes?

"Any idea where I should start looking?"

"Wherever Yasa pointed."

"Are you gonna tell me your client's name?" I asked.

He hesitated. "Sava. His name is Sava Kosanovic. Do you know it?"

"Means nothin' to me," I said, but wrote it down anyway. "I get fifteen dollars a day plus expenses, an extra hundred when I find him, and I need three days in advance." *For Sadie then,* I rationalized. It couldn't hurt to get a paycheck while I was looking for him, anyway.

He stood up, peeled off five tens from a roll in his pocket, and moved in close enough for me to smell the garlic, the cigarette smoke, and his body odor.

"No police," he insisted. "This is some private matter."

"I'm a curious guy, Marko: Just how much money are we talkin' about here?" I asked, standing up and pocketing the cash. "These ideas, these missing papers, are they really worth all this trouble?"

"This value ... this fair value is many millions, possibly beyond imagination. Tesla was our country's great imaginer. But I tell you this, Jack Hammer, when you find Bosko take care not to scare him. I do not want to 'spook him away,' as you say. He is so easy to disappear, and I must speak with him, and he must give to me some answers. Remember: Bosko is key."

Face to face, I thought. *What trouble was that going to be?*

"Tell me, Marko, have you ever heard about something called a Cvito device? Maybe something Bosko invented?"

Or stole, from Tesla?

He put a hand on the doorknob, eyebrows lowered. "What is this word, *device*?"

His hand was still. The other held another cigarette, unlit.

"How do I contact you?" I asked.

He hesitated. "Is difficult," he said. "We should have some signal. So, I think you have your flag, yes? Some American flag?"

I nodded.

"Hang your flag in window at your office. I myself will be checking ... and we will contact you."

"We?"

He busied himself with the cigarette and ignored me. Was that a slip of his tongue or a problem with speaking English?

"You know my office location?" I asked.

"Of course! Yasa told me everything."

20

Police Impound Lot
3:15 p.m., Wednesday, July 21, 1948

But I hadn't told Marko everything.

He was in the dark about my ambush at the Beeline, and he didn't seem to know who Sadie was. I left things that way. I wasn't sure what to make of those lapses, except that it made sense that there was somebody else who wrote notes without signing them, somebody else looking for Bosko, and somebody else threatening me with harm to Sadie. Maybe it was the same somebody else who killed Yasa. *Bad people.*

He dropped me off near Tiny's, and I caught a city bus headed downtown. It let me off on the corner, near the police impound lot where a tall, thin, duck-tailed Officer Kissell had my car ready.

He walked to his guard shack with long, loping strides.

"Just sign here ... and here," he said. "You'll find it over there."

"Keys?" I asked. He pulled them from a pegboard behind him.

I slipped my office key back on the chain with the others.

"Can I give you some advice, Hammer?" he asked.

"Everybody tries."

"Take better care of your car. Radiator's half empty, and there's a bunch of loose wires tucked up under the dash."

He was right.

"You changed your oil lately?" he asked.

I winced and added automobile maintenance to my list of things to do.

On the way back to my office, I stopped in the basement at ZCMI and bought flowers from the Japanese florist downstairs. Red roses might work.

My car fit nicely into a shady spot in the alley. I walked up the back stairs to the third floor, taking my keys this time. My furniture and belongings, piled in a heap on the floor in the office, could wait.

Sleep eluded me, and after a few hours I gave up on the cot and washed up in the sink. I pulled Bosko's damaged picture from the drawer and walked downstairs, leaving my jacket and gun behind. When I came out of the alley onto Main Street, the huge square clock next to Arden's said 5:40. The sidewalk was filled with workers from upstairs offices, hurrying to catch seats on buses home.

I turned north toward Peter Pan Billiards. Yasa said Bosko spent time there with the "little balls": *Peter's place.* I thought I'd stop to see if Bosko had shown his face lately, then head over by Sadie's and try to patch things up with her before going to work.

The pool hall was in the basement of a building wedged between a shoe store and a sporting goods shop. A barefoot kid was hawking papers out front. Moss grew on the concrete steps. A guy named Gene ran a three-chair barbershop at the bottom of the stairs. It smelled like tobacco and bay rum and went by the same name, Peter Pan.

I stepped past it, through the open door, and into the pool hall.

2I

Peter Pan Billiards
6:25 p.m., Wednesday, July 21, 1948

The wall art in the Peter Pan always spoke to me: an elk head, decades' worth of old fight cards, and framed photos of boxers—some local standouts, even a signed Joe Louis—tacked to the grimy, plastered walls and columns. Mementos like that played on me like they would anyone, raising darkly hidden questions about whether I measured up man-to-man. A layer of cigar smoke kept a tight lid on things, hovering just above the table lights.

Off to the left, a four-panel wooden door to the poker room was closed. I could hear shouting, arguing, and profanity. A game was going on.

The Peter Pan had a reputation for two things: serious pool, and money pool. The tables were top-notch, Brunswick Medalists, ten-foot-long pocketed slabs with green felt. Two or three games were in progress in the back, cue sticks moving the wooden number tags along a wire above the tables to keep score.

A skinny guy with a garter on one arm and rimless readers called to me. "What's new, Jack? I haven't seen you in a while." It was Bobby. He'd been running the place since before the war, along with boxing, billiards, card games, you name it.

"Yeah, well ..." I said, thinking before I answered. "I been stayin' away. Seemed like you set me up. Remember last time I was here?"

He had a puzzled look.

"I set you up? I didn't tell you to get a game going with that guy," he protested. "Besides, I've seen you play. You don't need me to ride around in your back pocket and tell you when to take a game."

"Funny you remember *him*, but you didn't warn *me*."

"Everybody hits a lucky streak now and then."

He pulled some receipts out of his pocket and walked them over to the brass register, where he slipped them under the cash drawer. Then he walked behind the counter and sat down on a high stool.

"You lookin' for a game?" he asked.

I pulled out Bosko's picture and laid it down in front of him.

"I'm looking for this guy. You know him?"

He twisted nervously on the seat.

"Don't do that, Jack ... you know I can't remember faces so good."

"C'mon, Bobby, he was here last week, getting himself thrown out," I coached. "Nothing comes to mind?"

He laid the photo under the desk lamp and squinted through his glasses. "Somebody said he was here, did they?" he asked without looking up.

"They did."

"Then why are you askin' me, if you know about it?"

I handed him a Lincoln from my pocket.

His eyes flashed anger.

"Settle down, it's not a bribe," I said. "Set me up with a table and give me the change. I'll ask around on my own." I took the photo back and slipped it into my shirt pocket.

He was lying, and he knew I knew it.

"Don't go bothering my customers, Jack," he said. "They come here to get away."

"Look, the guy went missing over the weekend," I said. "His niece hired me to make sure he's okay. That's all."

I walked to the wall and pulled down a house stick. I wondered how many hen-pecked husbands depended on Bobby to keep their secrets.

"Take that back table," he said. He handed me my five back and pointed to the corner.

"What's this for?" I asked him.

"You make me feel guilty," he said.

22

Peter Pan Billiards
6:40 p.m., Wednesday, July 21, 1948

I walked to the bar, leaned between stools, and asked for a Coke. Three guys took turns at a table across the room, insurance guys by the look of them. One of them had skills. The other two were there just to prop him up. I showed them Bosko's photo, but they didn't know him. Claimed they didn't come around much. Watching them play, I believed them.

Two younger guys played at a table further back, drinking beer. Easy money, probably college kids who drove here in Daddy's car.

"Sure, I seen that old geezer in here a few times, trying to hustle some poor sap. Not for a while though. I played with him, about three months back. Took me for two bucks! I learned a lesson there."

They didn't know anything else. I headed back to my corner and set the Coke down on the bench, then racked up a nine-ball spread for practice. I was trying to learn how to break, leaving the cue ball dead in the center of the table.

He's been here, but Bobby's holding back.

After my second or third shot, I felt eyes on my back. Some guy was staring at me, leaning hard on his right arm against the bar and smoking a cigarette. He must have come out of the card room. I hadn't seen him before.

"You're doin' it wrong," he said.

I ignored him and shot again.

"I said, you're doin' that all wrong."

"Excuse me?" I said.

He blew smoke out to his left shoulder. "You're working the nine-ball break? So, you shouldn't be hitting the one head-on like that, unless you're tryin' to send the whole rack to the rails."

"Is that right?"

He was mid-forties, wearing work boots, faded jeans, and a white t-shirt that had seen better days. He kept a pack of Lucky's in his shirt pocket, the round target showing through. Oiled down, his red hair was almost black. I couldn't place him, but once I'd seen him, I couldn't forget him.

I thought he was a jackass.

"How would you play it?" I asked.

He stubbed out his cigarette, pulled a house stick off the wall, and came over.

"You gotta use the angles. Set up your cue ball along the head-string to the side a bit and use a little softer touch." He shot at the one and sent two balls to the far rail. The cue ball died in the pack.

"There. You try it."

I set it up like he showed me. The cue ball struck the one, but I failed to put any balls to the rail. A foul.

"Takes practice," he shrugged.

I tried it again and did better.

He took a copper lighter from his pants pocket and lit another smoke. "Name's Red," he said, "on account of the hair."

"I wouldn't have guessed it."

"You up for a game?" he asked. He spun a ball on the felt.

I checked my watch. It was almost seven.

"Bobby says you're looking for a game."

I glanced at the counter, but Bobby was looking away.

"You're talking about a money game?"

"I don't play much for money," he said. "How 'bout we just shoot around, see if we match up?"

It was a hustler's approach. Everybody here plays for money, but I could give up a little while I worked the room.

"Alright," I said. "You like nine-ball?"

He kept playing with the house stick. I studied his stroke. He was smooth and steady, but he mishit a few shots, off-center on the cue ball. Maybe that was his cover.

I sent the low ball on the table to the side pocket.

"What do you do in your real life?" he asked.

"You don't think I hustle pool for a living?" I asked.

He laughed, making the raspy sound a long-time smoker makes before he coughed. "You might, Jack," he said. "But you won't catch any action back in the corner, playing alone."

My face couldn't hide the surprise. Bobby must've told him my name. I pulled the photo from my shirt pocket and handed it to him.

"I look for things, people sometimes. Ever seen this guy hanging around?"

He studied it while I lined up a shot on the one.

"What happened—"

"—to his eyes?" I finished.

"Yeah, I seen him around. Why are ya looking for him?"

He handed the photo back.

"Family thing," I said. "His niece is worried about him. He went missing a few days ago."

He scratched the back of his head, sideways.

"Not payback, for some pool cheat?"

"No."

"Mostly I play at the Mecca, up by Lamb's. There's a tournament up there this weekend. You know it?"

"A little," I said. I meant it as a joke. The Mecca was hidden in the basement of the Hotel Little. He didn't get it.

We shot back and forth for ten minutes, and I let him talk. He ran a blast crew at the mine at Bingham. Said he came to town every week, but he had nothing more to say about Bosko.

The room filled up steady, without much noise or fanfare.

Eventually, he put the nine in the side pocket, ending the game. We weren't evenly matched, but I could play with him. Two young guys watching from the bench stood up and came over.

"You guys are done, right?" one said in a declarative sort of way.

He was cocky, sure of himself, an early twenties hotshot. A little on the heavy side, he had the suntans-Florsheim-button-down look of a college kid.

"You wanna play?" I asked, chalking my tip.

"How much?"

"Ten cents a ball," I said. Marko's money burned a hole in my pocket.

"You guys ever played a ring game before?" Red asked.

"Sure, we have!" The bigger guy spoke for both of them, their eyes growing large.

"No playin' it safe, and every shot counts."

The big kid went first. His break scattered nicely and dropped the five, but he was too eager, and he failed trying to sink the nine off the one on the next shot.

I went second, putting the one, two, and three in before selling out to Red.

He ran the table. The younger kid never even got in the game.

Red had a nice touch, and now I could see just how much he'd been holding out on me. I stepped away for a minute and showed Bosko's picture around some more. A few guys had seen him, but nobody knew where he was.

In the next hour, I got in gear but still came up short, still down a fin to Red. The two kids gave up more than that and called it quits after three innings.

It was eight-thirty.

23

Peter Pan Billiards
8:30 p.m., Wednesday, July 21, 1948

"I gotta be someplace else," I said, thinking of Sadie.

I pulled cash from my pocket and handed Red a five. I'd already spent a good chunk of the money Marko fronted me.

Red took the money and racked up another nine.

"How 'bout this, Jack?" he said. "Let's go one more game, double or nothin'."

I shook my head. "Suckers' bet," I said. "I watched you play, and I didn't stop in tonight just to torch my whole bankroll. Truth is, I didn't even walk in intending to play at all. I just gotta find this guy, Bosko."

He held up my money, straightening it. "I got a confession to make too."

"I know. I spotted you, right off."

"Not that," he said. "Bobby sent me over to talk to you, about your guy."

"Yeah? You didn't have much to say, and since when has Bobby been lookin' out for me?"

He lit another cigarette and took a long pull. "You know, I don't mind clippin' those hot shot kids for a few bucks. It's a good lesson for them. They'll end up better players, or drift away. But I worry if Bobby hears I took money off you, he'll make my life miserable."

"That's your problem," I said. "I ain't takin' it back."

"I wasn't saying you would. I'm just thinkin' you and me should have one last game. Maybe I can work my way out of a jam with Bobby, and you might get back that cash."

"Or you end up deeper in my pocket and higher on Bobby's list."

He laughed and chalked his cue. "You're okay, Hammer," he said. "How about this? What if I play left-handed?"

"You'll tell me what else you know about Bosko?"

"It ain't that much."

"But that's the deal: win or lose, you tell me what you know."

It was getting late, but left-handed? I could really use that cash back, and I couldn't help myself, even if double-or-nothin' was a sucker bet.

"One last game," I said. "You play southpaw ... and no push-outs."

He hesitated.

"Or not," I said.

He worked more chalk onto the tip. "Okay," he said. "Let's do it."

I shook the rack, and when we lagged for break, I won. I put the cue ball off to the side, managing a safe break. Three balls grouped along the rail; the rest huddled up in the center with the cue ball.

"See that?" he said. "You're better already. Got your money's worth, I'd say."

He walked around the table figuring angles. A minute passed. He lined up on the one, touched it, and dropped the six in the corner, leaving the one in an easy place. He lined up on the one again, dropped it, and walked around the table.

The game started to draw attention. A few guys drifted over to watch.

I realized right off that I was in trouble. "You shoot as good from the port side as you shot all night long," I said, feeling lost.

He looked up, from lining up on the four.

"That's because I've been playing left-handed all night, Jack," he said. "You're gonna need to pay better attention to details if you're gonna survive as a private cop. And when it comes to pool, don't ever go for double-or-nothing."

He ran the table without a miss.

I knew better than to protest. I pulled out another Lincoln from my pocket, peeling it from a jumble of ones.

"You got promise, kid. Don't be so hard on yourself," he said.

"You still owe me," I said. "What about the guy in the photo?"

Red held up his drink like a toast, left-handed.

"I seen him, a couple of nights ago out in Bingham. He tried hustlin' some boys out there and almost got hisself killed."

"Bingham?"

"Sure. Near the mine out south, thirty miles or so."

"You're sure it was him?"

"Looked like him ..."

I pulled out the photo again and he stared at it.

"It coulda been at the Diamond," he said. "Maybe the Copper King ... I'm a little fuzzy there. Just don't use my real name if you head out that way."

I wanted to ask why he didn't tell me all this before, but he turned away, counting his cash.

Bobby walked out of the card room and raised his head in an upward nod. His expression was blank, but it was a blank I could fill in. It cost me another sawbuck, but in his eyes, we were as even as we were gonna get.

I laughed to myself as I left, at something Red said.

Don't use my real name.
He never told me his real name.

24

In Transit
9:30 p.m., Wednesday, July 21, 1948

I followed the stairway up into the hot, rain-threatened night. Arden's square clock across Main reminded me I was late. Streetlights flickered on and store displays teased, *Come back tomorrow*. My car waited in the alley. In the back seat I found a dozen roses, forgotten. Their thorny stems, weakened by the heat, couldn't support the deep red flowers.

I drove south, toward Sadie's.

She deserved an explanation, and I wanted to smooth things over. I turned right onto Layton Avenue, stopped two houses away, and walked to the family's back porch, but the house was already dark. A cat screeched behind the fence line, then another cat, then crickets again. I left the roses at the door with a hastily scrawled note: "I'M SORRY, JACK."

I slid back in the car and sat silently, looking at the neighborhood in the darkness. Everything was so tidy, so well-manicured, and so right. For a moment, I imagined the life Sadie and I could have together in our own little brick bungalow, with a garage out back. My mind conjured up an image of me coming home from work, from some uptown office ...

But that was never gonna happen.

I skipped tapping on her window and headed back to town. The gas gauge bounced and caught my eye, almost on EMPTY. I reached into my pants pocket. The remains of Marko's advance might be just enough to get me out to Bingham and back, tomorrow.

25

Auerbach's Department Store
9:50 p.m., Wednesday, July 21, 1948

"Where've you been?"

Jonny had on my Bees cap, ready to leave. I grabbed it off his head and tossed it back on the coat rack. The office smelled like a diner.

Chili?

"Anything I should know?" I asked.

He grabbed his lunch box and turned to the door. "Should be a quiet night, so try stayin' awake," he said. "No gunshots or wild stuff, okay?"

I wanted to ask him about Sadie, and what he thought I should do, and I wanted his advice on Marko, and Bosko, and on what to tell Uncle Jim.

"Last night," I said, "you know, that question I wanted to talk over—?"

"About Sadie?" he asked. "Did she say yes?"

Before I could answer, the door slammed, and he was gone.

I made my rounds through aisles of kitchen appliances in the basement, over to fine china, headed up through men's wear and women's fashion. The words *Bring me Cvito Device* kept running through my head.

I made my way back to the security office, set up Bosko's picture on the little desk, and stared at it, hoping for inspiration.

How are you the key?

Around midnight, I wrote down a list of possible leads I had for his whereabouts: BINGHAM and POOL HALLS. Looking back through my notes, the word WORKSHOP reminded me I had a third lead: Marko had been searching Bosko's cellar when I found him, and Yasa wanted me to see the workshop.

I made a spur-of-the-moment plan: I could leave the mannequins in charge, slip away for a few minutes, and take a look around. Technically, I was on duty the whole night, but this would be like a lunch break, and I could count on the dummies to keep quiet about my absence. I checked that every door was locked, grabbed my flashlight, and slipped out the employee entrance, heading east. I figured I could pick the old lock on Bosko's back door if I had to.

Maybe I didn't know exactly what to look *for*, but I knew there weren't any answers here in the bargain basement, and Bingham would have to wait till tomorrow.

26

Bosko's House
12:30 a.m., Thursday, July 22, 1948

I parked on McClelland, where the service alley past Bosko's house emptied next to a white clapboard house with dark windows. Gravel crunched under my feet as I walked past his damaged garage. Storm clouds pushed in from the north and west, but overhead the full moon was high and bright.

A printed sign at the back door said, "KEEP OUT BY ORDER OF SLC POLICE DEPARTMENT." The screen was unlatched, but something was jammed in the skeleton lock, just under the door-knob. Whatever it was, I couldn't get it out. I walked around the house checking every window I could reach. They were all latched except one: a tiny basement window too small for me to fit through. The front door boasted a new Yale deadbolt.

I walked back and sat in my car, thinking, until a light flicked on in the clapboard house and startled me.

I started up and drove north, circling the block and ending up one street east, across from Bosko's place. The spot was partially hidden under a canopy of bushes next to the Beeline. I pocketed my keys and pulled a tire iron from the trunk, along with a blanket to deaden the sound of breaking glass.

It was my best idea.

I passed the front porch and headed around to the back door, where I planned to break a small pane in the door itself. With luck, I figured I could reach through and turn the lock from the inside. On the side of the house, partly hidden by ivy, I noticed a shiny patch on a dark metal hatch that caught the moonlight. I moved vines away. *An old coal chute!* I stepped back into the alley and peered at the roof. A tin vent with a Chinaman's hat meant the furnace had already been converted to natural gas.

The chute door was locked but popped open with the help of the tire iron. I knelt in the garden and turned the flashlight into the opening. Coal dust covered everything, making it hard to tell exactly how deep the coal bin was. I dropped a piece of gravel inside. From the time it took to hit something, I guessed the floor was only five or six feet down. I laid the tire iron on the ledge, pushed the torch into my waistband, and lined the framed opening with the blanket as best I could. Kneeling down in the grass and flowers, I backed my way through the opening. It was a tight fit. I hung on the edge with both hands and dropped through, feet first.

It was deeper than I thought.

The concrete floor hit me hard, and I couldn't quite reach back up to the ledge at the opening. I switched on the flashlight and took stock of the empty room, black as night. The only door opened a foot above the coal room floor. I followed the beam of the flashlight into Bosko's basement workshop.

Edna hadn't exaggerated. Even without power, the setup of electrical equipment was dazzling. Three long workbenches spanned the depth of the cellar, front to back. Bare copper wires crisscrossed the space just above hat-level, connected to aluminum cylinders and large electrical tubes by multi-colored glass insulators. Broken glass littered the tables, tubes shattered by my gunshots from above. A longer, crystalline tube spiraled around a dark shaft.

Could something here be the Cvito device?

I found a pull chain attached to one of the bulbs hanging through the mess of wires, but it didn't work.

I ran the flashlight across the ceiling where floor joists, dark with age, were decorated with expired license plates. Several small holes through the aging floorboards above boasted sharp white slivers of gunshot damage from my earlier exchange with Marko. Water had dripped down from the bathroom and spotted across the tables, but everything was dry now.

A surplus combat radio and headset sat on a desktop along the far wall. Writing materials on the desk blotter suggested it was the room's primary workspace. An empty file drawer stood open, like somebody had been interrupted and walked away. A gray, pocket-sized notebook had fallen partly between slats of the rough, wooden floor. I picked it up and stuck it in my shirt pocket.

Thumbing through the pages of an open reference book on the workbench, I flipped to a marked page with an article about wave theory and electricity. Next to it, a legal notepad contained hand-written scribbles that I couldn't decipher, in an alphabet I recognized but couldn't read. I tore off the top sheets and shoved them in my back pocket, then tried making sense of the other equipment. Any of it could have qualified as the Cvito device—or not.

I glanced at my watch. I needed to get back to work, to sign onto my rounds again. On the short side of the cellar, two tall cabinets flanked the makeshift door that I'd noticed from the outside yesterday. It swung inward. I grabbed the spring lock handle, pulling it open, but noticing too late the electrical wires running upward from the strike toward a coiled wire at the lightbox.

A force jumped from the latch through my arm, momentarily paralyzing my whole body.

In an instant, everything went black.

27

Bosko's House
2:30 a.m., Thursday, July 22, 1948

Sand ground against my left cheek.

Sadie was there, with her back toward me. I couldn't see her face, but I knew it was her, and she was saying something to her dad as they walked away.

A soft light was shining. I opened one eye. Sadie vanished. I closed it again, but she wouldn't come back. From far away I felt pain hammering at my right hand.

I opened my eye again.

It was moonlight.

I tried sitting up but laying down seemed better. I closed my eye and took a breath, trying to remember something. *Bosko's place.* Moonlight streamed in through the high opening of a window. *Not a window ... a coal chute, but how did I get back in here?* I sat up and remembered looking through Bosko's things, reaching for the door latch.

After that, memories seemed just out of reach.

Somebody had booby-trapped the cellar door!

They wouldn't have expected visitors coming through the coal chute, so it must've been set up to discourage entry from the outside. *Why hadn't the cops disengaged it?*

I rubbed my left hand across my face and through my hair and stood up, unsteady. I reached for the door to the lab, but it was locked now, from the lab side. That was wrong. *Who put a lock on a coal room?* Everything seemed backward.

Only one explanation made sense: Somebody else had been here, hiding in a cabinet or behind the old furnace when they heard me open the coal chute. Maybe they were still here.

Bosko? Marko? Someone ... bad?

I reached for my gun, then remembered it was back in the Karrick Building. There was a crackling sound and the continual pulsing hum of some electrical mechanism, sounds I hadn't heard before.

I went to the chute door. It was still wide open, and I still couldn't reach it by a few inches. Straining for height, my fingers were short of the ledge.

I walked back to the locked door. "Hey!" I shouted. "Who's out there?"

There wasn't any answer.

I tried pounding on the door, feeling a stab of pain in my right hand. Nobody answered.

Instead, there was a loud bang and the humming stopped.

I listened in the dark for someone to come to the door. No one did.

The crackling got louder.

A moment later I smelled acrid smoke coming from the edges of the locked door. I couldn't see it, but it was there, and it wasn't wood smoke.

It was the pungent smell of an electrical appliance shorting out.

2 8

Bosko's House
2:45 a.m., Thursday, July 22, 1948

I pounded on the door again. "Who's out there?!"

No answer. I yelled out the chute, but the opening faced the alley and a tall, board fence.

Nobody could hear me.

Stay calm.

I stepped back and leaned against the foundation wall under the opening. I reached up to the chute ledge again. If I hopped straight up, I could hook the ledge with the top joint of my fingers. I pulled on it. Adrenalin surged. My nose came up to the bottom edge. Outside, the blanket was still in place across the metal frame embedded in the sill, but I couldn't reach it. My burned right hand gave out, recoiled, cramping, suffering from the electrical shock, and I collapsed against the wall under the opening.

The wall opposite the chute, between the coal room and the cellar, was clay-fired brick, several layers thick. The door was solid wood but might not last long in a hot fire, even though it held out against my repeated kicking. In any case, smoke was my worry.

I was !

Slivers of flickering light appeared around the door, highlighting shadows of thin smoke. I took off my shirt, rolled it, and laid it along the door bottom, but I could still see light at its top and edges. I needed the blanket. Maybe I could roll it up along the door edge and keep the smoke at bay until the fire department came.

Outside, clouds moved across the moon. I stepped back away from the wall, took two steps, and jumped, trying to hook the blanket with my good left hand, but in the darkness, I slammed into the wall. I tried again, moved it slightly toward the ledge, but it caught on the frame with a clank from the tire iron, just under the blanket's edge.

I took off my shoes, putting one on top of the other to create a makeshift platform I could stand on. Stretching as far as I could, I could almost touch the end of the blanket, just inches away.

I took off my pants, filthy with coal dust, rolled them tight, and placed them on top of the shoes. It gave me another inch or so. Not ingenious, but workable.

Flattening my back against the wall, I perched tiptoe on the makeshift step, reached back with my left hand, and hopped. The blanket snagged firmly on the chute door-latch, but the movement dislodged the tire iron and it hit my arm, clattering to the floor.

I knelt down and found it in the dark, then hurried to the door.

Inserting the sharp edge of the steel between the door and the frame near the strike, I pushed hard toward the wall. I could feel screws stripping out in the old wood, resisting, then giving way. The door popped open. A light was shining, over by the desk. The lab was filling with smoke, making it hard to see. The fire was building across the room, near the radio cabinet.

I picked up my rolled-up shirt from the door sill and covered my nose and mouth.

Without touching the electrified latch, I used the tire iron to pop the cellar door lock, ran up the few steps, and exited through a now unjammed, unlocked back door.

When I reached the grass, I dropped to my knees and sucked in the fresh night air. Lightning flashed nearby, illuminating the dead tree and the clothesline. The slack white shirts were gone.

Nobody was in sight.

Neither were my pants and shoes.

29

The Beeline Gas Station
3:15 a.m., Thursday, July 22, 1948

I yanked the blanket out of the coal chute, ran up the grassy side yard in my underwear, and sprinted to my car. I glanced back at the house. *No sign of smoke.* The fire station was just around the corner, but I'd left my car keys and Marko's cash rolled up in my pants. I dug into the car seats, the jockey box, and the ashtray, and found a dime and three pennies, then hurried to the payphone at the Beeline.

"Firehouse Five. Is this an emergency?"

I told him where the fire was burning.

"What's your name?" he asked.

I hung up, tiptoed delicately across the rock-strewn asphalt lot, and jumped back in my car. Reaching under the dash, I untwisted a couple of the loose wires, then touched them together. The car cranked and started noisily. I headed north past Jim and Edna's house. In my mirrors, a fire truck, no siren, turned the corner and pulled up to Bosko's place. I turned on my headlights and headed back towards town.

Without keys, I couldn't get through the back door at the Karrick. I couldn't get back into Auerbach's either. My lock-pick tools were in my pants pocket.

I wasn't wearing pants.

My mind raced. I grabbed the tire iron to pry the office door lock but remembered I'd opened the windows in the afternoon before falling asleep. I hurried around to the south-side fire escape and worked a few minutes to get the first-floor ladder to drop. It landed on the pavement with a clank. From there I climbed the rickety iron stairway to my open window on the third floor.

I was dirty and smelled of smoke. I peeled off the filthy shirt, washed up as best I could in the sink, then changed into some clean clothes and pulled my spare set of keys from the cigar box. I took a moment to wrap a clean, white handkerchief around the two fingers on my right hand that had been burned, and then headed back to work. It was faster to leave the car parked, so I crossed Main and rounded the corner onto Broadway.

That's where I stopped.

Two black and whites were parked out in front of the store, red lights flashing.

30

Auerbach's Department Store
4:45 a.m., Thursday, July 22, 1948

How many other nights passed when these same four hours had been quiet?

As I got closer, I could see two large, broken display windows. The mannequins inside were toppled over. The cops were busy looking at the damage out front. I crossed Broadway at the Judge Building, ran down the service alley, and made my way to the employee entrance at Auerbach's.

I unlocked the outside door with my spare key, slipped into the short hallway, and opened the door to the security closet. Jonny sat there in my chair, eyes closed, wearing my Bee's cap.

"Where ya been, Jack?" he asked.

"Is that your pajama top?" I blurted out, breathing hard.

He opened his eyes.

"You smell like you've been camping ... and what happened to your hand?"

A patrol officer in blue came through the door behind me. "Is this the guy?"

Jonny nodded and said, "Give us a minute." The cop stepped back outside and closed the door.

"I want to hear what you have to say, Jack, before I fire you."

I tried to cover the bandage on my right hand with my left. "What happened out front?" I asked. Nothing seemed to have moved in the office since I left it.

"What happened was that my night guy was AWOL," he said, staring me down. "Vandals took out the plate-glass windows. A stranger called it in. The cops raced over, and when they couldn't raise you on the office telephone, they called me and woke me from a fantastic dream. That's what happened."

I said the first thing that came into my head. "This could have happened whether I was here or not."

"And it happened when you weren't so, where on God's green earth have you been?"

I leaned into the wall and slid to a sitting position on the floor, head down. I'd let him down.

"You're right. I never should've left. Sorry."

"You oughta be sorry," he said, raising his voice. "You know, the cops had to swing by my place and pick me up in the middle of the night." He stared at the bandage on my hand. "Is this more about Sadie?"

"It's not what you think ..."

"Isn't it?"

I was tired. The adrenaline was wearing off, and we both sat silent for a moment. I could feel him staring at me.

"But it's what you wanted to talk to me about?"

I nodded.

He leaned forward. "I'll give ya three minutes then, starting right now."

I started with Edna and Yasa in my office. I told him about the threatening letter and ended with my visit to Bosko's house a few hours earlier. I didn't mention Marko. I left out a lot.

"Is this Bosko?" he asked. I'd left Yasa's photo of him on the desk when I left.

"I'm still looking for him," I said. "He's my only connection to the device."

"Do the cops know about this?"

"Jim told me the cops want me out of the case."

"But they know about Sadie and the letter?"

"How could I say anything? The letter said, 'No Police.'"

"Then, have you shared any of this with her?"

"I started to," I said, "but the words didn't come out right."

He sat back, thinking for a moment. "You can't keep a secret like that, Jack. It's not just about you."

"Yeah, well, me'n her are kinda on the outs right now," I said. "And I've been afraid if she catches wind of what's really been goin' on, I may never see her again."

"Wouldn't that be better than finding her floating in a bathtub with her eyes wide open, or worse?"

I had to admit, it would.

"Just what makes you think this Bosko character didn't already take off to someplace like California before Yasa even came to see you?" he asked, tossing the photo at me.

"Because," I said, "I just talked to somebody who put him in the south end of the valley yesterday, out near the copper mine. They said he was in Bingham, playin' pool."

"Bingham! That ain't even on the road to *someplace!*"

"I know," I said. "So, I figured he's stayin' close for some reason—just not too close. Maybe there's something he left behind, in the house."

"You're guessin', aren't you?"

"Maybe. But Yasa told me to check out his workshop. I don't know where else to look."

"You should have talked to me—"

"I tried, if you'll recall."

"So, you thought you could just take the night off?"

"I wasn't gone the whole night," I said.

"I already checked the sign-in sheets, Jack. You haven't been on the third floor since around eleven-thirty."

I ignored that.

"Look, I had to get back inside the house because I knew the day-shift cops would be all over the place."

"You *had* to? You just decided to leave your regular job and break into a crime scene at midnight, lookin' around in the dark for something, when you don't even know what that something is? You wanna know what I think?" he said. "I think you're putting all your eggs in the 'Jack fixes everything' basket."

He stared me down 'til I looked away.

"I guess when you put it that way—"

"That's the way anybody would put it, Jack. Did you find anything?"

"Lots, but I guess I don't know exactly—"

"See?" he interrupted. "That's exactly what I'm talking about."

"Look, I'm just trying to keep Sadie safe."

"Baloney, Jack. That's just what you're telling yourself. You're wanting to be the hero when you're supposed to be the night watchman."

There was a knock, and the door opened.

"Sorry to butt in," said the cop. "We're done out here, so you probably ought to get the sidewalk cleaned up. Maybe pull those dummies inside for now. Looks like it might rain."

"Right. Grab a broom, Jack."

We stood up and followed the cop out through the door. On the sidewalk, the wind picked up. Jonny and I cleaned up the broken glass and brought the mannequins inside to the sales floor.

He was right about Sadie.

"Jack, I'm not sure what to say about the rest of your case, but you have to tell her about the letter. Let her make the decision about whether you call in the cops or not."

Outside, the rain came down in sheets.

"And you're still fired," he said.

31

Karrick Building
11:20 a.m., Thursday, July 22, 1948

I'd come up the back stairway, put Bosko's photo away, and fell into my cot around five-thirty without setting my alarm clock. I hadn't really planned to sleep late the next morning, but I did. Street noise through the open window eventually made sure I wouldn't waste the day away. I decided to head up to the gym to shower off the smell of smoke, then follow up on Red's lead, out in Bingham. But while brushing my teeth at my own sink in the back, someone started pounding on my door.

Two guys in dark suits stood in the hallway, sweating.

"John Hammer?" one asked.

"I go by Jack," I said, stepping back. "Like the construction tool."

They looked at each other.

"FBI. Agent Tompkins, and this is ... Carter. We have a few questions." He flashed a badge as I ushered them in. "We just need to confirm a couple of things regarding the story you told the police. It'll only take a few minutes."

"Swell," Jim said these were the guys who were trying to keep me out of the investigation completely. "I'll have to uncover a couple of chairs here ..." I started unstacking some of the things I'd piled against the wall.

"You have an interesting office here, Hammer. Smells like ... smoke. Anybody ever tell you, you need an elevator in the building?"

"No," I lied. "You're the first one."

I only found one chair, so Carter stood, back to the wall. He kept his hat on and found a plaster crack that interested him near the door frame.

"I'll get right to it, Hammer. We're here about your involvement with this guy goin' by the name of Bosko Cvito. Eastern European accent, slight build, mid-sixties, five-feet seven inches. Do you know him?"

"Nope."

Tompkins glanced back at Carter and asked, "But you're Captain Burt's nephew, right?"

"That's right," I said with a smile.

He didn't smile back. Instead, he closed his notepad with a snap and sat back.

"You think we're here on a lark?"

"What?"

Carter walked over by the window on my right and raised the blinds. More traffic noise followed the fresh air inside.

"I know you already went through it with the local cops, but we're just trying to fill in a few holes. You were hired to do some investigating for a woman goin' by the name of Yasa Cvito, recently deceased. What do you know about her?"

He pulled a picture of her from his jacket pocket and slid it across the desk toward me. She was younger in this photo, maybe by ten years. Even in black and white her eyes picked up a sparkle of life in the sunlight. I remembered them, brilliant green, and a pang of remorse passed through me like an icicle, stabbing at my conscience.

"Tell me what you mean, 'goin' by the name of'...?"

"Don't get cute with us Hammer, you know exactly what I mean."

"Settle down—"

"You think that license you carry is really yours?"

"I paid the fee."

"So what? One bad report from me to the cops and it's gone. And you know what else? We've already read the police report about you finding her body in the bathtub and shootin' up the place on 11th East."

"Then it sounds like you have everything you need."

He leaned forward. His voice was restrained but carried a tone that was threatening.

"Look at me good, Hammer. I represent the special investigative powers of the United States government. We're here on an issue of national security, and if I were you, and if I wanted to keep my life in some semblance of order, I'd pay a little more respect to that flag you fought for and cut out the wisecracks."

Carter moved around behind me. I tried to keep an eye on him, poking around in my stuff. If it was an intentional tactic to keep me on edge, it worked.

"I'm answerin' your questions," I said. "I just wanna know what you mean when you say 'goin' by'." I tried to sound cooperative, but I didn't like being pushed around. I wondered what other notes he had about me, written down in his book.

He sat back again, relaxed, and smiled, then reached in his jacket and pulled out a pack of cigarettes.

"I'm just asking questions, Hammer. You know the drill."

A pile of office papers slid to the floor behind me.

"Hey! Don't touch that stuff!" I said.

Carter smiled sheepishly and stepped away. Tompkins lit his cigarette and searched for an ashtray.

"I don't smoke," I said, irritation in my voice.

He stood up and took a paper cup from the water cooler.

"Look, Jack ... can I call you that? We're just tryin' to locate this guy, Bosko Cvito. We know Yasa had you lined up to search for him."

"What's your interest in him?"

"It's our job," he said, vaguely.

I pulled his photo from the desk drawer. "You mean this guy?" I laid it on the desk.

"I thought you said you didn't know him," he said.

"I don't."

He looked at the photo and shook his head.

"Somebody else did that," I said, about the scratches. "Bosko was Yasa's uncle, but I never met him."

"She said 'uncle'?"

"Are you sayin' he wasn't?" I asked.

Tompkins sat back down, opened his notepad again, and took out a pencil. "Did she give you any ideas about where she thought he went?"

"She said he had gambling issues. I'm sure that's in your file already. She seemed worried about the time he spent playin' pool, but that was about it. She was ... puzzled, about why he left, and a little afraid."

"This was in your office—"

"Monday."

He wrote that down. "And that's when you started lookin' for him?"

"No," I said. "I went to the ballgame that night."

He looked up from his notepad. I slid around in my chair, guilty.

"Rained out," I said.

"So, Tuesday, you started looking?"

I pulled on my ear and glanced sideways. "Not exactly. I went back to see Yasa that afternoon, to get a look at Bosko's things and follow up on a few questions I had. At that point, I figured Bosko was sleepin' it off in some juice joint."

There was an awkward moment where we both sat listening to horns honk through the open window. It was getting warm. I switched on the desk fan.

"You guys want some water?" I asked.

We all had some. Tompkins put his smoke out in the wet cup.

"I found *her*," I answered. "And a guy with a gun."

I told them about my encounter in Bosko's house, how somebody crashed through the garage door, and about gunshots coming from the basement. I was detailed, but I didn't share Marko's name. It was a judgment call. He was my client now.

He stopped for a minute, reading over his notes. "What else do you want to tell us?"

He was fishing now. I decided to keep last night's visit to Bosko's house a secret, in case they tried to pin the fire on me.

"I think Yasa had more to say," I admitted.

"Like?"

I shrugged.

Tompkins paged back through his notes. "Tell us about getting punched. The report said you were making a call from the pay telephone."

"I was trying to call my uncle, to let him know something at the house smelled fishy."

He looked at me. "What do you mean, 'fishy'?"

"Well, Yasa said Bosko was her only relative. That didn't square with the other guy's claim about being her brother. Plus, he was carryin' a piece, in a shoulder holster. I figured maybe the cops knew something, so I made a call and ended up on the ground. You have the report."

"You didn't see anybody, talk to anybody?"

"Nope. These guys were smart. They turned me around, right into the sun, where I couldn't see a thing. They hit me twice, and I went down on the pavement. When I looked up again, they'd already driven off. Frankly, I didn't even know it was two guys, but that's what the kid at the Beeline said. He got a good look. You should talk to him."

He looked at me, suspiciously.

"So, what's the FBI's interest here?" I asked again.

He answered something else. "Let me just say, Jack, those guys are dangerous. You need to leave this whole thing alone."

Carter nodded.

"You think they're workin' with that mustache guy I saw in the house?" I asked.

"That'll be the day," said Tompkins.

"What does that mean?"

"Nothing." He put his pen away.

"Okay, are you guys gonna tell me what's goin' on here?" I asked.

They looked at each other again. "You were in the Army, right?" asked Tompkins.

"Third Army, under Patton."

"Then you should understand, it's a need-to-know situation, Jack, and you don't need to."

"C'mon, what do you know about Bosko? What's his story?"

"We'll track him down. He won't go far."

"You know that?" I asked.

He straightened the picture of the Indian as they walked out.

32

Back to the Beehive Café
12:30 p.m., Thursday, July 22, 1948

I left a message for Jim, telling him the FBI stopped by for a visit. Then I headed up Main Street where banners and flags in red, white, and blue lined the streets, marking the route for the big Pioneer Days parade. Saturday marked the hundred-and-first anniversary of the Mormon pioneers entering the valley.

I ducked in for a shower at the Deseret Gym, then walked back down to the Beehive, figuring I might as well come clean with Sadie sooner rather than never. Plus, I needed to see what I could work out with George about the hole in his floorboards. I stepped down from the sidewalk and opened the café door.

Suits and dresses filled nearly all the booths, a different crowd than at breakfast. George was helping out in the dining room, taking an order from three ladies in the back booth. I claimed an empty spot at the counter and ordered a Coke from a new girl.

"Where's Sadie?" I asked.

"You a friend of hers?"

"Most days."

"She hasn't been here today. Do ya need a menu?"

I waved her off and paged through the stack of papers to see if the *Trib* had picked up anything about the fire. It had: There was a short notice on page twenty-one, right next to an article about cows' reduced milk production due to the extreme summer heat. "Fire Department personnel declined to comment on the cause of the early morning fire ..."

George noticed me and held up a finger, which I took to mean "wait a minute," but I wasn't going anywhere. I ordered a grilled cheese sandwich with mayo and tomato, then studied the sports pages like there might be a quiz. The stool next to me opened up, and George came over and sat down. He put a hand on my arm.

"What happened to your fingers?"

"Burned 'em on my hot plate."

"Hah! By the way, I talked with somebody who thinks he can fix that hole in the floor for five bucks."

"Sounds fair," I said. I reached in my pocket to pull out the cash, but he held up both hands.

"I didn't say I was fixin' it," he said, grinning.

"What do ya mean?"

"I'm leavin' it. It's too good of a story, Jack, waitress with a gun and all. I think I'll just talk about it for a while, but I won't use your name or nothin'."

"Suit yourself."

His smile flattened out under his mustache. "Listen, you haven't spoken with Sadie today, have you?"

I shook my head. "She won't talk to me right now." I folded the paper and set it down on the counter. "I was kinda hopin' to catch her here."

"She didn't come in this morning. Never called in sick either. Left me a little short at breakfast."

"And I haven't talked to her since yesterday," I said. "We chatted about the gun situation, but it didn't work out. She was pretty upset."

The new gal stopped back and pushed my sandwich across the bar on a white plate. It had too much mayo, so I scraped the bread on the edge of the plate. Then I peeled the top off and peppered the insides.

"I heard about the gun—" the new gal started to say, but George waved her off.

"You're a smart guy, Jack," he said. "I don't know what's up between you two, but don't let her get away over something like this."

"Tip of the iceberg, George," I said.

A car horn sounded in the street outside the door.

"That reminds me ..." George started, then popped up from the stool and walked around the end of the bar to pick up something from the back counter.

"Your uncle stopped by this morning lookin' for you," he said. "He left these. Said they were yours."

Three keys on a familiar chain, and my lock-pick, from my missing pants pocket. It meant he knew I'd been in Bosko's house, but why was he sending them back without a lecture?

"No cash?"

"Cash?"

"What'd he say?"

"He said to come by the house later. Edna's fixing dinner."

I gave the new gal a buck without asking her name and headed back to my office, where I rolled around on my cot for a few hours, chasing sleep.

Eventually, heat and horn honks drove me out of bed. I grabbed Bosko's picture from the drawer and locked up. Halfway to the stairs, the telephone started ringing back in my office. I ran back down the hall, but by the time I picked up, all I heard was dial tone.

By four-thirty, I was in my car headed over to see Edna but stopped off at Dick and Jay's for gas. The filling station on the corner was an art deco concrete structure painted white, with a canopy out front and lube bays in the back. A cashier's office with huge, corner-glass windows and a high ceiling fit in between. I slid my gun in the glove box with the matching shoulder holster I'd found and laid my hat and jacket on the seat.

The kid pumping gas stepped over. "What'll it be?"

"Fill it up, with kerosene," I said through the open window.

He gave me a puzzled look. "Or Regular, if you got it," I said, and leaned down below the steering wheel to make sure the ignition wires were twisted back together properly, tucking them up under the dash.

"You got a restroom?" I asked.

"Inside. Key's on the doorframe."

The restroom door had a colored flyer announcing the Gene Autry Championship Rodeo at the fairgrounds and the Days of '47 Parade on the twenty-fourth. Business cards were thumbtacked to the wall by the pay telephone.

I added mine. Last one.

On the way out, I noticed a poster advertising the big copper mine out in Bingham Canyon as a place for tourists to visit. "World's Largest Open Pit Copper Mine."

Bingham. It was the only real lead I had left.

I walked out on the concrete apron. The kid was kneeling down by the back tire. "Listen, if I wanted to head out to Bingham, which way should I go?" I asked him.

He ran back and grabbed a free map from the office, spread it on the hood, and helped me trace the route going out the Bingham

Highway, west from Midvale. "Looks like it's only about twenty-five miles, but I hear it's a hot drive. I bet it'll take at least an hour."

I still had time to stop by to see Edna.

33

Jim and Edna's Place
4:45 p.m., Thursday, July 22, 1948

Edna was out in her yard watering roses. She had on a pair of dark glasses, the kind a blind man would wear if he were tapping out a sad song with a cane on a corner. When I pulled alongside the curb, she waved hello and hurried back to the house to turn the water off.

"Jack, I am so glad to see you again!" She threw her arms around me in a bear hug.

"It's good to see you too."

She held on a little longer.

"You okay?" I asked.

"Let's get out of the sun," she said.

We went inside and sat down in the parlor. We talked about her flowers, what she was fixing for dinner, and her new church calling. Eventually, she got around to talking about Yasa. That's when she took off the dark glasses and I could see her eyes were swollen. She tried to pass it off as an allergy from being out in the roses, but I knew she'd been crying.

The whole neighborhood was in shock about what happened, she said. Especially her. I sat alone on the sofa. She sat by the window, in an overstuffed chair with doilies on the arms. A wicker basket full of uncompleted sewing projects sat on a many-colored ottoman next to her.

"Jim says she doesn't have any family, so they'll end up burying her in a pauper's grave. Someplace on the west side of the river." It bothered her to think of Yasa being separated from her kin.

"She still has Bosko," I reminded her.

"Have you found him, then?" she asked. "Because Jim says you gave up on the case."

"That might be what Jim thinks," I said. "He actually told you I gave up the case?"

"Didn't you?"

"He suggested it."

Concern changed to a scowl. "That's not what I asked you."

I settled backward, uneasily. "Well, Yasa's dead. Bosko's still missing, and the FBI is lookin' for him now. What help would I be?"

"So that's how you private investigators operate?" she scolded. "Answering questions with questions? A person would think you were in politics."

"Okay," I said, "here's how I heard it. I was ordered to get out of it, direct from the chief. The FBI is gonna handle things."

"So, did you?"

"No."

She smiled. "Well, you're going to make a fine detective. That's what Jim says."

"He does?"

She told me more about her neighbors, how they were angry that a brutal crime like murder had been committed there, on their street. She said one of the neighbors, next to the Beeline, thought about putting her house up for sale and moving away.

Through the front window, I noticed Jim pull his pre-war Packard into the drive. He glanced at my car in the street and came through the door with his hat on. I stood up.

"Hello, Jack," he said. "You here for dinner?"

He took the hat off and hung it on the rack by the door.

Edna stood up and he kissed her cheek.

"Oh my gosh, I got so wrapped up talking with Jack that I didn't get the vegetables on!" she said, hurrying into the back of the house. She left me and Jim alone.

"Sit down, Jack," he said, in a tired voice. "I want to hear what you've been up to, lately."

There was nothing in his tone that sounded angry, but I knew where the conversation was headed. "I have a question or two myself," I said.

"Did you get your keys back?" He took off his jacket and settled into the chair where Edna had been sitting. He wasn't wearing his gun.

"Thanks," I said. "I had to leave in a hurry."

He nodded at the bandaged fingers on my right hand. "Uh-huh, what's that?"

"It's nothin'," I said.

We sat in silence.

I could hear the clock on the fireplace mantel in the other room tick away. He rubbed his chin with his hand.

"Look, Jack, I thought I told you to stay out of this investigation." He waited for me to respond. I didn't.

"You know, my guys showed up this morning with a pair of pants and shoes from a certain crime scene, just about your size? You wanna tell me what's goin' on and what you were doin' in Bosko's basement without your pants on?"

Edna came back in the room, asked if we wanted beans or peas, and then disappeared with the answer.

There wasn't a good lie to tell about my pants.

"Okay, I was there last night," I said, "before the fire. I felt like I owed it to Yasa, at least to her memory, to check out Bosko's workshop. I told her I would."

"You have a new client, don't you?" he said.

I met his eyes but kept my mouth shut.

"Just get to the pants part."

He pinched his lips together as I told him how I went in and couldn't get out, and how I used the pants to get a couple inches on my reach for the tire iron, and how I pried the coal room door open. He started shaking his head when I told him about poking around the lab and nearly getting electrocuted. I squirmed on the sofa like a kid, waiting for him to take his belt to my backside.

"Who dragged you into the coal room?"

"My guess—and it's just a guess: Bosko, back looking for something." *Or maybe Marko's bad people.*

He pointed a finger at me.

"You know, we found a note hidden in your pants pocket, something written in one of those Slavic languages. I'm guessing it's something you picked up along the way, stealing evidence off a desk somewhere?"

I'd forgotten all about it.

"Well," he said, "you're damn lucky you grabbed it when you did. There wasn't any notepad when we got there, but it's sent everybody who cares looking in other directions, away from you."

"How's that?"

"Since it was Bosko's house, they're thinking it must've been his pants we found. Especially since the note was written in another language and said something about Highland Boy."

"Highland Boy?" I asked. "Who's that?"

"Not who, Jack, where. It's a fork in the road, out near the copper mine and up past Bingham. A couple of our guys are headed out there in the morning to talk with the local sheriff."

Bingham!

"I thought you guys were handing this case to the FBI," I said.

"I thought so too, but they're not investigating much. More like they're obstructing any investigation, really. The fire's a new crime, so we're gonna poke around a little bit more. Did they ever stop by to question you?"

"Nobody gives you your messages?" I asked. "FBI didn't seem to know much more than me."

"Who's hired you now?" he tried again. His eyes locked onto mine.

"You know I can't say."

"You're putting me in a hard spot, Jack. I'm supposed to bring you in for questioning again—about the fire this time. And when I do, I'm gonna catch hell from the chief for not keepin' you out of this thing."

It smelled like Edna was frying pork chops. She called for us to wash up.

Jim stepped into the washroom next to the kitchen and closed the door, saying "I'll just be a minute."

I took that as a hint and bolted out the front door without a word.

34

On the Road Again
5:25 p.m., Thursday, July 22, 1948

I roared off, hoping to get out to Bingham and ask around before the cops showed up and sent Bosko running. I checked the sky. There were still a few hours of daylight left, so I turned south and headed past Sadie's place first. Part of me wanted to come clean and explain everything, to try to regain the ground I'd lost during the week. Part of me argued she'd be better off not knowing. Jonny's words broke the tie in my head.

"I'm sorry, Jack," said her mother, without inviting me inside. "It's dinner time, and Sadie isn't here right now."

I could smell something cooking and regretted missing out on Edna's pork chops. In the background, Sadie's little sister shouted that she'd gone out on a date with another boy. Her mother turned red, turned away, and then turned back.

"I thought maybe she told you," she said. "Sadie seemed pretty upset yesterday."

"Do you know who she's with?"

"Jack, now really ... I don't think it's my place to say." The color in her cheeks grew brighter.

I could hear cars coming into the neighborhood behind me, husbands coming home from work. Two doors down, a whirring sound meant somebody was mowing their lawn.

"Sure, but it's somebody you know, right?" I asked.

She went silent. Sadie's sister pushed to the doorway.

"He's a boy from the ward," she said. "He sees her at church and flirts with her all the time, and his name is Sherman."

"Shush your mouth," her mother said. "Jack, I do need to go now. It's dinner time."

She'd already said that, like the phrase "dinner time" could work magic on par with "abracadabra." Only I wouldn't disappear.

I shifted my weight from one foot to the other while she blinked at me through the door screen.

"Look, I think I gave her the wrong impression yesterday. I just want to be sure she's okay," I said.

"Then you need to come back some other time." She was getting flustered, putting walls up between us.

"Just promise me you'll tell her to be careful," I said. "I couldn't live with myself if somebody tried to hurt her."

As soon as I said it, I wanted to take it back, but it was done.

Her mother's hand went to her mouth, dropped, and her face turned from red to white. "Who would ever try to hurt Sadie?"

"Not me!"

Her eyes widened.

"I didn't mean me!"

"Why would you say such a terrible thing?" She closed the door and left me standing on the porch.

I ran back to my car and headed further south before her dad got home, and the other half of the bridge burned.

In Murray, I stopped at the Piggly Wiggly for a Coke, and when

I pulled onto State Street again, I noticed a dark blue Ford behind me, hanging back. I slowed down, turned west toward the smelter, and pulled into a parking lot. I slumped down, killed the engine, and watched in the mirrors as the taillights went by. I couldn't make out who was driving.

When he disappeared down a side alley, I doubled back to State Street and headed toward Midvale before turning west again on the Bingham Highway. It was a paved country road with long, straight sections through sparsely irrigated farmlands growing alfalfa and wheat, no fences needed. A parallel line of power poles ran off into the distance ahead.

I kept my eye on the rearview mirror.

The road was empty.

35

Bingham Canyon
7:00 p.m., Thursday, July 22, 1948

Shadows in the canyon stretched over the two-lane highway, all
the way to the top. I motored through the lower town, past ram-
shackle garages, wooden boarding houses, and brick storefronts that
nestled into ravines, squeezed between pavement on one side and
mountain on the other. Dirt pathways gave way to concrete sidewalks. Laundry hung in front yards behind short picket fences, and
children played street ball on the side roads.

I eased over to the road's edge, slipped on my jacket, and stepped
out in front of a squat, two-story building where the upper floor
leaned out over a set of red and blue gas pumps belonging to the
CANYON MOTOR COMPANY. It guarded the downhill corner
of the road into a smaller side canyon called Markham Gulch. A
massive steel trestle framed the roadway, and dump trains were
running close to the hillside, parallel to the main highway.

There was movement behind me in the street.

"Who are you?" Three boys in striped tee shirts and torn denim folded their arms, looking me over.

"Roy Rogers," I kidded. They looked at each other.

"Well, Roy," said the shortest of the three, not getting it. "You just ran over my friend's bicycle."

Another car sped past.

"What?"

"Right there," he said, "under your car."

"Yeah, that's gonna cost you," said his friend.

They were right. There was a bicycle, rusted and missing spokes on the front wheel, but nobody rode it here. It was bent in all the wrong places. I admired their spunk. I'd been rubbernecking the train and hadn't heard them slide it under the street-side running board.

"Okay, you got me," I said. "What do you boys think we oughta do about it, me bein' new in town and all?"

I put my hands on my hips, pulling back my jacket just enough so my shoulder holster was in clear view.

Color drained out of their faces.

"Probably we oughta report this, so which one of you can tell me the name of the sheriff here in town?"

"Police chief," one of them whispered.

That started a quiet and desperate argument between them. I walked into the street and pulled the bicycle out from under my car, then carried it behind the trunk and laid it up on the curb.

They were gone when I came back around the other side.

I headed out again, west and south. It was hard to get a good feel for the size of the town from any one spot. The map said Bingham was seven miles long and two lanes wide, an upward lazy curve unraveling a hundred feet at a time. More cars roared past, the opposite way. I drove by the post office, a couple of drug stores, and an ice cream parlor. Power poles sprouted randomly from the road, connected by drooping lines that hung low across the street at every possible angle. More bars advertised pool. They all offered BEER ON TAP in red neon.

The road split near the top of the canyon. Carr Fork was off on my right, another crowded side canyon with its own series of elevated train bridges. TO HIGHLAND BOY, a sign said.

Narrow sidewalks along the main road were steep and cracked, choked with miners at the crossroad. Blue denim overalls and long-sleeved shirts seemed fashionable; I was overdressed in a white shirt, tie, and jacket.

Protocol suggested I ought to find the cops right off, to let them know I was in town, but I was hungry. I parked on gravel, near the tunnel to someplace called Copperfield, and felt for the bullets in my trouser pocket. Loaded guns make me nervous. I decided to leave my pistol locked in the glove box until I could talk to the local cops. I left my hat in the back seat and set off in search of a good meal.

Downhill from the car park, I crossed the street and followed my nose into an eatery called The Pastime, where the smell of a home-cooked meal was stronger than the smell of cigarette smoke and beer. The dining room was filled with workers of various ethnicities and trades, none of whom I could easily identify. They overran the dozen tables, milling about in small groups connected by similar dress codes, rarely mixing. A card game in progress animated the back corner. An empty table stood near the window. I skipped it and sat at the bar, preferring to keep one eye on a room through the mirror.

"Good choice," said the bartender, close to my age, with dark greasy hair, unshaven cheeks, and an easy smile.

"Is it?" I asked.

"The bar ... I saw you checking things out. What're ya drinkin'?"

"I'll have a Coke," I said, "and a steak sandwich."

"That's it?"

"I'm workin'. Put some mayo and garlic salt on that sandwich."

He called it back to the kitchen, reached under the bar for a soda glass, and set me up with an eight-ounce bottle, minus the cap.

"You from the City?" His accent was local, not Greek.

"I just drove in," I said. "I'm tryin' to pick up the lay of the land, here."

"Lay of the land?" he repeated, laughing as he walked down the length of the counter and served a few more drinks.

I looked around for pool tables. There weren't any.

Loud voices over by the card game erupted into a louder pushing match, and the whole table stood up at once. I couldn't understand the insults. The rest of the room got meanly quiet. Two guys swung at each other and missed, falling in a heap on the empty table. Abruptly the whole group pushed through the doorway onto the street to resolve the matter. I thought back on my days as an MP, wading into crowds of drunken soldiers with a billy club, pulling guys apart.

"See what I meant?" said the bartender. "The counter was a good choice. Seems like it always ends this way."

"They come in here a lot?"

"Every night, but they know well enough to get it out on the street. Another Coke?"

He added ice, confident I'd say yes.

"Sure, why not?" I was on Marko's expense account now.

I pulled Bosko's picture from my shirt. The bartender came back with the sandwich, and I put the photograph on the bar in front of him, partly covering the greenback. It was a long shot, I knew.

"You seen this guy around here lately?" I asked.

He set the plate with the sandwich down on top of the snapshot. A gray-haired bartender with olive skin and a black mustache moved toward us.

"Watch what you say," the younger guy whispered, inching away.

"What have we got over here?" gray-hair asked. "Everything okay?"

I took a bite from the sandwich.

"This is good," I said. "Sirloin?"

The younger guy spoke carefully. There was unspoken tension between them. "He's new in town, looking for a place to spend the night. Isn't that right mister ...?"

"Hammer," I said. "Jack Hammer."

I sat at the long end of a short bar. I set the sandwich down, wiped grease off my chin, and stood up, offering him my hand.

The guy with the mustache smiled back. His two front teeth were gone.

36

The Pastime
8:00 p.m., Thursday, July 22, 1948

"Jack Hammer?" he repeated. "Like in the mines? The rock-breaker, jackhammer?"

"I guess so."

He didn't seem glad to meet me, and took my hand, squeezing it, rolling the bones. I could smell tobacco on his breath. I'd taken the bandage off the burn, but my fingers were still tender. I winced. He kept the serious face and wagged a tobacco-stained finger at me.

"You don't look like a rock-breaker. And you don't feel like a rock-breaker. Have you ever worked a day with a real jackhammer?"

I rescued my hand and sat back down, rubbing it.

"Leave him alone, Papa," said the younger guy. "He's just having dinner."

The older bartender stayed close while I took another bite of the sandwich. "You don't deserve a name like that," he said. "I don't think so."

The front door opened and the crowd from the card game started pushing inside again. Everyone was everyone else's best pal again. The older guy gave me a parting look and moved away to supervise reseating at the corner table.

"He probably thinks you look like management," said the bartender, "wearing a jacket and all."

"Management?"

"Up on the hill, the brick building. Superintendent's up there, and engineering, I think. Papa doesn't like any of 'em."

"He's a union man?"

"Was ... he had a run-in with the company back in the twenties, when he worked on a rail crew. One year everybody was on strike, tryin' to force a decent wage for dangerous work. The copper bosses called up a crew from some other state, a bunch of Mexicans, to take their jobs. They brought in professional thugs callin' themselves cops. Eventually, they went around to people's houses, askin' questions, trying to scare everybody off. A few people got hurt. It was a bad time and Papa never went back."

He nodded to the plate hiding the picture of Bosko. "This kind of thing would set him off."

"I thought I already set him off."

"You a cop?" he asked.

"That was carefully worded."

"No use beatin' around it."

"Private cop," I said. "On a family matter. A missing uncle."

He glanced to the corner of the room. My eyes followed him in the mirror. A new argument was developing. Nobody at the table seemed to remember whose beer glass was whose. A few were full, but most were empty. Nobody would touch the empties. The old guy was helping out with a pitcher, but I would have given even odds they'd be on the street again in a few minutes.

I moved the plate aside, slightly, exposing the photo.

His eyes asked the next question.

"His niece hired me," I answered. "That was Monday. Last night I met this guy who said he was a blast crew foreman at the mine. Said he saw my guy out this way getting' the bum's rush out of one of the bars, maybe last weekend."

"Has this uncle got a name?"

I told him.

His hand smoothly pulled the dollar from under the plate and pushed it into his pocket.

"I'm Chris," he said. "Sorry about Papa."

"It's okay. How 'bout you, though? Have you seen him?"

He glanced down, disinterested like I was asking him to look at my family vacation photos. He pushed it back at me, shaking his head slowly. I put it back in my shirt pocket.

"Too old to be in the mine," he said. "And he probably wouldn't drink here at The Pastime, not unless he liked cards. But that truck in the photo looks familiar. Wooden sideboards. I think I have seen it around town, or one like it."

"Any ideas?"

"Did you try The Diamond, or the place next door?"

"Not yet." Shadows overtook the street, outside. Neon signs came to life, and fewer people stood around on the sidewalk. "But you're right, he's not a miner. Fancies himself a pool player, but I don't know if he's any good."

Chris nodded his head like he was listening.

I asked about hotels in town. After a moment, he left me to take care of business. I chewed the sandwich and thought about Sadie, wondering who this Sherman kid was, drifting off to uncomfortable memories of her mother on the doorstep. I pushed that last image away and retraced my conversation with Uncle Jim. The last one.

What was Bosko doing out here? I wondered. *Hiding?*

When Chris came back my way, I asked him about Highland Boy.

"Highland Boy? It's just around the corner and up a ways. Some old mines there ... gobbled up in the expansion. Not much left except a few boarding houses on the old road ... it used to be a lot bigger. The place was full of Serbs and Croats, but the mine's closin' in on it. Why are you askin'?"

"I just heard the name. Boarding houses?"

"Maybe a few left in the lower Fork. If your guy's a Yugi, I guess he'd blend in. Might make him hard to find though."

I looked in the mirror for Papa. He was out in the tables, enjoying himself and laughing with his customers.

"If you go searchin' up that way, keep the photo to yourself. They won't take kindly to it."

I finished the Coke, slid cash across the bar, and asked for a receipt. Papa noticed and came over to examine the quality of my bills.

"I have some advice for you, Mr. Jack Hammer," he said, as I opened the heavy door to leave. "Don't come back."

37

The Bingham Hotel
9:00 p.m., Thursday, July 22, 1948

Chris told me The Bingham Hotel was decent but said he hadn't been inside since the war ended. I crossed Main at City Hall and headed toward my car as clouds drifted over the moon. The passenger door complained with a squawk, and I popped open the glove box, strapped on my gun, and realized that in my hurry I'd left my shaving kit back in the city.

The hotel lobby was grand, with a threadbare Persian covering a clay-tile floor, two battered leather sofas, and a potted palm that was turning brown. The room had a high ceiling, decorated along the edges with plaster fruit, carefully painted. I'd already walked past two other rundown hotels to get here. I signed in as John Smith and paid cash.

The thin-faced clerk barely glanced up. He slid a skeleton key wired to a tooled leather fob across the desk. The diamond-shaped piece of cowhide smelled like wood smoke and was stamped 307. It was too big to fit in my pocket. I carried it up the main stairway and unlocked the door. The room had a private bath in the back. I looked forward to soaking in a hot tub, later. For now, I unhitched my gun, leaving it hanging behind the radiator. The key went back to the clerk on my way back out.

"You know," I said, "you could use an elevator around here."

"We're gettin' one," he lied. "But I can call somebody to help with your bags."

"Not this time." I was traveling light. I headed back down toward The Copper King.

Just past the Telephone Building, two doors down and across the street, some of the local ladies of the evening sat outside fanning themselves in the heat.

"You look lonely, Mister," one called. "You need some company?"

I kept to my side of the road. "Thanks, but no," I said. *Not their type of company, anyway.*

Two of the gals were smoking cigarettes in an animated fashion, like they were practicing for a scene in a Bette Davis movie. "So, you're *that* type, are you?" one said. "Too good for us here?" I guess I thought I was, but I didn't think about it much until it dawned on me: *They just might have run across Bosko.* I crossed the narrow street to get a closer look.

They all started cooing to each other, like pigeons.

The loud talker wore an appropriately loud, low-cut, silky blue dress. Her blonde hair came from a bottle, and she wore enough rouge and red lipstick to blend into a stop sign.

"My, you are a skinny one," said another, with black hair, brown skin, and an accent. Maybe Mexican. "And you are not from the town, either."

"Are you keepin' a list?" I asked.

She raised her eyebrows.

"I saw him first—" one started, but I interrupted.

"Ladies, I'm workin' right now." I flipped open my wallet and flashed my license, unreadable behind the cellophane. I wasn't too sure any of 'em could read it, but they all wanted to look. Their faces went a practiced kind of blank as I folded the wallet and stuffed it back in my jacket.

"Just so you know," said one, looking around for support from the others, "we are all well acquainted with the local police force."

"Especially the ones with unusual tastes," said another.

"Even though we don't know anyone's real name," said the first, laughing. "And yet between us four girls, we've met every Smith in the phone book!" Now they all laughed.

Considering how I signed in at the hotel, I felt foolish but smiled to be sociable.

"I guess that's a rule around here?" I said.

"What's a rule?"

"Nobody uses their real name." I pulled out a five-dollar bill from my pocket, folded it lengthwise, and held it up with Bosko's picture.

"Ladies," I said, "I'd like to introduce you to my good friend, Mr. Lincoln, and that *is* his real name. First person who can tell me where to find the guy in this picture takes Mr. Lincoln home for good."

They all wanted a closer look.

"He looks familiar ..."

"Well, I certainly don't know him," said the gal in the blue dress. "Not in the Biblical sense, and not in any *other* way either."

The others pulled back, exchanging looks. Somebody wasn't talking. The photo and the fiver went back in my pocket.

"What'd he do?" another asked. They all avoided my eyes.

"A sad case," I lied. "They were a wonderful family, but there was so much blood."

She snorted, short and loud, and covered her mouth with her tattooed hand.

"You ladies know where I'm stayin'," I said, as I tipped an imaginary hat toward the hotel. "If you think of anything ..."

They cooed and cackled behind my back as I headed downhill toward the bar.

38

The Copper King
9:30 p.m., Thursday, July 22, 1948

Shops were closing now.

The street was empty, like the west desert was empty; when you rolled over rocks, dangerous things were hiding underneath. Music and laughter splashed out the open windows of bars, punctuated by shouting and profanity. A second glance showed small groups of stooping mine workers milling around open bar doors, and drunks slumped against shop doors. Pole-mounted lights painted yellow circles of haze on the sidewalk.

I pushed my way into the Copper King, where a cherrywood bar with animal figures carved along the edge ran through the room and curved into the back wall, making room for a door to the toilets. Black-and-white photos of prizefighters adorned the walls, and ceiling-high mirrors behind the bar were divided by exhibit cases showing off rifles, handguns, and knives for sale. Neon beer signs on the walls announced SCHLITZ and HAMM'S: FROM THE LAND OF SKY BLUE WATERS. Two bartenders kept things moving.

Through an open double door on the right, I laid eyes on an underlit room with a half dozen ball-and-claw footed pool tables. A few sober-faced miners held up the mahogany wall paneling, sipping beer and contemplating geometry while they worked out pool hall physics in the shadows. Felt tops radiated green under cut-glass Tiffany lamps that hung from a tin panel ceiling. Noise from the bar mostly buried the clacking of balls.

I stepped inside the pool room, and everyone looked over but the shooter.

I stayed at the room's edge, trying to keep out of their way. After a couple of minutes, a thin little man with brown skin and jet-black hair approached me. He wore a carefully manicured mustache, like two tiny golf clubs resting back-to-back. He wore a bolo tie, with a copper and turquoise clasp that kept his shirt from sliding down his neck and falling onto the floor.

"You play pool, my friend?" he asked quietly, guiding me toward the barroom.

"Some. Maybe not tonight."

"You sure? Because I can get you a game," he offered. "We play a nickel a ball."

I pulled the fin back out of my pocket and folded it in half again, then slipped it back inside my pants. His eyes followed it, like he was trying to memorize the serial number.

"You got plenty of money."

"Thanks, not tonight. I'm tryin' to find somebody. Maybe you could help me out?"

His face clouded. He glanced back at the other players. Nobody was paying us any attention now. He moved around until his back was toward them.

"I know all the cops in town—" he started.

"Everybody seems to."

Cheers and clapping broke out behind me as two guys stood up and competed to see who could down a pitcher of beer the fastest. The small guy won, not counting what he poured onto the table and into the floorboards.

He shifted on his feet, angling. "And you might be ...?"

"Private."

He kept his eyes on me and put a hand to his chin.

"But you can call me Jack," I said.

"Danny," he said, nodding. "You work for the Company?"

"Nope, just somebody's family. You?"

"On strike," he said, "some days, anyway. Why do you look for him?"

"You know how family matters are," I said. "He's old, and he matters to his family."

He looked behind him, touched my elbow, and walked me further into the bar crowd.

"Tell me," he said.

I slipped the picture out of my pocket and held it under his eyes. There were faint signs of recognition, a tightened jaw, quick eye movement.

"Somebody else from the mine told me he was out this way, causin' trouble," I added.

"He's called Bosko," he whispered and turned away, casually.

"You know him?" I asked.

He crossed his arms. "What's in it for me?"

I started to pull the five out again when he stepped back and slapped at my hand, missing.

"Don't be doin' that in here," he said. "We'll both get carried out on a board."

Beer was flowing. Nobody was paying us any mind. I stared at Danny's friends until one feigned interest in what his pal and I were up to. I smiled at him and lifted my hand, empty. He turned back to the table.

"Here is how it could happen," he said. "I could tell you what I know, right now while I have a chance. You could find yourself a spot at the bar, and when I come over to get another drink, you can slip me the sawbuck you'll owe me."

"It was a fin," I said.

"But I'm gonna collect a sawbuck, or I walk back to nine-ball and forget I ever saw you."

I weighed what I had in my pocket against getting back to the city and collecting expenses from Marko.

"It better be worth it," I said.

He lit a cigarette with a copper lighter and pushed smoke from his cheeks toward the tin ceiling. "Relative of yours?" he asked.

"Not even close."

"Good, because that guy didn't make any friends. It was almost like he didn't care about friends. Or enemies. But I talked to him. Two or three nights ago he was in here trying to hustle some of the house players. He said he lived in New York before he moved West. He had an attitude problem. I warned him to hit the street. Instead, he tried bringing a pair of the ladies from 520 down here. It wasn't long before he found himself outside on the sidewalk, face down."

"Dead?" I asked with some alarm.

"Not dead, maybe wiser."

"Who do you mean, ladies from 520?"

"Hookers. Prostitutes, up the street."

I nodded. I thought Bosko would be more ... discreet.

"Do you know where he went after that, where he stays?"

"I saw him driving an old truck up near the rec center one time, the Gemmel Club. He could be staying at one of those boarding houses up Carr Fork. Lots of Yugis are up that way."

"Could be staying?"

He shrugged. "I haven't seen him for a couple of nights. I heard some talk he's been banned from all the bars along this stretch. But then, I am not his keeper."

A chorus of laughter broke out at a nearby table.

"Did he have any friends? Besides hookers?"

"Not around here. He always talked about how smart he was, bragged about having meetings with the mine bosses up on the hill. He said they were going to make him rich, and he was gonna leave us all behind, like we were trash. He was full of himself. Nobody liked him."

"Why would the mine bosses make *him* rich?"

He paused, pulling his head back and looking down his nose.

"That, I do not know. But no one took him seriously," he said. "In fact, no one took him at all until they caught him cheating, moving the cue ball around. Even the ladies couldn't see their way to back him after that move—"

One of his buddies from the pool room took his arm and pulled him away, saying, "You're up." I never heard the end of his story. Instead, I turned and worked my way to the back wall. Two young guys helped each other away from the stand-up bar and shuffled off to the door. I moved in before the spots vanished.

"Coca-Cola," I said to the bartender. "No ice."

He looked at me like all bartenders do. "You sick or somethin'?" he asked.

I smiled and nodded. It was an explanation he could understand. Before I could turn back to face the room, a blonde in a black dress inserted herself in the space next to me. She set her drink on the bar, then leaned toward me and tossed her head back with a quick smile.

"I saw you come in," she said. "You're new here."

"That's honesty," I said. "Does everybody in town keep some kind of a list?"

She wasn't thrown off. Instead, her eyes traveled from mine, down to my left hand and back again. She had a fresh face, not one of the girls from up the street. Her smile was controlled. Her eyes were blue. She looked down into her drink with them, then back at me.

"Don't I know you?" she asked.

39

The Copper King
10:30 p.m., Thursday, July 22, 1948

She was the kind of woman that might have made me forget Sadie, forget my name, and forget myself. She was exactly that kind, and the longer I stared at her, the more I forgot. I even forgot to feel guilty about it.

"That's a line I recognize," I said. "Does it ever work?"

"Always."

I shuffled around to face her. "My name's Jack."

She smiled and touched my arm. "Well, do you have something to write with, Jack?"

"What?"

"Pen, pencil ... you know."

I was entranced by the movement of her lips as she formed the words but came to and gave her the pencil I carried to write in my notebook. It was a stub, with my teeth marks on it. She took it in her left hand and wrote something on a napkin. Then she folded it in half and slid it across the bar.

"Now you can call me some time," she said.

I put it in my shirt pocket, behind Bosko's picture, and briefly lost track of the room while chatting. When I checked the mirror for my new friend from the billiard room, he was still "ridin' the nine" with his friends.

"Here's your Coke, pal," said the bartender behind me. "That'll be two-bits."

I handed him a quarter and turned back to the blonde.

"You must be on duty." She sipped at her drink through a paper straw.

"You think I'm a cop?"

"I hope not."

"Well, I'm not. I just like cola drinks. What's your name?"

She looked around like her name was a big secret and she didn't want anyone around us to hear. "Fay. I like to tell people I was named after the actress Fay Wray," she said, "because she was so pretty. Maybe you remember her. You know, the one who starred in *King Kong* a few years ago. Besides the monkey, I mean."

"I remember."

"But really, I wasn't," she said, "because that would only make me fifteen!"

I hoped she wasn't fifteen. I sipped on my Coke and listened. She went on about how she lived in town all her life, and how her daddy was a rail worker. She said she worked at the drug store down the street, in the pharmacy by the post office.

"I can get anything down there," she said. "Cigarettes, rubbers, beer ..."

The enchantment began to evaporate as I wondered what might be in her drink. "Sounds like you hit the jackpot," I said, as alarm bells started going off in the back of my brain—just not the part I was thinking with at the moment.

Somebody dropped another nickel in the music machine.

Something I liked, a smooth song by Sammy Kaye, played in the background.

I felt a tap on my shoulder.

"You're in my spot, fella," said a deep voice.

The interruption seemed out of place. I couldn't hear the music anymore. Time moved in fits and starts. I had my back to the toilets.

"Well?" said the voice.

Fay looked across me, over my shoulder. "Go away, Charlie, you've had too much to drink." I turned. He was big. His eyes were angry cuts in a red-rock face. I stepped away, offering him the spot next to Fay.

"I'm fine," he said to her while staring at me. His breathing reminded me of a bull getting ready to charge, with exaggerated exhales from wide-open nostrils. Over his shoulder, I could see Danny pushing toward us, bringing a worried look from the billiards room.

Instead of taking my spot at the bar, Charlie squared up on me, blocking my way to the door. He was through talking. He raggedly shook his head, like a punch-drunk boxer. He dropped his right shoulder to throw a looping roundhouse at my head and opened up his body, thinking too slowly. I stepped inside of it, watched his arm go by, and brought my balled fist up hard under his chin. His head snapped back, and I smashed the right side of his jaw with my trailing elbow. He tried grabbing at me while we were standing close, but his arms lacked direction from his brain, and he went down wobbly to his knees.

I stepped away.

I could have finished him there, but this was his backyard. For all I knew, he was the president of the local Sunday school, and everyone here attended.

"See ya around, Fay," I said, with a salute.

I started to make my way over to the front door and the street outside.

Somewhere, I heard Danny's voice saying my name.

Somebody else grabbed at my arm.

Something hard hit my head in front of my left ear, and my head jerked to the right.

There was a bright light.

Not again, I thought as the darkness took me.

Sometime I was going to get it right.

40

Outside the Copper King
11:30 p.m., Thursday, July 22, 1948

I woke up smelling pavement—something like dirt and dog shit, only sharper and drier. Lightning blew up the sky to the south again. I waited for the rumble of thunder, but it never came. I was lying in a heap against the building on the sidewalk. A dog found me, his long tongue investigating my ear. I shook my arm to move him back and caught him on the neck. He squealed and ran off.

The bar door opened and closed. Feet shuffled in and out. Nobody bothered me but the dog.

It was still nighttime.

The impact to the side of my head had opened a cut on my ear, but it was still attached. I forgot about the soreness in my fingers, now that my head hurt. I touched the ear with my hand and was surprised at the absence of blood.

The dog.

After a moment, I sat up and leaned against the building for support. I could hear the crowd inside the bar through the open windows. My eyes closed, and I took a deep breath, checking for pain in my ribs or kidneys. It must've been one crack to the skull that put me down, no body damage. I stood up, like a newborn colt finding his legs, and leaned hard on the wall for support.

"You are one lucky hombre," said a voice. "And a stupid one."

It was Danny. "You have a place to spend the night?"

"What night is it?"

"Same one."

"How do I look?"

"Ehh ..." He flattened his hand and wiggled it.

Two tipsy local boys stumbled onto the sidewalk and across the street.

"What happened?" I asked.

"You wandered into another fistfight on your way out. Stepped right between 'em."

I reached in my pockets for my cash and bullets and felt my jacket for my wallet. "I owe you ten bucks then, probably more, keeping watch and all."

"Don't worry about it. I helped myself," he said.

I wasn't gonna argue, but I was getting low on walking-around cash. I looked through the noisy window and couldn't see Fay or Charlie.

Danny put out his cigarette and crushed the stub out under his shoe. "They already left," he said. "Where did you learn to punch like that?"

"Bar fights ... in France, mostly. Military Police."

A car across the street started up and backfired.

"I have a suggestion for you, my friend," he said. "Don't come back here for a while. Nobody likes troublemakers, especially out-siders. You won't be welcome."

I was having a hard time making friends. I nodded and turned back up the street toward my car when something came to me, and I turned around.

"Hey, Danny, what if I wanted to talk to your mine bosses?"

He stopped at the doorway. "Why would you want to do that?"

"This guy, Bosko. You said he bragged about talkin' to mine bosses. I want to ask if they know where he is."

He took a long draw on the cigarette and exhaled with a loud puff.

"Well, I can't say where any of them live. Prob'ly Copperton, outside the canyon. But they work on the hill, in that brick building, on the bench. The mine superintendent, somebody Chapman, and a Mister Hepworth, something like that. They like looking down on the rest of us."

"How do I get up there?"

"Fancy dresser like you? You can ride the inclined tram, over past the Merc. Otherwise, you take the stairs. It's a nice view if you have the time."

41

The Bingham Hotel
12:15 a.m., Friday, July 23, 1948

Most of the hotel lobby lights were off, but a door was still open. A handwritten sign at the front desk said, "RING BELL FOR SERVICE."

I rang it.

When nobody came right away, I pulled my room key off the pegboard behind the counter and headed to the third-floor guest room where I'd left my gun. The room offered a double bed, a nightstand, and a three-drawer dresser, in case I decided to stay for a month. I wished I'd asked for a room on the east side, so the morning sun would wake me early. I walked into the bathroom and turned on the water. Nothing came out. Nothing brown, nothing clear.

I slipped on the gun, took all my stuff with me, and walked back into the hallway, checking the doors all along the east side. Some were missing the tarnished, brass numbers, but it was easy to figure out what the missing numbers were. Wood floor at the edges of the carpet runner showed the hotel's age, fading and slivering. I hiked back down to the empty lobby.

Somebody must've come out after I'd left and turned the rest of the lobby lights down. I invited myself behind the desk a second time and examined the keys still hanging on pegs, unused. Number 312 and 314 were both on the east side, and either one might work. I took a chance on 314 and hurried back upstairs to make sure nobody else had taken the room.

I knocked quietly, out of breath.

Nobody answered. I used the new key, opened the door slowly, and switched on a corner lamp. The room was furnished just like the previous one, except the cheap walnut dresser was missing a drawer. I moved my things in, locked the door, and turned the hot water handle on the bathtub. I let it flow until it ran hot, then plugged the drain and drew a bath.

Only one bulb burned in the light fixture over the sink. The mirror reflected a face that needed sleep, but my ear didn't look so bad.

I left the bedroom curtains closed and switched off the lamp as I undressed by the light coming through the bathroom door. I still had a headache. I sat on the bed and pulled the cash from my pocket. Thirty-two dollars. I set the bills down with my notepad, bullets, and wallet on the nightstand. I had both sets of room keys now: one from 307 and the new set for 314.

I'll deal with it in the morning. Nobody will care.

When I pulled Bosko's picture from my shirt pocket, it brought out the paper napkin that had Fay's telephone number written inside. The Copper King logo was printed on the napkin in orange: a crown, with the chemical symbol for copper inside. Cu.

I stared at it.

"C ... U ...."

Something jumped in the back of my mind.

"C ... U ...." *See you!*

It was Bosko's little joke to Yasa. "See you," he'd said, leaving her alone last weekend.

Copper! Copper bosses

I turned the napkin over.

A telephone number was there, written in light, round strokes, but her autograph was missing. She probably guessed I'd remember *King Kong* and Fay Wray. Her boyfriend probably guessed too. Below the number was a short, penciled message: "Someone is following you."

She'd dotted the *i* with a tiny heart that seemed out of place with the message. *Someone?* Was *she* following me?

I thought back to the bars, the miners, the faces, the voices. *The blue Ford?*

It was quiet inside the hotel, a slow night in a place where you could hear a toilet flush two floors down. Outside, dry lightning flashed again, and thunder rumbled through the canyon, closer now. I loaded my gun and hung it in the holster over the sink, near the bathtub. Then I switched off the light at the mirror and eased into the warm bathwater to think things over.

4 2

The Bingham Hotel
1:35 a.m., Friday, July 23, 1948

I dozed off, then jolted awake in a bathtub full of tepid water. Was I dreaming? Had I heard something? The dark of the night was a magnifying glass for sound.

I held still, on high alert. Somewhere a door opened. Not mine. My wet hand moved to find the gun. Faint light crept under the door to the hallway and illuminated the bedroom to my night-accustomed eyes. I slowed my breathing, straining to identify any shred of life outside in the hall. There were no creaking floorboards. No muffled voices. Just my own heartbeat, pulsing in my ears like muffled footsteps on the far-off stairway.

I waited a minute, then let go of the gun and raised myself slowly from the water, dripping. I dried off, pulled on my pants, and drew the gun again. Somewhere outside, a dog barked. I peeked through a gap in the curtains. The town stretched out below, tunnel lights marking the edge of the dark mountainside. The moon's glow reflected from rooftops in the downhill canyon.

A row of cars slept quietly along the hillside, my own included. A dark shape, human, but hard to see at distance, crept among them. I squinted to be sure until clouds covered the moon, the street darkened, and I lost sight of him.

Far away a car engine rolled over, caught, and roared. Red taillights winked on and then vanished.

I pulled on my shirt and shoes and slid back the safety chain on the door, then stepped into the hallway without making a sound. Glass wall sconces offered dim light.

My heart went into my throat.

The door to 307 was wide open now.

I brought my gun up in both hands, one finger along the trigger guard. I stepped back, behind the door frame of the new room, my new room, to take a breath. I was totally dependent on my five senses for safety, but four of them were useless at this distance. *If only I could see through walls.* I waited and listened, trying not to make a sound.

Silence filled the third floor.

Someone had come looking for me. Was it the guy Fay noticed, in the bar? One of the girls from the street, looking for the five-dollar bounty? Charlie, hoping for payback? Or somebody else, driving a dark blue Ford and looking ... for what?

I took a breath and moved again from the doorway, edging down the hall with my gun still up in two hands. My weight shifted over a floorboard ever so slightly, resulting in a muffled, creaking sound. I froze again.

Nothing. I moved closer.

At the door's edge, I pushed inside, gradually widening the arc of my view. The bed and the dresser came into view. No one was inside, and nothing had changed, except the faint smell of stale cigarette smoke that gave shape to the darkness.

I switched on a room light.

The door to the bathroom was open. A cigarette butt lay in the dry sink bowl, half-smoked and cold. It hadn't been there when I checked for hot water. The butt left a tan-colored burn mark on the white, porcelain finish. I picked it up.

No lipstick.

I backed into the hallway, pulled the door closed, and considered checking out the floors below, but something told me it would be a useless gesture. Instead, I went back to my new room, locked the door from the inside, and left the key in the keyhole. Still listening, I hung my shirt on the bathroom doorknob, pulled back the blankets, and laid down on the cheap, wire-spring mattress.

The burnt-out cigarette in the sink occupied my thoughts until I fell into a restless sleep, leaving the light turned on.

43

Copper Bosses
7:40 a.m., Friday, July 23, 1948

I spent the rest of that hot, muggy night getting comfortable under a thin sheet. Bird chatter woke me before the sun, pigeon talk from the roof just above. I stepped into the hallway, barefoot. The door to 307 was still closed. I could hear a few people down below, flushing toilets, closing doors, but the third floor was quiet still.

I walked back into my room and gargled with tap water. The stubble on my chin needed attention, but the cut on my ear didn't look so bad, and the burn on my fingers had faded to a red patch. I combed out my haircut, put on my jacket, gun, and tie, and headed downstairs. The desk clerk collected my complaint about no water and took both keys.

Near the tunnel entry outside, a dozen trucks waited for the access light to turn green. I unlocked my car door, grabbed my hat, and stayed a pedestrian. At Main, I cut over to a side road next to the Copper King and headed up Carr Fork to look around. A barber pole swirled above the sidewalk near the corner. I gauged the stubble again with my fingers: an expense that Marko could pay. One shave later, I walked out feeling whole again and checked my watch. It was only 8:28.

Stairs on the sidewalk invited me up past a grocery store, a few occupied boarding houses, and a big Catholic church. The street sign pointed to Highland Boy and Yampa up ahead. The towering Carr Fork Bridge connected train barns, perched on one side of the gulch, to the mine offices and switchyards on the other.

Two men wearing straw hats were mowing a brilliant green lawn next to the yellow—brick Gemmel Club. Behind it, I spotted the inclined tram. It ran two hundred feet up a hillside covered with scrub brush and weeds. The tram cars were a matched pair of small, orange cabooses pulled by steel cables, one up, one down. Halfway up the incline, the two cars passed on a side-by-side track. According to the sign, it took almost a minute to make the ascent.

The down car was empty and waiting.

I approached the open door with as much attitude as I could muster and walked inside with two other men who joined from the platform. Nobody looked twice. An attendant flashed a light to the upper level and the tram started its slow climb up the hillside.

As we rose up toward the mine offices, I had a bird's-eye view of Bingham's upper canyon. Cresting the roofs of the taller buildings I could see the hotel, the tunnel, City Hall, and in the distance mine operations disappearing into the hillsides that still separated the mine from the town. Trains moved everywhere, collecting material blasted from hillsides and picked up by gigantic steam shovels. To my right, multiple bridges spanned the gulch to connect train traffic from mining out to the hillside dumps.

The tram stopped roughly, and we all walked over a wooden deck onto a sidewalk that led to the main office. The other two guys headed over to a single-story train building on the far side of the tracks. I walked in the front door of the brick office building without an appointment. My plan was to show Bosko's photo around and see what developed—although, I guess that was Edna's plan, really. So far, people didn't know much about Bosko, except that he knew the copper bosses and cheated at pool.

A pleasant, middle-aged woman in a pink-flowered dress sat behind a reception desk. She greeted me but didn't get up. There was no lobby to speak of, and no chairs to sit in while important people kept you waiting.

"You must be the detective," she said.

"I am," I said, taken back. Maybe she heard about the fight in the bar? I took off my hat and held it by the brim.

Something buzzed in front of her, and she rearranged cords to make it stop.

"We heard you might be late. Mr. Chapman is expecting you."

"Mr. Chapman?"

"On the top floor. His secretary will meet you at the stairway. I'm sorry, but we don't have an elevator."

"Thanks," I said, and smiled politely.

More things buzzed, and she turned her attention to making them stop.

When I turned the corner on the top-level stair, I came into a high-ceilinged hallway, dimly lit by copper pendant lights and a window at the far end. I was intercepted immediately by the silhouette of a young woman, slim and wearing a dark skirt and jacket. Her high heels clattered, echoing in the tall, empty expanse. My eyes adjusted, and I saw that her dishwater blonde hair was pulled back tightly behind her neck, held there by a copper clip. She was clearly attractive but trying her best to make it look like she wasn't. I gave her credit for not wearing horn-rimmed glasses, a dead giveaway. She held a clipboard at her chest in a way that implied she was worried I'd try to steal it from her if I had the chance.

She wasn't gonna let me get close enough to have that chance.

"Good morning, Detective ...?"

"Hammer," I said.

"Yes, Detective Hammer. I'm so sorry, your office didn't give us any names. You're from Salt Lake City, aren't you?"

"I am," I said, obviously jumping Jim's detectives' appointment. I didn't have much time if they were driving out from Salt Lake.

"You're early, but Mr. Chapman can see you now. When your office called yesterday, they said you needed just a few minutes of his time?"

She let it hang as a question.

"Okay," I said, being careful with words.

"We thought there'd be two of you."

"No, just me."

She frowned.

"Just to be thorough," she said, "can you show me some identification?"

I dug into my pocket in a way that made sure she saw the gun under my coat. As I pulled out my wallet, a mahogany door opened from an office on the street-facing side of the building. A tall, gray-haired man wearing a white shirt, striped tie, and suspenders holding up expensive gray trousers came into the hallway.

"Come on in," he said in a hoarse voice that spoke volumes about spending too much time in mining. "I have a tight schedule today, no time for formalities. Anyway, I thought we already gave the FBI everything they needed. Don't they talk with you boys?"

He was waving his arm, showing me the way in.

I opened my wallet and flashed my license to his secretary as I walked past. There was no way she could see anything that mattered.

"My name is Chapman," he said, extending his hand. "Have a seat."

I was drawn to the window instead, a window that looked out over the town. He handed me his business card. I studied it briefly and stuck it in my shirt pocket. I'd tacked the last of my own cards to the service station wall.

"That's quite a cut," he said, pointing hesitantly. "On your ear, there."

"It's nothing." I reached up and touched it. "Stray dog cleaned me up."

"What?"

"Thanks for your time," I said, turning back. "You have a great view here."

"All for show," he said. "But show counts, at least in my world. Helps me play the part, if you know what I mean."

"Only too well," I said. "My name is Hammer."

He offered me a leather-covered wingback chair and sat in a matching one himself. He made sure I admired the view out the window over his shoulder, where I could watch electric ore trains moving along the lower hillside on the south side of the canyon.

"Detective, I'm afraid I don't have much time this morning. Why don't we skip the pleasantries and get right to it? I understand you're here looking for information on the whereabouts of Bosko Cvito."

44

Copper Bosses
8:45 a.m., Friday, July 23, 1948

The sudden mention of Bosko caught me off guard.

"That *is* why you're here, isn't it?" he asked.

I set my hat aside and pulled out my notepad. "After a fashion," I said, "and since we're dispensing with the pleasantries, I'm also investigating events related to a murder that occurred earlier in the week. The victim happened to be the niece of Mr. Cvito." It was what I imagined Detective Nichols might say if he were here. "She lived in his house and died there. He disappeared, right around the same time."

"Is he a suspect?"

"Just a person I'd like to talk to, someone who needs to answer a few questions."

We paused as the dame in dark blue brought in a tray with a pitcher of lemonade and two crystal glasses.

"I'd have her bring out something stronger, but since you're on duty I thought perhaps lemonade would be nice." He was smiling but talking down.

"Sugar?" she asked, pouring the mixture over ice.

I declined.

He watched her walk with interested eyes as she left the room.

"Are you single, Detective?" he asked.

"Not married, if that's what you're asking. Why?"

"No reason," he said. He crossed his legs at the knee and settled back. "Where were we?"

"I was saying that I have a few questions for Bosko," I said. "If I knew where to find him, I'd ask him myself. Have you seen him since Saturday?"

He swirled the ice around in his glass, mesmerized. "I haven't, no. I don't make it my business to keep track of him. He's an odd character, hard to pin down, but then many brilliant minds are. He'll turn up, I'm sure."

"You don't know where he might be?"

He shook his head slowly, thinking about it.

"What makes you think he's brilliant?" I asked.

Now he pretended not to hear me, or maybe he just hoped Cvito was brilliant, but those were cop questions. I still needed answers to my own.

The lemon flavor was strong, almost overpowering. The muscles in my mouth involuntarily moved in reaction to the sour juice. I should've taken the sugar. I wondered if he'd instructed his assistant to bring lemonade to help mask his facial reactions to my questions. Or maybe he always drank lemonade before nine in the morning. His cheeks puckered as he sipped at the drink, while I told him about Yasa.

"So, help me understand. Are you suggesting Bosko's in danger too?"

"That's right."

"I hate to think it, but I believe I see what you're driving at." He held up his glass and studied it. "That lemon is quite strong, don't you agree?" He worked his lips around his teeth.

I decided to take a chance and be more direct.

"Listen, I've heard the term, 'Cvito device' bandied about," I said, ignoring his question. "What is it?"

"You mistake me for a scientist, Detective." He smiled. "That's way above my pay grade."

But he had heard of it.

"Then maybe you can clear something else up for me," I said. "Word on the street is that you two have been working out the details of a business deal ... a very substantial deal."

He stood up, walked to the window, and stared at the town.

"You must understand, Detective, this is a highly confidential business transaction you're digging at. I've been instructed to put you into the picture, so to speak, to the extent it might help your investigation. And we're all interested in Mr. Cvito's safety, I'm sure. But you'll have to give me your word that you'll keep what we discuss in the strictest of confidence."

"Of course," I lied.

"I don't know how much you know about our Mr. Cvito. And I don't really know that much myself. In fact, I'm not at all sure that Cvito is even his real name. In any case, you're aware that he worked with Nikola Tesla, before the war. You've heard of him, I imagine?"

Twice this week. I nodded.

"It seems Mr. Cvito was some sort of assistant, although to hear him tell it, it was Tesla that took direction from him. The FBI verified that they worked together."

"Go on," I said. *FBI?* I thought.

I wrote down his comments.

"Some time back, one of the fellows on our research and development staff first ran across Cvito. Introduced, I should say, by a colleague at the university. Cvito told our man about how he'd worked with Tesla to develop a method of moving power that would revolutionize the electrical world by safely transmitting electrical energy without wires! Naturally, we took an interest in the project."

"Without wires? How would that work?"

"I'm not at liberty to give you any details. Not that I fully understand them myself, but the invention uses a type of open-top vacuum tube array. It sounds rather impossible, actually. Quite unusual."

"So, what's the connection between a copper mine and this invention? Seems like it'll put you guys out of business."

He sat down again and leaned forward, energized by the discussion. His forearms rested on his thighs. We were drifting away from police-type business, but I let him run with it.

"Think about it, Detective. More than half the copper we produce here out of the Bingham mine is eventually used to make wire—electrical wire that connects things, and carries electricity here and there, hither and yon! It brings raw power from coal-fired plants and from hydroelectric dynamos all around the country and connects these power sources to every small town and big city across America. It's copper wiring that makes music and ball games alike possible in your own radio at home! Copper wire is our largest single market and we, right here, are one of the three largest copper producers in the world."

I thought maybe he'd written all this down before, in a speech for his investors.

"So, here's your connecting link, Detective. Although we sit near the top of the heap as far as worldwide copper production goes, we also live in a world of finite resources. Things have limits. We've managed recently to pull as much as two pounds of copper from a ton of overburden, and we're getting more efficient all the time. But the plain, unvarnished truth is that industry projections for copper usage tell us that the world's known supply of new copper will be exhausted in as little as thirty-five years! And not just the resources found here in Bingham, but also those found in South America and Asia as well, whether it's us, Anaconda, or Phelps-Dodge doing the digging."

His office was filled with elaborate furnishings purchased by cash from copper. I looked out the window and across the canyon at the huge investment in copper mining, railroads, milling sites, and everything related to production. I could only see a fraction of the process from here. I was beginning to get an idea of the dollars Marko hinted at, and the real value of such an invention: something that had the potential to replace all this with thin air.

"So, you're looking at Cvito and his wireless invention as a sort of business hedge?" I asked.

He didn't answer right away but pulled back, touching his pointer fingers together. "I guess you could see it that way."

"Then let me reframe the conversation the way I *do* see it. Cvito, from your own description, has a valuable idea, even a great idea. In fact, it's so good that somebody might be willing to kill for it. Am I making the right connections now?"

He set his glass aside but didn't comment. Bells clanged outside the window.

"Remind me again why you're here, Detective," he said.

"I'm looking for Bosko Cvito. Straight up, can you point me in his direction?"

He stood and walked to the window again.

"I hope you're not suggesting the death of his niece had anything to do with us, or with any purchase of his invention on our part?" he said. "That troubles me."

He was the kind of man who turned everything into something about himself.

"I'm just saying that after hearing your story, it occurs to me that a device with the potential to replace half your business with thin air could be mighty interesting to a whole range of buyers," I said. "Even to the point of violence."

His hand went to the back of his neck. "You'd best speak with the FBI about anything like that. I know they've been checking into Mr. Cvito's other connections, but that possibility truly troubles me, Detective."

"Don't protest so much," I said. "You already said that."

45

Copper Bosses
9:15 a.m., Friday, July 23, 1948

"What else can I tell you, Detective?" He didn't sit back down, but looked conspicuously at his watch, a gold and silver chronograph. I took it as a signal.

"Cvito's been noising around town that this deal is gonna make him rich," I said. "True?"

He leaned against the edge of his big mahogany desk. "I'm betting he makes us all rich," he said flatly. "Who did he say it to?"

"Pretty much everybody in town."

His face said nothing. His fingers played at the edge of the desk and the glass top.

Clearly, he was holding back. I knew he had an idea where Bosko was, and likely as good an idea about where he'd been. Twice I'd asked him where I could find Bosko. Twice he'd avoided answering. Somebody with an item as valuable as what Bosko was selling usually ends up being prisoner to it at some point. At least until his jailer trades cash for it. I had another card to play.

"Tell me about Highland Boy," I said.

His eyes darted up at the mention of it.

"Highland Boy? It's just a little area around the corner," he said. "Why do you ask?"

"It's a name that keeps comin' up," I said. "And I'm wonderin' why."

He regained control of his face, screwed a cigarette into it, and struck a match.

"Highland Boy was one of the early mines in the Canyon," he explained. "Utah Copper bought them out, and Kennecott bought out Utah Copper. Now, as the mine grows in size, Highland Boy is in its path. The Upper Fork is going away. We're closing it down a piece at a time, the old community center, the power station, and a bunch of old houses. You're free to drive up that way and have a look around, but up high there's not much left to see."

He walked behind the desk to find an ashtray. *Copper.*

"I have a hunch maybe Bosko's stayin' somewhere in Highland Boy," I said. Through the window, on the far side of the canyon, I could see an electric engine pulling a load of ore toward the Copperton depot. "You wouldn't know which boarding house he's stayin' in, would you?"

"I rather doubt he stays up there, but like I told you before—"

"I know," I said. "You don't keep track of him."

He put out the cigarette and walked over to where I sat. "Is that all, Detective?"

"Just one last question, Chapman, about something you said earlier. Why would the FBI be involved in your business like this, checking out Bosko's connections for a private company and all?"

That brought a deep-throated chuckle to the surface.

"I'm sorry. I thought you knew all about that. You see, this thing with Bosko was an FBI deal right from the start. The colleague I mentioned earlier, the one at the university? He was one of their local field agents."

I stayed in the leather chair a moment longer.

46

To City Hall
9:45 a.m., Friday, July 23, 1948

He was through answering questions. If he knew where Bosko was, he was hiding it. He walked me out to the hallway, where his assistant took charge.

"Are you heading back to Salt Lake right away?" she asked.

I nodded. "Why? Do you need a ride?"

Color rose in her cheeks, and she turned away.

I hadn't meant anything by it.

I hurried down the steps, past the front desk, and out to the tram loading area. I waited a few minutes for the lower tram to load, admiring the stepped mountainside mining operation beyond town.

The light flashed, the tram jolted and started down the hill. At the halfway point, I looked across the track at the upcoming tram car. There were two passengers watching the city fall away as the tram rose. One of them turned. A face stared out through the window, a face I knew. It was Detective Nichols. His eyes widened as he saw me, then passed out of sight as the cars crossed.

At the bottom, I skipped down the stairway to the road, but instead of heading right back to town, I hurried over to City Hall to introduce myself to the local cops, and to ask after Bosko. The building was a grand, two-story brick structure and, I hoped, the last place in town Nichols might look for me. The officer in charge drooped, fighting sleep at the tail end of his shift. His tie clip boasted a 45-caliber bullet and his wrinkled uniform carried a brass nameplate over his heart: DEPUTY WHITE.

"Take your hat off," he said.

I told him my name, and that I was in town looking for an old man named Bosko. I described him but left out the part about Yasa being dead.

He sat back on his chair, studying me, fiddling with a toothpick in his mouth. "Can't say as I know him. When did you say you got in?"

"Last night, late," I lied. "I stayed up at the Bingham Hotel."

"That fleabag?" he said, laughing.

"It had a bath."

"Well, here's a pad. Write it all down for the sheriff. You carryin' a piece?"

I pulled it out and laid it on the desk.

"Loaded?" he asked.

"No."

He picked it up, racked back the slide to check, and studied the eagle and swastika on the handle.

"Souvenir?"

"Something like that." I tried keeping one eye on the street, just in case Nichols turned back down the hillside and stopped in looking for me.

"How long are you going to be stayin' with us?" he asked.

"Only today."

"Well now, don't that beat all," he said. "There was this other fellow in here, not long ago, askin' questions about your Mr. Bosko. Only here for the day, too. Some hotshot detective from the Salt Lake Police Department, named ... Penny? No, that's not it."

"Nichols?"

"Could be. Friend of yours?"

I shook my head. "Hardly."

"Good, 'cause I didn't appreciate his attitude, comin' out here all high-and-mighty with a chip on his shoulder, tellin' me how a police station ought to be run. He was headed up the hill to talk to the mine bosses. You got any idea what that's all about?"

I figured I could give him either the truth or a version of it. The right answer was whichever one got me out the door the fastest, but a third option popped out of my mouth without thinking. "If I find out," I asked, "do you want me to let ya know?"

That seemed to satisfy him.

"Get out of here, Hammer, before I change my mind and hold you over for failing to register that gun when you got in town."

Before I could answer, he'd already turned away.

I hurried down the steps and over to my car. I wanted to get out of town before nightfall, but I still had a few more leads to check out. I could only hope Nichols took his cues from Chapman's girl and headed straight back to Salt Lake to look for me. I made it about a block down canyon, headed east, and then pulled over. There on the north side, past the J.C. Penney's, was a drugstore.

I decided to stop in, to see if Fay was around.

47

The Drugstore
10:45 a.m., Friday, July 23, 1948

I edged my Ford into a short space on the downhill side of the road, rolling up the windows in case it rained again.

The bell over the front door jangled when I walked in. No one took notice. The smell of cosmetics and school supplies combined into a familiar odor, comfortable and clean. A soda fountain and lunch counter hugged the right side of the store. The pharmacy window was in back, at the opposite corner from the front door. I seemed to be the only customer.

I walked straight back to the pharmacy.

Fay was there, dressed in a white blouse and jeans, with her back to the counter. Her hair was pulled up in a ponytail.

"Is this where I come to buy cigarettes?" I asked.

She turned to me across the window, smiling. "Jack, isn't it? And *you* don't smoke."

"Don't I?"

"What are you doing here?"

"I came by to check on Charlie," I lied. "How's he doin'?"

She frowned and turned to the racks of pills and bandages behind her. "I'm taking a break," she said to someone I couldn't see. She disappeared and reappeared from a door two aisles over.

"You want a Coke?" she asked. "On the house?"

She filled two glasses with ice and poured from the fountain. We sat on leather stools at the empty counter like high school kids. Stacked, empty glasses stood along the mirror and the freezers hummed, hiding ice cream. A green porcelain malt machine sat in the center of the counter.

"It gets busier," she said, "after school lets out."

School was already out for the summer, but I didn't push it. She tossed her head casually, rearranging her hair.

"You never told me your whole name, Jack."

She reached over and touched my leg in a familiar sort of way. Maybe I grinned. I sipped at the edges of the Coke glass without a straw.

"Hammer," I said. "Jack Hammer."

She leaned back and narrowed her left eye as if I were kidding.

"Well, I thought you'd probably call me, Jack Hammer," she said. "But I didn't expect a personal visit, you wearin' a tie and all."

My right arm rested on the counter. She put her left hand on my arm, casually.

"Ooh, let me look at that cut on your ear." She fussed over it for a minute. "You've sure come to the right place. I've got a little salve, something to help it mend."

She stepped in the back, then returned with a jar of cream and rubbed it on lightly. I almost forgot why I stopped by, but I didn't. I remembered Sadie back in the city.

"Actually, I came by to ask you about that note you sent. About somebody followin' me last night?"

Her eyes flicked up toward the front door and settled back again.

"What about it?"

"Well, who was it?"

"Nobody *I* know. I noticed him when you first walked into the bar," she said. "Into the pool room, actually. You came in and talked with that little Mex, but this other guy, the one I saw, came in a minute after and turned his back real quick when you drifted back out into the bar. He had his eye on you, good."

"What did he look like?" I asked.

"Nothing special," she said, smiling. "I had my eyes on you."

"No, Fay ... I'm serious. Can you remember what he looked like? Tall? Short? Mustache? Bald? You know?"

I pulled Bosko's picture out of my pocket and handed it to her.

"This guy?" I asked.

She stood up, walked around to the back of the counter, and put her Coke glass down.

"Not him," she said. "The guy I saw came in wearin' a hat and a jacket, like you. Maybe wider, but not taller. I didn't pay much attention. But he was watchin' you."

Marko?

"And you're sure he *followed* me inside?"

"Hey, I've had private cops followin' me before," she said. "I know what to look for."

I wanted to ask her why, but a guy in a white jacket stepped out from behind the back door to the drug counter and held it open.

"Telephone," he said. "It's for you, Fay." He spoke in tones suggesting the call was one she might rather not take.

"I need to get goin' anyway," I said. "I've got a few more things to check out before I head back to Salt Lake."

She spoke to the white jacket. "Take a message. Tell 'em I'll call later, will ya?"

He nodded his head and walked into the back room.

"So, you thought *he* was a private cop?" I asked.

She leaned across the counter, so I could get a view down the top of her blouse. She was compelling.

"You never told me what you do," she said. "Are you a cop?"

For a moment, I didn't care about Bosko or his Cvito device. I felt like I was on holiday here in Bingham, just taking in the scenery, and she was the best part.

"Sort of," I nodded.

A voice from the rear yelled, "Fay, he's callin' again! I think you better take it or he's just gonna come down here."

"Not now!"

She closed her blue eyes and sighed.

"Is it Charlie?" I asked.

The corners of her mouth turned down.

"Charlie's a flat tire, if you know what I mean. After you put him on the floor last night, I took him home and left him there feeling sorry for himself. I just don't see myself hitched up to a big, dumb miner like him anymore. I've been tryin' to explain it to him for three weeks."

"*Anymore?* You and Charlie ...?"

She stood up straight, the expression on her face warning me not to ask why.

"How long?"

"Since May," she said. "I keep tellin' him it was a mistake, but he won't listen."

I stood up, too, and pulled out a dollar bill. I wrote my name and number on it and left it on the counter.

"Look me up," I told her, "if you ever get into town and need a good private eye."

I paused under the bell and glanced back.

She really was a beautiful gal.

48

Highland Boy
12:45 p.m., Friday, July 23, 1948

I turned the car around, then took a right at the Carr Fork sign. I crossed under the first railroad bridge, supported by riveted girders standing on concrete piers as tall as a house. The crisscrossing steel and ironwork soared ten stories to support a single track crossing the canyon. Up ahead on the hillside, oak brush and June grass battled to maintain control of the landscape.

The road here was even narrower than the main canyon. There were no picket fence yards. Laundry hung across front-facing balconies. I drove slowly, keeping an eye out for Detective Nichols and searching for Bosko's truck, with its conspicuous sideboards. It was a long shot at best. He could've easily parked inside a garage somewhere, out of sight.

A hawk soared high above in the blue sky.

A rusty pickup truck filled with sunburnt men sitting in the bed passed by, none of them Bosko.

I sped up. If he was in one of these run-down buildings, I'd need more than luck to pull him out. Thunder rumbled through the canyon, echoes of blasting just over the ridge.

Somewhere between the second and third dump bridges, the road stopped. Pavement continued, but chain-link ran across the cracked asphalt and headed up both hillsides. A padlocked gate halted car travel further north. I stopped and got out to read the fine print on the signs.

"PRIVATE PROPERTY. NO TRESPASSING!"

The signs were new but recently modified with .22 caliber ventilation. In smaller letters, they read, "CONTROLLED ACCESS WORK AREA. CALL FOR AUTHORIZATION."

Demolition had taken its toll on the upper canyon. Beyond the fence, a few shacks and boarding houses were empty. Concrete foundations stood as reminders of where other structures had been. Chapman hadn't lied. The mine was taking over, swallowing everything in its path. I looked back down the road. The whole town was on borrowed time.

Highland Boy. What was Bosko doing up here?

I could hear a steady pounding in the distance. I turned back north to where the road rounded the hillside and disappeared west. Another truck headed downhill and stopped at the gate. The truck was unmarked. I stood aside as one of the passengers hopped out with a key.

"What gives with the road closure?" I asked.

He swung the wide gate out to let the truck pass. It came through and he locked it again.

"This section's been shut down for almost eight months now," he said. He was sweating, but not dirty.

"You guys tearin' down the houses up there?"

"Nope," he said. "Working on that new substation, around the hillside there."

"Substation?"

He turned away. Somebody in the truck had said something to him.

"Can't talk," he said, turning back. "Loose lips sink ships." He climbed inside again, and they drove off.

"Have a nice day," I said to no one in particular.

Midday sun beat on me. When he was out of sight, I peeled off my jacket and hat, and put the gun and holster in the glove box. I pulled the car over to a wide spot of gravel, took the keys from the ignition, and climbed over the fence.

Three abandoned houses sat undamaged on the uphill side of the road. Behind them, a hillside of rocks and scrub brush widened into a plateau, rising sharply into layered, dump-line contours with electrical towers feeding power to trains.

I walked behind the buildings and scrambled up the loose rocks to a group of boulders set deep into the west-facing slope. Small gray lizards scattered, then hesitated, their heads twitching mechanically. I copied them as they hurried from lounging in the sun to the cover of mounds of sage and scrub brush.

The pounding noise stopped. I picked up the distant grinding of earth-moving machinery. I looked for a better vantage point and picked out a mound of oak brush, lower on the hill. I half-ran, half-slid, and finally tumbled down the dry, grassy slope to its cover. Two hundred yards ahead and beyond the curve of the road was what the guy in the truck had called a substation. Equipment sat on a concrete pad a little larger than the footprint of the three houses I'd passed, surrounded by a chain-link fence topped with barbed wire. Several larger trucks carrying shiny ten-foot-tall metal cylinders were being offloaded. An orange crane truck lifted them to the ground. Inside the first fence, rows of ceramic insulators rose on spires, like trail markers. In the center of the pad was what appeared to be an enormously tall, thin radio tower.

Past the substation were a few other abandoned buildings in

various stages of demolition and decay. Discarded wood siding and bricks sat in piles at the edge of the road, waiting for transport away.

I stood up to move closer when a gunshot cracked and skipped off the ground in front of me. I put down roots, searching the hillsides for the shooter. After a moment, I started forward again, and another shot echoed through the canyon, this one closer.

"Hold up there, friend!" said a voice that seemed to come from the sky.

There was movement across the gulch.

"Keep your hands where I can see 'em," it said. "Walk down to the road."

If I could keep from getting shot, walking down to the road was what I wanted to do anyway.

49

Highland Boy
1:30 p.m., Friday, July 23, 1948

The voice came from a little man with a big rifle.

"What brings you up this way?" he asked. He worked his way down the hillside, eyes on me. He wore blue jeans, a white shirt, and a cowboy hat, and carried a military-style walkie-talkie. Field glasses hung heavy around his sun-dried neck. He showed me a badge: KENNECOTT SECURITY.

"This here's a fenced-off area now," he said. "No trespassing."

I just stared at him.

"What's your name?"

"Nichols," I lied. "Just came from a meeting on the hill with Chapman. He told me I could head up this way, have a look around."

The little man stayed back far enough that I couldn't knock his gun away. It was leveled at my knees. My identification was with my own gun, in the glove box, on the other side of the gate.

I motioned toward my shirt pocket. I handed him Chapman's

card and he scratched his head, lowering the rifle. "Nobody told me there'd be visitors."

"Go ahead, call up to his office and talk with his secretary if you want."

But I hope she's at lunch.

"Radio's line-of-sight," he said. "We'll have to walk down to the office. They have a landline."

And he'd have to walk me outside the gate to get a look at my credentials. I'd already pretended to be a cop once today. Doing it again wasn't gonna get me in much more trouble than that. He examined the card, unsure.

"Look, Tex, I'm a police detective," I said. "I'm up here lookin' for another guy and figured he might've come this way."

"What other guy?" he asked, passing over the nickname I stuck on him.

"Some two-bit shamus, goes by the name of Hammer. And he's tracking down another fellow, somebody named Bosko."

"Let's see your badge."

"It's in my car, back at the gate."

He looked up from studying Chapman's card. I had too much information, knew too many names, and it made him uneasy.

"Bosko?" he asked.

"Some kind of scientist or something, up this way. I have a message for him too," I said. "One of his relatives died. He doesn't know it yet."

"Let's go," he said.

He lifted the radio to his ear. The sound of the crackle in the voices took me back a few years, when I'd carried one like it.

"Could I get that card back?" I asked. "When you're through, I mean."

He motioned with his gun toward the bend in the road.

I walked in front of him and chatted about the heat and the rain.

He had to feel it, skin turning to leather, sitting out on the hillside all day. The power plant was clearly visible now. Workers were constructing a large concrete pad with all sorts of conduit and pipe poking up from the ground. They were preparing the cylinders to be lifted into place on the various smaller pads arrayed around the center. A brick house next door was being used as a site office. It had a covered porch, recalling days when upper Highland Boy was alive with miners' families.

"Inside," he said.

Workmen glanced my way, but nobody glanced twice. Inside, most of the walls had been torn out, like a hollowed-out jack-o'-lantern. There were a few filing cabinets and two tables with drawings on them, plans for whatever they were building. A telephone sat on a desk by the back door.

"Stay here," he said, pointing to a wooden chair. He left the front door unlocked. Either he had some doubt about my intentions and was testing me, or he knew there was nowhere to run. He put his radio on top of a filing cabinet across the room, but kept the rifle slung over his shoulder.

He walked into the back of the house where I could hear him talking. I couldn't make out what he said because the pile driver started up again just outside. It was likely they had more security guards outside on the hillside, connected by radios. I decided to stay put and play out the ruse I'd started. Relaxed security inside the house and the close proximity of the workmen coming and going suggested this wasn't someplace I was going to get sapped or taken for a long ride.

I walked over to one of the plan tables and scanned the papers but couldn't make heads or tails of them. I glanced around, then folded up one of the loose top sheets and stuffed it down the back of my pants and shirt like a back-brace. I drifted over to the window. I could explain watching the activity on a construction site, but studying blueprints might seem suspicious, no matter what my story was.

In a few minutes, Tex reappeared, bringing another guy in a white shirt, one with rolled-up sleeves, gray hair, and an unlit cigarette in his mouth.

Cigarette Guy stepped forward.

"Detective Nichols, is it?" he asked.

"That's right."

He handed back Chapman's card. "Just who is it you're lookin' for?" His head was looking down, but his eyes looked up and back at me.

"Some private eye named Hammer chasin' another guy named Bosko."

"You said something about a message for Bosko?"

"His niece died a few days ago. I don't think he knows about it."

"I see." He thought about it for a moment. "He never said anything about a niece."

"Well, I've never met the guy either."

"Look, this is a restricted work area, even for cops," he said. "I understand you don't have your badge with you?"

I noticed Tex's gun was off his shoulder.

"Like I told Tex here, it was hot outside, so I left my jacket in my car parked back by the fence."

He seemed concerned.

"And my gun," I added. "I wasn't expectin' trouble. Me and him could walk down and get it—"

"Uh-uh. Look, why didn't Chapman's office call ahead to let us know you were comin'?"

I turned away, scratching the back of my head.

"Not their fault," I said. "He suggested I could head up this way to look around, but he probably didn't expect me to be hoppin' your fence here."

His face muscles were still and unmoving. Sweat was making an appearance on his brow. Mine too. It seemed hotter inside than out.

"Just so you know, I tried calling Chapman's office to verify your story," he said. "He's at lunch, so I'm waitin' for a telephone call back. I hope you won't mind sittin' tight until they get back with us? I have a deadline to meet and a few other issues to get working on just now."

I did mind. I couldn't see that working out too well for me and I couldn't spare the time just sitting around waiting for the ax to fall. Instead, I pitched my own plan.

"You know, with all due respect to your deadline, I have somebody I'm looking for who's puttin' more space between him and me every minute that passes."

"Nothing I can do, Nichols," he said. "I'm sorry, but we're under some government scrutiny here, especially with regards to security at the work area. Nobody should be out this way, not without clearance."

"Well, Chapman," I said, "he told me all about the project here, and Cvito's device."

His head jerked up when I mentioned it. He glanced at Tex, then me. "Then you know it's a government secret," he said, "not up for discussion here."

I'd boxed myself out of more questions. I couldn't bring up the device again without betraying my own ignorance.

"Look," I said. "I didn't mean to trouble you, so why don't ya just call my office in Salt Lake? Ask for the boss, Captain Burt. He'll verify who I am, and I'll get out of your hair and back on Hammer's trail."

He lit his cigarette with a copper lighter. I was starting to think I was the only one in town without some kind of copper accessory.

"And I checked in here with Deputy White, too, down at City Hall, but ... he's probably off-shift until midnight."

He thought it over. I was clearly an interruption in his busy day.

"Okay, let's find out what your story is," he said, turning to Tex. "Hand me that telephone directory for the city and let's get this done with. I need to get back to work."

50

❧

Highland Boy
2:30 p.m., Friday, July 23, 1948

Uncle Jim hadn't answered my calls all week, but even if he wasn't in, I wasn't gonna be any worse off.

"The number's 4-6581," I said. "Ask for the Detectives Bureau, Captain Burt."

He checked the number in the book anyway, looking back at me when he found it.

"Maggie," he said. "Get me 4-6581 in Salt Lake. ... Of course, I know it's the police."

Tex sat across the room resting the gun on his knees. He looked at the electric clock on the wall and compared it to his watch.

Somebody picked up.

"Good afternoon, my name is Peter Cardwell," said Cigarette Guy. "Yes ... yes ... I'm calling from Bingham. That's it, Kennecott Copper. I'm tryin' to reach Captain Burt, maybe in the Detectives Bureau. ... Yes, I'll hang on."

Chapman had said he was working a deal with Bosko, set in

motion by the FBI, to beam electricity through air. Marko was right: this idea was going to be worth more money than I could even imagine. This had to be their test site, or at least a part of it. These guys knew Bosko by name and had at least heard of his device. So, what was it? Things weren't any clearer, but maybe Cardwell knew. Maybe this whole place was Bosko's device. How would I ever deliver if that was the case?

"... I have a man here," Cardwell was saying. "Claims to be one of your detectives ... named Nichols. Uh-huh, yes ... that's right. We picked him up inside a government-restricted security site ... We thought it was strange too. ... I'm not at liberty to say, Captain. ... No, we have a test scheduled for tomorrow night, so I'm under a little pressure to get back to work."

Outside the house, another explosion rocked the valley and rattled the windows.

"I'm sorry, we're almost in the mine itself," I heard him say. And then, "He doesn't have it with him, says it's in his car back at the gate."

He listened for a moment and looked back, my way.

"Says he wants to talk to you."

I walked over to the desk.

"Nichols here," I said.

Silence.

"Sorry to bother you, Captain," I said.

"Nichols, my ass," he said quietly, in a measured voice. "You're still after Bosko, aren't you?"

"I followed that private dick, Hammer, to a fence line in Highland Boy," I said. "I've probably lost him now."

"What? What fence line?" Jim said through the earpiece. "What are you sayin'?"

Cardwell and Tex were trying to follow the conversation from hearing my side.

"I did, yes." I was improvising. "I met with Chapman this morning. He told me to drive up here and take a look around. Told me Bosko spent time up this way."

Our conversations were out of sync. It was hard to track what was being said while I was inventing a make-believe conversation on my side.

"Whatever you're up to," said Jim, "get your butt back to town pronto. By the way, you didn't happen to take Sadie along for the ride, did you?"

"No—What?!"

"She's dropped out of sight; nobody knows where she went."

I felt the wind knocked out of me. I wanted to ask but couldn't think what I could say. I tried to keep the trouble off my face, but I couldn't do that either.

"Out of sight?" I managed.

"We're lookin' into it. Now, you get yourself out of there and call me back when you can talk."

"I left my jacket and badge in the car," I said. "You'll have to vouch for me with these guys."

He paused. "Get 'em back on the line."

I handed the phone to Cardwell and sat down in the chair. I didn't hear the rest of the conversation. I needed to get away from here. I'd been too slow for Yasa. Now I was too slow for Sadie. I remembered the look on her face, and her running down my back stairway the last time we'd talked. My mind was racing to possibilities, none of them good.

Cardwell shook my arm.

"Nichols, are you okay?" he said.

The telephone call had ended.

"Was he that hard on you?"

"Never supposed to go anywhere without my badge," I mumbled.

The thumping sound outside went on and on. "Don't know how you guys work with all that pounding."

He went in the building rear and came back with two aspirin and a cup of water, before sending me back to the fence line with a chaperon.

"Make sure you get him through the gate and on his way," he said to Tex. "And you—"

He was talking to me now.

"I'm gonna have to file a report about this. You have Chapman call ahead the next time you're nosin' around."

"What's a 'Cvito device'?" I blurted out, growing bolder as I thought about Sadie.

He frowned. "That's one question too many, detective."

"Then what about Bosko? Where's he at?" I asked.

"He's gone," said Cardwell. "It's the weekend. I'd check the pool halls if I were you." Then he headed into the far end of the house to finish whatever I'd interrupted.

Outside, the sun had melted the tar at the road's edge. We walked beyond it, in the loose gravel where it seemed slightly cooler. The hillsides were still, and I wondered if other watchers had a view of us. Tex unlocked the gate, and we walked through to my car.

He tapped my side with the barrel of his rifle.

"As long as I'm here, how 'bout you give me a look at your buzzer, Detective?"

"What?" I was worrying about Sadie.

"I don't stutter," he said. "You might have fooled Cardwell, but I don't take you for no regular city cop. I want to see that badge, or we can dicker over how much cash you'll part with to keep me quiet."

I hadn't expected that.

The hardest thing in life is figuring out what's right in any given situation. I was time-pressured, anxious about Sadie, and needed to get back to the city. *Fast.* The cops didn't know about the letter.

I unlocked the passenger side door, sat sideways on the front seat, and opened the glove box.

"It's right here somewhere," I said. "I put it in here with my gun."

Curiosity got the best of him, and he leaned in.

I kicked the door out, knocking the gun barrel away and catching the side of his nose with the edge of the door. One hand went up to assess the damage as he fell backward. Before he could think different, I stepped over him. I grabbed the rifle out of his hands by the barrel, swung it around, and flung it as far as I could onto the other side of the fence.

"Here's my take, Tex."

He was on his back, holding a handkerchief to his face to soak up the blood from the cut.

"You keep your opinions to yourself, and I won't kick your ass, haul you back to Salt Lake, and put you in *my* jail for tryin' to extort money from a cop."

His eyes showed contempt, but he held up a hand as if to say, "Good enough."

That's all I needed to be: good enough.

Doing the right thing; that was always the easy part. I didn't wait for him to get up. If anybody turned in a bad account of the afternoon, it'd have Detective Nichols' name stamped on it. I chuckled to myself.

Then I turned the car around and drove back down the canyon.

51

Midvale
4:10 p.m., Friday, July 23, 1948

The smell of burning brake shoes filled the canyon as I came up fast behind a flatbed, geared down and wove around him, and cleared the canyon tunnel exit. I ran through the little town at Copperton, watching for speed traps, and came out onto dry-farm flatland where grasshoppers popped and stuck on the windshield, catching under the wiper blades. It was a hot ride into Midvale. I stopped at a Texaco to gas up and cool down the engine.

"Hold it to a buck," I told the attendant. "Regular ... and check the radiator."

He scraped off the bugs, squirted a blue stream on the glass, and wiped it off with a white towel before raising the hood. I stepped out, checking my pockets for change.

"You got a payphone here?" I asked.

"Out on the corner." He pointed to a glass box with a blue sign next to a light pole. I forced a nickel in the coin slot while he worked. My hands shook, and I dialed deliberately.

o ...

"Number please," said the woman's voice.

I told her.

"That's a long-distance call. Deposit another twenty—five cents for the first three minutes, please." After a minute of talking to the police operator, Jim picked up.

"Fill me in," I said, in a hurry. "I'm at a payphone and I only have two minutes left."

I kept one eye on my watch. My stomach was turning flip-flops.

"I'll come over—"

"No, I'm in Midvale. Just tell me what you know about Sadie."

The kid was pulling the gas nozzle from the car and looking my way.

"Okay," he said. "Last night, around the time you bolted from my place and left dinner on the table, Sadie left home with some other guy from her neighborhood, a kid named Sherman. He's a college type, comes from a good family. They went out with another couple to see some new Randolph Scott picture at the Capitol Theater. The other couple said she acted real jumpy, like she was afraid they were gonna run into you, maybe."

"Did *she* say that?"

"Capitol's right around the corner," he said. "So, halfway through the first picture, Sadie says she has to go to the ladies' room and never comes back. The guy in the ticket booth said he never noticed her. Neither did any of the kids runnin' the snack bar."

"You think she just walked away?" I asked, hopeful.

"That's what the kid she was out with thought, and the other couple too. But somebody found her purse, one of those small things with a brass snap. It was in the alley, behind the bank."

That was the same alley where I parked, behind my office.

Was she headed my way?

"You're sure it was hers?"

"Had your picture inside," he said. "Her parents identified it."

There was a clicking sound on the line.

"Are you there?" he said.

"Yeah. What else have you got, besides the purse?" I asked.

"Nothin' solid. Somebody saw a gal Sadie's age gettin' in a yellow cab in front of the building next door. We're lookin' into it."

"Geez," I said, under my breath. "Okay, I'm headed back. I'll call ya when—"

A woman's voice cut in. "Please deposit another twenty-five cents for another three minutes," she said.

I didn't have it.

"I'll try ya in an hour," I said, over the top of her. I didn't know if he heard me or not. I pushed the folding glass door open.

"You're all set!" shouted the kid by my car.

I handed him the dollar and turned left onto State.

52

Karrick Building
4:40 p.m., Friday, July 23, 1948

The city took on a busy, festive feel for the upcoming parade, with red, white, and blue-striped flags hanging from cables stretched across Main. People crowded on sidewalks, buses crowded in streets, everyone anxious for the weekend. I didn't feel festive. I parked behind my office, ran up the stairs, and unlocked my office door. I stepped through the opening onto a white envelope, face down. My heart raced but slowed a bit when I picked it up—a Minnesota postmark. I ripped it open, and a ten-dollar bill fell out with a note: "SORRY ABOUT THE CAMERA."

Some people are good, just deep down.

I telephoned Jim's office to see what he could tell me, but he was out on a call. If I showed up there, I risked being held over for questions related to the fire, so I stayed put.

I took Sadie's photo out of the frame, taped it together as best I could, and stared at it.

Where did you go?

I put her in my shirt pocket, next to my heart, and searched through piles of stacked furniture and boxes until I found a flag to hang in the window facing the street. Forty-eight white stars on a dark blue field, another souvenir of my European holiday courtesy of the War Department. I needed Marko to show up and cover my expenses for the last two days; and with what I'd found out in Bingham, he owed me a better explanation for his own behavior.

Maybe she was just clearing her head—

I couldn't sit still. I walked into the back room and checked out my ear in the mirror. Sore as it was, it was going to be okay. I picked up some of my clothes and hung them in a cabinet. Then I took them out again and moved the cabinet into the back room with my cot. I rehung the shirts, rolled my wool carpets across the floor, and hung up a couple more pictures on nails left behind. My nervous energy needed an outlet.

I called Uncle Jim again. He was still out.

I dialed Sadie at home but hung up on the first ring.

I needed to be out too, somewhere, looking for Sadie or Bosko, but where?

I picked up the coal-damaged shirt and a pile of dirty underwear that needed laundry service and stuffed them in a pillowcase. I carried the laundry out and drove over to the Beehive to see what, if anything, George knew. I slotted the Ford in a diagonal spot across the street at the Belvedere Hotel, when a black-and-white unit rolled by. It didn't stop, though. I plugged the meter and jaywalked across four lanes to the café.

The Beehive was slower in the late afternoon. The dinner crowd hadn't shown up yet. People dotted the booths in twos and threes, eating pie or hamburgers, but the place lacked the energy and brightness of the morning rush. I put my hat on the countertop and stood by the register. A couple of Sadie's waitress friends glanced over but looked away when I stared back.

George spotted me and came out from the kitchen. "We missed you this morning," he said. "Have you talked with Sadie?"

"Not since she gave me back my gun. I spent last night out in Bingham, and just got back."

I noticed him staring at my ear.

"Bingham? What were you doin' there?" he asked, guiding me to a booth. "Never mind. Let's sit down ... how about a piece of pie?"

"No, thanks. What's the story with Sadie?" I asked. "What do the other girls say?"

He sat across from me as I stared out the window.

"I probably shouldn't tell you, but talk is, she went out with somebody her mother wanted her to date—some rich kid." He spoke quietly. "I hear she walked out of the picture, halfway in, and just never came back. I'm thinkin' she's still upset over the whole episode with the gun."

"Maybe," I said, "she doesn't care for Westerns."

He looked at me to see if I was joking. "I expect she left to find you, Jack. I heard somebody saw her at the pay telephone, in the theater lobby—if it was her."

I could feel his eyes on me.

"She's probably holed up somewhere, thinking things through," he continued. "She'll be back." He reached over and put his hand on my arm, in a fatherly sort of way.

"I hope you're right, George," I said. "I gotta go."

Keep moving. Stay busy. Do anything.

"But you haven't told me about Bingham yet."

I was already standing up. "It's a damn big hole in the ground." I grabbed my hat, walked back out the door, and ran across the street to my car.

Rain clouds were piling up again.

A small cleaner operated in the shops on the downhill side of the Belvedere, in a single-story stucco building past the Teamsters Hall, next to a locksmith who worked on lawnmowers and sharpened ice skates on the side. I grabbed the pillowcase from my car and walked in the front door.

"What have ya got for me?" asked the stout, graying woman behind the counter.

"Just laundry. A couple of shirts, but one of 'em got a little coal dust on it."

She reached in and pulled it out. "A little?" Her eyes widened.

"Light starch," I said. My stomach was still churning.

"You shouldn't *ever* put a dirty old thing like this in with the rest of the clothes," she said. "It makes the rest of the things harder to clean."

She counted the pieces out, then went back to the damaged shirt and unfolded it.

"Here," she said, "you'll prob'ly be wantin' this."

She handed me a gray, pocket-sized notebook—the one I'd found on the floor in Bosko's workshop.

53

Auerbach's Department Store
5:20 p.m., Friday, July 23, 1948

Buses lined up on Broadway, waiting to make the tight turn onto Main. Traffic cops roped off long segments of street parking for the parade. I managed to find a parking spot in front of Brook's Arcade, sprinted across the roadway, and entered Auerbach's through the Broadway entrance. Plywood covered the broken display windows. I turned right past women's handbags and made my way over to Jonny's backroom office.

He wasn't there.

I waited in the doorway a moment, but soon sat down at the desk and thumbed through the morning paper. Still nothing about Yasa, or Sadie. The Bees dropped a game to Twin Falls. I didn't care to know more and set it aside.

I pulled the small, gray notebook from my pocket. It was well worn, with a silver, foil-stamped oval image on the face. The words NEW YORK CENTRAL SYSTEM barely read through.

Lined pages were filled with carefully inked numbers, diagrams, and cryptic writing. The back sheets were highway and railroad maps. I paged through the handwritten notes, looking for something I could understand. *Numbers?* I found penciled writing near the back, and a dollar sign followed by the number ten thousand. I could guess which ten-thousand-dollar amount it referred to, even without translation.

In the front, hand-drawn diagrams showed rectangles with arrows and dots. They resembled trick pool shots, mapped out for practice later. On the back cover was an unusual name, Zoric, followed by the English notation "1st Av." A telephone directory stood in a slot at the back of the desk. I pulled it out and opened to the Zs. Nobody named Zoric was listed, not on First Avenue and not anywhere else. I heard a noise in the hallway outside and put the notebook back in my pocket.

The office door opened, and a tall man in a tan suit with wide lapels gave me a surprised look. He had a correspondingly tall face, and wore his blond hair slicked back and his necktie loose, with the top shirt button undone. He paused, seeing me, and leaned against the door frame with folded arms.

"Can I help you find something?" he asked.

I closed the directory and pushed it back in its slot. "Sorry, this used to be my office. That's my ball cap hangin' over there."

"So, you're him?" he said, looking me up and down like he was measuring me for a new suit. I tried to sit up straight, just in case. His face stretched into a slight smile, like I was the punchline to a joke he'd heard.

"I just stopped in to see Jonny," I offered.

"I heard all about you."

"Good things, I'm sure. Where is he?"

He pulled a watch on a chain from his pants pocket and studied it, like it held the answer. "How 'bout you stand up and give me back my desk?"

He managed to keep the smile while he said it, but a kind of caged smile that exposed a few teeth and betrayed a certain hostility. When I stood, he moved past me and sat down in the same chair. He pulled an envelope out of a file cabinet drawer and handed it to me. It was white, like the one someone had left before. This time my name was typed.

"Jonny's takin' nights for now, fillin' in your old spot, I guess."

"He hates nights!" I said. "So, you're the new day guy?"

"You can call me Vic," he said. "That Jonny's a company man through and through."

He leaned back in the chair, one elbow resting on my old desk.

I stared at the envelope, my heart racing. "He told you to give this to me?"

He shook his head. "Nope, it was just here. Showed up sometime after lunch."

From Sadie?

I tucked it into my jacket, and we shared an awkward moment, with nothing to say and no reason to say it.

"Well, nice to meet ya, Vic," I said. "I guess I'll come back another time."

"I'm already lookin' forward to it," he said, twirling a pencil between his fingers.

Outside again, thunder boomed to the east. My mind leaped to several competing explanations for the envelope as I stepped off the curb and dodged traffic. In my car, I pulled it from my jacket pocket. There were no marks on the outside to indicate who delivered it.

I opened it carefully.

Inside was a check from Auerbach's, for my last week's work.

54

Karrick Building
6:00 p.m., Friday, July 23, 1948

I stuck the key in my office door and turned it to the left, but the bolt didn't move.

It was already unlocked.

I stepped back and reached into my pocket for shells that fit the Walther. Popping the clip out as quietly as possible, I reloaded and turned the knob, slowly.

"For hell's sake, Jack, just get in here!"

The room was dark, the flag still draped over most of the front window. I stepped inside and switched on the floor lamp in the corner. Jim was there.

"You're here about Bingham, I guess?"

"Later. We need to talk."

His hat was on my desk, his coat behind him over the chair. A shoulder holster kept his shirt in place, but his revolver was out in his hand. I sat down in the chair that Yasa had used, and faced him, across the blotter on top of my own desk.

"Sadie?"

"Your phone keeps ringing," he said. "I answered it once, in case it was you ... or her. I said hello, but whoever it was hung up. I didn't pick up again."

"I did try callin' you earlier."

"Here?"

"Over at *your* office," I said. "Why would I call here?"

"You heard anything from her?" he asked.

"Nothing. I've been out since we talked. How'd you get in here, anyway?"

He stood up and walked over to the window, peering out beyond the flag. "Door was open."

He holstered his gun and sat down again, facing me. Thunder boomed again, rattling the window.

"What's with the gun?"

"Getting more cautious in my old age, I guess," he said. "Open door and all."

"So, what about Sadie?"

"You know how this works. She's barely gone, officially, so don't jump to conclusions. Unless ..."

"Unless, what?"

Outside, thunder echoed again along the still dry streets.

"What's goin' on, in here?" he asked, waving his hand. "With your office décor, I mean."

He picked up a stack of files from the floor and landed them on the corner of my desk.

"I been rearranging stuff," I said. It was vague, and he knew it was a dodge.

"Your desk is in the same spot."

"Yeah, I'm a lousy decorator. Listen, tell me what you know. You got me on pins and needles here."

His answer threw me off. "Remember that kid at the Beeline, across the street from Bosko's place?"

"The one who called the cops for me?"

"Looks like there was a stick-up there. Somebody smashed the till with a crowbar. The kid tried to stop it and ended up with a bullet in his head. I don't think he's gonna wake up."

"No!"

"I just came from there. Parents said he was getting ready to leave on a mission—Mexico or someplace like that. Nobody's ever robbed that place, and now this."

This was the same neighborhood Jim had lived in for the past twenty years. Now there'd been two violent crimes on his street in one week, and this one was just a kid. It was having an effect.

"Edna can't go to sleep at night," he said. "She's already talking about moving someplace else."

I reached over and flipped the desk lamp on. "Bullet to the head ... doesn't sound like any stick-up I've ever heard of. What else?"

He nodded to the empty brass frame on the desk.

"Like I was sayin', as far as Sadie goes, she's barely been gone twenty-four hours. Maybe she's just out doin' some thinking somewhere ... unless you know different." He looked at me carefully. "There's no ransom demand. The family's on edge, but they're not a good target for ransom anyway. They don't have money. And she's not your typical snatch for the flesh trade either—too old. So, if it is a kidnapping, it doesn't add up. Maybe she just walked away? I mean, with you two fightin' and all?"

"You know about that?"

"I heard about it. What do you think?"

"Wouldn't explain the dropped purse."

"Maybe not," he said. "The girls at the Beehive give odds she's either gone off by herself someplace, to think things over, or ..."

"Or what?"

"Or they think maybe she went out to find you." He paused. "Is there something you oughta be telling me?"

"I told you. I was in Bingham."

We were both trying to keep a positive spin on things, but his hand gestures and his face telegraphed his thoughts. Young gals vanished from time to time, I knew. Sometimes they were just unlucky, at the wrong place, at the wrong time. And when they turned up—if they turned up—it often wasn't pretty.

"Fine," he said, "I'm still gonna need to ask you a few questions."

I stood up and moved toward the door. "I don't have time for questions. I ... we need to get on the street and find her."

"You think she's on the street?"

"Well, I—"

"Sit down, Jack. Better me, now, than somebody else, later." I knew that tone in his voice.

"Am I gonna need my lawyer?"

"You ain't got a lawyer."

I'd been evasive, I knew that too. I sat back down facing him again.

"Sadie's mother said you stopped by last evening lookin' for her ... she said you made an odd remark, when you found out Sadie was out with another guy. Something about somebody hurting her?"

"So what if I stopped by? It was on my way to Bingham, from your place. I just wanted to smooth things over, about the gun and all. I wanted to say I was sorry, but Sadie wasn't there ..."

He leaned forward again. "Okay, but what about your comment, somebody might hurt her?"

I thought back on the doorstep visit. It *had* unfolded a little different than what I'd intended, and nobody else knew about the letter,

"What'd you say that for, Jack? Somebody might hurt her ... because in the hands of the wrong DA it could sound like a threat. Especially if Sadie's really gone missing."

He was just pointing out things I should have considered: *Hammer, the jealous boyfriend who carries a gun.*

"You coulda picked her up in the alley—"

"But I didn't. Her mother just took it wrong," I said, shaking my head. "She was so intent on *not* telling me where Sadie went, that she never listened to anything I said. Check with Sadie's little sister. I'll bet she tells it different."

He picked up the empty brass frame.

"And maybe I was a little jealous," I said. "Maybe I just used the wrong words."

"That's what her mother thought, until Sadie didn't come home last night." He paused, looking for a reaction. "Jack, I believe you. And I hope Sadie's just tryin' to clear her head somewhere, but tell me how she took it all wrong?"

He wasn't on a side, but he was only looking at it from one point of view, not mine. I thought again how hard it was to know what the right thing was.

"Look," I said, "after I left your place ... and Sadie's ... I headed straight out to Bingham Canyon. One stop in Murray. Plenty of people saw me, one stop to get somethin' to eat. Lots of people can vouch for me, including the cops in Bingham."

"That's right," he said. "You were out there bein' Detective Nichols' stand-in, lookin' for Bosko. I thought I warned you off that."

He pulled out a pad from his jacket and started making some notes.

"So, this is an official interview now, is it?" I asked.

"If you think so."

The phone rang, interrupting our family get-together. I reached across the desk and picked up the handset.

"Hammer Investigations," I said. "Hammer here."

"Jack ...?"

It was Sadie's voice.

I heard a sound like a squeal, and then someone else had the phone. Jim was watching me.

"Where have you been, Hammer? Time's runnin' out," said the voice.

"Who is this?" I asked. "And what are you doin' with Sadie?"

Jim's brow creased, his eyes steady.

"Get rid of the cops. We'll be in touch," said the voice.

The line went dead.

I hung the phone up, slowly.

"Sadie?"

I nodded, trying to memorize the voice and every word.

55

Karrick Building
6:30 p.m., Friday, July 23, 1948

Jim watched while I took her mended photo from my pocket and slipped it back in the empty frame. Then I repeated back the conversation. "'Get rid of the cops,' they said. I couldn't place the voice."

"Why are they callin' you, Jack? You're not family."

I couldn't think up a lie fast enough, so I told him the truth, the way I knew it.

"Look in the drawer, the white envelope," I said. "Maybe I should have said something before, but until now, I wasn't sure about it."

He slid back and opened the long drawer above his knees.

"How do they even know you're here?" I asked. "You drive an unmarked car."

"They're guessing. Or they could be talking about the black-and-white down at Sadie's house, sittin' outside," he said. "Unless you think they're watchin' your place, here?"

I stood up and walked to the window, looking out from behind the flag. He unfolded the note and read it. Below, on the sidewalk, people huddled under umbrellas, and traffic slowed up with the quick, cloud burst. Buses ran with their lights on, even though sunset was hours away.

"Where'd you get this?" he asked, looking up. There was a touch of anger in his voice. He folded the note with his palms to guard against leaving fingerprints.

"The other night, after you dropped me off. I came up the stairs and found all my stuff in the hall. Krogue, the old watchmaker down the hall, had it. He had my office key too. I guess the guys who jumped me at the Beeline told him they were cleaners, moving my furniture around while I was down at the station answering questions. They told him it was my bill."

He laid it on the desk by the picture frame.

"They took Sadie's photograph," I said. "They scratched her eyes out."

"And you weren't *sure* about something?"

"That was then. And it said, 'No Cops'."

I thought about the kid with the pimply face pumping gas at the Beeline. I could see his face, barely out of high school. And Krogue, with his Coke-bottle glasses, walked himself into my brain, handing me my keys. He couldn't see more than the two feet in front of him, usually things involving tiny springs and gears—

But they wouldn't have known it.

I ran out the office door and down the hall. Rain pounded on the roof above. I knocked on the door to his workshop, panicked. There wasn't an answer. Light slipped into the hallway from under his door. I knocked again.

Please be out!

But I knew he wasn't. He wouldn't have left the light on. I tried the door, but it was locked.

"What is it, Jack?"

Jim came up behind me.

"Krogue," I said. "He saw 'em too."

I kicked the door just below the knob. The frame splintered and gave way, and the door flew open.

He was sitting at his workbench, his head resting on his left arm. A gold pocket watch was in pieces on the desktop. He looked like he'd fallen asleep, except for the small, round hole in the back of his head and a little blood.

I was too late, again.

"Don't touch anything," Jim ordered, looking around the room.

I picked up Krogue's telephone anyway and called over to the Beehive.

"Let me talk with George," I said.

"Who is this?" said the girl's voice.

"Tell him it's Jack. It's an emergency. I need him, right now."

The phone went silent for a few seconds. It seemed like hours.

"Jack? What are you up to?" Jim asked.

I held up a finger.

George came on the line.

"George, don't say anything, just listen. You're in trouble. Is the Café busy?" I asked.

"Trouble?" he said. "What are you talking about, Jack?"

"Close it. Get everybody out and lock the doors until the cops get there!"

"Lock the doors? You're talking crazy, Jack. I have customers—"

Jim was listening.

"I'm not joking, George. Sadie's missing. I'm sure of it now, and if I'm overreacting, we'll have a laugh about it later, but I think who-ever snatched Sadie is going around killing everybody who could identify them, anybody who could tie them to her, or to me. They got to the watchmaker in my building today, and to the kid over at the Beeline too. And you saw 'em!"

"Who's 'they'?" he asked, "I didn't see anybody."

"I don't have *names*. It's probably the two guys who jumped me on Tuesday; the same two you saw Wednesday morning before I came in. Remember those two guys you said were makin' Sadie laugh?"

Jim leaned over the desk and grabbed the telephone out of my hand.

"George," he said, "this is Captain Burt. Just tell everybody you're going out and they should go home. Then get your shotgun and sit tight in the basement. Best if everybody thinks you're gone. Do it now, and I'll get a black-and-white over there. Jack's right—maybe nobody's coming, but it's better to be safe. I'm hangin' up."

He pushed down on the hookswitch, then dialed the direct line to the police. I moved to the door while he waited for someone in his office to answer.

"Where do you think you're goin'?"

"To find Bosko. I can't stick around here doing nothing," I said. "Sadie doesn't have the time."

"You can't leave, Jack. This is a crime scene."

"So, what are you gonna do, shoot me?"

I ducked out the door and ran down the back stairs without my hat.

56

Oxford Manor
6:58 p.m., Friday, July 23, 1948

Evening sunlight sliced through the rain clouds and made a rainbow. The movie house where Sadie vanished had a gigantic neon sign hanging above the entry. Another sign arched over the street, spelling out CAPITOL THEATER.

I knew I needed a plan, but I didn't have one.

I should never have left her alone.

I pulled into a parking spot and stayed behind the wheel, watching the movie house in my wing mirror. If Sadie walked out of the picture and headed to my office, she'd likely have crossed the street mid-block and entered the alley a few feet from where I sat. The alley was narrow, running behind the tall, gray-bricked Continental Bank Building on the corner. Garbage trucks ran down the alley and passed the Karrick, further south, before exiting on Broadway.

Rain slowed to a drizzle, then stopped. I stepped out and walked between buildings to what I thought was mid-block. According to Jim, her purse was found well back from the street. The dark sides of the alley pushed in and out, any of them good hiding places for somebody intent on kidnapping. Smells of rotting vegetables floated through the humid air.

A back door stood open to a noodle house that fronted on Main. Inside, a thin Chinaman in white, wielding a meat cleaver, was chopping heads and feet off dead, plucked chickens. A bone pile lay at his feet, next to a bucket of chicken heads. He ignored me until I stood at the door, filling the frame.

"What're you doing back here?" he asked in perfect English.

He smoked as he worked, stopping to pick up his cigarette from the edge of the butcher block, but replacing it every few swings of the cleaver. His straight, black hair danced with his chopping motion.

"I thought they'd be alive," I said. "When you chopped off their heads, I mean."

"What? Why?"

"I'm looking for a girl," I said.

He didn't stop chopping. "What girl?"

"Last night, there was a girl back here, brown hair, about five-foot-two. Carryin' a white purse."

He looked out to the alley. "Chinese girl?"

"No."

He thought for a moment but shook his head. "Lots of people come and go back there."

His cleaver took the cranium off another dead chicken. He pushed it from the table, into the bucket. I pulled Bosko's photo from my shirt pocket and held it under his nose.

"How about this guy?" I asked. "Have you seen this old guy around?"

"Sorry, no."

Someone called to him in a sing-song language. He gathered his piles of chicken parts onto a tray and carried them into the kitchen.

I walked back and sat down in my car. Krogue's face came to me again.

Don't panic. Make a plan.

I rolled down the window, reached in my jacket, and pulled out the gray notebook again. I scanned the pages, starting in the back this time. Some entries were dated, the latest from June of this year. I didn't recognize the language but could make out a few letters. They were similar to Greek, maybe Cyrillic. In the middle of a page, the name Zoric caught my eye for the second time. Next to it was a pair of English words: Oxford Manor. What was Oxford Manor? A hotel? I thumbed back to the inside cover—Zoric again, and the note that said "1st Av."

I pushed the starter and pulled the car back onto the street.

The Avenues in Salt Lake sit close to downtown, north and east of the Temple. Majestic houses, corner markets and brick apartment buildings mix together under a shady spread of stately sycamores.

I doubled back on First Avenue, behind the Elks Lodge, and drove slowly, reading names on several apartment buildings. Brigham Young, the Mormon prophet, was buried along here under a thick slab of granite in a private cemetery surrounded by a wrought-iron fence. I pulled over next to his gate, across the street and up a few doors from building number 125, Oxford Manor.

A hand-lettered sign read "APARTMENT FOR RENT: INQUIRE WITH MANAGER." The Manor was a three-story garden apartment house with its pretentious name etched into a cut glass door. Four white porthole vents penetrated the dark, brick frontage, just above a third-level cornice trimmed in white. A matching white Georgian entrance framed the doorway and connected the brick box to the sidewalk. There was no doorman, just a small, locked entry hallway. From the mailbox, I gathered there were dozens of people living inside. I glanced down the list of names written in pencil.

Nobody named Zoric was listed, but the manager's name was Grumbladt, number 102.

I rang the buzzer. A woman's voice came through a speaker. "Can I help you?"

"I'm lookin' for somebody named Zoric," I said. "I don't see his name listed on the mailbox."

"And who might you be?" she asked. Organ music played faintly in the background.

I didn't know anything about Zoric. Old, young, male, female, so I guessed.

"My name's Hammer. I'm here about a check he wrote," I said. "To Auerbach's."

There was a pause.

"I'll come out," she said. "Let me put something on."

After a moment a woman appeared from a doorway next to the stair. She was almost as tall as she was wide, wearing a kitchen apron and a faded yellow scarf that mostly covered the bald spot on her head. She passed judgment through the decorative cut glass in the doors. My hat was missing, but I was otherwise presentable. After a moment, she stepped to the locked door and opened it.

"I'm sorry to trouble you, ma'am. This was just the address printed on his check."

I pulled out the gray notebook and acted like I was double-checking the address.

She peered at me over the top of her glasses. They were perched on a triangular, bent piece of tin covering the spot on her face where her nose should have been. It stayed there thanks to a string around the back of her neck. It must've been what she had to put on. I tried not to stare, but she noticed my discomfort.

"Don't pay it no attention," she said. "My nose had the cancer in it. The doctor did his best, and they cut it out three years ago."

"I ... well ... Mr. Zoric, anyway. How'd he pronounce his full name?" I asked, fishing.

Her beefy hand pulled her glasses closer to her eyes.

"You don't even know his full name, do you?" she asked. "Who are you really?"

My real credentials didn't require any follow-up lies. I pulled out my wallet and handed it to her.

"Like I said, the name's Hammer—easy to pronounce and hard to forget. I'm a private investigator. I work for Auerbach's."

Maybe the part about Auerbach's was a stretch, now.

She took out my license and read each word.

"Well, you shoulda come by early last week, Mister Jack Hammer, because that's when he skipped out. Most of his personal belongings are gone and he still owes me rent for this month ... and for June too. Gave *me* a bad check too, he did. That's why I put his apartment up for rent in the first place."

Her teeth clacked loosely in her mouth as she talked. She took out her top dentures, wiped them on her apron, and put them back in.

"You keep a nice place here," I said.

I deliberately looked toward the stairway. She caught my meaning and shook her head. "I know what you're thinking, but I can't just be lettin' anybody go upstairs by his self."

I made a face like I was suddenly sad. "Well, what if I was thinkin' of renting your room?"

Her left arm folded across her chest while her right hand scratched her elbow.

"How serious might this thinking be?"

I reached into my pocket and found a few crumpled ones. They did the trick.

Her fat hand reached into an apron pocket and brought out a room key.

I turned, studying the inside lobby.

"I know," she said, "it's a walk-up, but we're gettin' an elevator pretty soon. I probably could still manage the stairs passable good, if you really need me."

"Don't bother. I won't let on to anyone."

"He was in the center room, top floor in the back. Now, that there only bought you five minutes," she said. "Take more time, and you'll be stretching my patience. I'll be down here, listening to my radio program."

I headed up a stair that rounded back on itself several times and ended in a wide hallway on the third floor. The passageway was decorated with brown-and-white striped wallpaper below a chest-high oak rail. Number 302 was already unlocked.

I knocked, just to be sure it was empty.

Inside were a few stuffed chairs, a floor lamp with a tasseled shade, a round wooden table with a single kitchen chair, and a cast-iron double bed. There were dishes in the sink, but no clothes in the closets. The kitchen cupboards were bare, and the whole apartment smelled like stale cigarette smoke and garlic.

The walls were without pictures, but nail holes in the plaster suggested they'd been there. Dead flies gathered on the windowsills and never left. Mr. Zoric, whoever he was, hadn't been a great housekeeper.

I walked into the washroom and opened up the medicine cabinet. A bottle of blood-red Mercurochrome sat on the bottom shelf next to a discarded toothbrush. The toilet tank was full of water and nothing else. Out in the hallway, a drawer to a built-in cabinet gave up an empty box of pool chalk that bore the Mecca name.

I pulled the drawer all the way out and turned it over. Nothing stuck to the bottom, but something was hanging in the gap between the drawer side and the rail. It fell, hit my shoe, and bounced to the ground. It was an acetate photographic negative. I picked it up and held it to the window. The reverse image appeared to be a woman, suggestively posed, but I didn't recognize her face, at least not in the negative. It was a photo that would have to be developed privately. I tucked it in my shirt pocket.

I locked the door on my way out, walked down the stairway, and found the landlady still standing in her open doorway, listening to her program.

"Well, did you find anything?" she asked.

"Nothing that helps much. What else can you tell me about him?" I asked.

"I thought you said he wrote a bad check?"

"That's right."

She hesitated. "I been thinking ... when he moved in, he had a woman with him. Younger, brownish hair, and quiet. I thought they were married, him always opening her door and such, but after a month or so she never came around again. He didn't want to talk about her, and I didn't want to pry into his personal affairs. He had a few men visitors from time to time, and he acted kinda secretive, if you know what I mean. What's this really about?"

I wish I knew. I reached in my pocket and pulled out the negative. "Was this the woman?"

She adjusted her glasses, held it to the light and practically dropped it when she recognized the subject.

"How dare you show me a photo like that!" she said. She handed it back and wiped her hands on her apron. "I don't know what you think—"

"Sorry." I pulled out Bosko's picture. "How about this guy. You ever see him come around?"

She looked at the photo, shaking her head. "No, who are they?" she asked, rubbing the side of her metal nose like it had an itch.

"He's just old," I said. "And missing. Her ... I don't know how she fits."

"What'd you say your name is, again? Jack Hammer?" she said, chuckling to herself.

She turned to go.

"So, Zoric just moved out," I prodded, "no forwarding address?"

"That's what skipped means," she said, looking back. "I cleaned out his mailbox earlier this morning. For another buck, I'll let you look through it before I send it back with the mailman. Course, you can't keep any of it."

She was cleaning me out too. I gave her a greenback, and she brought out a short stack of letters. The second envelope in the pile was pale blue, addressed in a woman's handwriting. I'd seen it before, clipped to a tin mailbox. It was addressed to someone named Zoric Markosivich.

Markosivich.

"Marko?" I said out loud. "Is he a short guy, with thick, black hair?"

"He was thick alright, and his hair was black as the night."

I made a show of paying attention to some of the other pieces. She was trying to listen to the radio through her open door.

Marko?

If Sadie's life hung in the balance, I wasn't gonna let postal procedures dictate who found clues and when. I handed her the mail, palmed the blue letter when she wasn't paying attention and walked up the street to my car.

57

Napoli Café
7:42 p.m., Friday, July 23, 1948

I slid across the front seat of the Ford and pulled my pocketknife out of the glove box. When I cut the edge of the envelope, a letter written on tissue paper fell into my lap. It was wrapped around a snapshot of the Karrick Building, possibly taken with Yasa's camera. The letter was one page, covered in foreign characters similar to the ones scribbled in the notebook in my pocket. It was unsigned and written in a feminine hand. The letter and the notebook were puzzles, and there were only three people I knew who could translate them: one was Marko, one was Bosko, and one was dead.

Then I remembered someone I *didn't* know: the waiter at the café where Marko bought me lunch. He'd spoken with Marko in their shared language. I slid the photo and the negative inside the letter and tucked it all behind the visor as I headed out.

Diners stood outside the front door of the café, chatting as I drew up to the curb. Streetlights flickered on in the humid twilight.

I pulled the blue letter down again, debating whether to surface it just now. *But how could I explain to the waiter why I had a letter addressed to Marko?* Instead, I copied a few lines from the gray notebook onto my own notepaper and folded it into my shirt pocket, leaving the notebook and letter in my glove box. I sat in the car until the group out front said goodnight and drifted away in twos and threes.

I walked across the street, where muffled laughter came from the open café door. A Glenn Miller recording played in the background. The place was different after dark. Lights hidden at the back of the room painted a soft, red-orange color on white plastered walls meant to keep customers out of the kitchen. The black-and-white risqué photos, coupled with the dim light, made the dumpy little café feel sophisticated and adult. All eight tables were filled. Heads tilted as I entered, conversations paused and restarted.

I took a seat at the counter and pulled a menu from the clip on the napkin holder.

A tall waiter with a white apron folded below his waist filled a clear glass with water and set it in front of me. I'd seen him before, somewhere. His ears laid flat against his head, unlike the little waiter I was hoping to find. He waited for me to speak.

When the awkward moment passed, he said, "Are you having dinner with us?"

"Just a cheeseburger and a Coke."

"Not ćevapi?" He seemed surprised.

He carried the order to the kitchen, and when he didn't come back right away, I figured I'd offended him by skipping the beer.

I turned on the stool and faced the small dining room. In the back corner, the door to the parking lot stood open. A guy outside was smoking a cigar, doing his best to hold up that side of the building with the flat of his back. A couple at the near table argued about whether or not the parade would go on if it was still raining in the morning.

"Would you care for *frites*?" said a voice behind me.

I turned back to see the waiter again. The corners of his eyes turned down slightly. He had a bump on the bridge of his nose. He stood with both hands on the bar, leaning forward. Like Marko, he spoke with an accent, but softer, less harsh.

"What?"

He leaned in, close to me. "French fries?"

"I'm looking for the waiter who was here the other day," I said, "the short one, with the big nose and the big ears."

"You mean Danko? He works only days. Did someone say for you to come here?"

"Well ... I'm also looking for my friend, Marko. You know him? He might go by the name Zoric. He and this Danko fellow were pretty chummy the other day."

He focused hard on my face, like he planned to sketch it later, from memory. I pulled the copied lines from my pocket, unfolded the page of notepaper, and slid it across the counter.

"And something else. I need help reading this," I said. "Can you tell me what any of these phrases say?"

He looked down at the paper without touching it, then walked to the cash register to make change for someone else. In the mirror, another couple stood up from their table and walked out the back door. A handgun, on the shelf under the register, was visible in the reflection.

"You been robbed lately?" I asked.

He ignored the question but held out his hand, taking the paper from me this time. He read over it quickly, stopping from time to time to look up at me.

"Where did you get this?" he asked.

"I copied it out of a book," I said. "Can you read it?"

"Of course." He carried it into the kitchen and came right back. "Follow me," he said, motioning toward the rear of the building. "Marko is coming, the boss man." I fell in behind, stepping through a swinging door with a round moon window. A few diners followed us with their eyes.

"Just through here," he said. I saw my burger frying on a griddle and nodded at the kitchen help, all dressed in white. I walked past food prep tables and counters to a storage area in the back. The kitchen smelled of grilled meat and fresh bread.

He pulled open the door to a small office, illuminated by a single red bulb with a string pull. As I stepped inside, I was surprised by a sharp smell entering my nose, coming from a cloth over my mouth, and what felt like a pistol in my shoulder blade. I wanted to fight back, but my knees buckled too fast. I lost consciousness as I dropped. Someone must've kept me from hitting the floor. A comfortable darkness filled my head and I buzzed off into blackness.

When I woke up, my hands and feet were tied to a metal folding chair. My mouth was gagged, and my stomach was queasy. The short walk through the kitchen came back to me. Whoever the waiter was, he didn't waste time. The clock on the wall said it was eight-twenty. If that was right, I'd only been out a few minutes. My hamburger sat on a small table just out of reach. *Out of reach like Sadie.* I struggled against the ropes, tensing every muscle to no effect. There was no way I was going to leave a tip.

My gun was too, but I couldn't reach it either. *Why tie me up?* I couldn't put the pieces together, and I felt sick. The chemical on the rag irritated my sinuses, making it hard to breathe. People were arguing in that language I didn't know, just outside the door. When it opened, it hit the chair leg, just missing my knee.

It was Marko, and he wasn't smiling.

58

Napoli Café
8:40 p.m., Friday, July 23, 1948

"What is this thing going on here?"

Marko stayed in the doorway because there wasn't room for both of us in the office.

"Ha wha I ..." I tried talking but the towel wrapped around my mouth kept me from saying anything coherent. Then I realized he wasn't speaking to me anyway. There was somebody just outside my line of vision, in the kitchen.

Marko pulled the gag off me and threw it over a short clothesline stretched between the office walls. I breathed in through my mouth, noticing he carried a carving knife in his left hand.

"Why are you doing here, Jack?" He reached down with the knife, and I tensed every muscle. "I said for you to hang your flag in your window. Then I could contact you."

He slit the cords holding my hands and stepped away.

"I need water," I said. A faint chemical smell lingered in my nose.

I pulled out my own handkerchief and spit into it repeatedly. "I think I'm gonna throw up."

He moved back into the kitchen, leaving me to untie my ankles from the chair. Before I finished, he came back with a glass of tap water. I swished it around in my mouth and spit it out on the floor.

"The flag is up," I managed. "It's been up for a while."

He saw the hamburger and shrugged.

"Jack, I must apologize for my friends," he said. "They are so eager to help, but they do not know you. Perhaps they are too eager."

"To do what?" I asked.

The night waiter appeared behind him, hesitant, as I finished untying my ankles. Marko turned. They spoke intensely in their private language, arms waving and pointing my way. I didn't know the words, but I could tell from the tone it wasn't a friendly conversation. The waiter looked at me and narrowed his eyes, sneering. But in a moment, there was silence. Marko stepped aside, and the waiter filled the door.

"Mr. Hammer, it is I who must apologize," he said, without looking me in the eye. "I am called Aleks. I work for Marko, here. My action was ... an error of judgment."

I stood up, holstered my gun, and lifted the top bun off my burger. It was cold.

"You see, I thought perhaps you were—"

I hit him with my right fist before he could finish, and he fell backward, into a stack of pots. "You thought I was what?" I asked, shaking off the impact to my knuckles. I could see now in his eyes that I hadn't endeared myself to him with such an impolite response. He wiped blood from his lip with the back of his hand.

"Get up," whispered Marko, looking down at him. Something unspoken passed between them. "Russian," he said out loud, after turning my way. "He thought you were some bad *Russian* person."

"Because I showed up here asking for help translating a few lines on a scrap of paper?" I shook my head. "Do I *sound* like a Russian to you?"

"I cannot answer it, Jack. How should some Russian sound?"

"Not like me!"

Part of me felt bad I'd hit him like that, but not a big part, and not for long. Aleks climbed up from the pots to his feet and spat out something to Marko in clearly bitter tones.

Marko nodded and put a hand on his arm.

"You see, Jack ... Aleks is my associate. He is hard worker and patriot to our country, but sometimes he acts without thinking deeply."

Aleks stepped away and scowled back at him. "Living here has made you soft," he said. Then he pointed at me and rambled off another full minute of foreign talk that I didn't have any hope of following.

This time Marko lifted his right hand and stopped it with a chopping motion. They glared at one another until Marko turned, indicating I should walk out ahead of him through the kitchen.

"What was that all about?"

We headed out the side door into the parking lot. Gravel moved under our feet.

"He thinks you are trouble."

"How? For who?"

Marko tugged my sleeve and we faced one another, between parked cars. Raindrops fell again in the darkness.

"Yasa said I could trust you. For me, that is enough."

Marko was driving a sleek, green Hudson. He seemed to have a variety of automobiles at his beck and call. We left my car sitting out in the rain and headed east toward the mountains.

"Where are we going?"

"For some discussion, in private," he said. "So, tell me you have found some clue for Bosko already?" It was a question, as though nothing had happened. "You have good news for me?"

"Not good, no. I headed out to Bingham, and somebody grabbed Sadie while I was gone."

"What does this mean, *grabbed*?"

I watched his hands tighten on the steering wheel.

"Where is she, Marko? Did you take her?"

"Jack, why would I—"

"The last time we talked, you didn't even know who Sadie was."

"I know she is someone you care about, yes?"

I spoke slowly. "That's right."

"I have also heard about this place called Bingham."

"I'll bet you have," I said. "Have you been there? Because I think you owe me an explanation."

"What explanation?"

I thought about the half-smoked cigarette in the sink, out in Bingham. *Marko's style.* "Why don't you start off by telling me why you and these Russians you're so worried about, are both looking for Bosko?"

He kept his eyes on the road ahead without answering.

"Dispute about inheritance?" I asked.

"I told you, Bosko made enemies to some bad people. They also want what Tesla made—what belongs to my own client—but for bad purposes."

"What bad purposes?" I repeated.

He was driving slowly with the wipers on. "Maybe they can make some weapon."

"Can they?"

"I tell you, at first, they tried to buy these wonderful ideas from Bosko," he said. "They offered him much money. So, he made—how you say—some *deal* with them, some contract. But your government, I think, discovered their plans and made better offers."

"Let me guess," I said. "Better than ten thousand dollars?"

He nodded. "Of course, and Bosko had no choice, so it was better."

It made sense now, the money I'd found just sitting on the counter. "He couldn't just give money back to the Russians?"

"No."

Off in the distance lightning flashed.

"How do you know about all this?" I asked.

"Yasa knew this, from Bosko's own mouth."

But Yasa never mentioned it to me.

He watched the road closely, driving in what seemed to be larger and larger circles.

"You followed me, then?" I challenged. "To Bingham?"

He fumbled for a cigarette without answering.

"You know what, Marko? Or is it Zoric? Every day I think about turning this whole thing over to the FBI, to see what they make of it."

He glanced at me, quickly. I knew the use of his name, Zoric, would have some effect, and he covered it well except for that glance. "That might make your Sadie be in more danger," he said.

"Do you know where she is?"

"How could I know this?"

"Then, that was a *new* threat you just made?"

He put the cigarette down, rethinking his comments. "Jack, that is not how I intended for you to understand."

"No? Well, I can only hear what you say, and here in America, we say what we mean. We don't talk in riddles, and we don't waste people's time. Tell me straight: What is this device everybody's looking for? You know what it is, don't you? Are you looking for it too?"

"My English words ... sometimes they do not say what I am thinking. But is much better than how you speak my language."

"That's about the answer I expected," I said. "Speaking of language, where's that paper? The one I gave to the waiter, Aleks?" I held out my hand until he reached into his jacket pocket and gave it back to me. At a stoplight, I unfolded it for him. "Did you read it?"

"It says only personal things, nothing important. Where did you find this?"

"I copied it, from something I found."

He was suddenly interested. "You should bring it all to me, so I can read it."

"When hell freezes."

The car behind us honked and Marko pushed on the gas.

"Why are you angry, Jack? I have not asked you to do anything illegal."

"I'm not angry! I'm talking about Sadie and her safety. I ask simple questions and you talk around the answers. I need to do the right thing here, Marko, for her, but what if I make a mistake? At this point, I have to wonder whether involving the *cops* would actually be the right thing."

We drove in silence for a few minutes. The rain let up as we crossed into Sugar House. The street was wide and well lit, but Marko looked constantly into his rearview mirror. He pulled into a parking spot on the street and turned off the engine. I could feel my heart race.

"Jack," he said, "you know my true name." It was a statement, not a question, not a threat. "How?"

"I know a lot more than your true name," I said. "And for whatever reason, I know you're making this job harder than it needs to be; people are getting hurt. You talk in riddles, and I think you're keeping a lot of information from me."

"You are not hurt."

"Not *me*! But that kid at the Beeline gas station is dead, and now a guy in my office building ... they both took bullets today, probably because somebody thinks they saw something they shouldn't have. Maybe you know what. I can't help thinking if I knew what you know about things, maybe they'd both still be alive. And now, Sadie ..."

I was breathing short and fast.

"*That* is how I expect Russians will act, with violence and death. Perhaps you can understand why I must find Bosko."

"And why I need to find Sadie, fast!"

"Jack, we can still help each other so much. Do you need more money?" He flashed a spread of ten-dollar bills that I pushed back.

"Can you help me find Sadie?"

He considered it for a moment. "Perhaps, I can make some inquiries."

I hit my open palm on the dashboard. "*Really?* And just how do you think you can help find *her*, but you can't find Bosko?"

I could see the wheels in his brain digest what that meant.

He lit a cigarette without asking whether I cared. He was stalling again, preparing some new version of the truth to cover whatever he was up to.

"Marko, how do I know you're not a Russian yourself?" I asked. "Or your 'friends,' as you call them, back at the café? Because honestly, *you all* sound like Russians to me."

"Is not my café."

I opened the car door suddenly and stepped out onto the sidewalk. He hesitated, watching me. I turned and walked toward the Safeway store to call a taxi.

He honked the car horn. "Jack," he called out, "we can still help each other."

I wasn't sure about that.

"I am not Russian!"

I kept going and hoped he wouldn't shoot me.

59

Safeway
10:05 p.m., Friday, July 23, 1948

Inside the grocery store, a kid with greasy hair was sorting pop bottles into divided wooden crates. The store had a fire exit in back that led to a side street. I put a finger to my lips and walked past him, stepping into the alley. I headed east and hailed a cab, telling the driver to take me back to the café and to step on it. I figured Marko would show up there as soon as he realized I ditched him out the back way.

"Drop me off by that old Ford."

But there was no sign of Marko or his Hudson. I handed the cab driver two bits and continued downtown in my own car. Headlights in the rear window drew my eye right away. I'd picked up Marko's habit of constantly checking for tails, so I slowed down and turned down a side alley. A green '46 Chev pickup drove by. When it passed, I cut back and idled through the alley behind my office, where the off-and-on rain had raised the stink of rotting garbage.

A police car was parked by the fire escape, and the back door to the stairway was propped open. I slouched down and kept driving ahead, slowly, until I was past it. The back door to the noodle house was open. I pushed on the clutch pedal and rolled to a stop without braking. Through the doorway, the heavy cleaver was embedded in the cutting block. Nobody was chopping parts off anything just then.

I circled the block and pulled into a spot on the street, in front of Auerbach's. Traffic was brisk; it was Friday night. I pulled my keys, grabbed the notebook from the glove box, and cut across the backside of the store behind the tire shop. I entered through the service entry.

Jonny was sitting in my chair, wearing my Bee's cap, listening to the radio. The smell of pot roast and onions hung in the air. He looked up like he expected me. "You still have a key?"

"I came by earlier," I said. "Who's your new guy?"

"A Pinkerton temp. Expert in pretty much everything except night work. Won't work past nine. I won't even tell ya what they're charging to have him handle days, and now I gotta cover graveyard until I fill your slot."

"Sorry how that worked out," I said.

Jonny said his wife was spittin' bullets about him having to work nights, and that if I ever saw her on the street, I'd better cross to the other side. He caught me up on all the latest workplace gossip and I let him talk, not really listening. *I had Sadie in my head.*

He stopped after a minute and played with the radio tuner.

"Listen," I said finally, "I need your help."

He reached for his wallet. "I can give you a few bucks ..."

"Not that. I mean help with Sadie."

He tilted his head questioning, at an angle. "I thought you took care of that."

"She's gone," I said, shaking my head.

"What do you mean, gone?!"

"I mean kidnapped! That's what," I said. "Jim told me."

"Dammit, Jack, I warned you about this—"

"Well, I still need your help."

"Yeah, more than I can give."

The story poured out of me, all the parts he didn't already know. I told him about her phone call in my office, that I wasn't really sure until then. Then I told him about Krogue and the kid at the Beeline, and about my trip out to Bingham.

"But the cops are in on it now, right? You're not still trying to solve this all on your own?"

"I told Jim most of it. And he was there when the phone call came."

"Jim's on it, then," he said. "I would be."

"But they're still way behind."

"And you're way out in left field if you think you can find her on your own."

"That's why I'm here."

He stood up and paced back and forth in the small office. "Let's walk."

We headed up to the top floor, starting his rounds.

"There's more to it, isn't there?"

I told him all about Marko.

"You're sure he doesn't have Sadie, using her as leverage?"

"I don't think he knows anything about her besides her name. And he's only hired me to find Bosko. He's never said anything about finding the device, so how would snatching her help him?"

"Maybe he's mirroring your idea: using Sadie, so you'll chase Bosko."

"Then why bother paying me anything?"

He checked his watch, signed the floor sheet, and headed to the stairway. On the way back down, we stopped and sat on the velvet chairs in the Women's Department.

"Anything else?"

"Discrepancies. Marko said he'd just arrived in town, but I found out he's been in town for months, going by the name Zoric. I even found the place where he'd been living."

The crystal chandeliers danced when the ventilation fans kicked on.

"And he has his own client?" Jonny asked.

"He says he does."

"Seriously, Jack, do you think Russians are involved?"

"Somebody's out there. They took Sadie, and they called me!"

He went quiet for a minute and stood back up. "Any idea why Marko really hired you? I mean, he tried shootin' you, the first time you met."

"He claimed he didn't know it was me upstairs. He thought he was shootin' at Russians ... at the bad people, he called 'em, but I don't know ..."

"I assume the FBI already knows about Marko."

"They know something. They said they'd been watching him, until I chased him off from Bosko's place. They weren't too happy about that, either. But you're the only one who knows all the pieces now."

Jonny stopped into the hall outside his office. "Sadie's only in this because of you, Jack."

"Don't rub it in. I'm worried sick about her. More every hour."

"I'm just sayin', if somebody out there started eliminating witnesses, whether it's Marko and his buddies or Russians or whoever, Sadie's on their list too," he said. "She's probably seen 'em better than anyone by now. And as soon as they get what they want, you know what'll happen."

"I do," I closed my eyes. "So, are you gonna help me or what?"

60

Auerbach's Department Store
11:00 p.m., Friday, July 23, 1948

"Anything else you want to share?" he asked.

I handed him the gray notebook. He flipped through the pages, turning it sideways to look at the maps.

"This is what you took over to the restaurant tonight?"

"I found it in Bosko's house, the night of the fire. It gave me the address for Marko's place in the Avenues." I showed him how I'd pieced things together. "That's how I found the blue letter again."

"What blue letter?" I'd left it in my car.

"Something Yasa mailed the day she died, clipped to the mailbox at Bosko's." I ran out to the parking spot on the curb where I had a cold feeling, like somebody was watching me. I looked around but couldn't see anything out of place. I checked the visor, pulled the letter from the glove box, and locked all the doors.

Jonny was still studying the notebook when I got back.

"Bosko and Marko know each other?"

"Marko said they met a long time ago. I think he hired me so he could stay in the background. There was a photograph too," I said, "inside the letter."

I pulled out the photo of my office, and the acetate negative fell out in my lap.

"What's that?"

I felt a little sheepish. "Take a look. It's somethin' I found stuck in a drawer at the place Marko rented. I can't make out who it is, not at that scale. But you can't just take a negative like that over to Shipler's and have it developed."

He held it to the ceiling lamp, moving it around. "You think it's connected to Marko?"

"Maybe. Or it could have been there for years before he rented the place."

He handed the negative back, and I dropped it in my pocket.

"Why would Yasa send Marko a crosstown letter? And why include a picture of your building?"

The notebook bent in his hand while he thought about it.

"I know a guy," he said, "one of the maintenance crew, on days. He's from over there someplace. Only been here a few months. He might be able to read this."

"Can we call him now?" I asked. "I'm runnin' out of time. Sadie is—"

He picked up the phone and called a number penciled on the wall. No answer. "Don't know where he lives, or I'd send you there now."

"Look, here's my key," I said. "I'm leavin' the car parked out on State."

I handed him the registration.

"What's this for?"

"Just a feeling," I said, thinking of Marko. "Somebody's watching for me tonight. As soon as your buddy gets in, drive the notebook over to him, to see what it says."

"Are you askin' me, or tellin' me?"

"It's for Sadie," I said. "I've got to check out everything."

"You don't wanna spend the night here?" he asked.

It felt like home, and the tug of familiarity was strong.

"I've got a long night ahead, thanks. Bosko's out there, some-where." I pulled my gun out and checked the clip. It was still loaded. "Cardwell said look for him in the pool halls."

"In Salt Lake?"

"He already got himself kicked out of every billiard joint in Bingham."

Jonny walked me down the hallway.

"Thanks for doing this."

"It's not for you," he said. "I'll do it for Sadie."

A few minutes later I slipped across the street and rounded the corner, heading up Main. Red mentioned he played a lot of pool up at the Mecca. If Bosko was around, Red might know.

Assuming Red *was* there.

61

Mecca
11:30 p.m., Friday, July 23, 1948

A barber pole hung motionless by the portico at the Hotel Little. Below it, off to one side, an arched neon sign said BILLIARDS and framed a steep stairway down to the Mecca. Next door, Lamb's Grill was closing up, despite flickering signs that warned lunch was being served, and ladies were welcome. The Mecca was smaller than Peter's place but didn't lack for patrons.

The main door was propped open, airing the place out while the storms paused. I pushed my way into the sauna of sweaty pool players. If the place had refrigerated air, it wasn't working. I searched the crowd for a friendly face.

Almost immediately a hand fell on my shoulder from behind. I flinched. My stomach tightened, but it turned out to be one of the kids I played nine-ball with earlier in the week, the heavy one.

"You come here for the tournament?" he asked. His white shirt was stained with green chalk dust.

"It slipped my mind," I said. I stretched upward, looking over the crowd at the tables.

"Too bad, 'cause you missed it. I mean, not all of it, but most of it."

"My loss."

"You don't remember me, do you?" he asked, disappointed.

"Sure, I do," I said. "But just now, I'm lookin' for that red-headed guy we played with at Peter's place the other night. You seen him around?"

"The lefty? Wasn't he something? Smooth ... But no, I don't think he's been here," he said, taking a long swig of his beer. "He would've been fun to watch."

I turned away, but he grabbed my arm. "Hey! Wait a second, though! I saw that other guy you were lookin' for—the one in the photo." He made it sound like a question, but it wasn't.

I pulled Bosko's picture from my pocket.

"You mean this guy?" I asked.

He grabbed it out of my hand. "Yeah, that's him. I saw him tonight. I remembered his face 'cause the scratched-out eyes in your photo here spooked me. Makes it a hard face to forget."

He handed it back, and Bosko's face looked up at me.

"I guess it is creepy."

A strawberry blonde, not legal by the look of her, came out of the crowd. She was dressed in a plaid dress and pulled her hair back tight from her forehead. Her face was pasty, beneath too much makeup, like she'd had one or two too many. She latched onto his arm, in case I was trying to take him away somewhere.

"Who's this?" she asked.

"My name's Jack," I said. "I was just askin' your boyfriend here about a mutual acquaintance ... from a couple of nights ago."

She glanced up with a fierce look on her face.

"Not that waitress again—?"

"I told you, there was nothing to that," he said. "Sorry, Jack. She's had a little too much tonight."

"I haven't had enough if you ask me," she said. "And I know what you're thinking, but I'm twenty-one, and I'm in college. Business college."

He was rolling his eyes, while he could get away with it.

"I like college," I said, smiling.

"Jack's a private investigator," he told her. "He's just looking for somebody. Somebody else."

She backed up behind him like she was hiding.

"So, he was *here*?" I asked.

"No. He was across the street on the sidewalk, just standin' there with these three other guys. They walked out of the Kearns Building, right there next to the movie house. They stood there lookin' at something on this side, way up at the top of the bank building on the corner. One of 'em had binoculars."

"When was this?"

He pulled the girl to his side. "What time did we get your mom on the bus?" he asked.

"Oh gosh, I don't know. Maybe five o'clock, five-thirty."

"Yeah, so later in the afternoon. We put her on the bus down by Montgomery Ward, then walked up here. That was probably around six o'clock, maybe six-thirty. He caught my eye because he was carrying a small suitcase, like the kind some guys put those three-piece cue sticks in, only a little bigger. I saw who it was. I guess my mind was stuck on pool," he said.

"These other guys, what did they look like?" I asked.

I was watching the girl. Her face was showing some inner discomfort.

"Let's go," she said, pulling on him. "It's hot as blazes in here."

"You better get her outside," I said. "Before—"

"Yeah, I know."

I started to back up. "Tell me about these other guys?"

"Just business guys in nice suits. Older, but not as old as your guy. They all dressed like bankers. Nice haircuts, hats in hand. I tried to see what they were pointing to, but it was just that big radio tower on the bank building. It's been up there for months now."

The girl was fading. I told him I'd look for him at Peter's place in a few days. I pushed through the crowd toward the stairs, then turned back. They were following but falling behind.

I ran up the steps, taking in the cooler fresh air.

I heard a noise like a splash on the concrete steps behind me, followed by somebody swearing.

I didn't look back.

The building Bosko and his friends stared at was two doors down, and sixteen stories tall, brown brick and terracotta. It was the same bank where Sadie's father worked.

I didn't go there.

Instead, I ducked under the parade ropes and ran across Main. I wanted the same view of the bank building that Bosko and his well-dressed friends had shared. Red lights were winking high above the penthouse level, pinned on the radio tower guy-wires. It was the tallest thing in town.

Behind me, the windows of the Kearns Building were dark. I put my hands on the plate glass to look inside. Lobby doors were locked, and a colorless neon tube flickered on and off, on a White Owl sign in the lobby. The building directory flickered with the neon. I could barely make out the building tenants: 5th FLOOR KENNECOTT COPPER CORPORATION.

Who had Bosko been meeting with?

62

Ace Billiards
11:55 p.m., Friday, July 23, 1948

I headed down the street, to where a crowd gathered outside the Peter Pan. Guys stood on the wet sidewalk and smoked, some of them still carrying cue sticks. Conversation was scarce. I spotted Bobby at the stairway.

"What's this?"

"Rain let up, so we're takin' a break," he said, flicking his butt across the sidewalk. "Are you coming inside tonight?"

"Maybe later. You seen my new friend, Red?" I asked. "He took twenty bucks off me the other night?"

A new cigarette came out of a pack in his pocket and went in his mouth. "Not tonight."

"What about this guy?" I showed him Bosko again, but he just turned away and struck a match.

"Thanks for nothing," I said to the back of his head and kept walking. He waved me off, holding up his middle finger.

My stomach growled. Bobby once told me how the pool hall

used to be part of a sit-down restaurant called the Peter Pan Café. It was back in the twenties, before hard times hit. He said the food was good, but the rent was high. It'd been gone for years.

I passed by the Karrick Building in favor of a quick supper at Ace. It was always less crowded and catered more to amateur pool, but they kept the grill open until 1:00 a.m. for the bowlers. There were a dozen lanes in the basement. I could hear pins scatter from the street.

Clouds parted, and stars peeked out, faint but pin sharp. Cars honked close by. I headed down the stairway and slipped onto a stool at the bar.

"We're closin' up soon," the bartender said. "What'll it be?"

I felt for cash in my pocket. "Make it a Coca-Cola," I said. "And a cheeseburger, with fries."

He looked up at the menu on the wall, across tall mirrors that made the place seem bigger, and called the order back to the kitchen. I waited until he moved away, then followed his gaze. He was looking at the clock on the beer sign.

Behind me, to my left, bowlers were swooping and spinning their heavy, black balls down the hardwood. I watched in the mirrors as pins clattered and smashed, reminiscent of thunder that followed lightning in the distance. Every crash was echoed by wildly enthusiastic cheering, an unusual sports rhythm given the skill of the bowlers. Paper notices taped to the glass blocked my view in some spots. I looked back the other way, surveying backward images of empty pool tables. A couple of guys sat at a table having a drink.

"One Coca-Cola," the bartender said, setting the tall glass down. He laid a knife and a fork on a napkin in front of me.

"You have a telephone I could use?" I asked.

He pointed behind me, to the lanes where bowlers sat chewing on sunflower seeds and emptying beer mugs.

"Go around that corner there and turn back down the hall. You'll have to pay."

"Watch my drink," I said. "I'll be right back."

I slipped around the corner into a hallway painted a dim shade of yellow. A tan padded bench sat in an alcove. Bowling team results and league standings were posted on the corkboard on the wall. The payphone was next to the men's room. I pulled the handset from the cradle, dropped a nickel in the slot, and dialed Jim's number to ask if he'd found anything new. I needed to know if I could go home without being picked up for questioning. And I needed sleep.

The door to the men's room opened. A face I knew stared out at me, and I hung up the telephone, slowly.

It was Bosko.

"You," he said, dropping his cigarette.

He turned around into the toilet room, trying to lock a door that didn't lock. I pushed him backward and stepped inside, closing the door behind me.

"You're a hard man to find," I said. I pulled my gun from inside my jacket, just in case he produced one first. He was carrying the black alligator case, gripping it in front of his chest with both hands. He reminded me of Chapman's secretary, holding her clipboard to her chest in some instinctive, defensive posture. I patted him down with one hand. He didn't carry a gun.

"Why are you following me?" His accented grammar was better than Marko's, but still foreign.

"Keep quiet," I said.

"You know, you can't shoot me. My friends are right outside."

He was bluffing. From what I knew, he didn't have any friends.

"Why would I shoot you?"

"You have your gun pointed at me."

Beyond the hallway, pins crashed. Predictably, cheering echoed through the room a moment later.

"Yasa hired me," I said.

His reaction puzzled me. He laughed.

"You find that funny?" I asked.

"She didn't hire you," he said. "Who told you that? Marko? One of the whores from 520?"

In Bingham?

"Yasa came to my office," I pressed. "Green eyes ... your niece. Remember?"

He was stroking the black case with his hand, as though it were a dog.

"She fooled me too," he said, "but she was not Yasa."

Not Yasa?

"Is that right?" I said, walking over and taking the case away from him. "And this must be the device I've been hearing so much about."

His eyes opened wide at its mention, and his mouth went round, but no sound came out.

"Get over in that corner," I told him. I put the case on the sink and undid the snaps along the edge. "Sit."

"Tell me who you work for?" he asked. "Marko, yes? Or Russians?"

The case popped open. Inside was an expensive pool cue in three pieces. Each piece was made of some rare and exotic hardwood, inlaid with mother-of-pearl and meant to be screwed together at a moment's notice. I closed the case and snapped it shut.

"You know Marko, then?"

"He is swine," he said. "He is traitor to your country and our country. Does he pay you well, to do these small jobs for KOS?"

KOS?

"Where's the device, Bosko?"

"I don't know what you mean," he said.

He became quiet again, his eyes shifting back and forth like a cat clock in a kitchen.

"I think you do. I've been hunting you down for days."

I considered my options.

"Move," I said, motioning to the door with my gun. He ignored me. He was playing for time, waiting for someone to come down the hall and find us. "Look, here's what we're gonna do," I said. "The two of us are gonna walk out of here together, down the edge of the alley like old friends. Then we're gonna head out the back door, walk up to my office, and sort everything out."

He stayed on the floor instead, so I took off my jacket, wrapped it around the Walther, and touched it to his leg.

He forced a smile. "You think that will make a difference?" he asked. He tried to act unafraid, but his eyes gave him away.

"It might," I said, crouching. "Because the next strike out there, the next crash of the pins is gonna be followed by a round of drunken cheering. And that's when I'm gonna make a mess of your kneecap and get my answers from you right here in the restroom. Even if they hear it, they won't pay any attention."

His eyes widened again.

"I don't have time to argue," I said. "People keep saying how you're some crackerjack inventor, but honestly, I don't even think your invention works."

He finally stood up. The attack on his ego did what the gun on his kneecap couldn't.

"Tomorrow night," he said defiantly, "you will see history, as if you were there when Ben Franklin flew his kite. And I will be there too, to claim the credit. At half-past ten the whole valley will see an example of what I've created, because yes ... it works."

I backed him off with the gun. "That's a little dramatic."

We walked out the restroom door, past the pay telephone to the bowling lanes. I switched the gun to my left hand, draped my jacket over it, and carried his precious leather case in my right hand. We came to the end of the hallway. I shoved the gun in his ribcage and told him to stay quiet. He started to veer off left, toward the front bar. I kicked his ankle, and he stumbled.

"Not that way," I said. "Straight ahead and keep thinking about your knees and how well they work right now."

Nobody paid us any attention.

A ball dropped on the hardwood. It was easy to imagine its travel from the low rumble heading away. The crash of pins was loud. Cheering rose and fell in a predictable pattern.

We passed through a doorway and walked by two boys and a woman wearing overalls busily resetting pins into numbered slots in the frame. I nodded, and they waved back.

63

Karrick Building
12:25 a.m., Saturday, July 24, 1948

A sign on Krogue's door read "CRIME SCENE, DO NOT ENTER." Bosko's eyes searched the hallway. The door to my office was still unlocked. I used my key to lock it once we were inside.

"Take a seat," I said, switching on the desk lamp. It wasn't a polite offer. I dropped his leather case by the coat rack, took down the flag at the window, and laid it across the top of a filing cabinet. I closed the Venetian blinds.

The lamp made a warm spot in the hot darkness.

"Cigarette?" I said, baiting him.

He shook his head. I didn't have one anyway.

I spread my jacket on the back of my chair and sat down across from him. Sadie looked out of the gold frame on the desk, smiling. I spun it around, keeping my gun leveled at him with my right hand.

"This is my girlfriend, Sadie. Her health and happiness are all I care about here. Not yours."

He held the photograph for a minute. "Who scratched out her eyes?"

"Bad people," I said, mimicking Marko's accent.

"I have nothing to do with her."

"Except that whoever took her said that I can get her back with your device."

I pulled Bosko's snapshot from my shirt pocket and slid it across the desk.

"And of course, there's this."

He picked up Yasa's photograph, his own likeness without eyes, and his hands trembled. He tried to mask it, but fear came back into his face. He looked at me in a different way, questioning. Part of me wanted to calm him down, to lessen his fear with an explanation. Another part of me wanted to use that fear. It was the second part that won out. I opened a desk drawer and pulled out a pair of stainless-steel handcuffs, then slid them across the desk.

"What is this?" he asked.

"I thought you were the smart guy here," I said. "Put 'em on."

His hands shook as he wrapped the steel around each wrist. I couldn't say whether the drops of sweat on his forehead were from fear or heat. *Could he stand up to physical pain, or even the threat of pain?* I wasn't sure I could do it.

"I guess your friends weren't watching the back door after all," I said, trying to sound tough. "But don't worry, I almost never hurt anybody in my own office."

If he caught any humor in my dark joke, he didn't let on. The Indian on the wall was tired, even in silhouette, head down. I knew just how he felt.

"So, your device—where is it?"

"I told you, I don't know what you mean." He started to wail and shout for help. I let him go on for a few minutes, to get it out of his system.

"The building's empty now. Nobody can hear you."

He took a moment and several short breaths before he quieted, resigned to his fate.

I picked up the telephone and dialed a number.

"I'm back in my office," I said, "with Bosko ... uh-huh, *that* Bosko. Better come now, before I do anything I'll regret."

I hung up.

"Who was that?" he asked.

"An old friend. It should take him about ten minutes to get here."

"What friend? Marko? Some Russian?"

I let him wonder. He struggled for control of himself and held onto the edge of the desk, breathing in shallow gasps. For a moment, he laid his head on the desk, resting.

"It doesn't matter now," he said. "People call it my 'device,' but it is just some private tool, for helping ... something I made. You will not understand."

"Try me. Where is it now?"

"I don't know. I don't know."

I stood up and walked around to his side of the desk. His eyes followed me sideways, like he expected my Walther to make a sudden imprint in the side of his face. *Dial it back,* I thought, *he's talking.* I didn't want him to die in my office from heart failure. I poured him a cup of water from the cooler.

"Tell me what it is I'm looking for," I said.

He swallowed and took a breath. "This tool, it is so complicated ... some integer-based alignment tool, for mathematically positioning electrons. It is abstraction really."

"Abstraction? As in, *doesn't really exist?*"

"Oh, it exists, but not in this real world. I told you that you wouldn't understand," he said.

"Then where is it?" I tried again.

His chin dropped to his chest, and he clammed up.

I decided to throw him a change-up instead of a fastball as a follow-up.

"Let's go back, then, since I clearly don't understand. Tell me about Tesla," I said. "Tell me about your time working with him."

"Nikola?" he said, looking up. "You know about him?"

He started out slowly, unsure of my reason for asking. He said Tesla had hired him almost thirty years ago. They'd met at Delmonico's, where Bosko worked as a busboy. He claimed to have helped the famous inventor develop the idea of alternating current before he sold it to George Westinghouse. He said Tesla depended on him to solve a lot of the difficult and practical issues that sometimes clouded his ideas. Mathematics was his specialty.

"I made Tesla's ideas real," he boasted, regaining some of his courage. "Without me, he never would have understood electron targeting, or how to control it."

"Electron targeting?"

"Yes, this means controlled acceleration of free electrons through non—vacuum mediums."

He was like lots of intellectuals I knew. He loved the sound of his own voice and the logic of his own worldview. He liked making it clear to me how little I knew. When he talked about electricity, it energized his whole body and he talked too much. He must have realized it because after a moment he stopped.

I followed up. "So, this alignment tool? This is the thing people call the 'Cvito device'?"

He'd said more than he planned, but hearing his name connected to it seemed to give him some measure of satisfaction. He smiled.

"Where is it, Bosko?"

"Missing."

"You know," I baited him, "I already saw the power plant at Highland Boy. I saw the transmitter tower being built, and at first, I thought that was your device—"

"Because you don't understand," he said. "And nobody can go in that part of the canyon. Not without clearance."

He stopped.

I pulled the blueprint from the work site out of the pile of stuff still sitting on the corner of the desk. "From Chapman?" I finished his boast. "He sent me up that way, to look around."

"Chapman?"

"That's right. He told me you'd sold him on the idea that electricity could be projected through the air, like a rocket. He told me you envisioned a fantastic world without wires—"

His head hung down.

I sat back down at the desk and waited.

"Perhaps, not so many wires," he said, finally. "And he told you this?"

"Big picture stuff. Nothing about the device, though. He said *you* were the scientist, not him. And he said they offered you a pretty good arrangement to make it all happen. You're lucky to be here, to make a deal like that."

"Yes. They reward me so handsomely—"

"I already heard it," I said. "Pretty much every miner out in Bingham told me you'd said the same thing."

"It is not only for money I do this."

"Of course not," I said, mocking him.

"This idea must be used for good things. Some others will not do good things. Even my own countrymen might ruin it, by making weapon."

That's what Marko said.

I looked at my watch, deliberately. "Look, let's cut to the chase here. Where is it? It sounds like it's probably some brilliant idea," I said, "and I really don't care how much you'll get paid. But you need to understand, I *have* to turn your so-called *device* over to whoever took Sadie, or they won't let her go."

"You would give secrets to Communists?"

"Spare me your patriot act, Bosko. How secret can it be if I know about it?"

He turned his face away. "I am sorry. There is nothing I can do."

"Can't? Or won't?"

"You will kill me, then?"

The question stopped me.

"I am not a bad man," he said.

"Cardwell said that too. But he also said you'd taken your best ideas from Tesla. He seemed annoyed that you leave him to do all the work in the canyon while you run off to hustle pool."

I was making it up as I went, trying to keep him talking.

"That makes no sense," he said. "Peter knows—he would never say such things, and if that were true, why would you be looking to me for this device?"

"You're implying that Cardwell has it?"

He laughed.

"Look, you can think whatever you want, but he flat-out said you stole Tesla's ideas," I lied, pushing back at him. "It's the classic story of an apprentice stealing the master's work. And he said if he hadn't been there, the whole idea wouldn't even work!"

Bosko's face was red. He'd gone from fear to pride to anger in minutes.

"You think I don't know what you're doing?" he said. "You think if you say these things, I will tell *you* about my secrets in some unguarded moment."

"You just confirmed that you *have* secrets."

"Secrets you'll never understand."

"Maybe," I said, pushing at his thin skin. "And yet I can't help but wonder if people won't remember you as the guy who let innocent people die so he could have his moment in the sun?"

"What are you saying?"

"I just showed you Sadie's picture."

He shook the handcuffs in frustration.

"She could die," I said. "Like Yasa. And for what?"

"I am sorry for your Sadie, but I was not sorry for this Yasa," he said, bitterly. "She deserved—" He stopped himself abruptly.

I eyed him, silently for a moment.

"It hasn't been in any of the papers, Bosko."

He looked up at the ceiling, at the window, and then all around the room. He wouldn't meet my gaze.

"You killed her, didn't you?"

Then he stared over my shoulder and smiled.

The cold steel of a large-caliber barrel pressed firmly against the base of my neck.

64

Karrick Building
12:35 a.m., Saturday, July 24, 1948

"Don't move a muscle," said a voice I recognized, a slow and easy drawl. "Put your gun on the desk, nice and careful."

Bosko quickly came over to my side of the desk and pulled the handcuff keys from the top drawer. The gun lifted off the back of my neck, and Bosko tossed the unlocked cuffs onto the desk.

"Now, put both hands behind your head and lock your fingers together, *Detective Nichols*."

It was Tex, minus his sombrero-sized hat and radios. He had a bandage across the bridge of his nose where my car door hit him, and his hair and shirt were soaked from the rain. He stepped around and slid the handcuffs onto my lap. His other hand propped up a .44 caliber cannon. It was a big gun for anybody, especially for him.

I didn't ask how he found us so fast, or what he was doing with Bosko. I didn't want to give him the satisfaction of telling me.

"Do you still wanna try and run me in?" he asked. "Lock me up?"

"You two know each other?" asked Bosko, surprised.

"Since lunchtime."

"I thought you worked for the copper company," I said.

"How 'bout that?"

"FBI?"

He didn't answer.

"You could shoot him, I think," said Bosko. "Nobody would hear a thing. He told me so."

"You need to cool down, old man. Me'n him are *friends* now ..." Tex seemed amused.

"I should have done it myself, instead of saving him."

Bosko, saving me? In his cellar?

"You don't even own a gun," Tex said.

"That never stopped him before," I said.

"Those whores, out in Bingham?" Tex gave him a nasty look. "I told you not to—"

"He killed Yasa," I said quickly.

"He's lying," said Bosko, "and he's in league with Russians."

"What is it about Russians? I don't even know any Russians," I said in desperation. "I'm just tryin' to save Sadie."

"Another hooker?" Tex asked, turning to Bosko.

"No," I answered. "Sadie's *my* girl. Somebody took her hostage, and they think I can get my hands on this thing Bosko stole or made or invented ... some kind of device. That's all I'm lookin' for, just a way to get Sadie back. I don't care about him."

He hesitated. Lightning flashed, lighting up the blinds. The glass in the windows vibrated as thunder rumbled through.

"You know what he's talkin' about?" Tex asked.

Bosko stood by the door, his ear to the wood panels.

"Project details. Classified things we should not discuss," he said. "He's trying to steal them."

"I meant about this gal, Yasa. You killed her?"

"He's lying. And I don't know anything about his friend, Sadie."

Tex rubbed his right thumb along the cylinder of the gun, looking at me. "So then ... you're working with the Russians?"

I didn't want to think about that. "Of course not. The old man stole the science from somebody else," I said. "It's not even his."

Tex wiped his hand down his face. "Well, my instructions are simple: Make sure Mr. Bosko here gets back in one piece, tonight. They don't say nothin' about gettin' involved with any Russians."

"I didn't say it was Russians. He did."

Tex picked up the gold frame, shaking his head.

"I'd like to help out your gal here," he said. "Really, I would, because I like helping people. But first off, I don't really know what you're talking about. Secondly, I've already got marching orders. And third, I just really don't like you all that much. Can't imagine what a cute gal like this sees in you. Did somebody scratch her eyes out?"

I hoped not.

"We should go," Bosko said, glancing back and forth between Tex and the crack of the door.

"Cuff your hand to the desk, there," Tex said, pointing with the gun.

I hooked one side of the pair to the top desk drawer. The other one fit snugly around my left wrist. I kept my eyes on the keys in Bosko's hand.

He handed them over to Tex, who slipped them in his pocket. Then he picked up my Walther from the desk, popped the clip out, and scattered the bullets on the floor.

"We need to go," Bosko whined.

"Souvenir?" Tex asked, admiring the markings on my gun. "You ever want to sell that thing ..." He slid it across the floor, out of reach, as he moved toward the front door.

"Not that way," said Bosko. "He used the telephone to call somebody, just before you showed up. They could be in the hallway right now."

"Who'd you call?"

"A friend." I shrugged. "There's plenty of other people lookin' for him."

"Get behind me," he said to Bosko. "We'll go out the way I came in, down the fire escape. And don't slip. It's wet."

He motioned with his head and came back to me. "I hope I can count on you not to say anything to Peter Cardwell. I mean about how you two got away from me and came this far?"

He stepped close and smacked the left side of my jaw with the .44, drawing blood from my mouth. With my free hand, I checked to see if my teeth were okay.

"That's for yesterday," he said. "Out at the fence line."

He didn't say, "We're even now," or anything like it. Instead, he just got one of those self-satisfied, cat-ate-the-canary grins on his face.

"Stop poking into things," he said. "You're testing our patience."

"We should go," whined Bosko.

"Count to a hun'erd," Tex said, waving his gun. He turned, and the two of them disappeared out the back window.

I pulled my lockpick out of my pocket and had the cuff off in less than a minute, then dashed back and stuck my head out the window to the fire escape. Fine rain wetted the back of my haircut as I scanned the drive below. Faint red taillights reflected in the puddles and the windows of the alley and vanished. Around the corner of the building, I could hear gears grinding.

Below me, a body lay motionless on the pavement.

65

Karrick Building
12:55 a.m., Saturday, July 24, 1948

I stood watching the rain fall, streaking down black and gray brick walls in the dark night alley. Then I closed the window, shook off the wet, and ran to my desk to reload the empty clip before heading down to check out the body. A knock on the door sounded first.

"Open up, Jack!"

I turned the key, and a tired-looking Uncle Jim stepped inside. I switched on more light. "You're too late," I said, reloading.

"I hurried. We'd already turned in."

"Well, you might want to call your boys over now," I said. "The two of 'em went down the fire escape. Looks like one of 'em didn't get past the alley."

He brushed past me on his way to the back room. "Two of them?"

"Somebody else came for him first. Somebody with a gun."

There was a bump, and I heard him cuss the window frame. "There's nobody down there now," he said. "Not that I can see."

"What?" I followed him back. "He was facedown, at the bottom of the ladder."

"Then I'd be lookin' right at him."

"You know what? Stay there," I said. "Watch the alley while I run down the stairs. Maybe he just crawled away somewhere."

I slammed the door shut and dashed down the hall. At ground level, I came around the back of the building on the south side. He was right. The alley was empty. There wasn't anybody lying on the pavement. I squinted up into the drizzle and spotted Jim watching from my office window, his head a dark silhouette.

"He was right here," I yelled. "I swear, he was lying face down."

"You see anything else," he called down. "Any blood, or shell casings?"

"No, but I never heard a gunshot either," I said. "Just saw the body."

"Wait there," he said. "I'll come down."

I kicked around in the darkness until he showed up with a flashlight from his car. We scoured the ground near the stair bottom, but it was no use. We stepped under an overhanging eave to get out of the rain. Jim pulled a broken cigarette from his pocket.

"I thought you gave that up," I said.

He cupped his hand around his lighter and caught a flame.

"I did," he mumbled, rolling the cigarette around with his tongue. "You have a guess about which one of 'em was down here?"

"I couldn't tell—it was too dark."

"But there were two of them?"

"That's right. I found Bosko over in the men's room at Ace Billiards and brought him upstairs to answer a few questions. We no sooner sat down than one of the guards from Bingham climbed up the fire escape and surprised me. Carried a .44 Smith and Wesson. Seems he had a second job as a minder, making sure Bosko stayed out of trouble."

"Wasn't so good at his job, was he?"

"Depends on how things turn out," I said. "Anyway, from what they said, they're headed back out that way tonight."

Jim crossed his arms and stared at me.

"There's only one road out that way," I said. "You could put out a call to pick them up."

"You didn't see what he was driving?"

"No, but it's not a busy road, not after midnight. They won't get far."

"You're sure he was up there?" He motioned to the open window.

"You're doubting my story?"

He leaned out from under the eave and looked up, like he could check whether the rain was going to stop by surveying dark clouds on a dark night.

"Listen, I know we—me and Edna—got you involved in this, but I'm getting pressure to bring somebody in to give us some answers, and it's not just Bosko. It's you that everybody wants to talk to, especially Nichols."

"Okay, but just listen. I swear he was upstairs. He even admitted ... well, he almost admitted he killed Yasa. And he's got some business deal going with the FBI."

"*Almost* admitted it?"

"That's right. He said she deserved to die, and she wasn't really his niece. It got me thinkin' back, how the FBI hinted at it in my office too."

"That she deserved to die?"

"Hell, no. That she wasn't his niece."

"And maybe you're just making stuff up."

"Just because you don't like the way I tell the story, doesn't mean it's not true."

He looked at me like I'd told him I had Bess Truman upstairs, in handcuffs.

"Are you gonna put out the call?"

He ignored me. "What else did you get from him?"

"Not much," I said. "Mostly electrical gibberish, and talk about his device being a tool, or an abstraction or something. Said it was missing."

"You mean, the 'device' from the letter you kept to yourself? You have any real evidence? Something to show that Bosko was actually here?"

"Well," I glanced around, "there's his pool cue, right there."

"With his name on it?"

I hesitated. "No."

He put his arm around me. "Look, I know you want to make it in this business, but look at it from my side, Jack. Me and Edna sent you over to Yasa's place to help look for an old man, and somehow you turn it into the *Gunfight at the O.K. Corral*. The next day you leave a loaded weapon with Sadie, and she manages to shoot up the Beehive."

"That's not tellin' it right," I protested.

"Then I tell you to stay away from Bosko, to let the FBI handle things, and you head right out to Bingham lookin' for him and impersonate one of my detectives. And to make it worse, you stop by Sadie's on the way there and get her mother all worked up before—lo and behold—Sadie actually disappears!"

I could feel my heart rate jump a notch with every comment.

"But you let me go—"

"Wait, I'm not done," he said, stepping away. "When you get back in town, two people you know take bullets in the back of the head. I find out you've been holding onto a key piece of evidence, which, I'll admit, not everybody believes is even real. And then you take off from a crime scene in your own building where your neighbor and good friend was murdered. The next thing I know, you're calling me in the middle of the night to come and pick up Bosko, who conveniently disappears, again, with a mysterious rescuer before I can even get here."

He had to stop to take a breath.

"Are you finished?" I asked.

He dropped his cigarette and ground it into the wet asphalt.

"No, Jack, but I wish I was. I've been cutting you too much slack, not holding you accountable for what's been goin' on this week. Too many holes in your story. People think I'm playin' favorites with you, especially now with this last shooting. I need to *at least* get your statement written down and on the record. You can't get away with ignoring *my* investigation anymore. I need evidence, Jack. Not just stories."

"*You* have an investigation? What have *you* turned up?"

"Well, you, for one thing."

"You know I haven't done anything wrong—not anything against the law."

"Impersonating a police officer?"

"I never said I was a cop, and who's looking for Sadie now, anyway?"

"Everybody I can spare," he said. "While you're off looking for Bosko—"

"Because I think *that's* the best way to find her. If I had some other lead, I'd be following it."

"And you think they'll just let her go?"

"If I can find the *device*, I do. Unless you have a better idea?"

"You know that isn't how these things work out," he said. "You can't pay ransom and think she'll walk away. And the device isn't yours to bargain with, anyway."

"My client claims it's his."

He shook his head and checked his watch. Far off and high we could hear my telephone ringing through the open window.

"That's probably Edna, lookin' for me now. You know, if I didn't need to get back to her, I'd take you to a holding cell and get the answers I'm lookin' for tonight."

"You wouldn't—"

"Because she's not comfortable at home alone at night. Said if I wasn't back inside of thirty minutes, I could sleep in my car."

"Your back seat wouldn't be so bad."

He gave me a look.

"You get yourself to my office tomorrow. I'll be tied up with the parade till lunchtime, but that's as much time as I'm gonna give you. And I'm going to need a full accounting of what's going on with you, and your client, and this Bosko character, and with everybody else you've dragged into it, starting with Edna."

"It was Edna who dragged me into this, because you wouldn't look for Bosko yourself."

He stared me down. "You can't keep doing this."

"Doin' what?"

"Blaming things on everybody else," he said. "Did it ever occur to you that maybe if we'd known about the threat, we could have protected her? We could've put somebody at her house."

"So, now you believe the letter is real?"

"I didn't say that. But as it sits, her mother is sure you've got something to do with this and wants to know why I haven't arrested you already. When that letter comes out, what do you think she's going to say?"

"I get it. I'm just tryin' to do the right thing."

"Me too," he said. "And you're making it way too hard. This is the last break I can give you. Come in tomorrow and let's get all this straightened out and put it on the record."

"Radiophone, Captain. Bingham Highway."

He put on his hat, stepped out into the rain, and headed back around the building. I heard the engine start and went back upstairs.

I know I saw a body.

I shook off the rain and went upstairs. When the door closed, I turned the key and looked around out of habit, but slowly now. Something seemed out of place. My handcuffs sat on the desk next to a stack of papers. My desk lamp was still on. The Indian still sat with his head tilted down on his horse, holding his war lance.

I pulled my gun out and took a minute to make sure nobody else was inside my office. I locked the back window, laid the gun on the desk, and walked back to look at the print by the door.

It hadn't moved for days.

66

Karrick Building
1:30 a.m., Saturday, July 24, 1948

I lifted the print from the wall and set it on the floor. Below the nail and off to one side was a hole, nearly as large as a dime. I slid a chair over to stand on, so I could get a better look. A red wire and a white wire, twisted together, poked out of the hole and connected to a square, flat piece of metal with three thin openings. It stuck out from the wall just enough to keep the picture from sliding when the door shut.

It was also capturing and sending my private conversations someplace else.

I'd heard about miniature listening devices but never expected anybody would care much about what I had to say. I tried remembering the last time I straightened the Indian print.

Sometime before I left for Bingham.

That meant every conversation here tonight could have been picked up by someone else, including my talk with Bosko. I made a mental list of everyone who had the means and a reason to do something like this.

The cops could, but Jim never came until I called him. Maybe Nichols?

The FBI, certainly.

Marko, possibly, but he didn't even seem to notice I'd hung up the flag.

And the Russians, or whoever Marko's "bad people" were.

I picked up the telephone, held the handset pressed tight against the cradle, and examined it upside down, carefully. I couldn't see any extra wires attached. I unscrewed the mouthpiece and the earpiece. From the little I knew about electrical things, they seemed okay as well.

The red and white wires on the wall went through the plaster surface and the wooden lath behind it, then turned down toward the floor below. I rehung the Indian, rummaged around in my drawers for a flashlight, and quietly slipped out the office door.

In the hallway, I stood still and quiet. The soft and distant roar from a car on Main rose and fell and vanished.

Walking slowly, stopping for a moment at every squeaky floorboard, I made it past the sign on Krogue's door. A single bulb burned dimly in the wall sconce at each stair landing. I pulled my gun out and headed down.

The dentist's office took up the north half of the second level. Until now I'd thought the rest of the floor was vacant, but a faint glow appeared in a window in a door in the back corner.

The frosted glass didn't have a name. I watched for movement, monitoring the hollow silence for sounds that were irregular, singular. Nothing. I took the lockpick tool from my pocket and went to work on the keyhole. It opened after a minute. Someone had recently oiled the hinges.

I stepped inside the single-room office and swept the flashlight across a gray card table with a red leather top. A radio transmitter the size of a bread box sat there, dials glowing in the darkness. One chair stood at an angle against the wall, two others were unfolded under the tabletop. The familiar red and white wires ran up the wall, entering a hole just below the ceiling. A third wire, the antenna, ran to the window.

Now what?

It would have been easy enough to shut it down, and I leaned down to unplug it, but a thought stopped me. Something whispered to me that maybe the listening device was a clue I could turn back against whoever put it there.

I relocked the door, twisting the egg-shaped knob to be certain it latched. Near the floor, where the door met the frame on the hinge-side I inserted a small scrap of paper into the gap. I stood up, motionless, watching the end of the hallway where it opened into the stairs. When I was sure nobody had entered the building, I hurried back to my office and quietly opened my own door. I picked up a few personal items, locked up, and headed out the back way, taking the alleys to Auerbach's.

Jonny met me in the hallway with his gun out.

"Just me," I said. "I'm takin' you up on that offer to have a sleepover."

I brought him up to speed and spent the night on a real mattress in the furniture department.

67

On the Street
7:08 a.m., Saturday, July 24, 1948

The next morning, I called Jim's place, but Edna said he'd gone out early.

The rain stopped, leaving drops of water beaded on the hoods of cars. Jonny's maintenance guy finally answered his phone and said he'd be glad to meet him for breakfast, but Jonny's wife let him have it when he called her and said he had an errand to run before coming home.

"Did you blame it on me?"

"You're already on her bad side."

"Well, thanks. Here's three bucks." I pulled two ones and some silver from my pocket. "Treat him to Covey's."

"Why don't you come with us?" he asked. "Talk to him yourself."

"I gotta be in the office in case these guys call again. If your guy can't read it, see if he knows somebody else who can."

The cops finished closing off cross streets at eight-thirty, setting Main Street apart as one long and downward-sloping parade ground. Normally four lanes wide, the street had been narrowed to two with the police barricades. Families staked out territory on the asphalt with blankets and folding chairs. Holiday banners fluttered overhead. Clouds covered the valley, but blue sky appeared out west, over the lake.

I angled my way across the parade route, then walked behind the Karrick so I could check things out in the light. Trash cans, some empty, lined the small turnout area where Jim and I had stood in the rain. The ground was still wet. I examined it for stains that could have been last night's blood at the bottom of the ladder, hard to see even now. The ones I found could just as easily be motor oil, or mayonnaise from some guy's hamburger. I walked over and pushed the ladder to the fire escape up as high as I could reach, then headed down the alley toward the Chinaman's chopping block. I could hear him working before I stepped around the corner of the building. He was gutting fresh trout, singing to himself.

"You came back," he said without looking up.

"Still looking for the girl," I said. "Are you always here?"

He glanced up with a sly grin. "Chinese girl?" He was toying with me.

"Sorry, no," I said. "Same girl."

I headed back toward my office but stopped.

"Say, wait a second," I said, turning around. "*Was there* a Chinese girl back here last night?"

He stuck the knife into the butcher block.

"Yeah, sure," he said. "With the old man who drives the bone truck—her father, I think. They scoop up bones and animal guts from all the restaurants in town, use it for fertilizer. He comes by here every night, sometimes late."

"How late?"

"Seven o'clock, eight o'clock, later on weekends. He backs into the loading dock next door and smokes a cigarette or two. Some-times he takes a little nap."

He signaled with a hand motion that he thought the guy pulled out a bottle while he waited.

"Were they back there last night, or the night before?"

"Every night."

"How do I find them?"

He stopped gutting and put his hand to the back of his head, thinking. I got the hint and pulled a couple of crumpled bills from my pocket.

"Wait here," he said, taking the money and heading inside. When he came out, he was carrying an open telephone directory. "They'll stop here later tonight, but she's too young for you."

"Yeah, how old would that be?"

"Twelve years old, maybe fourteen. Smart girl, though, talks like an old woman."

I copied down the address and telephone number for Huang Chou Li, Animal Product Waste Company. The address was eight blocks west. Maybe young Miss Huang had noticed somebody in the alley. Maybe I was grasping at straws.

I retraced the alley and took the stairs two at a time, headed up to my office. I stopped on the second level and looked down the hallway. Feeling for my gun under my jacket, I walked to the far corner. The scrap of paper was still wedged in the door frame. No-body had gone in or out. I started for the stair again when a door opened, and the painless dentist stepped out.

"Hey there!" said a chubby little man, dressed casually in a white shirt with sleeves rolled up and suspenders. "You have that office upstairs, right? The private eye?"

He seemed to be one of those people who were perpetually happy. Through the open door, I could hear voices and laughter.

I tipped my hat and started to move past, but he stopped me, his face turning solemn.

"Listen, I heard that watchmaker upstairs was killed in his office." He said it as a fact, but I knew it was a question.

Somebody, a woman, called to him from inside. "I thought we came to watch the parade!" she yelled.

"Did you know him?" he asked, ignoring her.

"Some. He was the kind of guy that kept to himself. And you?"

"Not really. He stopped down here yesterday, during the lunch hour. Said somebody from the FBI called lookin' for you. He thought it was odd and wondered if they talked to me too, but they didn't. I thought you'd want to know, given the circumstances."

"The FBI?"

"That's what he said."

"Listen, you don't happen to know who took that office, over in the corner?"

"Nope, I just see patients on this floor," he said. "Suits me fine, being in my business. The painless part, I mean." He winked, like it was an inside joke between us. Somebody called to him again from inside his office.

"I'd better get back. But stop by sometime," he said, handing me his business card. "You take care of your own teeth?"

I thought about getting smacked by Tex's gun and ran my tongue over the molars again to be sure. "I think I'm all set for now," I said. "But it's always good to know somebody in the business, just in case."

He pointed his finger at me like a pistol.

"Enjoy the parade," I said to him. "You've got great seats."

I backed away and went up the stairs.

When I opened the door, there was a large manila envelope on the floor.

68

Karrick Building
9:00 a.m., Saturday, July 24, 1948

I opened the envelope and held it on edge, between my shaking palms, to preserve any possible fingerprints. Jim had done something like that the night before. A note slipped onto my desk with letters cut from one of the local papers.

"Bring Device to Parade. 11:00 am in front of Post Office."

I sat back, calculating the size of something that I could bring to the parade. Were they going to show themselves? They were moving up their timeline. The first note from them said Saturday, not Saturday *morning. And what about Sadie?*

I walked to the back room and splashed cold water on my face. The cut on my ear was healing, but my face showed a purple bruise from Tex's gun.

The telephone rang. It was Jonny.

"That didn't take long. I was hoping it'd be Sadie."

"Sorry. But I figured you'd want to hear this, before you talked to—"

"I got it," I said, remembering there was still a working microphone in the room.

"First, the notebook's written in two parts. There's a lot of technical language, especially up front, and it'll take hours to translate it all. The back half is like a scratch pad with addresses, names, and a few random thoughts about life in the USA. And it even mentioned Yasa. My guy made a few notes, but nothing new really jumped at me."

"That's it?"

"No, that was first. We took another crack at the front part, trying to read some of the technical stuff. The handwriting is different, and it's all written in ink; mostly mathematics, and diagrams, and lots of equations. They're all jumbled together. But get this: He says the author refers to the equations with a word that could be translated as 'device.' It sounds like it's referring to some kind of mathematical tool. Does that ring any bells with you?"

He paused, waiting. I could hear him breathing through the telephone.

The notebook was the device?

"Are you still there? Because I think maybe it's *Cvito's* device. Not a physical tool—"

"Got it—" And as soon as I said it, I glanced up at the Indian.

"And those diagrams, those ones you thought were trick shots in pool?"

"Uh-huh ..."

"They're connected to the math somehow. The text says, 'electron bunching' ... 'electron gathering' ... depends on how you translate it," he said. "But they have nothing to do with billiards."

I reassembled the pieces in my head.

"Are you listening?"

"Yeah, I'm listening."

"Okay, so I had him look over the blue letter," he continued. "And remember how I kept tellin' you not to trust Marko?"

"Did I say I did?"

"Well, you're gonna be interested in this. I'm guessing Yasa wrote it Monday night. It starts out, 'My Darling Marko ...'"

"*My darling?!*"

"I know! Listen, it's short: 'I am writing with much hope that this will reach you soon. My heart is quiet again, your touch has calmed my fears ....'"

"So, they did meet," I said.

"There's more romantic stuff."

"Skip that."

"Okay, then here's the part about you: 'As for the investigator, I am sorry for acting in your absence. It is my hoping ... hope, that he will bring Bosko into the light again. I can handle him, when time is right.'"

"Handle *him?*" I said. "Did she mean Bosko, or me?"

"It's a rough translation, but either way, I think she meant to kill you. Rub you out, like in the movies. Listen to this part. She's referring to Edna: 'Her husband is policeman, so take much care. When Bosko is found, remove every connection that could lead to KOS and to me.'"

"'Every connection' certainly includes you and Edna. Then she signs off saying, 'Russians are near.'"

"Every connection? Leading to where?"

"KOS. K-O-S. You know what it is?"

"I heard it before."

"You've stumbled into a mess here, Jack. I think we need to bring in the FBI, now. You want me to bring these over to your office?"

"No!"

Now what?

"Are you still there, Jack?"

"Give me a minute."

I put the telephone down and walked to the window. I pulled the blind back and peeked outside. Street edges were filling with people, crowding for a good spot to watch the parade.

Yasa and Marko? Russians? The FBI?

I tried fitting the pieces together. After a moment, I cracked my knuckles and sat back down.

"I'm back," I said, staring at the Indian. "By the way, they finally got back in touch."

"Who got in touch?" he asked. "Russians? KOS? Are you talking for them? You are, aren't you?"

It was going to be another one-sided conversation intended for somebody else's benefit. Somebody was listening from behind the print on the wall. At least, I hoped they were.

"This morning, somebody slipped another letter under my door when I was out."

I was thinking as fast as I could.

"What did it say?"

"They want me and the device on the street by the post office in about an hour."

"How can I help, Jack? You're not gonna do it, are you?"

"Not without seeing Sadie first. Alive."

This was the message I had to sell, to whoever was listening in.

"Here's the way I see it," I said. "They've already murdered two witnesses, so once they have the device, Sadie will be as good as dead. If I follow through with the ransom, the way they've set it up, maybe I'll be dead too. They've got to understand that she's only good for leverage as long as I know I can get her back safely. I'm sending that back in a message. They'll have to do a live exchange— but I just don't know how."

"What if they won't agree?"

"Then I won't give 'em what they want," I said. "I don't have any choice here. They showed their hand when they killed Krogue and the kid. People's lives mean nothin' to them."

"And they're listening now, to you?"

"I hope so. Because I swear, this is not going to be another Lindbergh baby fiasco. I'm gonna send them back my own terms: something for something. I'll try to arrange a meeting, and if anything happens to me, you know what to do with it all."

"I do?"

"What would you tell me to do?"

"Take it all to Jim?"

"Right, do that," I said and hung up.

I thought about Sadie, tied up somewhere, and pushed it away as fast as I could. I didn't know if my tough talk would work, but I couldn't give up the device on a promise. If they thought they were still listening in to a private conversation, maybe they'd hear something in my voice suggesting the hand they're trying to deal me was another sucker-bet, and I wasn't going to play.

I took out a lined pad from the desk drawer and wrote on the empty page.

If you want the Cvito Device, Bring Sadie to—

I stopped and sat back.

Bring her where? Someplace where they felt like they could come and go undetected, someplace they could be certain they weren't walking into a trap. Naturally, they'd assume any place I suggested was covered. They were going to have to be the ones to choose.

I tore off the page, tossed it in the waste bin, and tried a new line.

"Skip the letter writing. Call my office today to arrange an exchange."

It was already past nine. I slipped the note into the tan envelope and twisted the string tie in a figure-eight to hold it closed.

A heavy knock pounded on my door.

69

Karrick Building
9:40 a.m., Saturday, July 24, 1948

I wasn't expecting anyone just now, least of all Charlie, the wannabe boxer. He carried a stained, canvas water bag over his shoulder; the kind people hung on the outside of their cars when they traveled long distances. He showed a bruise on his right cheek, but his face was missing the intense reddish hue of alcohol and anger.

"Charlie?"

He stepped inside and stood with his hands tucked in his back pockets, looking down. "I need water, for my radiator," he said. "I had to park out on West Temple, on account of the parade."

He was wearing denim overalls and a graying, white tee shirt that emphasized his muscular upper frame. I offered him a chair, hoping he'd take a seat. My heart rate kicked up.

He looked over at the water cooler against the front wall, past the Indian.

"Help yourself," I said. "I'll fill the bag at the sink in the back."

I walked to the back room with it, wondering why he'd come.

Payback for knocking him down, or for talking with Fay?

I used the moment alone to make sure my gun was loaded. My hands shook. *You can't shoot him*, I told myself. *You've got Sadie to worry about.* I filled the bag and walked back to find him staring at her photograph.

"Who's the dame with the scratched-out eyes?"

"That's Sadie," I said, taking a deep breath. "She's my gal."

He nodded and turned the frame back to face me.

"First things first," he said. He made a fist with his left hand and rubbed it inside his right. My own hand edged toward my gun. "I came here to say I'm sorry for comin' after you the other night," he said. "I guess I had a little too much to drink. And Fay's been givin' me a run for my money."

I sat down on the edge of the chair. He'd caught me by surprise. I didn't have an answer for him. He waited for me to say something, but after a few moments he couldn't take the silence.

"Speaking of money," he said. "What's this all about?"

He fumbled for a one-dollar bill from his pants pocket and smoothed it out on the desk. It had my name and phone number written on its face. He put both forearms on the desktop.

"This part here," he said, pointing to my name. Now his gaze was steady. His eyes were deep-set and blue, not at all like the narrow slits from the other night.

"Where'd you get that?" I asked, listening to my own breathing.

"Off the dresser at home. Your address is in the phone book."

The solid, chiseled steadiness in his face was breaking down. There was sadness and desperation tugging at the corners of his eyes and his mouth. I marveled at his hands, big as catcher's mitts, calloused and busy.

"Well ... I didn't have a business card handy," I explained. "I do that sometimes, to try to get my name out there."

"She didn't ask you?"

"I was there on a case, Charlie. She told me she noticed I was bein' followed that night, so she stopped at the bar to tell me about it. Said she knew something about bein' followed. That's when you showed up. That's all there was. Next day, I stopped by the drugstore on my way out of town, to follow up and see what else she knew. Now you know everything."

He was paying careful attention. I was trying to build him up. I avoided mentioning the note with her phone number and the little heart.

"It was purely business," I said. "In case she remembered something."

It was a small lie, to salve the hurt in his heart. She was a beautiful girl, the kind who could work magic in the hearts of any member of the male population that pumped blood. She'd done it to me by just leaning on the bar next to me, and I'd been happy to talk to her, until right now.

He pushed back away from the desk, head down. "She's a wonderful gal," he said. It was a comment addressed to no one.

"She seemed like it," I said.

"She's not, though, not really. I mean, I used to think she was, but she doesn't want to be married no more," he said. "I don't know what to do. I thought you were just one of those ... you know, one of those bar hounds lookin' for a little fun."

My pulse settled back into a more normal range.

"She took you home though, took care of you?" I tried. "Put you in bed?"

He nodded.

"There's something to that," I said.

"Is your girl like that?"

I wasn't sure anymore. I was anxious, afraid for Sadie, but I pushed it down. I had to. I wasn't hurting inside, like Charlie, but

I was scared out of my wits. He was letting his fears control him. I couldn't afford that, not with Sadie. That's what I told myself.

Be careful what you say here.

"I'm no family counselor, Charlie," I said. "And not to be rude or anything, but I have a business appointment downstairs in a few minutes. Just so we're square, you ought to know that she hasn't hired me or called me. I mean, if that's what you're worryin' about."

He rubbed the palms of his hands in his eyes like he was trying to jam the tears back inside. He stood up and walked to my window. He opened the blinds and looked down at the gathering crowd, his mind somewhere else.

"You ever do any boxing?" he asked, turning back. He wiped his nose with a purple plaid handkerchief.

"Military Police," I said. "Once upon a time. That's it. Sorry for the bruise."

He put his hand to the side of his face. "There aren't many guys could knock me down like that. At least I didn't think there were."

"Maybe not," I said, "but you'd had a little too much to drink."

I handed him the water bag and wondered if he was sad about Fay, or sad about the fact I put him on the ground in his hometown. Maybe both.

"Look, since you're here, why don't you head down and watch the parade," I said. "Everybody loves the parade. It'll be good for you; make you feel better."

I took my jacket from the chair, trying to herd him to the door when an idea hit me. "In fact, how'd you like to make a buck while you're at it? It'll help me out of a little jam I'm in."

He looked at me and rubbed the back of his hand across his nose.

"What would I have to do?" he asked.

70

Post Office on Main Street
10:45 a.m., Saturday, July 24, 1948

We left the side alley and came out onto the sidewalk. The parade was in full motion, a dozen drum-majors, wearing tall beaver hats, strutting pompously past Woolworth's. A high school marching band played "Stars and Stripes Forever." Crowds stood and cheered as Maw passed by, waving from a convertible. Overhead the rain held back. Anyone familiar with Utah in July would have said it was a perfect day for a parade.

I walked behind the crowd when I could, crossed Broadway, and headed down toward the post office. Charlie stayed at the back of the crowd and followed me at a distance. My eyes flitted around the parade, searching for someone I didn't know.

Who was I kidding? I didn't know these people. Would they be so bold?

I folded the tan envelope in half. Charlie's job was to keep his eyes on me. I wasn't keen on meeting Sadie's abductors, even their go-between, with nobody else around to back me up. Charlie was cheap muscle, not that I expected much to happen in public. But it might keep his mind off Fay for a while.

The post office building was gray-columned granite, built in classical Roman style. Old-timers associated it with federal control of Utah, symbolically balancing the granite Mormon Temple four blocks north. I picked a line from the front corner of the building, where the crowd thinned. Dodging onlookers, I worked my way toward the parade, trying to see everyone in the crowd at the same time.

Mounted riders from a club in Heber City executed precision equestrian routines. Another marching band strutted by, followed by a parade float with an Eskimo and a dog sled.

From the corner of my eye, I caught Charlie shadowing me, hanging back due to his size.

A top-heavy prairie schooner lumbered past, horses' hooves clip-clopping on the asphalt. Young boys with milk boxes strapped to their chests sold orange and cherry Popsicles for a nickel. Hatless men and women stood and clapped as floats and bands rolled by.

I checked my watch. It was 11:05.

A clown dressed in a leopard-skin outfit posed as a strongman. He lifted massively heavy weights, entertaining the crowd with his strength. At the end of his routine, a small boy appeared and carried off the bogus weights, to thunderous applause and laughter.

I searched more faces for someone, anyone, looking my way.

Spectators marveled at a sailing ship navigating its way down Main.

I unfolded the envelope.

Charlie was watching me and shook his head from side to side.

Where were they? I wondered if my plan had backfired. Maybe they'd been listening in and decided they didn't care for my attitude. Maybe they didn't agree with my change in plans.

My stomach twisted in knots.

I crossed my arms. There was still plenty of parade left, heading down the street.

Crosswinds lifted swarms of paper skyward, mixing high above the parade with runaway balloons. Seagulls swooped down and fought over spilled popcorn.

A crew of clowns dressed as street sweepers followed behind, cleaning up the horses' occasional gifts to the roadway, and taking practically everything from the crowd not tied down: hats, purses, cameras ... everything but trash.

Everyone loved the clowns, and everyone got their possessions back as the act moved on.

The first tug on the envelope was tentative, like a trout taking a dry fly and letting it go. As I looked down, the second tug slipped it from my grasp. Another street sweeper had come from behind, through the crowd. He dropped it into his wheeled can. I caught a glimpse of his face. He had huge glasses, a curly black wig, and a handlebar mustache three sizes too big for his rubber nose. Matching all the clowns from his group, he wore a white regulation, street-cleaner outfit.

I hesitated. *Was this my contact?*

In a moment, he was back in the street with three other clowns who could have been his twins. They twirled their brooms, lining up and falling down, and kept taking things from spectators like umbrellas and lunch boxes. The crowd laughed, and a band pushed behind them. They started to move on.

And suddenly, there was Charlie in the street with them, holding one of the clowns by the jacket. The captive clown frantically flapped his arms, to the delight of those watching.

"He took your envelope!" Charlie yelled to me.

People were looking my way.

The other clowns came to his rescue, beating Charlie off with their brooms. The crowd assumed it was all part of the act, laughing and clapping wildly, even more than for the weightlifter.

A tan envelope surfaced from somewhere.

Charlie reached for it, even as the clown holding it pulled it away. It tore in two pieces.

The crowd gasped. People pointed, then smiled. *It was a gag.*

Two clowns struggled with Charlie for the remaining piece. The action knocked over one of the wheeled waste cans, spilling a load of warm, fresh horse manure that had been gathered along the parade route. One of the clowns fell back into the dung. The others looked up at the rapidly approaching marching band. Drum majors in creamy outfits had already spotted the delay and held up the band, marching in formation a hundred feet back.

A uniformed cop stepped into the street. Charlie stepped back.

At first, the crowd laughed again, but then they stopped.

The clown with the envelope took the other half from Charlie and brought it to me with a sad clown face. A round of applause broke out.

People close to me smiled in sympathy. It was a great act but went nowhere.

More twirling batons started our way, and attention shifted back to the street and the royalty floats that followed the band. I walked away from the parade and sat down on the post office steps. It was ending soon anyway.

The Popsicle kid came over, and I gave him a dime. "Keep the change," I said.

Charlie watched me. I offered him half, but he stayed away.

The tan envelope was ripped and bent. I opened both halves and dumped out the contents in my lap.

My heart jumped.

A new note, written with newspaper letters, was folded in half. Somebody had slipped it into the torn envelope.

"AUERBACH'S OFFICE. 9:00 P.M. NO COPS!"

I folded the message, tucked it into my jacket and dropped the envelope in the trash.

How did they pull that off?

Down the street and three blocks away, floats and bands alike turned east toward Liberty Park, where the parade disbanded. The street cleaner act had vanished.

Police uniforms appeared out of the crowd, gathering up rope barricades. Real street cleaners went back to work. Cars returned, honking at pedestrians who'd already become accustomed to their absence.

I stood up, waved Charlie over, and walked back toward my office.

71

Karrick Building
1:35 p.m., Saturday, July 24, 1948

"I guess I should have let him alone, huh?"

"It's okay Charlie, no harm done," I said. I handed him two bucks, but he pushed it away.

"I can't take that," he said. "It was nice, just watchin' the parade until ... you know. I don't know what I was thinkin'."

The sky darkened, and wind picked up from the south. Rain spattered the ground with huge drops. We passed the Rialto movie hall and ducked down into Ace Billiards, where he let me buy him lunch. Outside, the sudden squall battered the streets. We sat at the counter, where he ate two burgers with extra pickles. I tried smoothing things over with the counterman, after walking out last night without paying for my Coke, but he didn't know anything about it. The bowling alley was quiet. Charlie checked his wristwatch repeatedly.

"Can we get back up to your office?" he said. "I think I'll get my water bag and head home."

We slipped out the back door into the alley and ran to my building. I stopped at the door to shake the water off my jacket.

"You wear a gun?" Charlie exclaimed.

"Tool of the trade, I'm afraid."

Footfalls sounded above on the stairs, heading our way. I slipped the jacket on again and we both looked up from the landing. A short man in a tan suit rounded the switchback, almost knocking Charlie over. He would have, too, if Charlie had been three feet shorter and a hundred pounds lighter.

"Watch yourself, pal," he said before he saw me.

It was Agent Tompkins, alone this time. His jacket was open, and he wore a green bow tie that was off-center from his neck.

"Hammer," he said, backing up slightly and rubbing his hands nervously. "Glad you're here. I was just up at your office lookin' for you."

He seemed flustered at Charlie's size, waiting for an introduction.

"I wasn't there," I said. "What can I do for you now?"

"I need to be goin'," Charlie said, talking across us. I handed him my keys so he could get his bag. I showed him twice which key opened my office door.

"Nice to meet ya," he said to Tompkins.

"Just leave it open," I yelled up the stairs after him.

Tompkins leaned on the handrail and spoke in quiet tones. "I understand you had the pleasure of entertaining Bosko Cvito in your office for a few minutes. Last night, was it?"

"Who told you that?" I asked. He could've heard it through Jim or Tex. Maybe he worked the listening device. We stood on the first landing, trying to maintain a comfortable space between us. He looked out the tiny window over the alley that threaded to Main. It was still pouring rain.

"You want to go back upstairs?"

He nodded. We started up. "Not a day off for you?" he asked.

"What's a day off?" I said.

"Me too."

Charlie slammed the door upstairs and bounded down to where we stopped on the edge, not wanting to get knocked over.

"Thanks again, Hammer," he said, handing me my keys. "It was already open."

"Getting careless, Jack?" said Tompkins. Lightning flashed outside.

"I thought I locked it," I said. "You need an umbrella, Charlie?"

"I'll be okay."

Upstairs, we went inside, and I opened the blinds all the way. Clouds and rainfall muted the sunlight. Thunder crashed and the wind blew.

"Looks like we just slipped the parade in," I said. "Did you see any of it?"

Tompkins shook his head. He sat down across from me and leaned the chair back on two legs, again.

"Can't guarantee that chair won't buckle."

He lowered it and sat straight. "I'm here following up on this Cvito thing," he said. "There's a rumor that you got your hands on one of Bosko's inventions, something called a Cvito Device."

"Who told you that?"

He answered with a shrug, crossed his legs, and held onto his kneecap; in case it was going to pop off. Then he started picking white flecks off his fingernails, waiting for my reply.

"Well, rumor's wrong," I said, truthfully. "I don't have it." Jonny did. I didn't say more.

Was the FBI listening in?

"The thing is, Hammer, I stopped by to let you know that this device that Cvito put together has been classified top secret. Sounds like Bosko lost track of it, so if you come across it, I'll need to come and collect it; get it back in the hands of the proper authorities. It's not yours to sell to the highest bidder, or whatever your plans are."

"Feel free to take a look around," I said, sweeping my hand around the room. "Like I said, I don't have it."

He stared at me, studying my face.

"You ever heard of a group called KOS?"

I couldn't hide the surprise.

"*Kontraobavesajna Sluzba*," he said. "The Serbian Counterintelligence Service."

"Just rolls off your tongue, does it?"

"Your buddy, Marko, is one of 'em."

"Who?"

"Marko. He runs a group of— What I'm telling you now is classified and needs to stay secret. You understand?"

"About Marko?"

"We're pretty sure he was here last night too."

"Where?" I asked, looking around. The surprise on my face was genuine this time.

"Don't be coy, Jack. You already told us you'd seen him in Bosko's house. Word on the street says he's hired you to flush out Bosko. Marko's real name is Markosivich, and he's connected somehow to KOS."

"Who is this 'Word' character that knows so much?"

"Smart. Look, they're here trying to get their hands on Bosko, a matter of national pride, so don't be foolish around them. They're dangerous. We heard they'd try to get in touch with you. I mean, since Yasa hired you to find Bosko already. Anyway, Marko's gone missing now too."

"Wait, Marko *and* Bosko?" I asked.

He didn't answer.

"And now you're looking for some device?"

"That's right," he said, looking away. "I might be able to arrange a cash reward if you come across it ..."

"One of a kind, is it?"

Outside in the hallway, I heard footsteps. Jonny opened the door and stepped inside, winded.

"Sorry, Jack. Didn't know you had company."

Tompkins stood up and turned to greet him. "I was just leaving."

When Tompkins' back was turned, I made a motion to Jonny to zip his lips.

"This is Agent Tompkins," I said. "With the FBI."

Tompkins stuck out his hand. "And you are ...?"

"Jonny. Jack and I share an office, over at Auerbach's." He wiped his palm on his thigh before gripping the FBI agent's hand.

Tompkins stepped back and looked him over.

"Thanks for lettin' me borrow the car," Jonny lied. "Mom's okay. She thought she was having a stroke, but it turned out to be nothing."

He tossed the car keys to me as Tompkins moved toward the door.

"Remember what I said, Hammer. Top secret. And if you run across it, or anything like it, call me. You still have my card?"

"Someplace. Hey, why aren't you guys lookin' for my girlfriend, Sadie? She's missing too, you know. Isn't that something you guys should be lookin' at?"

"I heard about that," he said and coughed. "Somebody else is lookin' at it. 'Course, maybe she just found herself a new boyfriend."

It was a cheap shot. He stopped at the door, listening to the rain.

"You don't mind if I take the umbrella, do you?"

Before I could answer he'd taken a gray one from the can by the door, the one my mother had given me last Christmas. It had my name engraved in the bone handle. My face must've turned red with anger.

"Relax, Jack. I'll make sure it gets back to you."

72

To Jonny's House
2:30 p.m., Saturday, July 24, 1948

When the door shut, I waved Jonny into the back room and opened the fire-escape window a crack. Cool air from the rainstorm washed inside.

"Now what?"

"Something's off here," I said. "Tompkins was one of the FBI agents who came by on Wednesday askin' about Bosko."

"So?"

"So, why would the FBI be coming around askin' me where Bosko was, if they already had him under Tex's wing?"

"Maybe he's gone off again, playin' pool somewhere. Or maybe they were just checking on you, seeing if you'd stepped back."

I considered it. "Maybe, but his questions were awfully pointed. He specifically said they were tryin' to locate Bosko. Now he's askin' about the Cvito device. And they've been keepin' an eye on Marko, when they can find him. And then, of all things, he brought up

KOS! He said it's some eastern European spy outfit, and Marko is involved!"

"So, call the FBI office. Check him out."

"They won't tell me anything."

"They might. Don't tell 'em what you want. Look, I need you to run me home before I end up as single and sorry as you are."

"You want to call Betty from here?"

"No," he said, with a short, self-conscious laugh.

We walked back up to the front, locked the door and headed down the stairs.

"You sleep on a cot, in a room with a sink and a toilet?" he asked.

"The store could've paid me a little better," I said.

I held my arm out and stopped him on the second floor. The dentist was gone, his office dark. I walked down the hallway, waved Jonny to follow and checked the corner door frame for the paper plug. It was on the floor.

I checked my gun and knocked.

"What're you doing?" he asked.

"I want to show you something," I said. I felt my pockets for the lock-pick.

"I thought we were leaving."

"We are," I said, "but I figured you'd want to see the radio."

"When I get home, I'm gonna blame you for everything," he said, hanging back.

Nobody answered the knock. I inserted the pick tools and swung the door open slowly. Jonny moved up and looked over my shoulder.

The radio was gone.

The red and white wires were gone.

The hole in the ceiling plaster was filled in.

The three chairs were gone.

Only the card table remained.

I pushed past him, ran upstairs, and opened up my office again.

The Indian print hung on the wall, crooked. I pulled it down and set it on the floor. That hole was filled in too, unpainted. The plaster was still damp and soft. I could smell it.

I made sure I locked up again.

"Where's my car?" I asked, meeting him on the stairs.

"Out back, where you wanted it."

He followed me down and back outside, in the rain. We headed north up the alley.

"They pulled the radio?"

"And patched the plaster," I added.

"You know what that means?"

"Somebody's closing off loose ends," I said. "They must think they're close and pulled it out while I was at the parade."

The rain was letting up, clearing over the lake.

"You didn't see what Tompkins was driving?" I asked.

"Tompkins? You think—?"

"Didn't you notice? His jacket wasn't even wet. He must've been inside the building before the parade ended, because that's when the rain started. That jacket would have been rain-spotted."

"Then somebody was with him," Jonny said. "They probably took the radio and left him to finish up."

I drove east then south to where Jonny and his wife lived in a small, red-brick apartment.

"I need to use your phone," I said.

Jonny's wife stood with her arms crossed and stared hard at me as I went through the front door.

"Wipe your feet," she said.

The telephone sat on a small table near the kitchen.

"Federal Bureau of Investigation, how may I direct—"

"Do you have an Agent Tompkins there?" I cut in.

There was a pause.

"I'm sorry, sir," she said. "How can I direct your call?"

"Agent Tompkins. Can you connect me with him?"

"I'm sorry, sir, there's actually no one else in the office at the moment. We're in Utah and they're celebrating a—"

I hung up. *Where did Tompkins go?*

"I hate to ask this of you, Jonny, because I know you need the sleep, but could you call my uncle for me? Tell him to check out this Tompkins guy? I'll get back with you later."

He nodded.

"You have the notebook?"

"It's behind your sun visor, with the letter."

"Sorry, Betty," I said, rushing past her again in the front room. "It's all my fault, go easy on him."

"Dammit, Jack, that doesn't make it okay."

I jumped in my car and headed west to the Animal Product Waste Company, to pay a call to Huang Chou Li and his daughter.

73

Animal Product Waste Company
3:35 p.m., Saturday, July 24, 1948

The address the Chinese kid gave me led me to a corner house with white clapboard siding and gray shutters. The front yard was a well-tended rose garden, without grass. A two-story garage and a gravel drive sat out back.

Nobody was on the street.

I jumped out and hurried up the concrete walkway, smelling the roses.

There wasn't a bell, so I knocked. A face came to the door, not Chinese.

"Hello!" I said, asking for Chou Li.

The face eyed me with suspicion. "Does he owe you money, too?"

"No, nothing like that," I said. I was getting used to long stares at doorways.

"In the back," he said. "Over the garage."

The garage door was up, and a small apartment spread over the top of the car park below. The truck inside said ANIMAL PRODUCT

WASTE COMPANY on the side. I headed up the outside stairway and knocked on this door too. A fly landed on the screen.

From behind it, I heard a voice speaking Chinese.

"I'm looking for Huang Chou Li," I called.

An aging Asian man in a gray work shirt appeared, stroking the stubble on his chin.

"What you want?" he asked. "You need pick up some bones?"

"Not right now," I said. "I'm a private detective. I'm looking for somebody you may have seen, and I understand you parked your truck in an alley behind Main Street last night."

He looked at me like I was speaking a foreign language. I tried again, slower this time.

"Who told you that?" he said. His manner was short and defensive. "I was working."

"Nobody said you weren't," I answered. Someone moved in the shadows behind him. "Look, I just need information. I don't care what you were doing there."

I reached in my pocket and came up with a fin. He watched it carefully.

"Two nights ago," I said. "A girl, dark hair. This girl?"

I showed him Sadie's photograph. He shook his head and squinted. "No."

"Maybe your daughter saw something?"

He opened the door, took the photo, and passed it behind him, saying something in Chinese.

"She not see this girl."

"You're sure? She was kidnapped, right from that same alley where you park. Maybe two guys put her in a car?"

He said something else in Chinese. The girl stepped up.

"My father said I may speak with you directly. We work in that alley every night. On Thursday night, we pulled in there around seven," she said in perfect English. "I didn't see any woman, though. I'm sorry."

"How about last night?" I asked. "Did you see any people last night in the alley? Later on, after ten? I mean, besides the guy chopping up chickens."

More Chinese discussion filled the moment.

"No," she said. "It was raining, so it wasn't a night we would've seen much anyway."

The father stepped forward again. "Last night I was feeling so sick," he said, looking at the money again. "I needed some sleeping. Maybe she saw something?"

He was smiling, but he didn't seem happy.

Sleeping it off?

"Something unusual?" I queried. "In the alley?"

"We only pick up bones," he said.

I considered the Lincoln. What was it buying this time? He reached for it with tobacco-stained fingers and held it to the light as though it could be counterfeit.

"There was *one* odd thing," the girl said. "There was this big truck, just sitting in the alley. Last night it was there pretty late." She looked back at her father, like she was betraying a secret. "Sometimes our Friday nights go till after midnight."

"What kind of big truck?"

"Bigger than ours, like a box truck. Big trucks don't come back there much, especially after dark. It's a tight space, too hard to drive. But the last two or three nights, this big truck blocked the alley for an hour or more, and then left in a big hurry. Last night it was there late, until after ten."

"Can you describe it? Anything to help find it?"

She thought for a moment. "Day and night," she said. "It said, day and night, in capital letters, on the side. I remember because the first night I saw it, the sun was still up. That would've been Thursday."

I said thanks and ran out to my car, repeating over and over, "Day and night, day and night, day and night ..."

When I got to my office, I ran up the stairs. At my desk, I took out the telephone directory.

Day and Night, Day and Night ...

It only took a minute to locate a business named Day and Night Storage Garage. That had to be it, on Richards Street, west of Main.

I called over to Jonny's house. Betty answered.

I hung up, then called again.

"Jack, I know it's you," she said, "so, cut it out!"

I didn't hang up.

"Jonny's asleep," she said. "You remember how it used to be, when you worked all night?"

"Okay, Betty, but this is life and death. I wouldn't be bothering him if it wasn't."

"Everything's life and death with you, Jack. Remember when you thought that dog had rabies?"

"Yeah, but—"

"And just last week you were chasing after that imaginary gold mine?"

"It's not imaginary."

I heard a voice behind her, and Jonny came on the line. "What is it, Jack?"

"Did you get a hold of Jim?"

"Yeah, and he wasn't in a good mood," Jonny said. "Chief made him stay in the office to deal with missing kids, from the parade."

"What about Tompkins?"

"Zero there. He did tell me the agent-in-charge here is some guy named Pocelli. Italian guy, transferred from Boston. Jim said he's been tryin' to catch up with you all week. This Pocelli guy, I mean. And get this: FBI says Bosko's missing again."

"No surprise, that's what Tompkins said. What happened?"

"Last night, when they left your place? They never made it back to Bingham. Nobody's seen him since. Same goes for your friend, Tex. Jim was asking me if I knew anything, because the cops never saw 'em."

"Maybe Jim never called it out. You didn't mention the listening device?"

"Never saw it," he said. "But look, I'm fading here. I'm not used to this schedule so I'm hanging up. You better call your uncle though, right away."

"I'm gonna try to talk him into checking something out with me."

Jonny hung up and didn't ask what.

74

Day and Night Storage
5:05 p.m., Saturday, July 24, 1948

Jim picked up on the first ring.

"Where in the Sam Hill have you been, Jack? You promised to be in here hours ago."

"Yeah, but just listen to me for a second," I said. "I think I know where Sadie is."

Silence. And then, "Where would that be?"

"Over at a garage on Richards Street. Maybe Bosko's there too. I heard he went missing again."

Through my office window, I could see sunshine spotting the eastern mountains. I switched on the desk fan to get some air moving.

"What's this about Richards Street?" he asked.

I told him about the Chinese girl, the moving truck in the alley, and how both nights it made a sudden exit—the same nights people disappeared from the same alley.

"Did she see anybody bein' pulled in the truck? Any suspicious people close by?"

"No."

"Did she see Sadie in the alley?"

"No."

"Bosko?"

I could see where this was heading. "No."

"So, this is just a guess?"

"If that's what detective work is ... it can't just be a coincidence," I said. "Big trucks don't wait around back in that alley. Especially not at night. They could've snatched Bosko and Tex and thrown them both in the truck and driven off. Sadie too. Nobody would know."

"So, you think they just sat back there in the alley, waiting to snatch somebody?"

"Not just somebody. Sadie. And Bosko ... they camped out on my doorstep, waiting for somebody to show up."

He paused. "Okay, why in your alley? And why not you?"

"Look, we don't have time to argue this out now. You need to get somebody over there!"

"What makes you think they took 'em to this particular garage?"

"The girl said the name panel on the truck was DAY AND NIGHT STORAGE."

"That business closed up a few months ago."

"Then it's even more likely," I said. "We're just wasting time, talking about it."

"You want me to move my people based on your guess? By the way, what's this about some FBI agent named Tompkins?" he asked.

"Did you check him out?"

"The guy we're dealing with is Agent Pocelli. Why?"

"Because this guy, Tompkins, showed up on Wednesday asking questions, him and his partner. He showed me his badge and everything, fine. But the more I think about him, the more I think something's not right about him. For one thing, why would he ask me where Bosko was? The FBI had him workin' out in Bingham. Look, I'll explain it all later. You need to scramble some guys right now to go over to this storage garage on Richards Street and cover the exits."

"Based on your hunch and what some fourteen-year-old Chinese girl said about a truck being back in the alley? That's pretty thin, don't you think?"

"Well, you got a better idea? What else are your guys doin'?" I asked. "Looking for speeders? Crackin' down on illegal fireworks?"

"Maybe they're out looking for witnesses that were supposed to come by and give statements but never did."

"Right. So, what you're saying is, they're not out finding Sadie? Fine, I'm goin' on my own. I think it's worth looking at, so unless you have a better idea, I'm headed there now."

I imagined his face turning red.

"You stay put, son. I'll see who I can raise on the radio first."

I hung up as hard as I could, hoping he could feel it on his end.

Marko flashed across my brain. I'd been ignoring him since I walked away from his car out in Sugar House. I wondered how much to believe of what Tompkins said. Maybe Marko was the one calling the shots.

Jim called back a minute later and said he had two patrol cars stopping by to check out Day and Night. I expect he tried telling me not to go over there, but we were having a bad connection.

"Jack!" he shouted on his end.

My fingers pushed the hook button over and over. "Are you there?" I asked, then hung up.

Sunlight spread itself across downtown and the rain clouds pulled back again. Downstairs, I sat in my car and saw the gas tank was less than a quarter full. Just like my wallet.

I put on a hat and half-walked, half-ran to Richards Street two blocks away.

I passed the seed store on the corner and stopped on the sidewalk at the entry ramp to the garage. A cardboard sign in the window said CLOSED. Gas pumps stood to the side, offering Ethyl and Regular on workdays. The guard shack at the gate was empty and locked. One of the roll-up entry gates was partially open.

I felt for the gun in my shoulder holster.

I walked up the ramp, ducked under the open gate, and took a look around. Skylights at regular intervals allowed daylight down through a plastered ceiling into the parking garage core. Windows in the back wall opened out over a graveled parking lot that emptied out between buildings on West Temple. The entire floor was empty. Doors on the far end entered empty business offices.

My footsteps echoed between concrete floor and plastered ceiling. When I out through a barred window, two trucks caught my eye in the alley behind the garage, down a half level and even with the street. They both had DAY AND NIGHT stenciled on the sides.

I walked back outside. The café next door was dark, closed for the holiday. I leaned on a parking meter while I waited, counting off minutes on my watch.

I got to twenty before anybody showed up.

75

Day and Night Storage
5:55 p.m., Saturday, July 24, 1948

Two cops pulled up in a black and white. They paused at the curb, then backed up the ramp part way, stopping where a wooden arm blocked their way.

"Did you put a car on the other side?" I shouted.

"What other side?"

"Where the lot opens out to West Temple."

A green Buick cruised down the street, its passengers staring. The older cop lost interest in me and walked down the ramp. A gray, pre-war Packard pulled up. My uncle got out and walked over to us.

"Put him in my car," he said to the cop next to me.

"What! No, I'm goin' in with you."

"You're not, Jack. We're gonna handle this. The last thing I need is your bullets flying around me and my guys. And I don't want you disappearing again before I can get your statement. Just sit tight."

"Your guys sure took their time."

He glared at me. "A little thanks should be in order," he said. "You're lucky we even bothered to show up."

The first cop walked me to the back seat of his car.

Another black and white pulled up, consulted with Jim, and went around to the other side of the block. A fourth car pulled up and stayed at the far end of the street.

Jim and two other plainclothes cops checked their weapons, kept them ready, and went inside. Everybody else checked their watches.

In the back seat, I pulled my own gun out of its holster, removed the shells from the mag, and dropped them in my pocket. I pulled back the action to make sure I hadn't left one in the chamber by mistake. I stared at the swastika on the eagle on the grip.

This has been an unlucky gun, for all its owners.

I slipped it back in the holster and waited. Jim was right. My bullets flying around would only confuse things.

I steeled myself for the worst. I imagined Sadie lying dead, a cord tied around her neck. I imagined a gunfight with Jim getting killed, Sadie getting shot, and all the cops getting killed. I imagined Bosko and Tex flying out through the glass of one of the second-story windows. I even imagined Marko inside with a band of Yugoslav fighters.

With the windows rolled down, a breeze floated through the back seat. I took off my jacket. My back was wet with perspiration, and my shirt stuck to my skin.

I was restless.

I opened the door. Every few moments a call crackled on the mobile radio in Jim's front seat.

I stepped back outside, feeling gravel through the sole of my right shoe.

And then, there was Jim, carrying something. From a distance, it looked like a rifle. When he got closer, I could see he was carrying a paper sack and my umbrella with the bone handle.

76

Public Safety Building
7:00 p.m., Saturday, July 24, 1948

"You recognize this?" he asked, holding out the umbrella.

"I loaned it to Tompkins a couple of hours ago."

He held my eyes with his for a moment. "Be honest with me. Have you been inside this building lately?"

"What? No! I told you—"

"Tompkins, huh?"

He kept staring, trying to see the truth in me. "Well, there wasn't much in there. Empty cigarette packs, some butts, and what's left of somebody's dinner. Otherwise, the place was empty."

"That can't be right," I said. "They must've been in there. Somebody camped in there, right?"

"Could have been hobos."

"Not hobos. The umbrella says it was Tompkins. They coulda had Sadie in there."

"Says you."

"Whad'ya mean, 'says you'?"

"Get in the car, Jack."

"What?"

"Get in the car. We're just gonna go take your statement, officially."

"What does that mean?" I asked, as I slammed the door.

"It means that everybody here came because you called me, and I called them. For this? Hobo litter? Sadie's still missing, and nobody's run across this character Tompkins but you."

"You were supposed to check him out," I said.

He shook his head at that. "Just like you claimed Bosko was in your office last night, but when I got there, he was already gone. Him and his friend with the .44."

"They were there," I said. "I swear it. You could check it out with your buddies at the FBI. And you heard Bosko was gone again, right? You never picked him up on the Bingham Road?"

"You're the one who said he headed that way. My guys never saw him."

I shook my head.

"The Kennecott boys called today," he said. "Bosko's supposed to be involved in some big test tonight. They think you've done something to foul it up."

"Everything happened just like I told you," I barked back.

"Did it? Like when Sadie went missing, right after the two of you had a big fight. In fact, it was right after she went on a date with another guy—"

"Now wait just a doggone minute, we talked about this."

"We did," he said, "and I've been giving it some thought."

"But I gave you the ransom demand."

"Which isn't exactly a ransom note, and nobody has even verified is real. For all we know, you just made that up to cover yourself and conveniently handed it to me like some get-out-of-jail-free card."

"You can't seriously think I did that?"

"No, but Detective Nichols went out to Bingham and found out you were in a bar with some other guy's wife. What would Sadie's mother think? Geez, what's your mother gonna think? And there's that incident last Wednesday with Bosko's house catching fire while you were there. You got yourself fired from a steady job over that one. And to start it all, you're the one who found Yasa dead in her bathtub."

"So, you think I'm some evil mastermind?" I asked.

He was silent for a minute.

"No," he said. "I've known you your whole life. I want to believe everything you say. But when you add it all up ... I told you before, I think you've been holding out on me and the department. I've tried to give you the room to be your own kind of guy, to spread your wings. Maybe I gave you too much room. Maybe you're just mixed up in things you can't handle."

"But why would I be doing all this? Me and Sadie—you know we have a great relationship."

"Don't you mean *had*?"

"Then what's my motive?"

"You tell me, Jack. Bad judgment? Attention? Some new girl-friend?"

I shook my head. "We're wasting time. Sadie's still missing."

He pulled into a "POLICE BUSINESS ONLY" parking spot, out front of the Public Safety Building. I left my hat in his car.

"Let's go in and get this over with," he said, glancing at his watch. "I ought to be home with Edna and the neighbors right now, having a barbecue on the patio."

Up half a flight, I sat down in an oversized leather chair in his office. I took off my jacket and threw it on one of the spare chairs. Jim had a picture of Edna in a silver frame on his desk. He handed me a pad and a pencil.

"Write it all down," he said. "And don't be leaving stuff out this time."

The door opened. Detective Nichols walked in and sat on the edge of Jim's desk.

"Well, well, well ... Look who's here doing his paperwork."

"Shut it," said Jim, looking over. "Just make sure he gives us a full accounting. I'll be back later." He was holding his hat.

I sat up straight in the chair. "What do you mean, you'll be back later?" I asked. "Where are you going?"

"It's a holiday, Jack. I'm gonna spend what's left of it with Edna, and then I'll come back here and figure out what to do with you, and what else to do about Sadie. By the book."

Nichols couldn't suppress the smile on his face, sucking on a toothpick. "What if he tries to leave? Can I shoot him?"

Jim turned on him, red-faced. "Cut the crap, Detective, or I'll have somebody else in here doin' your job."

"But—"

"Cuff him to the chair if you're worried about him getting away somewhere," he said.

"Wait a minute," I said. "You can't do that. Am I under arrest for something?"

"Jack, I keep trusting you and you keep disappearing on me. I still have plenty of questions that need clearing up, and I don't really want to put you in a holding tank, so just go along with me on this. At least until I get back. I think you can deal with it until then. Maybe I'll bring you a burger or something."

"I'm not hungry. What's everybody doin' about Sadie?"

"That's a great question," said Nichols. "We're hoping you'll give us the answer."

"Keep him in my office," Jim said. "I don't want him out there talking with anybody else until we know exactly what he knows."

"You left-handed by chance?" Nichols said.

He walked over and slipped the cuff around my left wrist and snapped it tight to a steel rail on the side of the chair.

"You're making a mistake here. This is putting Sadie in danger … more danger, I mean."

"Quit blaming everybody else, Jack," my uncle said. "I've been trying things your way, following your leads, but nothing's come of it. Just write it all down, maybe we'll find some way to help you."

"Uncle Jim," I said, resorting unashamedly to family. "I'm being completely honest here. I'm not supposed to say anything, but whoever has her is gonna give me instructions for an exchange, later."

They looked at each other, shaking heads.

"Jack, an hour ago you said we were gonna catch 'em at the garage," Jim said.

"And they were there. You guys were just too late."

"So, I guess you were in touch with them while I was in the warehouse looking around?" Jim asked. "And now they want you to do an exchange? With what? Your mysterious device?" There was almost a sadness in his gaze. "Better hold on to his gun."

Nichols walked over, slipped it from the holster, and pulled back the slide.

"Sorry Jack, but you won't be needing it tonight anyway," said Jim.

"It's empty," Nichols said, looking up. "You carry an unloaded gun?" He held it up and scowled at the symbols on the grip. "Don't go nowhere."

He laughed to himself as he closed the office door.

"You guys are making a mistake!" I shouted, but it latched before I could get it all out.

77

Public Safety Building
8:15 p.m., Saturday, July 24, 1948

The walls of his office were covered with honorary plaques, awards, and pictures of Jim with political big shots. The bag of trash from Day and Night sat on his desk. A leather-framed blotter was covered with telephone messages, a brass desktop lamp at its edge.

My chair wouldn't budge. I strained at the hardwood floor with my feet, but it was bolted down.

The pad of lined paper was brand new. I didn't write anything. I reached in my pocket and pulled out the two thin, steel lock-picks that had helped me into the office below mine.

Nichols surprised me and walked back inside. He sat on the edge of Jim's desk again, pulled out his nail clippers, and examined each fingernail, trimming some.

"You smoke, Hammer?" he asked.

"No."

"Me neither."

His right foot didn't touch the floor.

"But speaking of smoke," he said, "those mining boys out in Bingham were smokin' under the collar when they found out how you'd pulled the wool over their eyes!"

How long had he been working out that little gem?

"You about done with that confession?" He kept his eyes on his own hands.

"Sure, I wrote it all out in invisible ink here, about how I shot Lincoln."

He looked over and I caught his eyes with mine, diverting his attention while I slowly slid the lock-pick back into my right pocket. He didn't like my brand of humor. It brought him close, where he squatted in front of me.

"You think you're hot stuff? You think you're a better cop than anyone here? Better than me, better than your uncle? What've you ever done?"

He was close enough I could have stabbed the pencil in his eye.

Instead, I picked it up and started writing.

He knocked it from my hand. "You know what? Your uncle ain't here now," he spat. "Who's gonna give you cover for all your loose talk?"

"What do you want from me?"

"I don't want anything from you" he said, "except to make sure you stay chained up long enough to teach you a lesson about pretending to be a cop."

He stayed down low, balanced on his toes, his left arm resting on Jim's desk.

"You wanna hit me?" he asked, turning his chin my way. "You got a free hand. Go ahead, right there on my jaw. Take a swing. I hear you're a tough guy."

He tapped my cheek with two fingers. He tapped it again, harder. I knew what he was doing, trying to get me to hit him, so he could feel good about handing me a beating. He could do it anyway, at least while I was handcuffed, but he held himself in check.

I wasn't in near the trouble Sadie was, so I focused on her. He reached over and slapped the side of my face again and stood up.

"I thought so. I'll be back later, and you better have something for me to read."

He turned and headed back to the office door.

"I can't write without the pencil," I called.

He stopped, picked it up, and threw it at me. It landed on the floor at my feet.

"Pick it up," he said, smiling, and slammed the door behind him.

Instead, I pulled out the lockpick and went to work. It was awkward, working with one hand chained to the chair, but the cuffs were the same make as mine.

I had them off in minutes.

I slipped my jacket on, walked over to the office door, and locked it from the inside, taking care not to show myself through the hazy glass where Jim's name was painted. I'd been in here plenty of times, but never in handcuffs. Kneeling behind the desk, I used his telephone to call over to Jonny's place. Nobody picked up.

I moved the blinds and peered out the back window, behind his desk. It opened ten feet above the impound lot. I slid up the sash, climbed over Jim's credenza, and hung from the sill. I dropped into the gravel lot and crept from car to car, making my way to the exit. The impound lot was bounded by buildings with only one way out, and no gate. Lights were off or blinds closed in most offices bordering the lot.

Somebody was still at the guard shack.

"Excuse me," I said.

"You gave me a start," said Kissell, turning around. "I didn't see you standing there."

"You have a long shift!" I said, as surprised as he was. "Listen, my uncle didn't drop his badge down here by chance?" It sounded lame, but it was the first thing that popped in my head. "When he was down here earlier, I mean."

"His badge? You mean, his wallet?"

"Nope, he said badge."

"You lose your hat too?" he asked, picking up the telephone while rummaging around in his desk drawer. "How did you get in there?"

"You know what?" I said. "Forget it. If you haven't run across either one by now, they've got to be somewhere else."

"You want me to check up front?" He held the handset up for me to see.

"Don't bother, I'm headed up to his place right now for a barbe-cue, so I'll let him know."

I tapped twice on the counter and walked out onto the sidewalk whistling. I headed east and away from my office. As soon as I was out of his sight, I doubled back across town. I didn't take time to go to my office upstairs. When Nichols made it back into Jim's office, he'd be sending a black and white to cruise past my place. More than likely, he'd come in person.

I had only minutes to get my car and drive away from the area. I rummaged for my keys under the front seat, started the engine, and headed south.

The notebook fell into my lap when I adjusted the sun visor. I picked it up and put it in my jacket pocket, opposite my wallet.

Traffic was heavy near Liberty Park as people headed home from the holiday festivities with kids hanging out car windows. The evening wound down, waiting for fireworks. I detoured, taking the long way through empty neighborhoods to Jonny's place before circling back. Two boys next door were lighting sparklers with a candle and throwing them into the street.

I knocked, twice. There was nobody around back either.

The Karrick Building would be the first place the cops would head. After that, they'd almost certainly widen the search to include my old office at Auerbach's. Nothing I could do about that.

I needed my car to get to whatever rendezvous point the kidnappers dictated. They'd want the exchange to happen fast, before any police or FBI agents could move into place and cut off escape routes. I decided to risk parking on Exchange Place, a narrow street connected to the back alley at Auerbach's. I backed into an empty spot at the curb and stepped out on the pavement.

Bright lights came around the corner, dragging another car behind them. It was a car I recognized, and it pulled into the space next to mine.

But his timing was terrible.

It was Marko.

78

Auerbach's Department Store
8:55 p.m., Saturday, July 24, 1948

He flung his car door open and slid off the bench seat into the street. He was hatless, a white bandage covering his right temple and crossing his hairline. The gun attached to his left hand was familiar, but unexpected. So was the cotton sling cradling his right arm.

"So," I said, "it was *you* all along?"

He seemed puzzled. "Why do you say, 'it was you'?"

"You sent me a letter, to be here at nine."

"Jack," he said, raising his sling. "Have I been writing letters? I think you have not been checking your mirror when you drive."

"What happened to your arm? And how did you drive here with one hand?"

He walked a few steps toward me, a slight limp slowing him down. His jacket had dried mud all down the front. He was shaking his head from side to side.

"What are *you* doing here, Jack? Because I said to you before, *I want to help you.* Do you not want my help anymore?"

"You think you've been *helping* me? What are you doing here?"

"Last night, I went to your office and waited outside. You came back with Bosko, so I planned to join you, but someone else followed you. Maybe is Russian, I thought. He climbed your fire escape and entered your office through your open window."

Tex.

Marko leaned against the taillight on the driver's side of my car. "Of course, I am so patient. I waited to see what could happen next."

"You didn't wait long," I said, checking my own watch.

"Perhaps not. In our business, we do much waiting and lose time. Don't you think so?"

"Lose track of time," I said.

His eyes were wrong. Him being here was wrong.

"Speaking of business," I said, "tell me about KOS."

His eyebrows raised in surprise, then lowered again in a dark scowl. "Start walking," he said. "I am losing some patience now."

I moved slowly.

"You're part of your country's secret police?"

"If it pleases you to think so."

"Where's your backup man?"

"Why should I need this 'backup man'?"

He was a difficult man to question. I asked him another one anyway.

"What happened," I asked, "when they came down back down the ladder?"

He smiled, like a man who takes pride in his work and is pleased when others notice.

"I came up behind him and they turned to see my gun, but ..." He touched his forehead. "Someone else was in shadow," he said. "Some bad people. Perhaps people you know? They knocked me to ground, and when I raise myself up from your pavement, they were gone, all of them. My arm ..." He raised it like a chicken wing and winced.

"That was you, under the ladder?"

"Shall we go inside now, Jack?" He motioned toward Auerbach's door with his pistol.

"Put the gun away," I said. "You don't need it here."

"Perhaps not, but it feels good in my hand, at least until I see who is inside. Maybe it is our friend Bosko? And his protector? You have hidden them here, I think?"

"That's what you've come up with?" I said. "You can't be serious."

"Did you tell Bosko about me?" he asked. "Perhaps you are hiding him away? For Russians?"

My head swirled as I wondered what might cause him to think so.

"I think I must also ask to take your own gun, Jack."

I lifted my jacket, so he could see my holster was empty. "The cops already took it. They'll be here any minute," I bluffed.

His eyes surveyed the alley like a caged animal hoping to escape, but he spoke calmly and kept a smile on his lips. "Please, Jack," he said. He pulled the slide back on the 37M and chambered a round. "Tonight, I am weary of difficulties. My head hurts, and I find it leaves me with short temper. I have paid money to you, and now I am asking you for your report."

He glanced backward as a car passed on the street behind him.

"Where is Bosko Cvito?" he said. "Inside?"

I shook my head. "I don't know where he is. You're the one who saw him leave last night. Maybe he went someplace with those Russians you've been avoiding?"

He seemed confused. "If that is true, perhaps Yasa overestimated you."

"And you and Yasa were ... what?"

He paused. "Go inside, now."

Lightning flashed far off, behind the mountains to the east. Rainwater had puddled in the alley. It splashed as I walked up to the side entrance and unlocked the door.

"You're crazy if you think Bosko is here," I said.

"Step back."

I did. He stuck his head in and glanced down the hallway both directions.

"You be first," he said. The pupils in his eyes were large and black. He stayed just out of my reach as we stepped inside.

I turned the worn iron doorknob on the office door. It opened easily. I stepped through and moved left, next to the empty coat tree. It gave Marko a good view of everything inside the small room.

Vic was sitting at Jonny's desk, getting ready to leave for the night. The radio was tuned to a ball game. He spun around in his chair and looked at me, then at Marko and his gun.

"Jack?"

His own gun was stuck in its holster, lying on the desk. Maybe it was instinct that made him reach for it. Maybe he just grabbed at the edge of the desk to steady himself on the swivel chair. Either way, it was enough for Marko. His 37M barked once in the small office, echoing into the hallway. The bullet hit Vic in the left side of his chest, under his arm. He looked down at the wound, then up at Marko and laid back.

I moved quickly, slamming the coat rack down hard on Marko's left wrist, knocking his gun to the floor. He followed it onto one knee, and it slid under the desk, out of reach. There was confusion in his face when he turned back over his shoulder toward me. We both lunged for Vic's gun, smearing blood on the desk and floor. Marko's right arm was caught in its sling, useless, but his powerful left arm swung back at me, blocking my approach. He positioned his body between me and the desk, struggling with one hand and the holster. Vic's body rolled over the desktop, spilling dark red blood across paperwork.

My eyes searched for something, anything, to use as a weapon. A letter spike holding yellow and white receipts caught my eye. I took it and stabbed it into the muscle around the back of Marko's neck. He howled and brushed it away, turning on me and throwing me back against filing cabinets. I fell to the floor and watched him wiggle Vic's gun from the holster, turning it my direction.

Another gunshot exploded in the small space and a second followed like an echo. My ears were ringing.

Marko stood still.

He dropped the gun and brought his hand up at an awkward angle to cover a small hole in his neck. Blood came from his mouth and between his fingers. His eyes widened with fear, and he stared at me with a word he'd never say forming on his lips.

As I scrambled back to my feet, Marko fell back against the desk behind him, slowly settling to the floor. He was desperately trying to stop the blood flowing from his neck.

Jonny stepped through the door, his face white, hands trembling.

I rolled Vic's body back in the chair and felt his neck for a pulse that I knew was gone. His eyes stared up at the ceiling fan. I brushed them closed.

Somewhere, a telephone rang.

I breathed in short gasps.

"It's for me," I said.

It rang three times before I picked up.

79

Utah State Fairgrounds
9:05 p.m., Saturday, July 24, 1948

I listened to the voice giving me instructions, then hung up and knelt down on the near side of Marko. Jonny squatted in the blood on my right. Marko slipped backward to the floor, drifting in and out of consciousness. I worked the sling from his damaged right arm, wiped Vic's blood from my hands, and handed the cloth to Jonny, who pressed it hard on Marko's neck.

"Call the cops," he ordered. I reached for the handset again, when a siren pierced the night, screaming that somebody else must've beat me to it.

I found Vic's gun where Marko dropped it, put it in my own empty holster, and reached across him for the car keys in his pocket. His breathing was shallow, gurgling from inside. He smelled like cigarettes and garlic and blood.

"Did you see anybody with him?" asked Jonny.

"No." I stood up and nervously shifted weight from one leg to the other, watching him work. The sirens closed in. He looked up.

"Get out of here," he said. "Find Sadie. I'll deal with this."

Blood soaked the white shirt on Vic's lifeless body.

"Fair Park stables," I said. "But give me some time—"

"Go! I've got my hands full here," Jonny said, irritated. "Don't count on more than a few minutes."

I ran down the alley to Marko's Hudson, pulled it around my old Ford, and headed west past the Mining Exchange. In the rear-view mirror, I could see the cops pulling in behind me. I gunned the engine, eased off the clutch, and drove west.

Gene Autry's Pioneer Days Rodeo Celebration was going to end soon, spilling thousands of people into the Fair Park parking lots and flooding surrounding streets with cars. When that happened, traffic in the area would slow to a standstill, and whoever had Sadie could melt away into the crowd unnoticed.

I crossed the train tracks on North Temple and fell behind three city buses, then swerved around them. A motorcycle cop waited for speeders on the downhill side of the viaduct, but Marko's car meant nothing to him. I passed by and pulled into the gravel lot south of the grandstand. Straw cowboy hats and blue jeans trickled out in twos and threes, people leaving early to beat the rush. Between showers, the bright lights tacked on rough wooden poles attracted yellow clouds of moths and mosquitoes. The announcer's voice rose and fell, echoing away into the darkness beyond.

"And now ... now ... now ... from Morgan ... Morgan ... Morgan ..."

People cheered in unison, roaring like waves falling on some distant shore. I hurried across the back of the stands to where livestock and cowboys passed time in rows of canvas tents and outbuildings. A string of bare bulbs illuminated each one. Riders in felt hats with paper numbers pinned to their backs brushed their horses, chewed tobacco, and kicked in the mud. Flies buzzed around the moist smell of manure and hay bales, and at the far end of the buildings, men loaded struggling bulls into trucks and cursed.

A piece of paper tacked to the second tent pole fluttered in a breeze and caught my eye.

HAMMER, it read in block letters. It was a Coliseum poster with a line drawing of the domed structure.

I turned left, facing the huge building across hundreds of parked cars. Somebody was there, watching for me. Watching to see if I showed up alone. Watching to see if I'd show up at all.

The Coliseum was a mass of dark brick, domed and foreboding. It sat in the parkway crisscrossed by walks and flower gardens. Two white Doric columns framed the entry and supported a massive arch at the building's front doors. Inside was an empty arena, meant for exhibiting livestock or watching roller derby. I stepped back around a corner, out of sight. My hand reached for the gray notebook filled with strange writing and complex calculations—the Cvito Device.

My leverage, for Sadie.

Jonny's words came back. *You're trying to do too much by yourself.* He was right.

Sweat dripped down my forehead in the humid, nighttime air. I ran my fingers across my hairline and shivered. I pulled Vic's gun out and checked for bullets. There were six in the magazine, one in the chamber. Not even a full clip.

I flipped through the book and tore two pages of numbers from the center, folded them in half, and stuck them in my shoe, under my left foot.

Insurance.

I took a deep breath. The Coliseum remained silent. I beat a jagged path across the gravel lot and stopped under the arch. Carved doors meant for giants stood side by side. One was ajar.

I pushed it open and stepped inside.

80

Utah State Fairgrounds
9:45 p.m., Saturday, July 24, 1948

There was only blackness.

I moved away from the opening, Vic's gun in my right hand. I felt the cold, plastered wall as I picked my way ahead with my left. My eyes adjusted, registering faint light in the upper dome from the rodeo grounds outside. My heart pounded.

"Hello!" I shouted, hearing a hollow, echoing return.

I moved through the entry hall at a snail's pace. Two stairways wound their way upward. I found one and slid sideways into the opening, settling behind a riveted steel column that gave me protection and a partial view of the darkened arena floor. Outside noises found their way inside as people left the grandstands and spilled into the parkway.

"Thank you for coming," said a voice from the blackness. "I believe you have something for us?"

The voice was thin, the accent undefinable. I couldn't tell where it came from, or whether I'd heard it before. Then there was silence.

"I need to see Sadie," I shouted. My echo died out before I got a response.

"You don't trust me?"

"Do I know you?"

The black, hollow cavern was silent for another moment.

"Don't try to be clever, Jack. You walked through the front door unharmed. Isn't that enough for you?"

My eyes searched the void and came up empty. "We both know you didn't shoot me because you don't know if I brought the Cvito Device with me."

"You wouldn't be here without it, I'm sure."

"How do you know the cops don't have this place surrounded?"

"Jack, please, we are wasting time." It could have been Tompkins' voice. If that was true, he couldn't afford to let any of us leave here alive.

"I want to see her first," I said. "I need to know she's okay."

There was silence again. A single row of overhead lights clanked on, gradually illuminating the Coliseum's dirt floor and the domed roof above. Most of the building remained in shadows. Bosko was there, sitting on a folding chair at the center of the dome, forearms on his thighs. His head looked down, to his feet. A quick check around the empty room showed me three other pairs of doors: one across the room and one at each end.

I still couldn't locate the voice.

"I can't see her," I called.

"In the top row," said the voice, moving further away.

At both ends of the upper deck, I could make out figures balancing on the backs of folding chairs. Sadie was one of them. I panicked seeing her like that. My throat tightened. A man was at the other end. It was Tex. They were fifteen rows up and at least a hundred yards apart.

A rope was wrapped around each of their necks, tied to a roof beam above. Their hands were free, and they wiggled back and forth, steadying themselves by clutching the rope stretched tight above their heads. They were trying desperately to stay balanced. What appeared, in the dim light, to be cloth gags covered part of their faces and stopped them from crying out.

"Hand it over, Jack."

"Tell me–" I said, as my voice cracked. "Tell me your plan here, first."

"You bring it out to Bosko. Once he verifies it's genuine—assuming it is genuine—he'll bring it to me, and we'll disappear out of your life for good. You'll be free to help your friends, and we'll all go on with our lives. Of course, if it's not genuine, or if you don't really have it, you can see enough of our setup here to guess the other possible outcome."

He referred to "we" and "our" enough times to convince me he wasn't alone, but I couldn't see anyone else. I glanced toward both ends of the building. Hostages were like uncashed bank checks, only holding value until the moment of the transaction. Once the deal was complete, I wondered how any of us would get out of the building alive.

"What happens to Bosko?" I asked.

"You don't care about Bosko."

"Let him go," I said.

"I think their legs are tiring, Jack."

Two separated hostages complicated things. I couldn't get to them both at once. I didn't know how long they'd been standing there, struggling not to lose balance, not to slip off the chair-back and strangle. Once they came off, when the rope pulled tight, they might have less than a minute of consciousness, followed by only a few minutes to live. Everything depended on their arm strength and how long they could keep the noose slack. I stepped from the alcove and tossed the notebook toward Bosko. It spun around and landed in the dirt, short of where he sat.

"Go ahead and pick it up," said the voice that now sounded more and more like the FBI agent.

Bosko followed instructions. His feet shuffled up dust and his head stayed down, as though he'd been warned not to look one way or the other. His hands were tied together in front of him. He bent over from his hips, awkward and stiff, then walked directly under a light and studied the pages.

"*Da*," he said. "This is it."

"Are you certain?"

Bosko flipped through the pages again, looked over at me and tapped on his wristwatch. I glanced at mine in the dim light: 10:24.

"*Da*," he said. "But—"

Sadie held both arms up, stretched out above her head and holding the rope. I made a move toward her, away from the cover of the column, and a gunshot exploded plaster on the wall a few feet from me. I jumped back. The muzzle flash had been on the upper deck at the south end, near Tex.

There *was* someone else here.

"Not so fast," said the voice. I could tell now that it came from the location of the shooter.

Bosko flinched, looking up at me again.

"Šta još?" said a second voice.

"Postoje neke stranice nedostaju," Bosko said. "There are pages missing."

I held my breath.

"Missing pages?" said the new voice.

There was an urgent conversation between them. Bosko spoke rapidly, looking over to me again.

"With their lives literally hanging in the balance, you thought we wouldn't know the difference?" said the first voice, anger rising. "Jack, all you had to do here was the right thing, and we could all walk away."

"Or we could all end up with a surprise shot to the head, like Krogue or like that kid at the Beeline," I said. "I've seen how you guys work. Nobody walks away but you. I needed some insurance, some leverage, in case this turned out to be a setup."

"*Leverage?!*" the second voice shrieked. "You think you are boss-man?!" High and to my left a chair clattered to the floor and footsteps echoed away. I stopped breathing and peered around the corner, in the dim light, as Tex wiggled at the end of the rope, hanging on with both hands. His body weight was pulling the noose tight on his neck.

"No!!" I screamed.

"Leverage, Jack?!"

Bosko stood up, looking first at me, then Tex, and back at me again. I glanced at Sadie. She was still standing on a chair-back.

For now.

She was the leverage that mattered most, what brought me here. And as long as the threat to her remained, my options were limited. My options were also what kept her alive till now.

"Okay! The pages are here! I have them, here."

"You killed him, Jack!"

I took off my shoe and threw it out to Bosko.

"They're right there," I said. "Inside the shoe. Look inside."

He picked it up and anxiously pulled out the small, folded sheets. He separated and stared at each one. I thought about my next move, if I had one.

Tex was grunting and straining.

"Dobro," Bosko agreed, glancing toward Tex. "They're here." His eyes then met mine and he tapped his watch before he turned away and walked to the exit doors.

What was he trying to tell me?

My part of the transaction was done. Sadie was still holding tight to the rope around her neck. I looked helplessly at Tex, flailing at the end of the rope cutting into his neck and shutting off blood to his brain. I had seconds to choose.

Sadie watched me run up the stairs, *the other way*, toward the dying man.

Another gunshot rang out, glancing off the concrete platforms. I dived behind a row of bleachers, brought Vic's gun up, and fired a shot in return. But before I could crawl to the upper deck, a bright flash outside was followed by the boom and echo of nearby thunder. All the lights in the building blinked out, and the borrowed light from parking lots vanished. I heard voices yelling. A smothering darkness reclaimed the huge room.

I stopped moving, then reached out and found the concrete top at the edge of the stairway. I moved ahead, feeling my way forward along the rail with my right hand, gun in my left.

Doors in the lower arena opened and closed. Sounds of a car cranking up in the parking lot mingled with sounds of an argument, followed by the short crack of a small-caliber gun sounding twice.

Muffled noises from Tex's throat drew me upward. I imagined his arm strength failing, the rope cutting into his neck. I crawled up the concrete risers like a blind man, one-by-one, reaching for him at the top row. I could hear his struggling close by and rose up.

"Sadie, hold on!" I shouted, still heading away from her in the blackness.

Suddenly, something smashed hard into the left side of my neck, knocking me backward. It had to be Tex. I caught myself on the floor, nearly rolling back down across risers in the dark. Vic's gun clattered down the concrete stairway to the arena dirt below.

I'd come too close to his kicking legs.

"Hey, it's *me*—Jack! Hold still!" I yelled and tried to regain my sense of direction. "I'm right here. Stop kicking! I'll grab your legs and hold you up."

I reached out with my left arm waving in the dark, seeking contact again. When I found his leg, he flinched. I moved close, circled my arms around both legs and lifted, taking pressure off his arms and neck. A split-second later his entire weight hit me as he released his grip on the rope. I could hear him sucking in air through his nose until he pulled the gag loose. From his unseen movements, I guessed he was pulling at the noose.

"You gonna be okay now?"

I couldn't hear anything from Sadie now. Outside, cars were starting.

"Don't leave," he stammered, his voice hoarse.

My pocketknife was in my car, parked across town.

"I don't have anything to cut the rope. Is it a slip knot?"

"I ... loosened it ... can't get it off."

"And I can't hold you up all night," I said. "I've got to let you go for a second. That chair must be close, something you can stand on. Can you hold on with your arms for another thirty seconds?"

He made a sound that I decided meant "okay." I eased him down, then searched on my hands and knees in the darkness without success.

"I'm losing—" he stammered.

I crawled back to his voice and stood up, finding his legs again to relieve his failing arms.

"Sadie!" I shouted. "Don't give up! I'll be there!" If she made a sound, I couldn't hear it over Tex's rough breathing.

A newsreel in my head played images of her hanging lifeless, arms limp and dead eyes staring at me. I pushed it away as best I could and focused on Tex's more immediate problems: the missing chair and the rope around his neck. I said a short prayer in my head.

Dear God, what now?

Above me, another metal clanking sound drew my eyes. A short row of lights began to glow, humming a low, monotone buzz. Dim, orange light clung to glass globes hanging below porcelain canopies. It wasn't much, but it was enough to outline the shape of the balcony edge. I turned Tex around and scanned the grandstand for the missing chair. It had to be close.

New voices came from the darkness, hushed and far away. Red lights flashed through the high windows onto the domed ceiling. White lights danced on the dirt below, flashlights sweeping the arena.

"Up here!" I shouted. "We're up here!" My voice echoed.

An unsteady beam found us, and another.

Seconds later the voices were clear, and more lights switched on overhead.

"You, up there! Don't move!"

"At the other end!" I shouted at the lights. "Sadie's at the other end!"

The sound of footsteps on the concrete steps echoed throughout the domed hall. I tried looking in her direction, but somebody grabbed me from behind and pushed me to the concrete floor. He cuffed my hands. I could see the chair now, collapsed on the deck. Somebody else saw it too and used it to help Tex down from the rope. I tried to listen to what was happening at Sadie's end of the building but couldn't piece the voices and noises together.

"Did they get her down?" I asked, lying on my belly, arms behind me.

No one answered, but someone shouted, "There's a gun down here, in the dirt!"

I turned my head. Tex was on his back, his chest rising and falling as he gasped for air. Somebody asked if he needed a doctor. Two men in suits stood me upright, not cops.

"Take his cuffs off," one said.

"Your name?" asked the other. I told him.

"Who did all this?"

"I don't know," I said. "They stayed hidden and ducked out the west doors when the lights went out. Did you get the girl down? Sadie? Is she okay?"

Shadows vanished as the lights came up. I watched her direction but couldn't see much. Policemen and suits gathered at the opposite end of the building. More car engines roared to life outside the building.

I heard somebody say, "She's down."

A wail of sirens started out softly, rising, then falling, far away.

"Stay put," one of the suits ordered. I knew he meant me.

I felt useless, just watching. I walked down a few concrete steps, but a uniformed cop stopped me. "You know better than that, pal," he said.

I asked again about Sadie and how she was doing. He didn't know anything. More lights came on. I paced nervously in a small circle. More cops showed up. I settled for watching from the overlook by the entrance while Tex first, then Sadie, rode down the concrete stairways and out on stretchers.

When they brought her close, I called to her.

She looked up at my voice but turned away.

"Sadie?!" I called again.

A tug on my arm pulled me back from the edge.

"Give her some time," Jim said. "Be glad she's safe."

"Easy for you to say," I mumbled. "You just get here?"

"I've been following your breadcrumbs."

I paced back and forth, anxious to follow her out. "Let me just go talk with her," I said. "I need to explain—"

"There'll be time for that later," he cut me off.

I grabbed one hand with the other and looked for a way out. "But he would've died," I said. "Tex would have died."

"If you say so."

"You think she knows that?"

He shook his head and left me alone again with the uniform. He walked over to talk with somebody I didn't recognize. The man wore a baggy suit and kept his hat on. Jim turned my way and pointed. The man in the hat nodded.

A few minutes later, Jim came back, and walked me out to his car. "FBI," was all I could get out of him. We drove in silence back to the station and parked out front, at the curb.

81

Public Safety Building
11:15 p.m., Saturday, July 24, 1948

We ended up in a small room on the second floor, not his office this time. There were two mismatched chairs and a small round table. Jim sat down in one and pulled out a pencil and a pad.

"Sit down, Jack."

I did.

"You know, I had a warrant ready to pick you up."

"For what? Making a fool out of that jackass, Nichols?"

He didn't answer right off but shook his head slowly.

"How about fleeing from a police officer, withholding information, being an accessory before and after the fact, impersonating a police officer, and maybe obstructing an ongoing police investigation? And as far as Nichols is concerned—"

"Hey, I had things handled. If I hadn't busted out of your office, who do you think would've gotten to Sadie in time? One of your guys?"

"Fair point, Jack, and probably the only one keeping you out of a very small cell right now."

"Yeah," I said under my breath, "because *these* accommodations are top drawer."

He faced me across the table, his jaw set.

"Why don't you just tell me what happened?"

"Which part?" I asked.

"The part that keeps you out of jail." His fingers were laced together, his eyes locked on me.

"What happened back there with Bosko?" I asked. "You caught up with 'em, didn't you?"

"Jack, I called in a favor tonight with the FBI. That was their crime scene. I told them you're my sister's kid and I didn't want to be the second guy to hear your story, so why don't you do the explaining tonight. If I need something clarified, I'll ask."

He seemed distant, tired. He tried to relax by leaning his elbows on the table and rubbing his eyes with his fingertips. He reached for his notepad.

"So, that's how it is?" I asked.

He nodded.

I turned away, scratching the back of my head. "Okay, so when Edna stopped by to talk about Bosko, I figured he was just some old man off on a bender," I said. "Maybe if I'd gone by to see Yasa on Monday night, things would have turned out different."

"And you think Bosko killed her," he said. "You already told me that, Jack. What I want to know is, what am I missing? Jonny told us one of the dead guys at Auerbach's was your pal, Marko, that he was lining up to shoot you?"

"Right. I went there to take a call from the kidnappers, like I told you. Marko showed up with his gun out, waving it and accusing me of hiding Bosko in the security office. Vic was there. He just twitched at the wrong time, so Marko shot him. Marko and I wrestled for his gun, and when he pointed it at me, Jonny showed up to cover my shift and shot him dead. Just in time, if you ask me."

Jim stopped writing to sharpen the pencil with his pocketknife. "What about those other two dead guys?" he said.

"I don't know anything about other dead guys."

"On the west side of the Coliseum?"

Bosko went out the west side doors.

"I heard shots there, after the lights went out, but I had my own problems."

He made pages of notes.

I explained how Marko hired me after Yasa's death. I told him about the second letter, the one that took me to Tiny's, and how I found the notebook in Bosko's workshop the night his house caught fire. "The notebook helped me find his place in the Avenues, where the landlady knew him as Zoric. I guess Yasa was there too."

"In the Avenues?"

I told him where and thought about the blue letter.

He stopped writing. "If Marko was only looking for Bosko, and not the device, you think he suspected Bosko for Yasa's death?"

"Count on it. He and Yasa were close. He told me we could find Yasa's killer, together, after we found Bosko. He used me to sniff out Bosko at a distance, but he never even mentioned the device."

Jim sat back and flipped through his notes. "How did you know Marko didn't have Sadie?"

"He'd already hired me to find Bosko. Why complicate things? Plus, his handwriting didn't match the first letter. And I'm pretty sure he was out in Bingham following me when Sadie disappeared, so I figured there had to be somebody else in the mix, somebody I didn't see."

"Until they showed up tonight."

"I still didn't see 'em. They used Bosko as a go-between, to verify what I brought was legitimate. Marko blamed everything on Russians ... Russian spies ... but I never met any."

"Except at the Beeline?" he said, rubbing two fingers along his lower lip.

"Okay, but whoever set up Sadie and Tex could speak Bosko's language. You should ask them."

"You heard multiple voices?"

"Mostly one, from a distance. I thought it might have been that FBI guy, Tompkins—"

"You're back to blaming Tompkins again?"

"Well, it sounded like him," I said. "There's too many coincidences with that guy."

"Just so you know," he said, "I got a call back on Tompkins. The FBI does have a guy named Tompkins, but he's not a Russian, and he's not connected to this case."

"Yeah, not officially connected. 'Course, he doesn't have to be from Russia to be on their payroll."

"Fair point," he said, pausing. "So, what does your Tompkins look like?"

"About five-foot-six, dark black hair. Slight build, maybe a hundred and forty pounds. You need to check him out, see where he's been."

Jim's face darkened as he wrote stuff down. He sorted through his notes, re-reading parts out loud to make sure he had it all written down right.

"Definitely cold," he said, "how they used Sadie and Tex to keep you from following them outside."

I decided it wasn't a question.

"You know, I got off a shot or two," I bragged. "With Vic's gun. I thought they'd kill us all, but when the lights went out, they just took off."

He didn't comment, but sat there, thinking.

"What about Sadie?" I asked. "What did she say?"

"Not a thing. Tex said they were blindfolded most of the time." He stood up.

"Wait here," he said opening the door. "I need to step out and make a quick telephone call. The FBI is sending somebody over to ask you a few questions, so sit tight. I guess they've had eyes on this the whole time. And for what it's worth, Jack, you hit the witness jackpot tonight. You've probably just put a finger on all four dead guys."

"Four?"

"Marko and Vic, plus Bosko—and maybe your guy, Tompkins. He didn't carry ID."

"Tompkins?!" I shook my head. "I figured he was running things."

"Apparently not."

82

Interrogation Room, Public Safety Building
8:05 a.m., Sunday, July 25, 1948

I spent a hard night in the tiny room with two chairs, trying to get some shut-eye by using my crossed arms on the table as a pillow. By my watch, Jim's quick phone call took hours. The FBI agent with the baggy suit showed up around seven o'clock the next morning and looked in but saved his questions until Jim stopped by at eight to make an introduction.

"Jack, this is Agent Pocelli," he said. "Try to show a little respect, as a favor to me."

"Aren't you staying?"

"You're on your own here." He turned and shut the door on his way out.

"Have you talked with Sadie?" I asked Pocelli, straight out of the chute.

"As a matter of fact, I have. She's fine."

"Could she identify anybody?"

"Not so far."

"Who's keeping an eye on her? You know, nobody who's seen these guys survived much longer."

"I have people at the hospital, Jack. Don't worry. We'll take good care of her."

But that's my job.

"What else did she have to say?" I asked.

"About you?" He slumped down in his chair and played with his pencil, rolling it in his hand. "Let's just set her issues aside and focus on what you know about a few other things, Jack. Have you had anything to eat? Bathroom?"

I shook my head.

He knocked on the door. A uniformed cop took me down the hall and brought me back.

The FBI man was waiting.

"I already read Captain Burt's notes of his conversation with you last night. And I understand you tracked Bosko out to the copper mine, in Bingham," he said.

"That's right. You guys brought him here in '44, wasn't it?"

He held up a hand and smiled. "Let me clear up something here, Jack. I'm asking the questions this morning."

I rubbed the side of my face, wiping sleep from one eye. "Alright."

"You met a mining executive out there named Chapman, and you impersonated a police detective?"

"Now wait a minute, he asked if I was a detective and I said, 'yes'. I never said I was a *police* detective."

"But you told *Tex* you were. And Chapman shared some highly confidential information with you, information about the test site at Highland Boy and Bosko's work. He thought he was giving that information to a sworn officer, didn't he?"

I didn't answer right off. "I guess you'd have to ask him."

"We did. And sometime during the week you came across the notebook, the one Bosko calls—called his device?"

I noticed he wasn't taking notes like Jim did.

"Jack, when did you realize it was connected to the things Chapman told you about?"

"Not right then. I couldn't read it." I was stretching the truth, but he was starting to sound like the DA.

"Alright, but at some point, you struck a bargain with whoever was behind Sadie's abduction? You'd agreed to find the device and give it to him, so he'd let her go?"

"I didn't have a say in that bargain, if that matters any."

"It doesn't. Because you knew what the deal was, right?"

I nodded.

"So, at some point you hired out to Zorin Markosivich, calling himself Marko?"

I didn't like this line of questioning.

"I might have."

"At what point did you realize he worked for the Yugoslavian secret police?"

"He told me he was a private investigator, looking for things Bosko stole from his client, Sava somebody."

"Right, Sava Kosanovic. Turns out he's not just a communist, he's the Yugoslavian ambassador to the United States."

"Marko told me he was Tesla's nephew. That's it. I never had time to check him out."

"Then he only gave you part of the truth. You see, here's where I'm going with this Jack. When you give government secrets away, even as ransom, we call it 'espionage.' That's a crime. You conspired to give away government secrets, to someone you eventually came to suspect was an agent of a foreign government."

"I didn't conspire with anybody, and the secrets belonged to somebody else. Marko said Bosko stole that stuff from his client's inheritance, and it saved Sadie and it saved that guy, Tex."

"What was Jonny's role in all this?"

"Jonny! He didn't do anything. Why bring him into this? He just found somebody to translate things for me."

"Doesn't matter, Jack. The 'device,' as you call it, belonged to the government, no matter what Marko said. Jonny had it and he had it translated on your instruction. You could both go to jail for decades for something like this."

He let that sink in. I didn't know if he was telling the truth or trying to scare me.

"Well, I'd do it again," I said. "If it saved Sadie and Tex, I'd do it again."

"I'm sure you would."

He stopped talking, looked me in the eye, then stood up abruptly and walked out.

My watch had stopped. There wasn't a clock in the room. After a while, the doorknob rattled.

"Am I gonna need my attorney?" I asked as he came back in and sat down.

"You could call somebody, but to be honest, he couldn't help much. Not in a case like this."

He nervously tapped his pencil on the edge of the desk.

"So, it's checkmate, then? You're just going to send us to jail?"

His eyes came up and he cracked a smile—a slight one. "Look, that's really not what any of us are after here, Jack. What I want, what your government wants, is simply your total cooperation. We want this whole episode shut down now, with no public trials, no newspaper stories, and no publicity whatsoever." He paused while I tried to guess what he meant.

"Here's what we're proposing," he said. "You seem like a decent enough guy. You served your country, and people vouch for you. The chief speaks highly of you."

"The chief?"

He pulled a single folded sheet from his suit coat, set the paper down, and stretched his hands out, fingers apart like he was going to make a quarter disappear. "Prison doesn't work for us."

"It doesn't work for me, either."

"The problem I have—the problem we have—is that you've been privy to a lot of classified information. Too classified, and too much access, more than most of my agents here. You know, the War might be over, but the battle goes on. Similar struggles, different adversary."

"I read the papers," I said.

"Then I hope you understand why we're worried. All this has to remain secret, Jack, prison or not. Top secret. Not one word about it, any of it, for the rest of your life. Not ever, even with your uncle."

He rambled on about state security and state secrets and what was written on his paper.

"Agreed?" he finally asked.

"What if Jim asks me about it? What do I tell him?"

"You'll figure it out. Tell him you can't remember. Tell him we worked out a deal. I'll tell him. I don't care."

"What about the press? And the dead guys? How do you keep it all bottled up?"

His head nodded back slightly, satisfied. "Robbery gone bad ... shots fired, it's already in the works."

"So that's it?"

"When you sign here. You sign now, in order to stay out of federal custody, trial, and prison. Or I will take you to jail. Those are my orders and that's our deal. It's a generous offer, but the secrecy conditions have sharp teeth. You violate the agreement; you end up in prison."

He slid the paper across the desk.

"But you're saying, if I sign this, I can just walk out?"

His eyes stayed locked on mine. He put a pen on the table.

"I don't understand."

"We all want to come out of this looking good, son."

Self-preservation? A spy in his bureau didn't look good, but there had to be more to it than that.

"Can I still talk to you about it?" I asked.

"In private."

"But I didn't know—"

He held up a hand. "It doesn't matter, Jack."

I re-read the typed paragraphs and looked up.

"Now or never, Jack. Everybody wants this on the shelf."

"Jim doesn't know?"

He didn't answer, didn't nod or smile. He just stared at me.

"What about Jonny?"

"Depends on what you do here, but he'll have to sign something too."

I knew what that meant. I signed at the bottom. "Do I get my own copy?"

"Sorry, Jack, it's classified."

There was a knock on the door, and somebody handed in a cold cinnamon roll.

I asked him what he knew about Tompkins, and he gave me one of those guarded looks that came in sideways, with a good deal of suspicion.

"He was a good man," he offered.

"Then how did he get mixed up with something like this?"

"He shouldn't have been, not with any of it. He was an accountant, with a family. His involvement caught us all by surprise. He was always just one of those rock-solid—"

He stopped himself.

"A good man who fell in with thieves?" I said. "A guy who got drawn in and ended up as a loose end that needed to be tidied up?"

"She doesn't need to know any of that," he said.

"You mean his wife? You know, she could be the next target. Whoever's behind all this is still out there."

"We're looking into that. I have somebody at her house."

"Most of your leads are dead," I said. "Except ... Sadie and Tex. And they're loose ends too, don't you think?"

"I already said, *we're on it.*" He stood up looking irritated. "You traveled much, Hammer?"

"Some in the South. And the time I spent in Europe, courtesy of Uncle Sam."

"Then you know how big this world is, and you're just a little fish in a backwater pond."

"Is that some kind of warning?"

"Just be careful, Jack. Don't be sayin' the wrong thing to the wrong person." He chuckled to himself. "Which means pretty much everybody you'll ever know in your entire life."

He walked me out to the front desk where we collected my wallet and personal effects. The evidence room cleared my .38, and the desk sergeant had me sign for it and the Walther. My car was still parked on the street behind Auerbach's. Pocelli gave me a ride, along with my missing shoe.

His fish comment made sense of things now.

"You're using us as bait, aren't you? Me'n Jonny?"

He kept his eyes on the road and didn't answer.

"That's why you're letting us go. You're hoping we'll lure back the one that got away."

"Give it a rest, Jack. Your government would never do something like that."

But he wasn't convincing.

"So, what do you think the Russians or whoever want with the notebook?" I asked him. "I mean, out there, in the big world. You think they want to build some kind of electric death ray like Bosko feared? Shoot electricity through the sky?"

He gave me his best, *you're not gonna leave it alone, are you?* look.

"It's possible," he said, "in theory, but not in the short-term. Besides, those two pages you tore out? We found them, on the ground next to Bosko, unreadable. I'm guessing your foot smeared the ink right off the page. We're looking at them now, trying to see what they didn't get."

"But Bosko said—" and I stopped.

"Bosko said what?"

"He said it was all there." *And he had to have seen it wasn't readable.*

We pulled up next to my Ford, and he patted his chest pocket.

"Don't forget what you signed here, Jack. *Not a single word, ever.*"

"And if I run across any Russians?"

"Here's my card."

83

Jim and Edna's Place
2:05 p.m., Sunday, July 25, 1948

I headed over to Holy Cross, looking for Sadie, but the hospital staff kept me away. I waited in the lobby, hoping to see a family member or maybe a cop so I could tag along, but nobody came through. The robed Sister at the front desk stared at me through black-rimmed glasses while I sat and waited.

After an hour, I got antsy and left to find lunch. Since it was Sunday, most of the cafés in town were closed, and the ones that stayed open I couldn't afford. I headed over to Jim and Edna's place to take my chances there.

Nobody was home.

They must be at church.

I went around back and let myself in, then sat down on the sofa in the front room. I could smell a roast in the oven and yeast from rolls raising in a pan. It reminded me I needed to call home, to talk to my own mother.

The Sunday paper was in disarray on the ottoman. The front-page banner shouted, "Wallace Urges U.S. to Quit Berlin," but I wasn't in the mood for politics. I dropped it on the floor and rummaged through the pile. There wasn't anything about a shooting at Auerbach's or trouble at the fairgrounds, but an article on the bottom of B-1 caught my eye:

County Loses Power Saturday Night, Thunderstorm Likely Culprit

Nearly 200,000 customers of Utah Power and Light inexplicably lost power Saturday night at exactly 10:30 p.m., according to an unnamed power company spokesman. The outage caused chaos at traffic signals and movie theaters alike when electric power ceased, and then came back slowly between five and fifteen minutes later. Company officials were unable to explain why electric power failed simultaneously across the valley, nor did they have an explanation as to why it curiously continued at the Walker Bank Tower, located on the northeast corner of Main Street and Second South. The distinctive bright red glow of winking radio tower lights was reported to be visible from nearly everywhere in the startlingly dark valley, from Draper to North Salt Lake.

I shook my head and settled back into the sofa, smiling. *His invention actually worked!* Bosko would have been proud.

But who could I tell now?

I jerked awake at the sound of voices.

"Let yourself in, did you?" said Jim. He and Edna came in through the back way. I'd drifted off, trying to make up for sleep lost overnight on the hard table.

"There's our detective," said Edna. "Jim said you helped the police find Bosko."

I stood up and gave him a sideways look.

"He doesn't want to talk about that, Edna."

"Well, I don't see why not," she said. "Have you had supper, Jack?"

Jim looked at me with questions in his eyes, but kept his mouth closed.

"I probably shouldn't bother you," I said. "Especially after the last dinner I skipped out on."

"Nonsense," Edna said. "You think you can afford to be driving all the way home to Butlerville every few days just to get a free meal?"

"She's right, Jack. And you made her feel real bad the other night, the way you disappeared."

"Oh, he did not," Edna said, slapping him on the arm. "Course, it's still too early for corn on the cob, but the carrots are right out of our garden, and we picked a few early tomatoes."

I was an easy sell.

"Everything okay between you and the Bureau?" Jim asked as we sat down.

"We worked it all out."

The three of us sat in the kitchen instead of the dining room. Jim avoided any more talk about police work. I realized again how much I missed a good, home-cooked meal, but nothing came free. Edna, still full of her Sunday school lesson, quizzed me about the last time I made it to church.

"A few weeks ago, I guess. Anything changed while I was away?"

She frowned. "We talked about Samson today. You remember Samson and Delilah, don't you?"

Jim sat back from the table and chuckled, picking the roast beef from his teeth with a toothpick. Edna retold the story of Samson's downfall, brought down by a scheming woman. I realized again how nothing in life comes free, even dinner with family.

"A shameful woman can spoil a man, Jack. Make him turn away from a good life to something wrong and sad. So, who's the new girl you've been dating, by the way? Sadie? What's she like?"

Jim was careful with what he shared at home.

I smiled at the awkward transition. *That was Edna.*

"I think Jack probably wants to get back to the sports pages and relax for a bit. What do you say to that?"

I shot him a grateful look.

"Maybe I could help out with the dishes after?" I offered.

"Not a chance," Edna said. "That's my good china, right there. There's no way I'm gonna let either of you near it with wet, soapy hands."

We left her alone in the kitchen. Jim sat down and played with the tuner, looking for *Nick Carter, Master Detective* on the cathedral radio.

"You two don't talk much," I said.

"Not about work."

I sat back and fell asleep on the sofa, again.

84

Jim and Edna's Place
4:45 p.m., Sunday, July 25, 1948

The sound of a telephone ringing pulled me back from my nap in the parlor. Jim was talking in low tones in the other room.

"Sure ... I'll be right over ... No, I'm closer than he is. I'll handle it."

I sat up on the brown corduroy sofa and cleared my head. Jim walked back in the room and lifted his coat off the rack.

"Just a quick call," he said. "I'll be back in an hour or so. I'll stop by Johnson's and pick up some ice cream. We can all sit out on the front porch."

"Uh-uh. What's up?"

"It's nothing," he said, grabbing his hat.

"You always take *nothing* calls on Sunday afternoons?"

He looked around, like he was giving me some top-secret information.

"It's about your guy, Tompkins. His house anyway. Looks like something's going on over there," he said. "Probably nothing, but I'm gonna run over and check it out."

"Can I come along?"

He hesitated, like he was pretending not to hear me.

"For company," I said, putting on my own sports jacket. "It's not like I'm going to do anything."

"Jack, you know—" he stopped. "I'll probably regret it, but okay. Edna! Jack and I are headed out for an hour or so."

She didn't answer. Jim closed the front door softly, so she wouldn't hear.

Tompkins and his wife made their home just north of South High School, eight streets over in a red brick bungalow like Jim's. It was a five-minute car trip. Jim's two-way radio crackled.

"What's going on over there?" I asked, rolling his window down on the passenger side.

"A neighbor reported gunshots," he answered. "Could be a car backfire, but under the circumstances ... you know. You keep your mouth shut while we're here, especially around his widow. You're just company on the ride over, remember?"

I held my right hand out the window as he drove, pushing the angle up and down into the wind, like an airplane flap.

"I stopped over to see Sadie," I said. "At the hospital."

"I didn't know if I should ask. How'd that go?"

I kept my eyes straight ahead. "I didn't see her. They wouldn't even tell me what room she was in." We pulled up behind a black and white already out front. The front window of the house was cracked; diagonal streaks ran from the single bullet hole.

"I thought the FBI had somebody camped here."

"Me too," he said. "Stay put. I'll just be a minute."

I climbed out the passenger side and followed him in anyway. Two uniformed cops were already inside. We walked through the front door without knocking. It had two bullet holes of its own.

A woman with long, dark hair sat on a ragged, brown sofa in the parlor. She was hunched over, crying into her hands.

"We found this." One of the cops held out a 9mm pistol by the trigger guard. "Fired twice. She said it was an accident. And she's been drinking."

"Two shots?"

"It doesn't add up," said the cop. "Three bullet holes. And neighbors said they saw a car drive off in a hurry."

"You seen the FBI around?"

He shook his head.

Jim glanced over at her, then at the officer. "I guess you know she lost her husband last night, a career FBI agent. Where's the kid?"

"My partner's got her, back in the kitchen. She's okay."

"Mrs. Tompkins," he started. "I'm Captain Burt, with the Salt Lake Police Department. I just want to say I'm so sorry for all you've had to go through today."

"Are you?"

She looked up at him. In spite of the swollen eyes and a lack of makeup, I recognized her from somewhere. I wondered what he'd find to say to a woman whose husband had been uncovered as a criminal, just before he was killed. Jim had a gentle side I wasn't familiar with.

"Do you have family nearby—anybody we should call to come over and sit with you?"

A handkerchief appeared, and she blew her nose. She was still dressed in her morning housecoat. Her eyes focused on something far away.

"How about a pastor, or a priest or somebody?" he tried again.

She put her face back in her hands and cried quietly.

"It's all my fault," she managed between breaths.

"It's not," Jim answered in a soothing tone. He turned back to the patrolman next to me and spoke softly. "She's going to need somebody here to stay with her. See if you can round up the local bishop or somebody."

Neighbors gathered in small groups on the sidewalk.

"And see if anybody out there knows her."

I walked toward the voices in the kitchen. At the rear of the house a child was crying. An older cop was sitting at the kitchen table, trying to console a young boy with LifeSavers. The rear door stood open, and over my shoulder I saw Jim was still talking with the wife.

I stepped outside, looking around. A wooden swing seat hung from a chain to the limb of a large tree. The grass was dry, mostly yellowed, and dead. A pair of gray metal garbage cans sat on a wooden pallet, by the side of a small garage.

Near the back fence, a sliver of familiar, shiny, black wood poked out from an open fifty-five-gallon drum. Curiosity teased. I walked across the yard and looked inside. The intriguing wood was part of a broken picture frame, sitting on top of some burnt, dry trash. *The portraits at Marko's café had similar frames.* Remnants of a black-and-white photo lay in the debris, and despite the fire damage, some of the image was still visible: a silvery ghost image on ashes. It was artful, even striking, revealing more than enough to power black-mail. I reached inside the can, hoping to take a closer look, but the ash of the charred portions fell away at my touch, collapsing into dust. Only a part of the woman's face survived.

The art photos at the café had shown a woman in silhouette, tastefully backlit and facing away. The model in this image had gazed sensuously into the camera lens, wearing only a hesitant smile. I was the last person on earth to see it, and I recognized her at once and felt uncomfortable.

It was Tompkins' widow.

85

Napoli Café
10:35 a.m., Monday, July 26, 1948

The next morning, I skipped breakfast and stopped by the hospital again, but Sadie was gone. I called over to County General and asked after her, but nobody knew her there either. I cruised past her house on Layton Avenue. Deserted. An unmarked sedan parked across the street, facing toward the market. A sleepy cop slouched behind the wheel, watching traffic pass in his rearview mirror. Jim's advice haunted my thoughts: *Give her some time.* I drove out the other end of the neighborhood without slowing down.

On a hunch, I turned north and parked at the curb, just down from the Napoli Café. I pulled the .38 from the glove box, loaded it with shells from a box under the driver's seat, and dropped it in my pocket. I got out and stepped cautiously across the grassy park strip. The white stucco building was brilliant in the late morning sun.

Brick houses lined both sides of the road. Birdsong twittered from the shadows in the trees behind them. An outdoor patio, covered by a white-painted trellis, joined the stucco restaurant to a gravel lot next door, and every so often a car cruised past, headed downtown. I peered through the front window into an empty dining room.

A sign in the window said CLOSED, but the door was unlocked. I walked inside. The bell over the door jangled. I turned the thumb piece on the deadbolt clockwise, locking it. Chairs were stacked, feet up, on the tables. The kitchen was silent. I switched lights on in the dining room. My heels made a clicking sound on the tile floor when I walked over and stood in front of the cafe artwork.

Where was everyone?

I studied every photograph on the walls, satisfied eventually they were all the same woman. Then I sat down at the lunch counter where I could keep my eye on the whole place in the mirror. I pulled out a menu and tapped it nervously on the counter.

"I am sorry," said a waiter, walking out from the back, "we are not yet open." It was Marko's friend, Aleks. His left eye was still swollen slightly from my right cross that knocked him into the pots and pans. His white apron covered the front of his shirt now, and the tops of his trousers. His eyes blinked rapidly, coming from darkness. "Oh—" he said, stopping abruptly. "It is you."

"No lunch today?" I asked.

"Later. You should know, Marko is not here."

"But you expect him soon?"

He shrugged, pulled off a pair of rubber gloves and laid them out on the counter. A faint acidic smell, like vinegar, caught my nose and wafted away.

"Nobody has spoken to Marko since Friday."

"Well, he said I should meet him here for lunch," I lied, sliding the menu back in the clip. "Could I get a glass of water?"

"Marko said this?" He wiped his hands on his apron while he figured out what to say next. He pulled a glass from a green wire rack. "When?"

"Last night. You don't mind if I sit out here and wait, do you?"

"I have nothing to say with you," he countered. He slid the short water glass across the bar but kept his distance.

"You're still angry over that black eye, aren't you?"

"I must get back for work," he said, turning away. "The cooks will be—"

"The cooks will wait," I ordered. I wagged my finger toward the framed figures on the wall, a question on my face, unspoken.

He eyed me suspiciously. "Marko makes them," he said.

I slipped off the barstool, walked over to a photograph and pulled it from the wall.

"Is for sale," he said. "They are all for sale. Twenty dollars, for one."

I whistled. "Twenty bucks? For this type of ... work?"

"Some people will buy them. Is what you call, 'hobby'."

"Some people collect stamps."

"Yes."

I thought for a moment. "So, if taking 'art' photos of women is your hobby, I'm guessin' you can't just send them over to the local drugstore for developing, can you?" The red light in his back office, the chemical smell, and the rubber gloves on the counter all fit together now.

"I'm sorry," he tried again. "I must start kitchen preparation. Some cooks will be here soon."

I headed back toward him, sat down on a stool, and took the negative I found in Zoric's drawer from my pocket. I laid it on the counter at arm's length and tapped it with my finger.

"Could you make *this* into one of your slick art prints?"

He had a great poker face.

"It's the same woman, isn't it?" I asked.

He picked it up and held it towards the front window. "How did you get this?" he asked, coolly.

I slipped the .38 from my pocket, brought it onto my lap, and pulled the hammer back.

"The real question is, how did you get her to do it?"

"I do not know what you mean."

"Sure, you do. Wife of an FBI agent. Blackmail photos. Was it drugs? Booze? That's her on the wall, isn't it?"

"I told you, Marko makes them."

"And signs them with your initials, AK?"

He put the negative down.

"I'll bet you have more pictures, don't you? Dirty, smutty, little blackmail pictures you threatened to send to his friends, his bishop, and his bosses at the FBI if he didn't help you find Bosko's note-book."

"No."

"Too bad Tompkins was just a Bureau accountant," I continued. "He wasn't a field agent, after all." *Or Samson.*

"Who is this person, 'Tompkins'?"

"Somebody who tried, I'll give him that." I felt pity for him, now.

"You should wait for boss-man."

"Why? You seem to be your own man."

Beads of sweat began to drip down the side of his face and he brushed them with his hand. "I do what Marko tells me."

"When it serves you. You've had your own little game goin' behind Marko's back, haven't you? Blackmailing Tompkins, hoping he'd help you find Bosko? Then you kidnapped Sadie, to put pressure on me, but Marko didn't know anything about that either, did he?"

"Marko does what Marko does—"

"That's right, and after Yasa died, he was obsessed with finding her killer, even though the real prize had always been the note-book. He wanted revenge. That's why you said *he'd* gone soft, isn't it? But not you. You wanted the device. The notebook. Who are you working for, Aleks? KOS? Or the Russians?"

His eyes darted around the room as he edged toward the gun under the cash register by the front door.

"That's close enough," I said, bringing my own gun up to the counter. "Put your hands in the air, and don't move."

He stopped.

I stepped down off the stool and picked up the telephone near the register. Pocelli's card was in my shirt pocket. I took it out and dialed his number, keeping the gun pointed at Aleks.

"I'm at the Napoli Café, on Main ... that's the one. How fast can you get here? I've got somebody here—your missing man." I laid the handset on the counter.

"You must talk with Marko," Aleks repeated. "He and Yasa—"

"—shadowed Bosko for months," I said, finishing his excuse. "They'd been watching his work out in Bingham, waiting for the notebook to surface? Is it Tesla's?"

"What is 'shadowed'?" he asked.

Just like Marko.

"Then what? Bosko got suspicious and disappeared—so Yasa panicked and hired me?"

"You have only ideas, Mr. Hammer—"

"And this is all about ideas," I said. "Tesla's ideas. Do you love your country, Aleks?"

"My country? I do what *Marko* tells me. I am going to put my hands down now. And I will talk with your police when they arrive, if you like."

I stepped toward him. "Keep your hands up where I can see 'em."

Maybe he was telling the truth. Pocelli could sort it out. But it was something else that brought me here: the photos.

"I want to see that little office out back, before the cops get here."

He hesitated. "Marko must give permission."

I pushed him through the kitchen doorway anyway, back to the small office. I held the gun on him with my right hand and reached through the doorway with my left to switch on the red light. I must have interrupted his work processing some new "art" photographs. Three large prints hung from clothespins on the wire behind the door, drying. An exhaust fan was pulling chemical fumes from the room and sending them through the roof. I stepped in to get a closer look. The gun dropped for a split second.

What I saw felt like a punch to the gut.

The woman in these pictures was someone I knew well.

It was Sadie.

My eyes darted back to Aleks, who'd taken advantage of my distraction by diving behind a rack of cooking utensils. Anger rose up inside me. I felt rage gather through my chest and into my upper arms. I followed him in the near dark, down a narrow passageway between shelving and coolers. I could hear him knocking things off counters as he scrambled away.

I came around another corner.

His back was three-quarters toward me, only yards away. He stood by a grill holding a 30.06 with a telescopic sight.

I steadied my gun hand against the corner of a freezer and called out, "Put it down, now!"

He swung around toward me, pulling the bolt and racking a new bullet in the process, but the long barrel caught on a shelf post in the confined kitchen workspace.

I fired my own gun three times.

The first shot was off target, glancing off a pipe.

The second shot hit him in his shoulder.

He kept struggling with the rifle as the third shot hit him in his left thigh.

He dropped the rifle and staggered back, grabbing at his leg. Red splotches appeared, soaking into his white apron.

I grabbed the rifle and swung it across the floor by the barrel. It hit him in the face as I moved it away.

"Where is the notebook?"

Something hissed from the pipe.

"Gas," he said, coughing up blood.

His eyes blinked closed as he lost consciousness. The sulfur stink of leaking gas spread into the room from the damaged pipe. I grabbed the collar of his shirt and dragged him out the side delivery door, into the middle of the gravel lot.

His head settled into a pillow of sharp, crushed stones as the first small explosion shattered the café windows and knocked me to the ground.

86

Beehive Café
8:05 a.m., Friday, July 30, 1948

I sat at the counter again, back near the unopened door to the Twilight Lounge. One of the waitresses took my quarter and I punched out five spots on the nickel-board, all losers.

It had been five days.

Breakfast was busy at the Beehive. I found a paper and scanned the sports page, twisting the swivel seat while I waited. Every time the bell over the door rang, I looked up, betraying a foolish hope that somehow, she'd walk through the door. George came out of the kitchen and set a plate of pancakes in front of me.

"Still no eggs, Jack? You always were an egg man."

He laughed at his little pun, and I managed a smile as I worked the butter into the hotcakes. George told me Sadie hadn't come back to work, and he didn't know if she would.

"Nobody takes my calls," he said. "I'll have to drop her paycheck in the mail."

I poked at the bacon with my fork as he walked away to make change at the register.

The bell jangled, and I looked up again.

Jim stepped in, scanned faces in the room, and walked back to sit with me. He put his hat on the empty stool next to him to give us some privacy. I hadn't seen him since Monday.

"I hear you're working again," he said, smiling.

"That's right. Jonny got me my job back after Vic ... well, you know. I guess he told everybody I was some kind of hero," I said. "Told 'em they'd be lucky if I came back."

"So, that's a good thing. Right?"

"Sure." *Except I stay up all night, thinking about her.* "And he got me a raise," I said. "He told me he was embarrassed that I sleep next to a toilet."

We both smiled at that, then fell silent for a minute.

I had to ask. "Have you seen her?"

He shook his head.

"She won't take my calls," I said. "Nobody answers, and George told me they don't take his calls either."

"Then you ought to be encouraged that it's not just you. Don't keep goin' over things in your head. I told you it was going to take time."

"But I had things handled," I said.

He nodded and pretended to look at a menu.

"Maybe I should have surfaced the letter right off—"

"Maybe, Jack, but stop it. Life's full of maybes. No telling how things would've gone if you did."

One of the other waitresses showed up with his cup of Postum and some toast. He stirred in half-and-half with his spoon while figuring out what to say next. I picked up a piece of the bacon and took a bite.

We both stared at our food.

"So, what do you think about chances for a Boston versus Boston Series?" he asked, changing the subject. "Braves are way out front—"

"I don't think the Sox can pull it off."

He was careful not to ask any questions about the Cvito case, and I didn't offer any explanations. I assumed Pocelli warned him against it.

When he ran out of things to say, he invited me over for Sunday dinner, again. "Edna's been trying to get your folks to drive into town," he said. "We haven't seen them in ages. That'd be nice, don't you think?"

"Sure."

It was all small talk. Eventually, we talked about the weather, and I made some kind of sniffing noise through my nose and stood up.

"You want these, Cap'n? I haven't touched 'em."

I left a buck on the counter with the pancakes and walked back to my office, hoping to catch up on a few days of missed sleep.

At the top of the back stairs, Krogue's family was cleaning out the old watchmaker's office, carrying small wooden crates down to cars parked in the alley. The splintered door frame to his office had been nailed back together, but a large piece of the wood trim was missing on the latch side. I touched it, thinking I'd step inside to pay respects to his sister, and picked up a sliver in my middle finger. The sister was dressed in black, sitting in a wooden chair supervising the others.

"I'm Jack," I announced, trying to get the sliver out of my finger with my teeth. "Don't get up. We met, at the funeral—"

She stared for a moment. "I remember," she said. "You were the one who—who found him." She turned toward his workbench, brushing a hankie to the corner of her eyes.

"I'm truly sorry for your loss," I said.

Her reading glasses hung from a string around her neck. She

twisted the handkerchief in her lap, turning it over and over, like Yasa. "Twenty-six years he'd been here, right in this very spot," she said. "Did you know that? Ever since the First War, when the jewelers downstairs started sending all their watch repair business to him. He had such a gift with watches, and he could repair anything."

I wanted to say something comforting, so I showed her my own watch, an Elgin. I told her he'd cleaned it for me a few weeks ago, adding, "He never charged me a thing." But it wasn't true. He'd never really cleaned it at all, although he might have if I'd have asked. It was a harmless lie.

A boy too young to drive brought a box of small tools and set it in her lap. She moved things around inside before telling him to take it all downstairs. "I'll look through it later," she said and looked up at me, proudly. "My grandson."

I knew I was intruding and meant to go, but she spoke again.

"You know, it shouldn't have been him," she said. Her blue eyes were faded and grayed with age, rimmed now with a thin crimson line along her eyelids. "He kept to himself," she said. "He always did. It was just his way. He didn't involve himself with people and he certainly wouldn't have had anything to do with any Russians."

"I'm sure he wouldn't have," I said, shaking my head. We stood like that for a minute, in silence. "You know, I'm just down the hall if there's anything I can do." But it sounded hollow.

Somehow, I should have prevented all this. Could have, maybe.

I excused myself and headed to my own office, hoping a few hours' sleep would help me see things in a new light. I pushed the door open, hung my jacket on the coat tree and sat down in my chair, emptying bullets from my pocket into the long drawer under the desktop. For a moment I entertained picking up the telephone and calling her again but drew my hand back, not from pride but rather from the lack of it. My heart couldn't bear one more unanswered call.

I picked up the gold-braid picture frame from the desk, turning it over in my hand. Sadie's photo stared back at me.

But not the torn black-and-white image I'd left there!

Somebody had replaced that one with a new hand-colored image. I stood up, wondering who'd been here in my office and how, when the door opened again.

She was wearing a wrinkled cotton print dress, with her hair pulled back loosely.

Her brown eyes sparkled.

"Jack?"

But I couldn't answer. Not a word, not a question about where she'd been or how she got here. Instead, I ran to the doorway and wrapped my arms around her shoulders, holding her tightly. Tears burned my eyes as she laid her head against my chest and her body moved again with mine in the slow convulsive rhythm of her crying.

"Sadie," I finally managed, whispering it over and over. "Sadie."

THE END

Afterword

Story Notes: HINT OF COPPER is a fictional account. All of the people in the book are products of my imagination. The buildings described herein were, or are actual places, although I've taken some liberties with the interiors and the vast majority have fallen victim to decades of "progress." The Whitehall Hotel and the Beehive Café are gone. The billiard halls and bowling alleys along Main Street have long since disappeared. The Fairgrounds Coliseum survived as a concert venue into the 1990s but then fell to the wrecker's ball. The small family cafes and gas stations are gone, and even Auerbach's Department Store vacated the corner of 3rd South and State in the 1980s. Buildings that remain, such as the Karrick building, and the Auerbach's building have been repurposed. And pretty much every single thing in Bingham Canyon has been erased, swallowed by mining efforts.

I have taken some artistic license in portraying the layouts of some building interiors, often due to a lack of information. Photographs of building exteriors are easier to come by than plans or photos of interiors.

For example, I searched for weeks online, checking Salt Lake historical web pages and haunting sites frequented by billiard players, looking for any photos of the Peter Pan pool hall with no luck. Then one day, a good friend and capable amateur photographer, Jim

Davis, was reading an early draft of the story and excitedly texted me to let me know that he personally had five or six black-and-white photos he'd taken of the pool hall interiors before it was torn down. Who knew?

In a similar experience, I searched everywhere for plans or photographs of the interior of the old Fairgrounds Coliseum building, to no avail. While waiting for an unrelated business meeting at the Division of Facilities Construction and Management, I asked a member of the support staff if there might be some way to find old plans or pictures related to the now-demolished public building. She helped me to fill out and file a FOIA request, and two weeks later I received a call from the State Archives. They had two boxes of information for me to inspect. Opening the first box, I found a study of the building that had exactly the information I was looking for—floor plans and building sections—prepared more than a decade earlier by good friends and former partners of mine. If only I'd known ...

The Beeline gasoline brand never occupied the corner of 9th South and 10th East until more than a decade after the story setting, but I used the name because I liked the identity tie-in with the Beehive Café and the Bee's baseball club. Utah is, after all, the Beehive State. And as far as I know, Nikola Tesla never had a lab assistant spirited away to work for the copper companies, but the potential for copper shortages was a real issue before Congress in the late '40s.

Not being trained as a writer, I managed to thoroughly enjoy the writing process, especially the research and discovery. I want to thank employees at the Research Center of the Division of State History for guiding me to collections of photographs, Sanborn maps, Polk Directories, and other resources as I attempted to understand the city as it was in 1948. Although my memory doesn't reach back to the 1940s, I remember the '50s. The pace of change was slow back then. My hope is that readers will come to feel and appreciate what a special and wonderful past we enjoy, here along the Wasatch Front.

Visit www.mormondetective.com to get a look at additional background, photos, and some of the informational materials I used to create the story.

Notes About the Ridge View edition: In the hopes of finding wider circulation I've altered the way I've published the book. The change gave me a chance to correct a few minor errors; things like time and weather references. A sharp-eyed reader pointed out that the first edition referred to brake pads, instead of the historically accurate term, brake *shoes*. I fixed that. I also realized the Walker Bank tower light scheme showing weather forecasts by light color wasn't put in place until several years after 1948. I corrected that reference to reflect only the tiny red lights that warned airplanes of the radio tower's presence. Beyond that, the story is the same. I hope you'll watch for Jack and Sadie in the sequel to this story: *The Lost Pages*, coming soon.

About the Author

Steven R. Burt grew up in Salt Lake City during the 1950s and 60s, reading cereal boxes at the breakfast table and his favorite books under his bedspread with a flashlight. He continuously read from three different publications of the 'A' encyclopedia, because the $0.98 introductory copies sold in grocery stores were all that fit into the family budget. Eventually, he grew up and became an Architect, a profession from the 'A' volumes, but always felt books were his true passion so, he wrote one: the story of a young detective with a kidnapped girlfriend, Cold War Russian spies, and quite possibly the best idea Nikola Tesla ever had. He is an Affiliate Member of Mystery Writers of America.

Hint of Copper is his debut novel.

His second novel, a time-travel mystery titled *My Brother's Keeper*, will be released soon.

For updates and all things Steven R. Burt, go to www.stevenr-burt.com.